"I'm Marin the Red," Joel announced to the pitch-dark chamber, "the captain of the guard of Lord Xvim's throne room, and I demand to know who you are."

Raucous, high-pitched laughter rang through the hall. Leaving his backpacks on the floor, Joel drew his sword and moved forward cautiously.

"Watch out!" the high-pitched voice cried out.

The warning came too late as Joel tripped on something soft. He sprawled across the floor.

As he pulled himself to his aching knees, the bard's hands came in contact with what had tripped him—the legs of a human body. Joel ran his hands up the body. It was encased in plate mail. The bard felt around the body's throat. The flesh was cold. There was no pulse.

"That was the last captain of the guard," the voice announced matter-of-factly.

Also by Novak and Grubb:

THE FINDER'S STONE TRILOGY

Azure Bonds
The Wyvern's Spur
Song of the Saurials

THE HARPERS

Masquerades
Finder's Bane

FANTASY ADVENTURE

TYMORA'S LUCK

KATE NOVAK
and
JEFF GRUBB

This book is dedicated to our friends at The Game Guild, whose support in the past few months has helped keep us sane.

The authors also gratefully acknowledge the contributions of several other persons to this book.

For their fictional characters' thoughts on opera: Dave Cook, Elaine Cunningham, Ed Greenwood, Bob Salvatore, Margaret Weis, and Tracy Hickman (whose quote, even though in the end it was not used, made us laugh for hours)

For their expertise and advice: Sue Cook, Julia Martin, and the well-lanned Michele Carter, who shared the dark of the Outer Planes with us, answering our innumerable phone calls with much graciousness, even when we were fools enough to call during "Star Trek Voyager"

First Printing: December 1997
Library of Congress Catalog Card Number: 96-60814

9 8 7 6 5 4 3 2 1
8583XXX1501

ISBN: 0-7869-0726-6

U. S., CANADA, ASIA,	EUROPEAN HEADQUARTERS
PACIFIC, & LATIN AMERICA	Wizards of the Coast, Belgium
Wizards of the Coast, Inc.	P.B. 34
P.O. Box 707	2300 Turnhout
Renton, WA 98057-0707	Belgium
+1-206-624-0933	+32-14-44-30-44

Visit our Website at http://www.tsrinc.com

Ye wouldn't appreciate the poetry of the tale, or the subplots of the opera, would ye? I'll cut to the heart of the matter.

—Elminster to Alias

Overture

To the Sensates of Sigil, new experiences were everything. Like children hungering for knowledge of the multiverse, they streamed into the Civic Festhall, eager to perceive with every sense they possessed, impressing on their minds and bodies the bounty of life. Hundreds, sometimes thousands, of Sensates visited the private sensoriums every day, so that the arrival of guests to a certain private party attracted no special attention. Yet the private party in question would be very special. Tonight, fifty-seven Sensates in good standing and of considerable discretion had been invited to share an experience both rare and risky. Tonight these select few would spy on the gods.

The chosen audience took their seats in one of the largest sensoriums and began to look around with excitement. The leader of the Sensates, Factol Erin Darkflame Montgomery herself, was their hostess. The lovely, sinuous woman moved from guest to guest with a private greeting for each. Cuatha Da'nanin, Montgomery's handsome half-elven consort moved alongside her, handing each guest a small rounded stone, glittering with semiprecious minerals.

In the front of the room sat a lone woman, small and slender, with blue skin. She was a genasi, meaning someone in her ancestry was from the elemental plane of air. She, like the rest of the guests, held one of the small rounded stones. An orange-sized sphere of smoky gray crystal lay on a pillow in her lap.

Montgomery, having greeted the last of her guests, stepped to the front of the room to stand beside the blue-skinned woman. "I'd like all of you to meet my guest of honor, Ayryn Farlight," the factol said, motioning to the woman beside her. "Ayryn is a gifted sorceress with a few unusual abilities that make this evening possible. Something rather unusual happened when Ayryn joined our faction and attempted to make her first recording." Montgomery held up one of the glittering stones.

The members of the audience listened with breathless attention. The stones were known as recorders, and they could magically encode the full force of any experience and then "play" the scene back for anyone to experience anew. Recorders were one of the Sensates' most important tools in enticing people into the Society of Sensation. Each Sensate was required to record several stones as part of his initiation. The recorded stones became part of a vast library of sensations.

Montgomery continued her explanation. "Ayryn's sensations seem to be more incorporeal in nature than most, so much so that the instant they enter a recorder they waft back out again. Consequently, if Ayryn holds a recording stone in her hand, we can experience her sensations moments after she does, but only then. Her experiences cannot be stored . . . unless we do it for her."

The members of the audience nodded with understanding.

"Ayryn's gift of scrying is unparalleled," Montgomery continued. "She has cast her eyes where few would dare, yet her intrusions have gone, for the most part, unnoticed. Tonight, for our enlightenment, she will seek out and view what few mortals have witnessed—the gods themselves."

The members of the audience applauded with appreciation and excitement.

"As a security precaution, we ask that no one speak the names of any of the gods this evening, since we would prefer that no notice is drawn to these proceedings. Ayryn will not remain focused on any one god for longer than a few minutes at a time. You should also understand that there may be occasions when she attempts to view a god and something or someone else entirely different will appear due to some misdirection spell that god may have placed on his or her person or realm. To begin, we will be viewing the gods of Faerûn, which is a fairly large continent on a world called Toril, set in a prime sphere known as Realmspace. Ayryn has cast a spell so you can comprehend whatever language they might speak." Montgomery flung wide her arms and announced, "Let the experience begin!"

There were a few moments of silence while the factol took her seat beside Da'nanin and Ayryn focused her attention on the crystal ball in her lap.

From his position slightly behind and to one side of Ayryn, Bors Sunseed, a paladin, studied the faces of each member of the audience. Bors was the only participant who remained standing and who did not hold a recording stone. He was also one of only four people who had been allowed to carry a weapon into the room. There were certain people who might consider spying on the gods as a highly blasphemous activity and who would consider Ayryn the primary offender. Bors's job was to see that Ayryn came to no harm. None of the guests looked in the least bit displeased with what was to come. They had been carefully chosen, and Montgomery and Da'nanin had done their best to ascertain that none were impostors, but there was always the possibility of error.

There was also the possibility that one of the gods would detect the intrusion upon his or her privacy, resent it, and send a retributory strike. While it was impossible for any god to enter the city of Sigil, one of them might send a powerful proxy, or several proxies, to let his or her displeasure be known.

There was a collective gasp among the crowd, and Bors took an instinctive step backward as a goddess towered over the assemblage. According to folklore, which Bors knew to be true, entire cities could be, and often were, built on the corpses of dead gods. So Ayryn's projection of this goddess was by no means life-size, yet it was large enough to cause a sensation among the Sensates. If the goddess reached upward, her hands would appear to

brush the ceiling of the sensorium, some fifty feet overhead.

The goddess was notable for more than her size, of
course. She was lovely to behold. Her glistening white
hair, worn in a long braid wrapped about her head, suggested a woman of great age, yet her pleasing features,
the texture of her brown skin, the firm tone of her muscles, all suggested a mortal in her middle years. Her figure was strong and womanly. "A rose in full bloom" was
the phrase that Bors's people might have used to describe
her. She wore a short tunic of unbleached linen and her
feet were bare. Her only adornments were the ivy and
wildflowers entwined in her hair and a girdle embroidered with all manner of fruits.

Bors, who had been fully briefed on which gods Ayryn
would attempt to scry, recognized the goddess before him
as Chauntea, the Great Mother, patroness of agriculture,
symbol of Toril's fertility. Ayryn's projection included the
goddess's surroundings. Fittingly, Chauntea stood in the
midst of a recently plowed field. Insects and earthworms
on the surface wriggled and scrambled to bury themselves
beneath the dirt furrows before they were eaten by the
flock of robins that bobbed along behind the goddess,
chirping excitedly. Chauntea walked along the furrows,
sprinkling tiny yellow seeds onto the ground from a green
cloth pouch and nudging the dirt with her toes so that
each seed was covered. She worked with the speed and
grace of a practiced farmer. An unseen but undoubtedly
bright sun glittered in the sheen of perspiration that covered her bare skin. Mud and dust covered her feet and ankles and even her calves. Her lips curled up in a tiny smile
as she attended to her task. If she noticed she was being
scried, she gave no indication.

Chauntea turned about to plant another furrow. Bors
wondered idly just how long Ayryn would keep her eyes
upon this goddess. While spying upon any goddess was a
new sensation for him, he wasn't a gardener. His interest
in Chauntea's activity was somewhat limited, and the
field she was sowing appeared to be rather large.

Someone in the audience pointed to a spot behind Bors.
The paladin turned halfway about. Another figure had

appeared over the horizon of Chauntea's realm. As the figure approached Chauntea, Bors recognized it as that of Lathander Morninglord, another god of Toril and reportedly Chauntea's current lover.

Lathander appeared every bit as impressive as Chauntea. His face shone like the sun, and his hair burned a fiery orange-red. Were Lathander a mortal, Bors would have judged him to be a young man. The god's physique was slender and athletic, and his features were divinely handsome. He wore an opalescent robe of red, pink, and yellow, open at the chest and bound at the waist with a red and gold sash. The robe and sash billowed out behind him as he flew toward the goddess of the harvest. He made a magnificent spectacle, as lovely as the dawn itself. His magnificence, however, was lost on Chauntea, whose attention was focused on the ground and her planting.

Lathander smiled, apparently amused that Chauntea was so engrossed in her task that she didn't seem to notice him. He landed in the field just behind her.

Without turning from her task, Chauntea addressed her newly arrived companion. "Lathander, the seedlings' roots and stems won't be able to break through the earth if you compact it with your weight," the goddess chided.

"Sorry," Lathander replied, immediately levitating once again so that his golden sandals hovered inches off the ground. He floated about so that he and Chauntea were face-to-face. "Sweet dawning," he whispered near her ear. His voice held the husky tone of one lover to another.

"Sweet dawning," Chauntea replied softly. She brushed his cheek with a kiss. There was something perfunctory about the goddess's action, however, and she prodded Lathander gently so that he hovered to one side of her furrow. She continued her planting.

"A new universe lies aborning out beyond the worlds of the Tuhgri," Lathander said with a twinkle in his eyes. "The tiny crystal spheres are nested together like faerie-dragon eggs. Whenever a wave of phlogiston washes over them they bump against one another, and you can hear them chime over the humming of the void."

Chauntea laughed lightly. "Voids can't hum," she replied.

Lathander sank again to the ground before the goddess. His feet sank in the soft earth. He slid one hand behind Chauntea's back and with the other grabbed at her
braid of hair and wrapped it about his waist. "They do," he
insisted, "but you have to get very close to them and listen
very quietly for a very long time. Come with me and I will
show you."

Chauntea put her fingertips on the Morninglord's chest
to keep him from embracing her closer. "Lathander, it is
planting season. You know that I must tend this field to
insure the fecundity of the Realms."

"What will it matter if the crop is a day late?" Lathander whispered. He tilted his head and pressed his lips
to the curve of her throat.

Chauntea smiled, but when the god began pulling her
backward through the field, she broke away abruptly.
"Lathander," she reprimanded her companion sharply, "if
you do not stop churning the field with your feet, there
will be crop failure in Halruaa this season."

"They can buy grain from Amn. It will teach the wizard
kingdom something about cooperation," Lathander said
glibly. "Come with me, Chauntea. The growing season is
very lovely, but it comes every year. The birth of a new
universe, on the other hand, is not only beautiful but also
rare."

Chauntea sighed with exasperation. "Lathander, you
might just as well tell the sun to hold off rising in the
morning. My duties cannot wait."

"The last time I saw a new universe blossom," Lathander said sadly, "Tyche was my companion. We lay on the
back of a space whale and watched for a full year as the
crystal spheres grew larger and spread apart and the
stars inside them flickered to life and brightened."

"Tyche always did have too much time to fritter away,"
Chauntea muttered, scattering a handful of seed in the
furrow before her. "I'm sorry, Lathander, but my work is
more important."

"I want to share this with someone," Lathander insisted stubbornly.

"Well, Tyche is gone, and I am busy. You'll have to find
someone else. Why don't you seek out Tyche's daughters,

Beshaba or Tymora? Perhaps one of them has time to lie on the back of a space whale."

"Neither child is the same as her dam," Lathander complained. There was the faintest hint of a whine in his voice.

"But you are the same as ever, Lathander," Chauntea cried, throwing her arms up in a gesture of annoyance. "You're always looking for beginnings. Some of us have tasks that must be *finished!* Go! Let me complete my planting in peace!"

Lathander's face darkened like an eclipsed sun. "As you wish," he retorted hotly, and with that, he spun about and flew quickly away in the direction he'd come, disappearing beyond the distant horizon. There were black scorch marks where his feet had last touched the field. Halruaa's harvest would be poor this year. Chauntea sighed, then turned back to her task.

Ayryn covered her crystal ball with her hands and raised her eyes to Montgomery's face. The vision of Chauntea and her field vanished.

A moment of nervous silence followed. Then the room erupted with the sound of the audience's applause. They had witnessed two gods having a lovers' spat. Not a run-of-the-mill experience in anyone's book.

Montgomery held up her hand. The room grew silent again.

"Can you continue, Ayryn?" the leader of the Sensates asked the genasi scryer.

"Yes," Ayryn replied. She gazed once more into her crystal ball.

Darkness filled the room, complete blackness. There was the sound of water dripping in a cave. Then a red light shone up from the floor. The light came from a round pool of water—or perhaps blood—nearly ten feet in diameter. A drop of liquid fell on the surface of the pool and spattered like hot oil in water. The light from the pool flickered as the surface rippled.

Someone snarled a female voice, "Stupid eyewing, get away from here. Okim, Airdna, bat that beast out of here before it poisons my spell."

A figure sat down beside the pool and tossed back a

mane of snow-white hair, revealing the features of a beautiful maiden. She was quite tall, with a voluptuous figure and impossibly small waist. Her skin appeared red from the light of the pool, but Bors, whose catlike eyes could not be deceived by tricks of the light, could see that her flesh was as white as a corpse's, but flushed about her cheeks and throat with the palest blue and violet color. She wore a gown of the darkest black, which fit her like a glove, and a tiara of black pearls. The goddess raised her head, and someone in the Sensate audience gasped softly. The deity's eyes were rimmed with yellow and red and blazed with madness.

This, Bors realized, was the goddess Beshaba. No doubt Ayryn had been influenced by Chauntea's suggestion to Lathander that he seek out one of Tyche's daughters. Beshaba was known as Tyche's "unpleasant" daughter. She was also known as the Maid of Misfortune. She had dominion over bad luck.

Ayryn's projection of Beshaba was not gigantic. The form the goddess wore was human-sized. She was joined a minute later by two winged women of great beauty with demonic eyes. The women wore silken pants, silver breastplates engraved with the stag horns of Beshaba, and swords with serrated blades. Bors recognized the winged women as alu-fiends, creatures of evil from the Abyss, where Beshaba made her home.

An old man's face appeared on the surface of the pool of red liquid.

"There he is," Beshaba whispered with an evil smile on her lips.

The goddess was scrying on someone, just as they were scrying on her.

"Doljust," Beshaba said, "it is time to pay for slighting me."

The vision in Beshaba's pool seemed to move away so that the goddess, and those Sensates who spied upon her, could see more of Doljust and the landscape around him.

Doljust was old, as evidenced by his gray hair and beard and wrinkled features, but he was by no means feeble. He rode straight and tall in the saddle of a prancing mare. A handsome pair of hunting hounds circled his mount, barking with excitement. He wore neither fancy armor nor noble velvets, but his clothing was well made and sturdy, and his mare was a fine-looking beast.

Doljust began to dismount.

Beshaba reached down and touched the surface of the pool.

At that instant, Doljust's boot caught in his stirrup, and when he managed to free himself with his hands, he fell backward on his back. Doljust swore a common oath, not one that mentioned any god's name.

One of the alu-fiends giggled; the other merely smiled. Beshaba was not yet amused.

Doljust rose and brushed himself off. He followed his dogs to a cave entrance. At one side of the entrance lay the corpses of two children, mere toddlers. Doljust tossed his cloak over the bodies. Then he started a fire at the cave's entrance, drew his sword, and waited.

The dogs paced behind their master. Soon, forced from its lair by the smoke, a were-bat came hurtling toward Doljust with an awful shriek. The creature was in its hybrid form, with the wings and head of a bat but the torso of a man. It raked at Doljust with the claws at the ends of its wings. The man raised his sword and swung.

Beshaba touched the pool again.

Goaded by the goddess's magic, one of Doljust's hounds forgot its training and leapt toward the were-bat's throat just as its master's sword came swinging downward. The blade sliced across the hound's ribs.

The dog gave a horrible howl, which echoed about the audience.

The were-bat flew clear of Doljust and landed on the mare's saddle. With a cackling laugh, it kicked the horse in the ribs. Doljust hollered, but the mare was frenzied with fear and galloped off into the darkness.

There were tears in Doljust's eyes as he examined his injured and apparently dying hound.

Beshaba touched the pool again.

The other hound whimpered behind him. Doljust whirled about, slicing his sword into a small were-bat as it flew from the cave.

The bat crashed to the ground, dealt a mortal wound.

Then, before Doljust's eyes, it transformed to a small child, a little boy with curly golden hair.

"Grandpa," the boy gasped with his last breath.

Doljust's screams rang out through the sensorium.

Beshaba laughed a horrible, maniacal laugh.

The darkness dispersed.

Ayryn's crystal ball fell to the floor with a *clunk* and rolled toward the audience.

There was a stunned silence in the room.

Bors came forward quickly and put a hand on Ayryn's shoulder.

"Are you all right?" he asked.

"Yes," Ayryn replied. "I . . . I was shocked, that's all." There were tears in her eyes.

Montgomery came forward, holding out the crystal ball.

"We don't have to continue," she said softly.

Ayryn took her scrying tool and shook her head. "It would be a shame to end on such a sour note. Let me try again."

Montgomery smiled and nodded. She returned to her seat.

Bors stepped back and examined the audience. Many of them looked as shocked as Ayryn, but most hid behind impassive masks. One guest, though, was smiling.

Bors felt his body stiffen. The guest was a woman, small of stature and slender, with long black hair. She was attractive and appeared quite young, but Bors knew her youth was a lie. The woman's name was Walinda. Once she'd been a priestess of the evil, now-deceased god Bane. While the Sensates welcomed anyone who earnestly desired to be a member, Bors found himself thinking Montgomery must have temporarily taken leave of her senses when she invited Walinda into their midst, especially for so sensitive a performance. Walinda was, in Bors's opinion, a viper in woman's form. He could still feel the bump on the back of his head where she had clubbed him with his own frying pan. Had the paladin not sworn his undivided service as Ayryn's bodyguard for the evening, he would have challenged the woman's presence.

The room darkened once more, though only slightly.

Two figures appeared in the center of the room, a young man with red hair and a slightly older raven-haired woman. The pair were seated at a table, drinking ale. They were the size of ordinary mortals, but the woman sported a pair of copper wings, and her face was covered with black feathers.

While the audience was busy trying to guess which gods they were seeing, Bors realized something had gone wrong with Ayryn's scrying. These people were not gods. The man Bors recognized as a priest named Joel, a Prime from Toril, the same world whose gods they were currently spying upon. Bors had never met the winged woman, but from a description his friend Holly Harrowslough had given him, he guessed she was another Prime by the name of Jas.

"Jas, you're being ridiculous about this," Joel said. "Give me one good reason why you won't come with me."

"I don't have to give you any reasons," Jas retorted. "This is my business. Why don't you just let me be?" The whites of her eyes flared, and her dark brown irises began glowing green.

"You don't mean that," Joel argued.

The vision quickly faded. Ayryn looked up, shaking her head. "Misdirected," she whispered in Montgomery's direction. "I'm going to try one more time," she said.

The room dimmed somewhat. A god Bors recognized appeared in the center of the room. The deity was seated on a bench, strumming a lyre. He appeared as a handsome young man about ten feet tall with shoulder-length hair of spun gold. He wore a tunic of fine brocade with fur trim. Behind him was a great library, with shelves and shelves of books and scrolls. The god was Milil, Lord of Song.

Milil looked up from his instrument. "At last, an audience," he said with a sly grin.

Bors's body tensed.

"Welcome, prying eyes," Milil greeted them. "I expect you to pay attention now. It's the least you can do after peering into my realm without invitation."

Milil began to sing "The Baker's Daughter," a love song about a silver dragon's love for a mortal woman. His voice was deep and mellifluous. Several of the women in the audience sighed.

Next Milil sang "Pipeweed Dreams," a halfling drinking song. Many members of the audience joined in, while others just hummed along softly.

Milil sang "The Seven Sisters," a long ballad. Then he sang "Three Thayvian Roses," a bawdy festhall tune that brought a blush even to Montgomery's face. Finally he began, "The Purple Dragons of Cormyr," another long ballad. A few members of the audience began to nod off. Milil woke them with a little shout. The concert continued. Milil began singing several old Torillian folk songs one about the weather, another about crops, and even one about milking cows.

Bors stole a glance at Ayryn. Surely she cannot keep scrying for much longer, he thought. She must be exhausted.

Ayryn's blue skin was pale. There was a glazed look over her eyes. Although deities could not enter Sigil, somehow Milil had managed to get some charm through the crystal.

"And now," Milil said, "I have a truly special treat. "The finale from the opera *The Fall of Myth Drannor*."

Bors slipped up to Ayryn and yanked the crystal ball from her hand.

Mercifully, Milil's image disappeared.

The audience shook themselves from their stupor. Montgomery laughed.

"My, but wasn't that interesting," the Sensate leader said.

I've heard that people commit murders at the operas and no one notices because everyone on stage is bellowing at the top of his lungs.

—Olive Ruskettle

Act One
Scene 1

Joel stood at the end of his last song and bowed to the audience. His long red hair fell forward and brushed the floor. The applause was loud and long and spiced with a few shouts of "More!" Joel made an exit, stage left. Though a very young man, he had been a bard long enough to know the three main rules of the entertainer. Don't turn your back on your audience. Don't upstage the act that follows. Always leave the audience wanting more.

"And that was Joel, the Rebel Bard, at the end of his exclusive engagement here at Chirper's Seawind Theater," the master of ceremonies announced. "Coming up in ten minutes, our next performer, the renowned juggling act of Shar Nova."

One of the stagehands slipped Joel a note.

The bard perused the writing quickly. "Finally," he muttered. He slipped through the dressing room, tied back his hair, retrieved his sword and knapsack, and stepped out into the theater. Nonchalantly he followed a few members of the audience who were taking advantage of the break to leave the theater.

Chirper's Seawind Theater emptied into Chirper's dining room. At this hour, the dining room was still very busy, so it wasn't easy picking out the author of the note. A woman with wings didn't stand out from the crowd in a

place like Chirper's. As one of the most popular inns in
Sigil, the City of Doors, Chirper's catered to a clientele as
diverse as the multiverse. More than a few of the guests
possessed wings, not to mention tails, horns, talons, and
antennae.

The native population of the Cage, as Sigil was called
locally, was comprised mostly of humans, the humanlike
githzerai; the half-ram, half-human bariaurs; the half-
human, half-fiend tieflings; and a few elves and dwarves.
The transient population outnumbered the natives by two
to one. Creatures from every known world and plane were
represented, and they all seemed to visit Chirper's. Evil
fiends from the lower planes who stood several feet taller
than an average human dined beside halflings no taller
than human children. Creatures that looked like giant
frogs argued across the dinner table with women with six
arms and snake tails instead of legs. Beings whose bodies
seemed to burn with fire broke bread with foxes and bears
who walked upright and wore clothing.

The only way to enter or leave Sigil was through one of
the city's innumerable magical portals. Many of the visitors were stranded there, having stepped through a one-
way portal and been unable to locate a portal that led
home or been unable to find the right key to a portal that
led home. Other, more worldly, visitors had come through
one of the two-way portals as tourists to the city. Some
came to negotiate with their enemies in the neutral city.
And since, for some mysterious reason, the portals would
not admit beings of godly power, a few came to do their
god's bidding here, while others came to escape the gods.

Joel had come to Sigil the first time searching for an
artifact for his god. He returned to use the city's portals to
disperse the pieces of that artifact throughout the multiverse, and to fulfill a bargain made with one of the city's
natives. Both tasks completed, the bard was anxious to
leave Sigil, but not without at least saying good-bye to
Jasmine of Westgate, one of his companions on his last adventure. After fruitlessly scanning the crowd, Joel pulled
aside the *maître d'* to ask where he'd seated the winged
woman who'd sent the note. The *maître d'* directed Joel to
a small table by the bar.

Joel found Jas sipping an ale just where the *maître d'* said she'd be. She was not bothering to cover up her gargoyle-like wings of patina-tinged copper or the black feathers on her face. She wore a new outfit, consisting of leggings and a jerkin of black leather that clung to her slender, well-muscled frame. A short sword in a scabbard and an azure cloak hung on the back of her chair. Her dark black hair was cropped close to her skull, and it shone nearly blue in the amber light of the lantern hanging over the table.

"Where have you been?" Joel demanded, taking the chair opposite her. He set his pack and weapon beneath his chair. "Holly and I were worried about you."

"I hate just banging around," Jas explained. "So while you were away, I took some work as a private courier for a high-up. Blood wanted to have me at her beck and call. So I left Dits's to stay at her case."

Joel grinned at the amount of Sigilian slang the woman had managed to pick up after only two weeks in this foreign place. Of course, that was to be expected. Jas was an experienced traveler. She knew how to make herself fit in anywhere.

"So, did you and Holly unload all the pieces of the hand?" Jas asked.

Joel nodded. The artifact whose pieces he had dispersed throughout the multiverse had been known as the Hand of Bane. He'd done it to help a paladin, Holly Harrowslough. Holly's god wanted to be sure the hand could never be made whole and used to resurrect the evil god Bane.

"Holly's friend Bors showed us several portals to other planes where we could hide the pieces," the bard explained to Jas. "Holly spilled the pieces into the void out over the edge of the city. Then she was summoned to Elysium to give the ring finger of the hand to her god."

"What's Lathander going to do with a stone finger?" Jas asked.

Joel shrugged. "Use it for a paperweight? Who knows? Anyway, Holly was thrilled. She waited around for two days, hoping to see you, but she couldn't keep her god waiting. She left for Elysium this morning. She's not sure when she'll be back."

The bard nodded as Jas's waiter set a mug of ale down in front of him and a fresh one in front of Jas.

"She's probably secretly hoping Lathander will ask her to serve in his court or something," Jas said.

Joel nodded in agreement. That was his suspicion as well. As a paladin of the Order of the Aster, Holly lived to serve the god Lathander. "She said she'd send word back if she wasn't returning soon," Joel explained. "So we could return home."

"Joel, you mean you're not keen to stay in the Cage?" Jas asked with a grin, using the slang term for Sigil.

Joel gave a quick glance at the tables nearby to be sure he didn't offend any eavesdroppers. "No, not really. This city has more political intrigue than Waterdeep, the people are more arrogant than Westgate merchants, and the air's more foul than a Zhentil Keep sewer," he answered.

"But that's all part of its charm," Jas replied.

Joel studied the winged woman's expression carefully, trying to determine if she was serious. Jas came from the same world as Joel and Holly, a place Joel called the Realms, but which Jas referred to as the world of Toril in the sphere of Realmspace. Jas had traveled through the void to worlds in other spheres in a magical ship called a spelljammer. Joel found it hard to believe she was now prepared to settle down in this awful city, but their last adventure had changed Jas. Perhaps she had decided to give up her wandering.

Jas grinned. "It does have one thing in its favor," Jas said.

"What?" Joel asked.

"I don't stick out like a sore thumb here," she said.

"You don't stick out all that much," Joel said.

"Ha!" Jas retorted. "Back on Toril, it was bad enough when I just had wings. Wizards were always trying to capture me to study me. People in the Realms would mistake me for a succubus or an erinyes and run me out of town. Once there was this kid who thought I was a were-eagle and tried to get me to attack him so he would contract lycanthropy and become a were-eagle, too. One crazy lich tried to put me in his harem just because of my wings. Gods only know what would happen if I went back to Realmspace now."

"If you'd stay in one place long enough for people to get to know you, they'd feel differently about you," Joel pointed out.

"Joel, you're too nice. Your friendship has made you blind to what I am," Jas declared. "Look at me . . . No, don't look away. Really look at me. I have black down and feathers all over my flesh and a crest of green feathers sticking out of my forehead. If I don't stay calm, my eyes glow like an owl's. Yesterday some snotty Taker tried to tax me twice in one hour, and I got so angry that one of my hands changed into a claw again. If that Taker hadn't been spry, he'd be missing an eye instead of just the tip of his nose. I'm more animal than human now. If I go back to Toril, there isn't anyone who's going to welcome me, except of course all those priests of Iyachtu Xvim."

Joel took a sip of his ale, debating whether he should continue arguing with the woman. The priests of the evil god Iyachtu Xvim had transformed Jas with a curse, trying to make her a dark stalker—a hunter they could use for their own foul purposes. Jas had managed to fight the transformation and retain part of her humanity, a testament to her willpower. If she were to kill someone, however, Jas would transform completely and forever into a creature of evil. There was a way for her to overcome the curse, however.

"Finder said he would try to help you," Joel said, reminding the older woman that his god had offered her his assistance. "All you have to do is ask. I've found a portal from Sigil to his realm in the outer planes. We can go there now if you want."

Jas shook her head vehemently. "I'm going to handle this myself. I don't want any god's help."

"Jas, you're being ridiculous about this," Joel said. "Give me one good reason why you won't come with me."

"I don't have to give you any reasons," Jas retorted. "This is my business. Why don't you just let me be?" The whites of her eyes and her dark brown irises began glowing green.

"You don't mean that," Joel argued.

"Damned if I don't," Jas snarled.

"Damned if you do," Joel whispered softly.

The winged woman glared at Joel for a moment, then whirled about and grabbed at something behind her chair. Something yelped behind her. With a sharp yank, she pulled the something forward, depositing it on the table in front of her with a unceremonious *thunk*.

The something was a small man with pointed ears and a topknot of very long brown hair. Over his indigo home-spun trousers and shirt, he wore a scarlet vest covered with pockets and an orange cloak over that. He was holding a crystal paperweight full of some dark liquid, in which floated a thousand glittering specks. Joel recognized the paperweight. Holly had bought it for Jas as a gift to help remind the winged woman of the stars, which couldn't be seen in Sigil. Joel didn't recognize the small man. He guessed that he was some sort of halfling who'd just picked Jas's cloak pocket.

"You lousy little halfling thief!" Jas hissed. She had both her hands about the creature's throat.

Joel gasped, alarmed by the sudden transformation of Jas's hands into the talons of a bird of prey. Her claws were piercing the thief's flesh. Blood was trickling down his neck.

"Ow! Careful with those claws," the creature squeaked.

Joel put his hands about the winged woman's wrists and managed to pull one talon away from her prey. The little creature tried to pull away, but Jas caught a clasp of his vest with the claws of the other talon, and he was stuck fast.

"You're mistaken, lassie," Jas's captive said with an offended air. "I'm not a halfling thief."

"Halfling, tiefling, leprechaun—I don't care," Jas said. "It won't matter once I've put you in the dead book."

"Kender, lass. I'm a kender," the creature said proudly. "I don't think I'd fit in a book, not even a great mage's tome, though once when I was a child I managed to crawl into a magic pouch. Magic is tricky, though, you know, and I couldn't find my way back out. My parents searched for me for hours. Finally I kicked my way out. Tore a huge hole in the back, ruined it. The man who owned it was furious, but, really, he shouldn't have left it lying around where a child could find it. I might have suffocated."

Jas growled at the kender.

"I was just going to ask if this was yours," the kender concluded quickly, holding out the crystal paperweight. "It's very lovely. Is it magical?"

"Jas," Joel whispered softly, "think what you're doing. Let the authorities handle this."

Jas snarled, deep in the back of her throat. If Joel were to release her wrists, she could tear out the kender's throat with a single blow or even break his neck.

"For gods' sake, Jas, if you're going to lose your humanity, at least do it killing something your own size," Joel implored.

"It reminds me of the stars on my home world," the kender said, peering into the crystal, apparently oblivious to how close he was to death. "Funny you can't see the stars in this town, or the sun. I miss the stars, don't you? Of course, if you're from around here, you've never had them to miss. Which is a real shame."

As if they were a magical chant, the kender's words softened Jas's heart. Her eyes became human again; her talons transformed back to hands. She pulled her hands from Joel's grasp and pushed her chair away from the table. She put her elbows on her knees and her head in her hands so Joel couldn't see her face.

"Is something wrong here, sir?" a waiter asked Joel.

"Just a little misunderstanding," the kender said.

Joel might have asked the waiter to remove the kender, but the creature was still bleeding from the wounds Jas had left about his throat. Brawling would get a person bounced out of Chirper's, but if they suspected Jas had drawn a weapon and wounded someone, the staff would alert the authorities.

"No problem," Joel said coolly.

The waiter studied the bard's face, searching his even features for any sign of a lie.

"Except that we could really use a plate of sandwiches and an ale for our friend here," Joel added.

"Yes, I'm parched and famished," the kender said.

"As you wish, sir," the waiter said with a shrug. He hurried off to the kitchen.

"Um, I'm Joel, a priest of Finder," the bard introduced himself.

"Pleased to make your acquaintance," the kender replied. "My name's Emilo Haversack. Just call me Emilo." He held out his right hand.

Joel accepted the kender's handshake.

"Finder, hmm?" Emilo queried. "That's another god I've never heard of."

"He's a new god from another world," Joel explained. "Let me have a look at those cuts on your neck before our meal comes."

"I'd appreciate that," the kender replied.

There was nothing in Emilo's tone that was the least bit sarcastic or threatening. His voice and manner were soft and mild, rather different than one might expect from a thief, but also different from the behavior of an innocent man accused of a crime. It was as if the creature were completely indifferent to the violent skirmish his actions had caused.

Joel pulled a stool over from the bar for the kender, and Emilo slid down onto it. Very gently Joel laid his fingers about the kender's bloody neck. Emilo closed his brown eyes, as if he thought the healing might hurt. He reminded Joel of a boy waiting for a birthday gift to be set down in front of him.

Joel noticed Jas looking up at the kender. The woman's face was pale beneath the feathers that covered her flesh. There were tears in her eyes, though whether from shame or self-pity, he could not tell. Noting that Joel was watching her, Jas looked back down at the floor.

Joel returned his attention to his patient. He noticed there were streaks of gray in the hair gathered back from Emilo's temples and fine lines all over the kender's face. In a soft voice, the bard prayed to his god. A dim blue aura of healing energy illuminated Joel's hands and seeped into Emilo's body.

The puncture wounds sealed up easily, leaving little scars, like flea bites. Joel wiped the blood from Emilo's neck with a handkerchief.

"That's much better," Emilo said, opening his eyes wide, as if surprised. "You're good at that," he said to Joel.

Joel bowed his head modestly. There was an awkward silence as he realized he was stuck with a chatty kender when what he really needed to do was talk some sense into Jas. "So, where is it you're from, Emilo?" he asked politely.

"Well, I was born and raised in the East, about twenty miles south of Kendermore, in a small village called Tengrapes," Emilo explained. "I've been wandering most of my life. Before I came here I was in the lair of a dragon called Flayze somewhere near Thorbardin. I stepped through a magical vortex and ended up in this city. I've been trying to get my bearings ever since I got here three days ago. I've asked all sorts of people, but not one of them can tell me how to get to any major city or kingdom that I've ever heard of." The kender gave a tiny shrug. "Geography seems to be a lost art among the people of this city."

"True," Joel agreed. "Maps are not particularly meaningful to them."

"We don' need no stinkin' maps," declared a drunken man seated at the bar. He wore a chain mail shirt and carried a double-headed axe. He pointed the axe handle in Emilo's direction. "You don' like that, you clueless sod, go back to Prime."

Jas stood up, whirled around, and took two steps toward the bar so that she stood nose-to-nose with the interloper. If the man had been standing, he would have towered a head taller than the winged woman. In a harsh whisper, Jas asked, "Did it ever occur to you that if you were on a Prime world, *you'd* be the clueless sod?"

"Never happen," the drunk said with a grin. "Never be so addle-coved that I'd leave the Cage."

"The way you're drinking, it's only a matter of time," Jas retorted. "Some night you'll make a wrong turn and step into a hidden portal by mistake. Could be a one-way portal, or you might never find the key that opens it on the other side."

"Bar that. What would you know?" the drunk muttered.

Jas stepped back and grabbed the crystal paperweight

from Emilo's hands. Then she stepped back to the drunk. "Oh, yeah," she said. "Let's see, if you've got the guts to scan this." She shoved the crystal in the drunk's face.

The drunk moved his head back, trying to focus his eyes on the glittering flecks.

"What do you see?" Jas asked.

"Nothing . . . just little specks of light," the drunk answered belligerently.

"Ah-ha!" Jas said. "Those little specks are called stars."

"So?"

"So. Like I said, it's only a matter of time before you'll be seeing them." Jas snatched the crystal away from the drunk's eyes. She shook her head and *tch*ed sympathetically. "Oh. Here's our sandwiches at last," she said as the waiter returned with a plate piled high with cold meat and cheese sandwiches and a mug of ale for Emilo.

Jas returned to her chair, slid the crystal back into her cloak pocket, and grabbed a sandwich.

The drunk staggered up to the table. "Are you telling me that crystal can see into the future? Let me see."

Jas shook her head. "Sorry. Only one look per person. Any more and you're likely to go mad. Besides, it doesn't matter what you see. It's your fate. You can't change fate."

"Let me see that crystal!" the drunk demanded, yanking at Jas's cloak.

Joel looked up at the waiter. "*This* gentleman's becoming something of a nuisance," he said.

The waiter nodded understandingly. He raised his hand over his head and snapped his fingers twice.

"You sodding Prime. You're going to give me another look at that crystal ball," the drunk insisted, "or I'm going to nick you good."

"Nick me well," Jas corrected.

Two bariaurs, creatures with the torso of a man and the body and horns of a mountain ram, took up a position on either side of the drunk. Each bariaur took an arm and lifted him from the floor. Together they carried him off, despite his loud protests that he "wasn't doing nothing" and that it was all that clueless birdwoman's fault.

Jas took a bite out of her sandwich. "Mmm. This *is* good."

Joel shook his head with a grin. "You may not stick out like a sore thumb here, but you'll never fit in with these Cagers," he said. "Their arrogance will always get on your nerves."

Jas shrugged and took another bite of her sandwich.

"So you do come from someplace where you can see the stars, don't you?" Emilo asked.

"I don't just come from a place where you can *see* the stars," Jas said. "I've traveled *to* the stars."

Emilo's eyes widened with amazement. "Really? That must be interesting."

"Sometimes," Jas agreed.

"Is the magic crystal ball from the stars?" the kender asked.

"No. My friend bought it at Lizzy's Paperweights over at the Great Bazaar," Jas said.

"Then it's not magical?" Emilo asked with a disappointed tone in his voice.

"Magical enough. It banished that lousy Cager, didn't it?" Jas asked.

Emilo chuckled. "Emilo Haversack," he reintroduced himself to Jas, holding out his hand.

"Jasmine. Just call me Jas," the winged woman said, accepting the handshake.

As they ate their sandwiches, Emilo kept up the conversation, relating a long, complex tale featuring a mad magician, a dragon, a human boy and girl, a historian, and himself.

When they'd finished their meal, Joel studied Jas, trying to gauge her mood. He'd known the winged woman for a little less than a month, so she was still something of an enigma to him. She looked calm and happy enough. Of course, that could work against Joel. When she was calm, Jas was less likely to accept the fact that she had a problem controlling the dark stalker within her.

Her behavior toward Emilo had taken a complete about-face. While it seemed highly improbable to Joel that Emilo had only been looking at Jas's crystal and had not intended to steal it, Jas now seemed to find the kender's company quite acceptable. Joel wondered if he could use that. The kender might serve as bait, or at least

as a face-saving excuse for Jas to accompany Joel to
Finder's realm.

"Emilo, I was planning on making a trip to Arborea to
visit a friend of mine," Joel said, deliberately avoiding
Jas's gaze. "He's something of a scholar. He might be able
to help you find your home again. Would you care to accompany me?"

"That's a very gracious offer," Emilo replied. "I'd be
happy to take you up on it. Not that I'm unhappy wandering, even in this strange city, but one does like to have
one's bearings, you know?"

Joel nodded.

"Are you coming, too, Jas?" Emilo asked.

Jas shot Joel a sly smile, as if to let the bard know that
she was wise to his tricks. "I'll walk you to the portal," she
said. She stood up and tossed enough coins on the table to
cover the cost of the food and drink and a large enough tip
that the disturbances with Emilo and the drunk would be
quickly forgotten. "Let's go."

Outside of Chirper's, it was very dark. A foul-smelling
fog hung over the city day and night, making the days
gloomy and the nights pitch black. Once upon a time, or so
Joel had been told, the city's streets had been lit by magical lamps on poles. Then, so the story went, some enter-
prising street urchins had discovered a cache of magical
lights and used it to create their own industry. After dis-
pelling the light on every lamp pole in the city, they began
offering their services as "light boys." The lamp poles had
been abandoned, and light boys were now an institution
in Sigil.

Although he could create his own magical light, Joel
had been convinced of the wisdom of spending the change
it took to hire a light boy. For one thing, the native young-
sters knew their way around the city far better than he
did. For another, the natives of Sigil had a vehement dislike of stinginess, and persons too cheap to hire a light boy
were more frequent targets of Sigil's very large population
of pickpockets and muggers.

As they stepped away from the inn, Joel signaled to a
group of light boys on the corner. One broke away from a
crowd of his associates and ran up to Joel. The urchin held

a silver wand enchanted with a light spell, which cast an unnatural orange glow in a circle all around him. He was no taller than Emilo, but a good deal thinner.

"Where you off to, sirs and lady?" the light boy asked.

"The Civic Festhall," Joel said, handing the boy a small coin.

The light boy started off down the street at a quick pace; the festhall was quite a ways off. Joel and his companions hurried after him. The fog was thicker than usual this evening and carried the stench of both sulfur and burning animal fat.

As they hurried through the darkness, Emilo began quizzing Jas about her travels to the stars. Jas described her spelljamming journeys among the crystal spheres that surrounded the worlds. Emilo listened, enthralled. Apparently the kender's people believed the gods came from the stars or someplace beyond. The idea that mere mortals could visit where the gods lived intrigued him.

Joel, who'd already heard some of Jasmine's tales, was trying to think of some way to convince Jas to come through the portal to Arborea with him. While he was pondering this problem, he became aware of the footsteps that seemed to be following the group. At first Joel dismissed the notion that they'd picked up a tail. The citizens of Sigil hardly recognized the difference between night and day. The footsteps could have been those of any number of people hidden by the dense mist going about their own business. Indeed, they often crossed the paths of other persons traveling in sedan chairs or on foot, guided by their own light boys. Besides, in the fog, it was hard to discern which direction a sound came from.

Joel grew aware that there was a clinking sound following them, as if they were being pursued by a ghost wrapped in chains. When the light boy made a left turn, the clinking sound followed them around the corner.

Emilo tugged on Joel's shirt sleeve. "I think we're being followed," the kender said softly.

"It's just echoes in the fog," Jas said with a shrug.

Joel shook his head. "No. I think he's right."

Their suspicions were confirmed in the next moment. A grating voice mumbled some indecipherable words, and some fell magic extinguished the light from their guide's wand, leaving them in total darkness.

"Hey!" the light boy cried out. "What's the big idear?"

Joel's first thought was to get the boy out of the way of whatever was undoubtedly preparing to attack. He dashed forward to push the boy to one side, but it wasn't necessary. Joel could hear the urchin's boots slapping on the cobblestones, veering off to the right. The bard crouched low to the ground on the chance that their attacker would aim high.

Jas screamed, then shouted, "Let go of me!"

Joel heard a sound like a sheet beating in the wind and felt a luff of air. Jas had spread her wings.

Joel drew his sword and murmured a prayer to Finder. His blade flared like a torch. It wasn't as bright as the light boy's wand had been, but it was enough to see what was going on.

They were being attacked by five men. Four were common street thugs, undoubtedly hired just for the purpose of abducting Jas, but the fifth one wore the white and green robes of a priest of the evil god Iyachtu Xvim. Xvim's priests were determined to recapture Jas and enslave her as their dark-stalker slave. One of the thugs, an especially large man, weighted with chains, had grabbed Jas about the middle, making it impossible for her to take to the air. The three remaining thugs, scrawnier than their companion, were dragging forward a large weighted net to throw over the winged woman.

Jas began screaming at the top of her lungs. Wise to the ways of the city, she wasn't crying for help but screaming, "Fire!" over and over again.

If the priest were brought down, Joel realized, the others might abandon the attack. With his sword raised, the bard moved toward the servant of Xvim.

The priest held his hands out as if to ward off a blow. A dark shadow seeped from the priest's palms; then two whirling black blades of mystic force shot out from his hands. The blades spun toward Joel.

The bard was able to ward off one of the blades with his sword. It sparked against the naked steel and then spun off into the darkness. The second spinning blade sliced

Joel's chest and left shoulder, then it, too, spun away. A horrible searing pain gripped Joel's whole left side, but he didn't let it deter him from his attack.

The evil priest raised his hands again, and Joel's sword smashed into the bracer protecting the priest's left wrist.

Joel dropped the tip of his blade and lunged. His sword sliced through the fabric of the priest's robe and stabbed into the priest's inner thigh. Blood gushed from the priest's leg, and he screamed in pain. Before the bard could press his attack, two blades buried themselves in his flesh, one in his back, the other in his right arm, causing the bard to drop his sword.

Joel looked down at the weapon that had struck his arm. It was the same ebony blade that had whirled off into the night. As he watched wide-eyed, it dissolved like the mist. Blood seeped from Joel's arm, staining his sleeve red. At least, Joel thought thankfully, there's no sign of the other blade.

The priest of Xvim unslung a mace from his belt and whirled it over his head, charging toward Joel.

The bard leapt to one side and rolled away.

The priest of Xvim spun about. Keeping his back to a garden wall, his eyes searched for his foe.

Crouching in the shadow of a wall buttress across the street, Joel cast a hasty healing spell to stanch the bleeding from the wounds he'd received from the magical blades. Then he eyed his sword with irritation. It lay in the middle of the street, glowing from the spell he'd cast on its blade. Should he try to retrieve it, the weapon would only serve as a beacon, and he was by no means certain that he would be able to use it to any effect with the injury to his arm. Suddenly he was aware that Jas had stopped screaming. Joel scanned the street for any sign of his friend, but in the darkness, he could spot neither Jas nor her attackers. They'd disappeared into the mist. Emilo was nowhere to be seen. In fact, Joel couldn't remember seeing Emilo at any time during the attack. Was the kender involved in the ambush? he wondered uneasily.

The question was moot at the moment. The priest of Xvim was still a problem. Joel considered casting a spell to heat the metal the priest carried, but he wasn't certain if the foe wore any armor beyond the bracers about his wrists, and the handle of the priest's mace was wooden. Then Joel's eyes fell on the answer.

A thick clump of razorvine climbed up the wall behind the priest of Xvim; its tiny dark leaves glittered in the light cast by Joel's sword. Not only could the bard use it to immobilize his enemy, but also if his enemy fought against it, its razor-sharp stems would do grave injury to any flesh they touched. Joel began whispering a prayer, motioning toward the vine with his fingers.

The vines twisted and writhed, then fell forward, wrapping themselves about the evil priest's throat, his raised mace and arm, and his waist. The priest cried out in surprise and tried to pull away from the wall. Then he began to scream in pain from the lacerations inflicted by the vine's stems.

Joel dashed out from his hiding place and scooped up his sword. In the next moment, he stood before his attacker with his sword pointed at the priest's chest, ordering him, "Don't move, or the vine will cut through your flesh to your bone. It's called razorvine. You must be new to Sigil, or you would have known not to get anywhere near it. The citizens here grow it to keep thieves out."

The priest of Xvim glared at Joel. "You are too late, priest of Finder," he gloated. "We have captured the winged woman. My master's servant will come to claim her, and she will be our dark stalker again."

"Jas!" Joel shouted down the street in the direction he suspected the thugs had dragged his friend. "Emilo!" His voice echoed back in the fog, but there was no reply from the winged woman or the kender. "You're going to tell me where they're taking her," Joel insisted, pressing the point of his sword ever so slightly against the priest's belly.

"Never," the priest replied.

"What's going on here?" a voice bellowed.

Joel lowered his sword and turned around slowly. Five Hardheads, the city watch, stood behind him. One carried a wand enchanted with a light as bright as the sunshine.

"Officers, this man attacked me," Joel declared, indicating the blood and scars from the freshly healed wounds on his arm and shoulder. "His henchmen have just abducted my friend, a woman named Jas. It's imperative that I find her before they smuggle her out of the city, but he refuses to tell me where they have taken her."

The highest-ranking Hardhead stepped forward. "Is that right?" he asked the priest of Iyachtu Xvim.

"The woman indentured herself as our servant," the priest said. "We are only reclaiming our own."

"That's a lie. She's a free woman," Joel snapped. "You have no claim on her."

"We'll have to sort this out back at headquarters," the Hardhead leader said. "Tell us where the woman is," he ordered the priest, "so we can determine the truth of your stories."

"I have no idea," the priest said.

"He's lying," Joel growled.

"Mitchel, convince the witness to cooperate," the Hardhead leader barked.

One of the other Hardheads stepped forward. The priest of Xvim glared disdainfully at the man. The Hardhead began a chant.

The Hardheads, Joel recalled, had special magical ways to make witnesses talk.

"You will never force me to speak!" the priest shouted. "I will die first!" With the fanaticism of the mad, he lunged forward until the razorvine about his neck sliced through his throat. Blood gushed down his robes, and he collapsed to his knees. He hung against the wall, still trapped by the razorvine.

Joel blanched in horror. Even the Hardheads looked shaken. The one casting the spell stuttered and grew silent. One of the younger Hardheads whispered an oath.

"You'll have to come in with us, sir, and file a statement," the Hardhead leader said.

"Please," Joel asked, "couldn't I search for my friend while the trail's still fresh? I don't think they could have taken her far. They have her wrapped in a net, so they'd have to go to ground nearby or risk being spotted by your patrols."

The Hardhead leader considered Joel's words briefly, then gave a sharp nod. "We'll help you. Describe your friend and the men who abducted her," he ordered.

"She's got short, dark hair, brown eyes, and she stands about this high." Joel held a hand up to his chin.

"Human, sir?" the Hardhead leader asked.

"Yes," Joel said, "but she's been cursed by the priests of this man's god," he explained, pointing to the priest of Xvim. "She has wings, and her skin is covered with feathers." The bard didn't bother to mention that Jas had the wings long before the priests of Xvim had transformed her into a dark stalker. There was no sense in confusing the authorities. "The men were common street thugs in dirty clothes. Three were pretty scrawny, but the fourth was a big, muscular man with chains around his body. They must have taken her in that direction." Joel pointed back up the street.

"You three go with this gentleman," the Hardhead leader ordered three of his men. "Stop anyone coming in your direction. Ask if they've seen her. Mitchel and I will knock on doors."

Joel hurried down the street with the three Hardheads. His heart was heavy with the fear that he might never find Jas. Anger gnawed at his gut as well, anger born of the suspicion that he and Jas had been set up for the ambush, anger now directed toward a certain suspicious kender by the name of Emilo.

Behind the Scenes

Somewhere in the outer planes a fire flared in an empty brazier. As brightly as it shone, it could not illuminate the edges of the dark hall where it burned.

In a high-pitched voice, a small creature cried out, "The summons! The summons!"

From the shadowy recesses, a deep, spiteful voice announced, "Finally the summons is issued." Then the speaker commanded, "Fetch the makers and their infernal machine while I prepare for our journey."

There was a scurry of activity in the great hall as servants hurried to carry out the order.

In a more brooding tone, the speaker murmured, "My scheme has taken root. How appropriate that it should happen at this very moment. Tymora has just lost one of her favorites, and soon she will lose far more. Tymora's luck will be mine."

Act One
Scene 2

Emilo had heard the priest of Iyachtu Xvim mutter the words that would extinguish the magic of the light boy's wand. There was menace in those words, of that the kender had been sure. The moment the light went out, Emilo dodged to the side and crouched behind a wall buttress. Once Joel used his own magic to light the blade of his sword, the kender was able to observe the attack completely unnoticed. The attackers didn't bother to search for him. They must have thought he'd run off, or else they didn't really care if he was present, thinking he posed no threat to their activity.

Joel seemed to be holding his own in his fight with the robed attacker, but Jas was completely inundated by the four men intent on bringing her down with a net. She screamed, "Fire!" at the top of her lungs until the men unstoppered some sort of vial under her nose. Then she collapsed, unconscious. The men dragged her off in the net. There was no time to wait for Joel to finish his battle with the fifth man. Emilo took off after the four men abducting Jas.

The kender had no trouble trailing behind the men despite the dark and the fog. The man who had first grabbed Jas was wearing chains which weighted him down and made it impossible for Jas to fly off. The chains jangled as he walked, and he and his companions all complained about having to drag the weight of the small winged woman. Emilo simply followed the noise they made.

They turned into a small alley. Near the back of the alley, a short set of steps led down to a door in the rear of a building. One of the men unlocked the door with a key and opened it. The men dragged their prize into the building and closed the door behind them. Emilo slipped quietly down the steps and put his eye to the door's keyhole.

A lantern lit the basement room beyond the door. The men hung the net holding Jas from a hook in the low ceiling. Then they sat in rickety chairs surrounding a rickety table and began playing cards. Emilo put his ear to the door.

"Perr's going to be mad about losing his light," one of the men commented. "Going to expect a bigger cut for leading the gullies our way."

"Not our fault. Priest were the one what fizzed it out," another man said. "Let him ask the priest."

"That's cold. And him just a boy. Still paying for the wand, he was," the first man said.

"Think we should tell the priest to light it up for him again," a third man said.

"Right," the first man agreed.

"You ask him, Sladdy. I'm not asking that snake for anything more than the money he owes us. Got venom in his looks, he does."

"What's taking him, I wonder? Don't suppose that berk with the sword did him in, do you?"

"Not a chance. Probably just got lost. No matter. His boss will be here soon. He's the one with the purse anyway."

"The priest's boss is the one that gives me the shakes. There ain't no man under that cloak. It's a creature from the Lower Planes, if you ask me."

"No one asked you."

Emilo pulled away from the door. Even if Joel did defeat the priest, Jas wouldn't be safe. Someone else would be coming for her, someone undoubtedly very nasty, unless Emilo could rescue her somehow. Hastily the kender concocted a plan.

He pounded hard on the door with the back of his dagger. "Sladdy, it's Perr!" he called out in a fair imitation of the light boy's voice. Then he ran back up the stairs and hid in the shadows.

A few moments later the door opened and one of the men poked his head out.

"Perr? Where are you, boy?"

"Hiding," Emilo whispered in the darkness. "Hard-heads caught the priest. Priest turned stag on ya; told 'em where to find you and the girl. Hardheads are coming this way. Better run while you can," he called out. Then, keeping to the shadows, the kender ran back down to the end of the alley and ducked behind the corner.

Emilo had to wait only about a minute before all four men came tearing out of the alley and ran off down the street. He hurried back into the alley. It was a simple matter to pick the lock on the door and slip inside. The lantern was still lit.

Jas still hung inside the net on the hook. She was just regaining consciousness, stirring in the net and muttering some foul oaths.

"Jas, it's me. Emilo. You've got to hold still so I can cut you out," the kender hissed.

"Where are we?" the winged woman demanded as Emilo sliced at the rope net with his dagger.

"Somewhere we want to get far away from quickly," Emilo answered.

"Why?" Jas asked.

"The priest's boss is coming here. Someone from the Lower Planes, they said. Is that a bad place?"

Jas swore again. She grabbed Emilo's dagger and began slicing at the net in frenzied fear. Emilo worked more methodically with his sword. In a few moments, Jas tumbled to the floor, landing on her tailbone. As Emilo helped her to her feet, she grimaced in pain. "There?" she asked, pointing to the door to the alley.

Emilo nodded. They rushed out the door and hurried up the steps. Once in the alley, Emilo froze. From the end of the alley, he heard a noise, a croaking, gulping sound. There was a whiff of sulfur in the air.

The kender dragged Jas farther down the alley and pulled her down to crouch beside him in the dark shadows.

They'd left the door to the kidnappers' hideout open, so a faint beam of light streamed out into the alley. A giant creature stepped out of the mist into the beam of light. It resembled a frog, though it was several feet taller than a man. It made its way down the alley, walking on its hind legs. It seemed to be looking straight at them. Emilo felt a momentary sense of hopelessness steal over his heart.

Then the kender felt Jas stiffen and sway. Her eyes seemed to glow in the dark. She reached her hand out toward the frog creature. Fortunately the frog creature, standing in the light, could not see into the dark shadows where they were hiding. Nonetheless, its gaze seemed to exert some evil power over Jas. The kender slid his hands over the winged woman's eyes.

Jas's body shook, then relaxed.

The frog creature shimmered and shrank, then transformed itself into the shape of a man in a great cloak. In human form, it made its way down the steps, ducked through the door, and disappeared into the thugs' hideout.

Emilo grabbed Jas's hand and tugged her to her feet. They ran past the door, down the alley, turned, and dashed down the street, around another corner, and down another street. They didn't stop running until they bumped into a Hardhead with a light wand who ordered them to halt.

"I haven't done anything," Jas insisted. "I'm running from a creature who tried to abduct me."

"I know, miss," the Hardhead said. He blew a shrill whistle. A few moments later, Joel and two more Hardheads appeared out of the mist. Joel's tunic was torn and stained with blood, and his flesh beneath was scarred but not bleeding. He looked sick with worry.

"Jas!" Joel cried out. "Thank goodness you're all right."

"Thank Emilo," Jas corrected. "He helped me escape. If it hadn't been for him, I'd be a prisoner in Gehenna right now."

Joel looked surprised, but he was relieved to learn his suspicions about the kender had been incorrect. He broke into a smile and clapped a hand on the kender's shoulder. "Thank you," he said heartily.

"Show us where you left the thugs that captured you," one of the Hardheads ordered.

"I don't want to go back there!" Jas declared, her voice rising in pitch. "There's a monster back there who wants to take me to Iyachtu Xvim."

"Iyachtu Xvim?" the Hardhead asked, puzzled. The other two Hardheads rejoined the group in the street.

"Xvim's an evil god of one of the Prime worlds," Joel explained.

"The monster was an evil creature from the Lower Planes," Emilo added with obvious relish. "It was a giant green and yellow frog, ten feet tall. It shape-changed into a man in a cloak."

Joel bit his lower lip, wishing the kender were less extravagant with his description. No one is going to believe such an exaggeration, he thought.

But the Hardheads seemed to take the description in stride. "Hydroloth," one said.

"Undoubtedly," the leader replied.

"It's in a basement room in the alley beside the alchemist's guildhall," Emilo offered helpfully.

The Hardhead leader nodded. "Got it. You three can wait here," he told Jas, Joel, and Emilo. "Follow me, men."

The Hardheads followed their leader into the dark mists of Sigil, intent on apprehending the amphibian culprit.

"Let's go," Jas whispered.

"They told us to wait here," Joel replied.

Jas rolled her eyes and sighed. "They said we *could* wait here. They didn't say we *had* to. If you think I'm waiting around so I can testify against a hydroloth in a Sigilian court of law, you're nuts. I've had it up to here with this whole dark-stalker problem. I'm ready to do whatever it takes to keep from getting delivered to Iyachtu Xvim, even if it means asking for help from another god. Now, are you going to take me to Finder or not?"

"All right," Joel agreed before the winged woman had a chance to change her mind. "Let's go. This way," he said, heading down the street in the direction of the Civic Festhall. Jas followed.

Emilo trotted along beside Jas. "This scholar friend of Joel's that we're going to see—is that Finder?" the kender asked.

Jas nodded.

"Is he really a god?" Emilo asked excitedly.

Jas shrugged. "He and Joel seem to think so."

Joel turned and shot Jas an annoyed look.

Jas grinned. "But neither of them claim that he's a real important god," she explained.

"But he lives in a place called Arborea?" Emilo asked.

Joel nodded.

"Is that in the stars?"

Joel shook his head. "It's one of the Outer Planes. That's where our gods live . . . most of them anyway."

"Is that different from the Lower Planes, where the frog creature came from?" the kender asked.

"The evil gods dwell in the Lower Planes, one of which is called Gehenna. That's where the frog creature came from. Arborea is one of the Upper Planes. Finder is a good god," Joel explained. He shot a challenging look at Jas, but the winged woman made no comment. Her mind, Joel could tell, was on the evil god in Gehenna whose priests were trying to enslave her.

Act One
Scene 3

Bors Sunseed slipped quietly back into Factol Montgomery's private reception hall where she was evaluating the evening's performance with her advisers.

Montgomery's consort Da'nanin looked up at the paladin. "How is Ayryn doing?" he asked in a soft voice.

"She's resting comfortably. Just exhausted," Bors replied.

"Good, good," the bariaur Annali Webspinner said. As the registrar for the society, Annali had "discovered" Ayryn's gift first, and consequently felt a certain protectiveness toward the scrying genasi.

"More importantly, will she try it again?" Adviser Kenda Fretterstag asked.

"That's a decision she should sleep on, I think," Bors replied, keeping the tone of his voice completely neutral. Kenda charmed more people with her statuesque beauty than she did with her magic, but Bors did not care for the human sorceress. Her interests were always selfish.

"Just so," Quellig, a wizard, said. "Time for me to go, I think. I had a perfectly lovely evening, Erin." He took the factol's hand and kissed it, giving her consort a sly glance. The wiry-framed, blue-skinned Quellig was a tiefling, with all the love of mischief and flirting for which tieflings were renowned. "You throw such interesting parties."

"Thank you, Quell," Montgomery replied, rising to her feet. "And you are always such a perfect guest."

Taking the hint, Kenda and the other advisers rose and bid their host and hostess good night. Then they filed from the private reception hall. When the last one had gone, Bors closed the door behind them.

"My lady," he addressed Montgomery.

"What is it, Bors?" the factol replied.

"Two matters," the paladin said. "First, I was curious how that Prime, Walinda, managed to insinuate herself onto the guest list for this evening. Security is a very sensitive matter. That is why you asked me to serve this evening. Did you know she was a priestess of the god Bane?"

"Of course I knew she was a priestess of Bane. However, now that Bane is dead and Walinda has abandoned her quest to resurrect him, I am not overly concerned that she might rat on us to her god," the factol said with a grin. She curled up on the sofa beside Da'nanin.

"How do you know she hasn't already offered her services to the Baneson, Iyachtu Xvim, or one of the other evil gods who've filled in the void of power left by Bane?" Bors objected.

"I've spoken with her at length," Montgomery replied. "I don't think that's very likely. She's rather soured on gods of the male gender at the moment. She played by all his rules, yet Bane did not reward her as was her due. It's left a rather large scar on her. As a matter of fact, I asked her to come this evening to help her search out a goddess to whom she might be willing to offer her services. Frankly, I'm surprised by your reaction. She said your friend Holly Harrowslough recommended she come to us."

"Holly was taunting Walinda when she suggested that. Walinda was belittling our quest for sensations. She is too fixated on her own sick desires to understand a decent pleasure." Bors halted. He remained silent for several moments, trying to find how to put his feelings into words that did not offend.

Montgomery did not need his words to know his feelings. The topic of discussion between them was not a new one. "Walinda came to join us, Bors, and Annali was convinced of her sincerity. Annali has always been completely impartial in such decisions, and I am not about to override her nomination of a registrant. Walinda has made all five of her recordings for us, and they have been approved."

"I see," Bors said, lowering his eyes. All initiates were required to make recordings of worthwhile experiences that focused on the five senses. Once an initiate had contributed recordings covering all five senses and those recordings had been accepted, the initiate became a full member of the faction.

"Yes, so you should," the factol replied. "Walinda is a Sensate now and entitled to the rights and respect deserving of her position. I expect you to welcome her as you would any other member."

"Lady, she is not just any other member. If you keep this woman among us, you will regret it one day. You know that I have done my best to get along with persons whose greed or jealousy or hatred or lust for power has poisoned their souls. But Walinda's evil is different. Walinda takes pleasure in the pain of others. Walinda takes pleasure in inflicting that pain."

"That was obvious from the recordings she made for us," Montgomery replied. "You should consider experiencing one of them. Perhaps you would understand her better."

"I would prefer to understand sickness from a distance, lady. The sensation of putrefying my soul does not intrigue me in the least," Bors said coolly.

Montgomery's eyes flashed angrily.

Da'nanin set his hand down gently on the factol's and said, "Bors is entitled to his repulsion. Walinda's feelings could not, after all, coexist with Bors's specific specialization."

The paladin gave the half-elf a grateful look.

Montgomery calmed down somewhat. Like many of the more powerful Sensates, Bors specialized in a particularly esoteric range of sensations. The paladin was exploring all the aspects of purity of the heart. Da'nanin knew well that the factol was more than pleased with the paladin's work in the field. She enjoyed the recordings he made and collected from others.

The factol sighed. "You may be right. What was the second matter you wished to discuss?" she asked the paladin.

"I thought you might be interested to know the identities of the two persons Ayryn scried when she was misdirected," Bors said.

"Yes," Montgomery agreed.

"They are friends of Holly Harrowslough, the ones that were seeking the Hand of Bane. The winged woman's name is Jasmine, a spelljammer sailor, and the red-haired man is a bard named Joel. Joel is also a priest of a god named Finder."

"Finder? I don't recall any god called Finder. Is he a god of Toril?" Montgomery asked.

"A very minor new power," Da'nanin interjected. "There's a book about him making the rounds, as I recall."

Bors nodded. "It's a tale Joel told to a bookseller named Dits. To get to the heart of the matter, Tymora, the goddess of luck, is an ally of this god Finder. Apparently Lady Luck had a hand in seeing that Finder obtained godhood when he destroyed another evil god. When I asked Ayryn, she said she was indeed trying to scry for Tymora when she was misdirected to the two mortals."

"That's interesting," Da'nanin said. "Tymora's spell misdirected us to her ally's priest. Could there be meaning in that, do you think?"

Bors shrugged.

"Can you find these people, Joel and Jas, so we can speak with them?" Montgomery asked. "Perhaps Holly knows their location."

"Holly left for Elysium this morning," Da'nanin reminded her.

"Oh, yes. Called hence by her god. Now, there's an experience!"

Bors nodded in agreement. "Joel is still in Sigil. He's been staying with the bookseller I mentioned before, a bariaur named Dits."

The door to the private reception hall opened suddenly. Annali Webspinner poked her head in and whispered excitedly, "They're here! The man and the winged woman that Ayryn scried tonight. They've come to speak to Bors."

"Very efficient, Bors," Da'nanin teased. "How did you do that? Mirrors? Time travel?"

"Please show them in, Annali," Montgomery requested.

A few moments later, Joel, Jas, and Emilo found themselves ushered into a private reception hall. Joel looked slightly surprised. He had expected to speak with Bors alone. The presence of the half-elf and the lovely

Montgomery left him momentarily speechless. He was
agonizingly aware of how dirty and disheveled he must
look after his combat with the priest of Xvim.

Fortunately the paladin seemed to recognize the bard's
discomfort. Bors stepped forward. "Lady, allow me to introduce Joel of Finder. Joel, this is our factol, Erin Darkflame Montgomery, and her adviser, Cuatha Da'nanin."

"I'm pleased to meet you. Welcome to the Civic Festhall," Montgomery said to the bard. She did not seem to be
taken aback by Joel's appearance, but smiled warmly at
him.

Joel bowed. "Allow me to present my companions, Jasmine, and Emilo Haversack. Please excuse our interrup-
tion, but Holly led me to understand that you might allow
me access to your portal to Arborea. We were hoping to
travel there as soon as possible."

"Ordinarily we charge a fee for that, don't we?" Montgomery asked Annali. The bariaur adviser remained by
the door, too curious to leave.

"An exchange of a sensation recording," Annali said.
"An important one."

Joel hesitated. He was not shy about sharing his experiences with others; indeed, that was a large part of his
training as a bard. He had already related his most important experience to Dits the bookseller, who had
recorded it in a more traditional medium with paper and
ink. Dits had then made a tidy profit selling the story as
an adventure serial in three parts, and a small fortune
selling the collected serials. Joel had been glad to see the
tale get an audience, since it helped spread the word
about Finder. Making a Sensate recording would guarantee an even larger audience, but there were things about
the Sensates' recordings that disturbed the bard. They
could be made by anyone, since there was no particular
skill required of the person making a sensation recording.
They were also said to be so real that those who played
them back sometimes came to prefer them to the reality of
their own lives.

"Is it true you were a companion of your god Finder for
quite some time before he revealed to you that he was a
god?" Da'nanin asked.

"Yes," Joel admitted with a sheepish grin.

"That moment must have been quite wonderful for you," Da'nanin guessed. "It would be just the sort of thing we would love to have on a recording. But . . . you did say you were anxious to travel to Arborea as soon as possible. We'd be willing to send you through our portal now, and you can record for us when you return to Sigil."

The half-elf must have read Dits's book, Joel realized, and understood how he felt about Finder. Somehow that made the bard feel as if Da'nanin might be trusted. "Your offer is most gracious," Joel said. "I accept."

"Perhaps your companions would consider making a recording for us sometime as well," Montgomery suggested. She turned a winning smile on Jas and Emilo.

"Be glad to help out any way I can," the kender said with a low bow that sent his topknot sweeping the marble floor. "I've had lots of interesting experiences."

"And you, Jasmine? I'm sure you must have something to share with our audiences," Montgomery said.

"Not unless your audiences enjoy the feeling of being cursed by the gods and having their lives completely disrupted," Jas replied in a honey-sweet tone that mocked the factol's own, yet did nothing to cover her own bitterness.

Joel looked down at his feet, embarrassed by Jas's behavior, but Montgomery was completely unruffled by the winged woman's rudeness. "Some of them just might," she replied.

"Oh," Da'nanin said, "just one thing. In cases such as these, where someone owes us a recording, Annali usually insists we get a lock of hair or some such trifle as a token of good faith."

Joel nodded in agreement.

"Well, then," Annali said, "if you'll follow me, I'll take you to the portal."

"Thank you," Joel said, bowing low to the Sensates. Annali led the three visitors through a doorway in the back of the private reception hall.

When they had gone, Montgomery asked, "Cuatha, my love, what do we need with a lock of that young man's hair?"

"Give it to Ayryn," Da'nanin replied. "It will make it easier for her to scry for him."

"You clever, devious man," Montgomery said, tugging playfully on the half-elf's earlobe.

"Joel is a man of his word," Bors insisted. "He will honor the bargain. Why do you need to scry for him?"

"Bors, Bors," Montgomery laughed. "Think. Joel is going to Arborea. What is he going to do in Arborea?"

"Visit his god, perhaps. I believe Finder makes his home in that plane somewhere near Bright—" Bors paused, realizing what the factol had in mind. "You're hoping to scry and record their meeting," Bors said, realizing what the factol and her consort had in mind.

Montgomery nodded. "And who knows? Perhaps they'll visit Brightwater."

"Where Tymora makes her realm," Bors noted.

"Then we might get a glimpse of the elusive Realms goddess of good luck," Montgomery said.

Act One
Scene 4

Jas slid her dagger blade across several strands of Joel's hair near the nape of his neck. "I can't believe you're doing this," she muttered to the bard. Joel gave her a weary smile as he retied his hair back up with a strip of leather.

They stood before a doorway in some dark, secret chamber. Annali had brought them here via two magic portals, but Joel felt sure they were still somewhere beneath the Civic Festhall. He could hear music playing somewhere above. He took the strands of his hair from Jas and handed them to Annali.

"It's a lovely color," the bariaur Sensate said as she wrapped the strands around her fingers.

"Thank you," Joel replied.

"You need to take these," Annali said, handing Joel three acorns. "They act as a key to the portal. Simply step through. Your friends should follow right behind you before the portal closes. When you arrive, you'll be facing the Gilded Hall of the Sensates. It's a place of great beauty . . . some would call it a paradise. I do not think you will be visiting there, though, will you?"

Joel shook his head. "I have another destination in mind. Thank you again," the bard said, bowing briefly before the bariaur. He turned and stepped through the magic portal. Jas and Emilo followed close on his heels.

They emerged on a wooded hillside beneath a moonlit night sky. A mild breeze cooled, but did not chill, the summer air surrounding them.

"I can't believe you gave them a lock of your hair," Jas said, stepping in front of Joel. "They could use that in all sorts of magic spells," the winged woman lectured. "You know that, don't you? What were you thinking?"

The bard was temporarily distracted by the sight of Jas's wings. Whenever she traveled to a different plane, her wings took on a new form. Her face was still covered in the black feathers that had come with the curse of Iyachtu Xvim, but since she'd stepped through the magic portal, her wings were no longer hard and metallic, but feathered, as they'd been in the Realms where she'd been born. In the Realms however, her feathers had been white, tinged with pink. Here in Arborea, they were deep blue, brilliant green, and sparkling gold, in the pattern of peacock feathers.

"Joel, stop looking at my stupid wings," Jas snapped with exasperation. "How could you let them have some of your hair?"

Joel sighed. "Jas, Holly said I could trust Bors. I trust Holly's judgment," he said.

"It's the loveliest thing I've ever seen," Emilo said softly.

"What?" Jas growled, prepared to berate the kender for admiring her wings.

The kender pointed outward.

Jas looked up, then breathed in sharply in astonishment.

"The Gilded Hall," Joel said. "Annali didn't exaggerate. It is a place of great beauty."

In the distance, across a valley, on the opposite bank of a shimmering river, stood a castle that seemed to glow in the moonlight. It was crowned with several domed towers of varying sizes, from graceful spires that soared into the sky to massive halls that hugged the hillside. The reflections of the moon and stars sparkled on the domes and on a tremendous fountain outside the castle, which splashed as high as some of its towers. Waterfalls spilled from the fountain into a cascading stream, which glittered all the way down to the river. Fertile fields and lush woodlands covered the outlying lands like plush velvet surrounding a rare and stunning piece of jewelry. Although they were some distance from the castle, Joel could have sworn he smelled roses and petunias from the gardens. He even imagined he heard laughter and music wafting across the river valley.

Emilo tilted his head back and looked straight up. "It's good to see the stars again," the kender said, "even if I don't recognize any of them."

"Yes," Jas agreed. Suddenly she laughed and launched herself into the air.

Joel looked up at the sparkling lights in the black sky. Their pattern was completely unfamiliar, but they were lovely to look at. As he watched, a few of them shot across the sky and vanished. The moon was only a sliver, but bright and silvery as an elven blade.

Jas soared out over the river and arched back. In the peaceful stillness, the bard and the kender watched the winged woman in companionable silence. Jas landed beside them.

"Sorry about that. I just suddenly had to fly. I don't know what came over me."

"Perhaps it was simply the beauty of the place," Emilo suggested.

Jas looked around and shrugged. "Maybe," she said. She changed the subject, as she often did, to avoid discussing her feelings. "So. Where's Finder?" she asked Joel.

"His realm is between here and the town of Brightwater."

"I thought you said the portal led to his realm," Jas said.

"Well, near his realm," Joel said. "It's a nice evening for walking. We should be there before the moon sets."

"We'd better be," Jas said. "We don't have Holly with us anymore to help us live off the land."

"I'm good at that," Emilo said. "I can bring down a bird with a stone. Once I brought down two birds with one stone. And I can fish. I love to fish. And I can trap rabbits. That's almost too easy. If you want to know what berries are good to eat, you can't always rely on the birds because birds can eat poisonous berries, but people can usually eat what the bears eat. Bears also know how to dig for roots. If you're not sure about eating something, you should find a bear. But be sure the bear doesn't find you."

Jas laughed. "Well, we're lucky to have your wisdom

because Joel and I are both city folk and haven't a clue about trapping or what berries are safe to eat. And I certainly don't want to find any bears."

"I can create food with a spell," Joel reminded her.

"Bread. You can create bread with a spell," Jas corrected.

"It's good bread," Joel countered.

"When you can create stew and custard and berry pie, then you'll be creating food," Jas retorted.

Joel harrumphed.

"I like bread," Emilo said. "Especially herb bread. Though I'm also very fond of sweet rolls with raisins. Herb bread is good with little bits of cheese baked into it. Though not necessarily with stew. With stew, you want a plain bread you can use to sop up the gravy. One with a lot of bite to the crust, but soft inside. Of course, berry pie is always good. I know some people who won't eat raspberries because of the little seeds, but that's as silly as not eating fish because of the bones. The really good foods always have little annoying things like seeds and bones. Like life, I guess. Of course, bread doesn't have seeds or bones. But I do like bread."

"Well, it won't really matter if we reach Finder's for breakfast," Jas said. "Which way?"

"There should be a road leading from the Gilded Hall to the town of Brightwater. There's a path that heads away from the road that leads to Fermata."

"Fermata?" Jas asked.

"That's the name of Finder's realm," Joel said. "It's a musical term for a hold over a note or a rest."

"So which is it?" Jas asked. "A hold over a note or a rest?"

"Well, either one . . . both, really," Joel explained. "Finder's life and his music are sustained in his realm, and it's also a place where he can rest."

"There's a road leading off in that direction," Jas said, pointing along the ridge above the river valley. "I saw it from the air."

They made their way along the ridge until they reached a hard-packed dirt road. In one direction, it wound down into the valley to a bridge supported by seven graceful stone arches, then wound back up the valley toward the Gilded Hall. In the opposite direction, it led along the ridgeline into a dark forest.

"How about a light?" Emilo asked.

"I don't have the power to cast another one tonight," Joel said.

"Not to worry," the kender said. He pulled a small torch from his backpack and flint and steel from one of the pockets of his vest. With expert ease, he lit the torch from sparks in a matter of moments. Jas applauded his skill. Emilo bowed and handed the torch to the winged woman.

They plunged into the forest, moving at a quick pace down the road. The ground was dry, but not dusty. The canopy of leaves overhead blocked their view of the stars and moon, but the forest itself twinkled with fireflies.

They'd traveled for some time when Emilo reported he heard someone coming toward them from up ahead. A few minutes later, they saw lights and heard shouts and laughter. Despite Joel's protests that there could be no harm in greeting the natives, Jas was loath to encounter strangers. She insisted they put out their torch in the dirt and take cover. Once Emilo smothered the torch in the dirt, Jas flew the kender and the bard to a branch high overhead, then settled beside them.

The strangers, dozens of them, moved as one, not like a troop of soldiers but more like a mob of revelers. Occasionally one stumbled but was kept from falling by a companion. There were both men and women in the group, all shabbily dressed and dirty. They passed about wineskins from which they drank as if they were dying of thirst. Arguments broke out whenever one failed to pass a wineskin quickly enough to suit his or her companions. One of the women carried an enormous rat in her arms, which she stroked as if it were a pet cat. As the mob passed below the trees where Joel, Jas, and Emilo hid, the stench of wine and unwashed human bodies assaulted the adventurers' noses.

When the last of the strangers' torches had disappeared behind a bend in the road, Jas turned to Joel. "Not the sort of natives we really needed to greet, were they?" she asked with an air of the worldly wise.

"I take my hat off to your superior distrust," Joel replied.

Jas harrumphed. When they'd relit their torch and were once again safely on the ground, they continued through the forest more warily. Emilo traveled in the front since he had the best hearing of the three.

By the time they finally came out of the forest, the moon had set. Some distance ahead of them, the sky was noticeably lighter, as if from a well-lit city. The road now passed through meadows and fields planted with grain and grapes.

The road led through a grove of ancient oaks, and Jas tripped over a huge tree root.

"That's it," the winged woman said. "Time to make camp."

"But it can't be far now," Joel protested.

"Joel, I'm dead on my feet, and I'm willing to bet you've been overly optimistic about the distance we have to travel. Besides, in the dark we might miss the path to Fermata. I think we should rest here until dawn."

"I think she's right," Emilo said. "I'm beginning to feel stretched a bit thin."

Joel sighed. He was eager to see Finder again and excited about the prospect of visiting Fermata, but he knew Jas and the kender were right. It was too late to continue. He nodded in agreement.

Nestled between the roots of the largest oak tree in the grove and wrapped in their capes, Jas and Emilo were soon asleep. Joel, less tired than the others, sat up and kept watch. A trio of raccoons, a mother and her young, trundled past and climbed into their lair in a hole in a nearby tree, but otherwise the grove was peaceful save for Emilo's soft snoring.

As the sky began to lighten, Joel softly hummed a song to greet the dawn. Songbirds began to stir and chirp in the trees. Teasingly Joel began whistling back replies. He felt a gentle hand touch his shoulder.

"Good morning," he said, turning about, expecting to see Jas.

The hand did not belong to Jas, however, but to another woman. An elf maiden was Joel's first guess, until he saw that her curly hair was as deep green as the leaves on the oak trees that surrounded them. Still, she was very, very lovely, slender and graceful, with dark amber-colored eyes and skin as smooth as satin. She wore a gown pieced together of light, shimmering bits of fabric in a variety of colors, but mostly green, gray, brown, and pink.

"Greetings," the woman said in Elvish. Her voice was soft and deep, but there was a slight hint of disapproval in her tone.

"Soft light, sweet lady," Joel replied in the same tongue. The woman drew back a step and giggled.

Joel stood and bowed. "My name is Joel. These are my companions, Jas and Emilo. If you make your home here, lady, please forgive our intrusion," he said. His words came slowly, since he was taxing his knowledge of the elves' language to its limit.

"I am Ada," the woman said. "Your Elvish is not very good," she chided.

"I have very little practice," Joel admitted. "But so sweet a voice as yours could teach me well."

Ada giggled again, lowering her eyes to the compliment. Then she slipped behind the tree and disappeared from view.

Joel circled about the tree, but the woman had vanished.

"Ada?" Joel called softly.

Jas moaned and rolled over in her sleep. Emilo snored on.

Something tugged away the strip of leather that held back his hair. The bard spun about. Ada stood behind him, appearing as if out of nowhere. Joel grinned. "How did you do that?" he asked.

Ada stepped closer to the bard. A sweet scent rose from her skin. She stroked Joel's long hair and smiled with pleasure.

Without thinking, Joel reached out and ran his hand through the green curls that crowned Ada's head. They were soft and warm.

Ada brushed her lips against the bard's, then quickly drew back. Giggling, she disappeared behind the tree again.

"Ada, come back," the bard called softly, circling the tree once more.

Ada appeared suddenly before him and wrapped her arms about his neck. Joel embraced her about the waist. As if in a dream, he felt no embarrassment whatsoever about kissing this perfect stranger. Her mouth was as sweet as her laughter, and her caresses made his heart pound. Joel couldn't understand why he should suddenly feel so enamored of this woman, unless he was indeed dreaming.

That was it, he decided. He was more tired than he thought, and he'd fallen asleep. He really should stir himself awake, he thought, but he had no desire to do so.

From the edge of the grove, a familiar voice called out in Elvish, "Hold, sprite! Release him."

Ada and Joel turned to the speaker. Finder stepped into the grove. The god wore the form he had possessed when he'd been mortal, that of an older man, but one still in his prime. His bearing was strong and regal, and his dark brown hair and beard held only the slightest streaks of gray. Joel found himself unable to speak but wishing he could tell his god that he didn't wish for Ada to release him, ever.

"I'm sorry, Ada," Finder said, "but you cannot keep him. He is mine, and I have far more important things for him to do than fetch you honeycombs and weave clover crowns for your hair."

"You should have to ransom one so fair and sweet," Ada said, tossing her head saucily.

Finder held out his hand. In his palm rested a large golden acorn carved from an amber so dark it seemed to have blood mixed into it. "To match your eyes," the god said.

Ada kissed Joel once more on the lips and stroked his stubbly cheek. Then she ran to Finder's side and snatched the acorn gem from his hand. With a laugh as thick as honey, she ran back toward the largest oak and disappeared like a ghost into the tree's trunk.

Finder moved toward Joel and set his right hand on the bard's chest, just over his heart.

Joel felt a sudden shock, as if someone had splashed

cold water on him. Although the attraction to Ada remained, the enchantment he'd felt for her dissolved. "Finder," he gasped. He bowed formally, embarrassed at his behavior.

Finder chuckled. "Somehow I suspect that was the first dryad you've ever met."

"A dryad? That's some sort of tree sprite, right?" Joel asked.

The god nodded. "In my youth, you could always find a tree sprite in the Realms if you knew where to look . . . and were fool enough to do so. These days they are far more rare in the Realms. The ladies of the oaks wield one of the most powerful enchantments known to men. They like to use it on men they find to their liking. And here in Arborea, where passions tend to run strong, it's even easier for their enchantments to succeed. Sorry, but I had to rescue you."

Joel blushed. "Thanks . . . I think," he said with a sheepish grin.

"Fermata is less than a mile off," Finder said. "Wake your companions and bring them along. I'll see that breakfast is waiting." The god winked, then disappeared.

Cautiously Joel approached the large oak.

"La," Ada called out from above. The dryad sat in the crook of a branch, smiling down on the bard.

"Sorry, but I have to leave," Joel said.

"Come back sometime," Ada invited.

Joel took a deep breath. The memory of her caress was like a flickering shadow in his mind. "I will," he promised.

Ada giggled again and disappeared, melding into the oak branch.

Joel gave Jas and Emilo a gentle shake and called out their names. Emilo smiled cheerily upon rising. Jas was as grumpy when she awoke as Joel had always known her to be. When he told her that Finder had been there and promised them breakfast, her mood improved. Joel did not mention Ada.

They traveled through fields of oats and wheat and meadows of grass and wildflowers. Golden-fleeced herd animals somewhat larger than sheep dotted the meadows and viewed their passing without any apparent fear. They

spotted a shepherd on a hilltop playing a flute. It was a
tune Joel recognized, something from the Realms, but in a
strange key. Several of the herd animals flocked about the
hilltop as if they were an audience to their tender's performance.

Cedar trees began lining the road to their left. Then,
between two especially large cedars, there appeared a
road paved with cut gray stone. On either side of the road
stood a man-sized pillar constructed of similar stone. Both
pillars were marked with two symbols, Finder's white
harp and the bird's-eye shape of the symbol for a fermata.

"Finally," Jas murmured.

They turned onto the road, which was lined on both
sides with more cedar trees, forming a tunnel of green. A
hundred paces beyond, the tunnel opened out onto a vast
green blanket of short grass, at the end of which stood
Finder's home. Joel stopped to admire it. The other two
halted behind him.

In the nation of Cormyr, where Finder had grown up,
the building would have been referred to as simply a
manor house. Finder had built his new home, however, on
a scale far larger than any manor house that Joel had ever
seen, larger even than many castles. Two massive square
towers flanked the central hall. The towers were four stories high, the hall only three, and built of the same gray
stone as the road and the pillars, but the stone was merely
a framework for the dozens of great glass-paned windows
that sparkled in the early morning sunshine. Joel counted
twelve chimneys beyond the ornate stone parapet surrounding the roof.

"If it weren't for the sunlight, that place would look a
bit forbidding," Emilo noted.

"If it weren't for the invitation to breakfast, I don't
think I'd go near it," Jas declared. "But it does remind one
of Finder, I've got to admit."

"How so?" Emilo asked.

"It's very showy and, as you said, a trifle forbidding."

"Finder's not forbidding," Joel argued. For his own part,
he found the building much to his liking. It was grand,
magnificent, inspiring. But then, that was how he felt
about Finder.

"Just what is Finder a god of?" Emilo asked in a whisper.

"God of reckless fools," Jas declared.

Joel shot Jas an annoyed glare. While Finder had at one time called himself that, it had been a joke. "Finder is the patron to all those who seek to change and transform art, to renew art. He also has some limited power over the decay and rebirth of living things."

"An eclectic sort of fellow," Emilo noted.

"Yes," Joel agreed. It was one of the things that he admired about Finder.

Joel strode up to the manor, with Jas and Emilo following a pace behind him. The doors to the front hall stood wide open. Joel stepped inside. The grandeur of the front hall was breathtaking. The floor was of polished marble, in hues of white, black, and gray. In the center of the room, Finder's harp symbol was inset into the marble floor. The walls and ceiling were painted with intricate floral designs that created an illusion of movement when anyone looked at them for very long. Two huge curved staircases of marble climbed up to the next floor; pairs of closed doors on either side of the hall undoubtedly led to the rest of the manor. The only furnishings in the room were two carved marble benches.

The bard called out, "Hello!" His words echoed throughout the building. For several moments there was no reply. Then, from somewhere behind the staircase, a young woman appeared. She wore a simple short-sleeved smock of pink covered with a thin film of white-gray dust and several black smudges. She had blue eyes and long, thick, light brown hair, which she wore pulled back in a blue ribbon. She was small and slender.

There was something vaguely familiar about the woman, but for the life of him, Joel couldn't recall ever having met her.

"Welcome to Fermata," the woman said. "I'm Rina. Lord Finder has asked me to bring you right in to the morning room." Her voice was soft and husky.

They followed Rina through the doors on the right. She led them through several large empty rooms until they arrived in a room with windows on three sides. Chairs and

settees covered with cushioning and pale yellow fabric
were grouped about the room. In its center, on a small
round table covered with a quilted cloth of shades of green
and yellow, someone had laid out a breakfast worthy of a
king. Ham and sausages, fish and fowl, bread and muf-
fins, strawberries and raspberries, milk and cream, butter
and cheese, tea and wine, custard and pies filled the table.
Three places had been set with shiny white dishes, cups,
and saucers decorated with tiny blue flowers, silver table-
ware, linen napkins and shiny blue bowls filled with
water and rose petals.

Finder rose from a chair by the window and crossed the
room in long strides. "Welcome, my Rebel Bard," he
greeted Joel as he embraced his priest.

"It's good to be see you again," Joel said. He had been
friends with Finder long before he'd known the older man
was a god. He was comfortable in his god's presence and
happy to be reunited with him.

Finder turned to Jas and Emilo. "Jasmine," he said
with a nod. "I'm glad you've decided to come. And Mr.
Haversack, welcome to my realm."

Emilo bowed low, sweeping the marble floor with his
top knot. "Pleased to meet you, sir," he said, his brown
eyes as wide as saucers.

Finder nodded. "Thank you, Rina. You may go about
your work now," he said.

Rina bowed quickly and left.

Finder sat down at the table and said, "Please be
seated and help yourselves to breakfast. I'm a little short
of all kinds of staff at the moment, let alone waiters. Don't
much care for the magical kind."

"Who's Rina?" Joel asked curiously as he took the seat
to Finder's right and stabbed a slice of ham and a slab of
bread. Jas and Emilo followed suit.

"She's a petitioner," Finder replied.

"A what?" Emilo asked.

"A petitioner. Someone who worshiped me in her life, so
she ended up here after she died."

"You mean she's a ghost?" Emilo squeaked.

Finder shook his head. "No. Ghosts are people who, for
one reason or another, never come to the Outer Planes

when they die. They remain undead. Rina is one of the only two petitioners who have come to Fermata so far. She was a potter in Tilverton, working on uncovering the secrets of how the Kara-Tur make porcelain. Her skill went beyond mere craft, however. She created works of art from porcelain, encouraged by a speech Joel gave to some artists in a tavern once."

"She looks familiar, but I don't remember her," the bard said.

"She was a shy thing. Sat in the back, listening quietly but intently."

"How did she die?" Jas asked.

"She worked late at her master's shop every night to do her designs," Finder explained. "An enemy of her master's, intent on his murder, poured smoke powder into a chunk of coal that fired the shop's kiln. Rina was the only one in the shop when it exploded."

"That's horrible," Jas said.

Finder nodded. "Fortunately she doesn't remember it. Petitioners don't remember anything about their previous lives, but she's still an artist. When I don't need her to greet visitors, she's working with the kiln she's built."

"Did Rina make these?" Emilo asked, holding up one of the white dishes. "It's so light, and look, the sun shines right through it." The kender tapped the dish with his spoon and it rang like a bell. "Did you hear that? That's real pretty."

Finder nodded. "Rina made all the dishes, pottery, jewelry, statuary, anything porcelain you find here. The other petitioner was a painter named Springer who died of old age. He painted the front hall. He's around here somewhere, painting one of the other rooms."

Joel remembered Springer. The old man had gotten into an argument with an Iriaeban merchant over what should be painted in the merchant's hall. Springer had walked off the job and promptly offered his services at a cut rate to paint the hall of one of the merchant's rivals. The painted hall, and thus the rival, had become renowned throughout the region.

"So if you only have two petitioners, who cooked breakfast?" Jas asked.

"I've hired some local help for a while," Finder explained. "I'm not expecting many petitioners in the near future. With any luck, my worshipers will remain healthy and alive for years to come." The god snagged a strawberry and stood up. "I have something I'm working on at the moment, so I'm going to leave you to your meal. When you finish, climb the staircase beyond that door." He pointed to a smaller door than the one by which they'd entered. "I'll be in the room at the top of the tower," he explained. Then he vanished.

"He just disappeared, like a wizard," Emilo noted. "I guess gods can do all sorts of tricks, can't they? Your Finder seems like a splendid fellow."

"He is," Joel assured the kender.

"One of the nicest reckless fools you'll ever meet," Jas added, serving herself a helping of raspberries. "God or no god."

They proceeded to dine in earnest, speaking now and then only to comment on how good the meal was. Joel, anxious to speak with Finder, hurried through his meal. Then he excused himself from the table, insisting the other two not rush on his account. He received no argument from either of his companions. Jas was busy playing with the custard, and Emilo was creating a very artistic sandwich far too large to fit into his mouth. Joel hurried up the tower stairs.

The room at the top of the tower was nearly empty. Several books were spread out on a table on one side of the room. There was a single wooden chair in which Finder sat. The god was pondering a yellow crystal that hung suspended in midair in the middle of the room.

The crystal, an artifact known as the finder's stone, could locate just about anything or anyone even slightly known to the bearer. Once upon a time it had also contained spells, like a wand. The spells could be cast by any member of Finder's family. Included in the spells were illusions of Finder singing any of the many songs he had composed in his life as a mortal man. Finder had cleaved the stone in two, however, to get at the shard of para-elemental ice within. He'd used the ice to destroy the evil god Moander, after which he claimed Moander's power and godhood for his own. Each half of the finder's stone still worked as a magical locator, but the stone no longer held any spells.

Finder gestured with one hand, and blue fire engulfed the gem. Joel could feel heat radiating from the stone.

"Have you put it back together?" the bard asked excitedly.

Finder lowered his hand and the blue fire faded. The god shook his head. "I haven't quite figured out how to do it," he explained. "Any power great enough to reintegrate the crystal's structure is equally likely to destroy the magical properties the stone already has." He lifted the top half of the crystal from the bottom and tossed it to Joel.

Joel caught it. It felt warm, but not hot. "What will you do if you do get it back together?" he asked, admiring the stone's sparkle.

"Try to do what I did before. Put another shard of para-elemental ice in the tiny flaw in the heart of the stone, and then see if I can store magical spells in it, and music—mine and the songs of others."

Joel set the top of the stone back down on the bottom half. The two halves fit together perfectly. "Do you know why we've come here?" he asked.

"Jas's condition is getting worse," Finder said.

Joel nodded. "I don't think it will ever improve in a place like Sigil, but the way she looks, she doesn't want to go home."

"Sigil's restless atmosphere is only part of the problem," the god explained. "Iyachtu Xvim's power and influence is growing stronger throughout the Realms. Jas's condition is a reflection of that."

"You said you might be able to help her," Joel said.

"I'll try," Finder said, though he didn't sound hopeful.

Joel could read his god's mood. "You're not sure if you can, are you?" Joel asked.

"I suppose I'm just feeling less certain because I haven't yet succeeded in gluing this rock back together," Finder said. He took up both halves of the stone. "And, of course, Xvim *is* more powerful than I am. It's entirely possible the priests of Xvim just shape-shifted Jas's form and relied on Jas's own hatred and anger to transform her into a creature of darkness."

"But how can that be?" Joel asked. "Jas isn't evil and her will is strong."

"She was forced to watch as Walinda systematically tortured her friend Arandes and the rest of her crew to death. She was a victim herself of the priestess's sick practices. That changes a person, even one with a will as strong as Jas's. That doesn't mean there isn't some way to help her," the god added, mustering a little more enthusiasm. He juggled the two halves of the stone in one hand and gave Joel a wink.

"I also told Emilo Haversack you might be able to find his home and help return there," Joel said. "But then, you know that, too, don't you?"

Finder nodded. The god had the power to sense whatever occurred in Joel's presence. He didn't need Joel to explain how he'd met the kender. "Yes, I know of his world. Krynn, it's called. I can show him a magical gate that goes there," he said, "though I suspect he's not in any big hurry to get back. Kender spend a good portion of their lives in wanderlust."

"He did seem pretty curious about Jas's spelljammer stories," Joel recalled.

"I'm more curious about the circumstances that brought him to Sigil," Finder said. "Magical vortexes don't lead from Krynn to Sigil."

"So you don't trust him?" Joel asked.

"Let's just say I'm uncomfortable because I can't predict the outcome of his actions. The vestiges of a superstition from my mortal days remains in me. Halfling luck, they called it when I was a boy."

"But Emilo's a kender," Joel said.

"He's a short person with clever hands and a quick wit who's been thrust under mysterious circumstances into my priest's life. I can't help but wonder what will come of it."

"So should we just send him home?" Joel asked.

Finder shook his head. "Not unless he wants to go. Whatever or whoever brought him here isn't a force I want to trifle with."

From the stairway came the sound of Emilo's chatter and Jas's laughter. Finder stood as the winged woman and kender entered the room.

Jas looked over at Finder. She shifted her weight to one foot nervously. She was uncomfortable asking anyone for favors, and Finder was no exception.

Finder didn't make her ask, however. "Jasmine, there you are. Joel says you've agreed to let me take a stab at reversing your condition."

"If you're not too busy," Jas said without enthusiasm.

"My appointment calendar is empty. Have a seat," Finder said, pulling forward the chair from which he'd just risen.

Jas sat down with her ankles crossed and her hands in her lap, looking like a prim schoolgirl.

"I'm going to do a little metaphysical examination first," the god said. "Shouldn't hurt, but I'm going to have to touch you."

Jas shrugged.

Finder reached out with his right hand and touched Jas on the forehead lightly with his fingertips, then stepped back. He studied her for several moments.

"I'm going to attempt a transformation now," the god said to the winged woman. "Relax. Don't resist the magic."

"I'm as relaxed as I get," Jas said through clenched teeth.

Finder reached out and laid his hands on Jas's head.

Immediately the winged woman's form started to shimmer like the air over hot desert sand.

"It's working," Emilo whispered.

The feathers covering Jas, from the green crest on her forehead to the small black down on her face and hands, began to sparkle. Jas brushed at them irritably, and they fell from her flesh as if she were a molting bird. Her skin glowed softly, and the scaly pores that held the quills sealed over. She was left with the same rosy complexion she had when Joel had first met her.

"Why does she still have the wings?" Emilo asked Joel in a whisper.

"They weren't part of the curse," Joel explained. "She had them before that."

Jas's eyes were fixed on the floor.

Finder placed a hand on the woman's shoulder. "Are you all right?" he asked.

Jas looked up into the god's eyes and shook her head. "The dark stalker is still in me. I can feel it," she whispered. There was a trace of fear in her voice.

Finder looked surprised for just an instant. "Hmm," he said. "Well, let's try something else, shall we?" He reached out with both hands and laid them on Jas's head. His hands began to glow with blue light, which seemed to seep into the winged woman's body. Very gently Finder's hands touched Jas's forehead, her eyelids, her lips, her ears, and finally her shoulders. The blue light seemed to shine out of Jas's flesh, then faded. Finder stepped back with a smile.

Jas sighed. "That didn't do it either," she said. "It's still inside me."

Finder stroked his beard thoughtfully. Then he said, "It's possible, since Iyachtu Xvim had a hand in your curse, that you will need help from a god more powerful than Iyachtu Xvim."

Jas sighed. "It's never easy, is it?" she muttered.

"We can pop on down to Brightwater," Finder suggested, "and have Tymora take a look at you."

Jas glared up at Finder.

"Or not," Finder said.

"I need to think," the winged woman said. She stood up and strode over to the door. As she hurried up the stairs to the top of the tower, she called out over her shoulder, "I'll be back later."

"Should I follow her?" Emilo asked in a whisper.

"Can you fly?" Finder asked.

Emilo looked momentarily confused by the question. Then he understood. "You mean she's going to fly off to do her thinking?"

"That's what she usually does," Joel said. "Is there some reason she doesn't want to see Tymora?" he asked.

"She and Lady Luck have a history," Finder said. "It would be better if she told you about it herself."

"Why?" Joel asked. "Don't you know it?"

"Better for her," the god explained. "It will help her

decide what to do in the end. In the meantime, why don't you get some sleep? You kept watch last night while Jas and Emilo slept; you must be dead on your feet. I'll entertain Emilo. We'll call you when Jas gets back."

The moment Finder mentioned it, Joel became aware of his exhaustion. "There's a bed calling my name somewhere in this manor. I can hear it," he joked.

Finder led him to a room furnished with a four-poster bed and heavy curtains covering the windows. Then the god and the kender left him to rest.

Joel stripped off his boots and clothing and slid between the satin quilt and the featherbed. He couldn't remember the last time he'd felt so comfortable. Sleep did not come immediately, though. He spent a long while wondering about what kind of history Jas had with the goddess of good luck. Whatever happened, in the past or the future, the bard was determined to help the winged woman overcome the curse of Iyachtu Xvim.

Operas, like the gods they so often portray, are a mystery to me. They are a mystery wrapped in an enigma swallowed by contradiction and covered by a silken shroud of dark chocolate and best served with hot milk before a nap.
—Giogi Wyvernspur

Intermezzo

Holly Harrowslough watched anxiously as the petitioners and proxies of Lathander Morninglord bustled about the temple.

She couldn't believe she'd been brought here, but she hadn't dared argue with the messenger. Lathander had sent a deva, a creature of pure goodness made corporeal, to summon her. The deva had resembled a young man with milky white skin and silver hair and, of course, wings of shining white feathers. As he had approached her in the streets of Sigil, several persons had scurried off in fear, while others had stood staring in openmouthed awe.

The deva could have taken the last piece of the Hand of Bane back to Lathander, but the celestial creature had insisted that Holly was to bring it in person. Since then, the paladin had spent hours in fruitless speculation of what purpose her coming here might serve. Now that she had arrived and was possibly only moments from learning the answer, the suspense made her nervous. The honor was more than she'd ever imagined she'd be paid in her lifetime, and she was only sixteen. Morning Glory, Lathander's realm, was a land of perpetual dawn, and Holly found its rosy hues breathtakingly lovely. Yet the realm's beauty did not bring her a perfect peace. She was afraid that the thing she hoped for most would not come to pass.

The paladin's first vision from Lathander had awakened in her a desire to devote herself more fully to her god. Her arrival in Sigil and subsequent visits to other planes had opened her eyes to how much wider her world could be. Ever since Bors Sunseed had told her there were beings called proxies, mortals who understood their gods' purposes and desires and worked directly to achieve them, Holly knew that was what she wanted to be. Such a decision was not hers to make, however. Lathander alone could decide her worthiness. Yet Holly wasn't even sure if she'd been summoned to meet the Morninglord.

A freckled redheaded woman surrounded by a radiant aura came out of a room in the back of the temple. She wore the red-hued robes of Lathander's clergy. As she approached she smiled at the young paladin.

"Bright dawning, Holly Harrowslough. Welcome to Morning Glory," the priestess greeted her.

"Bright dawning, Dawnbringer," Holly replied. For some reason the paladin felt completely at ease in the priestess's presence. Holly's nervousness subsided. She found herself grinning uncontrollably.

"I am Aurora Brightday," the priestess introduced herself. "I've been asked to speak with you before the Morninglord is ready to see you. He's busy with a task of some importance at the moment. Let's walk, shall we?" the priestess suggested, leading Holly from the temple back outside into the dawn light. "How was your journey here?" she asked as they strolled through an orchard of peach trees.

"Fine," Holly replied. "I'm sorry I got a late start. I was hoping to see a friend before I left Sigil."

"But it only took you a day to arrive. You made good time," Aurora noted.

"I traveled mostly by riverboat," Holly explained.

"Any adventures?" Aurora asked with a gleam in her eyes.

"I rescued a little girl's doll that fell in the water," Holly said, jokingly recalling her minor act of heroism.

Aurora smiled. "Anything else?"

"Before I reached the river port, I spent a while speaking with an asuras who was guarding a bridge over the river," Holly said. She didn't really think Aurora would find the encounter notable, but for Holly it had been most interesting. She'd never met one of the flame-winged, talon-footed asuras before, and the one at the bridge had been the finest figure of a man Holly had ever seen.

"It is said that those who face the examination of the asuras at the bridge are blessed for a short while with his gift to tell truth from lie," Aurora said. "What did you talk about?" she asked.

"About the battle over the Hand of Bane," Holly replied. "Do you know about that? Lathander sent me orders to get the hand and destroy it, but I couldn't fight my friend Joel to take it away from him. His god wanted to trade it for his own stolen power, but the banelich they were dealing with betrayed them. They finally destroyed the banelich and the hand themselves."

Holly's voice wavered uncertainly as she explained. "Lathander sent me a vision telling me it was all right that I didn't fight my friend for the hand. I would have lost anyway, but that wasn't what stopped me. I owed my life to both Joel and his god. Bane was almost resurrected, which would have been a great evil, but then Walinda, a priestess of Bane, learned she couldn't trust her own god. So not only wasn't he resurrected, but Walinda also ceased worshiping him. So a greater good came out of not fighting Joel and Finder. Lathander said that it was more important to follow the spirit of his orders so that greater good is accomplished than to just follow the letter of the law."

"But even though it served goodness, you still felt guilty that you couldn't obey Lathander's instructions to the letter," Aurora guessed.

Holly nodded. "That's what I had to explain to the asuras when he asked me if I felt guilty about anything. The riverboat captain told me that the asuras was barmy, that he asked everyone that question before he let them pass. The asuras helped me clarify how I thought and felt about it all, though," the paladin explained.

"So an irrational asuras can also serve the cause of good," Aurora suggested.

Holly smiled. "I hadn't thought of it that way, but it's true, isn't it?"

Aurora took up Holly's hands in her own. "You are a quick learner. That is good."

The paladin's blush was evident, even beneath her dark brown skin. She grinned again.

At Aurora's bidding, they resumed walking, and Holly spoke in greater detail about her most recent adventure trying to thwart the resurrection of Bane.

The orchard gave way to a meadow, through which flowed a small stream. They crossed over the stream by way of an arched bridge. Birds twittered excitedly in the meadow, flying low over the grass to catch insects. From somewhere downstream came an odd hissing noise and an annoying clanging. Aurora directed Holly to travel in that direction.

There was a clearing where the stream intersected a second stream. In the clearing stood a great complex clockwork machine constructed of metal, marble, glass, and gemstones. The hissing came from steam escaping from a valve at the top of a huge brass barrel. Beneath the barrel burned a fire so hot its flames shimmered with white and blue. Attached to the barrel were pieces that moved up and down or back and forth, causing the clanking. The moving pieces disappeared into a giant sarcophagus mounted atop a pedestal. Rising from the sarcophagus were chunks of glass and crystals, which glowed and sparked.

"What is it?" Holly whispered to Aurora.

"My gift to the Morninglord," a deep voice answered. The voice rang throughout the clearing, but its source became obvious when a figure stepped out from behind the sarcophagus. The figure was that of a tall man whose beard and hair were flames and whose robes shimmered with the colors of fire. Holly was a tall girl, as tall as some men, but the fiery-haired figure towered over her. He had piercing green eyes, which for some unknown reason made Holly feel uncomfortable.

Aurora bowed respectfully toward the man, and Holly followed suit.

"My Lord Sirrion, allow me to present Holly Harrowslough," the priestess said. "Holly, this is Sirrion of the Flowing Flame. He is an ally of Lord Lathander's and a god of a people on a world in a sphere far from your own. Lord Sirrion is building a machine to help with a magical spell so that Lord Lathander can right an ancient wrong."

"What will the machine do?" Holly asked the foreign god.

Sirrion's fiery eyebrows raised in surprise. "Your people speak whenever they choose, don't they?" he asked Aurora.

Holly felt her blood rush to her face as she realized she'd just addressed a god so blithely, but Aurora came immediately to her defense.

"Holly Harrowslough is an honored knight of the Order of the Aster, Lord Sirrion," the priestess replied. "Lord Lathander encourages his followers to question what they do not understand that they might learn and so better serve the Morninglord."

Sirrion grinned. "And what service can one so young and tender perform for the Morninglord?"

"You told Lord Lathander that you would need help in assembling the materials for your . . . spell," Aurora answered.

"Yes. So?" Sirrion asked.

"Lord Lathander intends to assign Holly Harrowslough to the task," Aurora said.

"Her?" Sirrion laughed. "She's no more than a slip of a girl. I need warriors. Lots of warriors."

"Lord Lathander has every confidence Holly Harrowslough can accomplish the task at hand," Aurora replied calmly.

Holly could feel her heart pounding in her chest. Pride coursed through her every vein.

As he looked down upon the paladin, Sirrion's green eyes glowed for a moment. Holly was struck with a chill and the feeling that she had seen those eyes before, but she couldn't recall where or when.

"Well, since that's the case," Sirrion said, "I suppose she will do."

"Good," Aurora replied. She turned to the paladin and said, "Holly Harrowslough, it is the Morninglord's wish that you collect such materials as Lord Sirrion instructs you to. When all is in readiness, Lord Lathander will come to aid in the spell, and you will receive his thanks."

"I will serve faithfully," Holly said, making a formal bow.

Aurora nodded. "May the joy of the dawn give you strength," she said to Holly. She bowed to Lord Sirrion and turned to leave.

Lord Sirrion watched the priestess walk back upstream for several moments without a word.

"What does the machine do, Lord Sirrion?" Holly asked the god. "And what am I to fetch for you?"

Lord Sirrion looked down at Holly again and smiled. "Come closer, and I will explain all," the god said. "The machine will help with a magical spell so that Lord Lathander can right an ancient wrong."

Holly nodded slowly. Sirrion had repeated exactly what Aurora had told her, yet there was something different about the way he said it. Something rang false in Holly's ears. It was possible that she simply mistrusted the god because he had offended her pride. Perhaps, though, it was true that her talk with the asuras had left her for a short while with the gift of telling truth from lie. Whatever the case, Holly was sure that Sirrion had just lied to her and that there was malice behind his falsehood.

Opera is the sound of nightingales sighing in sympathy over the tomb of a maiden whose ghost weeps of its broken heart, lamenting true love lost and wasted—except when it sounds more like cats on a still summer night, yowling in heat right outside one's window.

—Storm Silverhand

Act Two
Scene 1

Joel awoke to a soft touch on his shoulder. In the dim light of the curtained room, he could just make out Jas's winged silhouette.

"Jas? Are you all right?" he asked, still groggy with sleep.

"Can we talk?" Jas whispered.

"Yes. Sure. Open the curtains a little so I can see," Joel said.

Jas pulled the curtains back. A stream of afternoon sun flooded the room.

The bard sat up and motioned for Jas to have a seat at the foot of the bed.

Jas perched on the edge of the mattress. She didn't say anything for several moments. Instead, she simply looked down at her hands.

"Am I supposed to do the talking or you?" Joel asked, trying to humor the winged woman into a less somber mood.

"What do you think?" Jas asked.

"About what?" Joel replied.

"About going to see Tymora about my problem?"

"It sounds like a good idea to me," Joel replied.

Jas was quiet again.

Joel sighed. "Jas, this beating around the bush just drives me crazy. Why don't you tell me about your history with Tymora, and then maybe I'll have some clue as to what's bothering you?"

"It's sort of complicated," Jas said.

"I'm a clever guy. I can handle complicated things," Joel said.

Jas took a deep breath and blew it out. Then she spoke. "My parents were adventurers, both paladins, like Holly. When I was just a girl, they were both murdered. They'd helped break up a ring of slavers, and in vengeance, the leader of the ring hired an assassin to kill them. A friend of my mother's fostered me. She was really nice, but I couldn't stand being in the city where my parents had lived. Everyone had known them and constantly reminded me about them. I loved my parents, but every time I remembered them, I remembered they were dead, and that just made me upset. So I ran away from Waterdeep."

Jas stared out the window as she spoke, never looking at the bard. There were streaks in the dust on her cheeks. They could have been from tears, but they might just have been from sweat. Joel could smell her perspiration across the bed. She'd flown until she'd worn herself out.

"I took a job as a hired sword with an adventurer named Carter," Jas said, continuing her tale. "He was a professional troublemaker. If you wanted to ruin a person's reputation or bankrupt a merchant firm or turn brother against brother, Carter was the guy you hired. He was good at what he did, and he didn't work cheap. He taught me a lot and paid me a lot. . . . It took a while, but slowly I began to realize Carter wasn't such a nice guy, and the things he did weren't either. Still, I couldn't bring myself to simply leave him. I was far from my home and friends. Carter often told me I couldn't survive without him, and I believed him."

Jas pulled her feet up on the bed and hugged her knees. "Then one day," she said, "everything in my life changed. I was in the right place at the right time, I guess. I was keeping watch over an alley door for Carter, waiting for two priests to go through the door. While I'm

hiding in this trash bin with a tiny peephole to look
through, this thief runs into the alley and tosses a sack
into the trash right on top of me. Then three other thieves
come barreling into the alley. They corner the first thief
and demand their share of the loot from Tymora's temple.
The first thief tries to feed them some story about the
heist not going off. In the meantime, I'm looking into the
sack. The contents are worth a fortune. There's platinum
coin and all this jewelry and a cape made of white feathers. Then I see there's something moving around among
the feathers. It's about four inches long, slimy and
writhing like a worm. Really ugly. Then I see there's this
cracked eggshell. The slimy, writhing thing has just
hatched, or maybe its shell broke when the thief tossed it
into the trash.

"Outside, the thieves are still arguing, and one of them
stabs the first one and the first one stabs him back. The
pair of them fall down, trying to hold their guts inside
their bodies. One of the thieves is a mage. He turns and
shoots five magic missiles in the back of the last thief.
When he's all alone in the alley, he starts searching for the
sack. I know its only a matter of minutes before he looks
into the trash. I come spilling out of the trash bin with the
sack in hand and take off down the alley, but the mage is
fast. He teleports himself into my path and blocks my way
out of the alley. He doesn't look human anymore. He's
changed into a shadow man with horns and bat wings and
fangs. I hold the sack up in front of me like a shield, so he
doesn't dare risk using his magic on me. He says if I give
him the egg, he'll let me have the rest of the loot.

"It wasn't that I was all fired up about protecting the
egg thing. I'm not an idiot. I know I'm dead the moment
this creature gets his hand on the egg thing. So I refuse
his offer, and I draw my sword, still holding the sack in
front of me like a shield. I don't really believe I can beat
the shadow creature in a fight, but I'm not letting it kill
me without one. Just then, two priests of Torm come into
the alley. They're the two priests I was supposed to be
watching out for when I was hiding in the trash. They see
the shadow creature, and right away they start calling out
to their god and casting bolts of light.

"When the bolts of light hit him, the shadow creature howls like a dog someone stepped on and disappears. The two priests are all solicitous, making sure I'm all right. They're sure the shadow is some sort of sign, so instead of going into the building to which Carter had so carefully lured them, they go back to their temple to pray. I know Carter's going to be furious, so I'm not real eager to tell him about any of what just occurred. Instead, I go to the temple of Tymora to turn over the loot the thieves stole.

"The priests at Tymora's temple go nuts with joy when I show up with the sack of loot. They say that Tymora must have guided my hand. I know Tymora didn't have anything to do with me hiding in that trash bin, but I keep my mouth shut. They hold this big party to celebrate the return of the loot, especially the hatchling. It's a baby faerie dragon they had sworn to keep safe. I'm still not keen to go back to Carter, so I stay for the party. There's this priestess at the party who takes me back into the temple to talk. There's something familiar about her, but I can't figure out what. The church wants to reward me. She challenges me to a game of cards . . . nothing complicated. Just a game of empress. If she wins, she'll choose my reward for me. If I win, I get to pick my reward. Anything I want. I agree. She shuffles. I cut. She deals."

Jas hopped off the edge of the bed and paced over to the window. She looked out across the fields of Finder's realm for a few moments. Then she spun around and looked straight at Joel. "Well, I win the game, but figuring out what I want isn't so easy. What I really want is for my parents not to be dead, but that's not going to happen. I also want to leave Carter, but to do that I need something to make me independent. I don't ask for money. Money can be stolen, and when it's gone, it's gone. I need a skill I can use. Suddenly this pigeon flies through a window of the temple up to a nest near the ceiling, and I say, 'I want to be free like that bird. I want to be able to fly.' The priestess gives me this sad little smile like I'm a kid who just asked for cake for dinner.

"I meant I wanted to be able to fly the way a mage does with a spell. I didn't mean I wanted giant wings sticking out of my back, but the next thing I know, I look like an overgrown pixie. I ask the priestess to take the wings back, but she says they'll serve as a reminder that I'm always flying away from my problems instead of dealing with them. When I learn to face my problems, she says, I'll be blessed with all the luck I need. Then she vanishes." Jas snapped her fingers. "Just like that. Gone. That's when I realize she wasn't a priestess. The reason she looked familiar is because she looked just like the statue of Tymora that's on the altar in front of me. Now I'm really angry, but I'm not so stupid that I'm going to fight with a goddess, so I just leave."

Jas turned back to the window and was silent for some time.

"Did you go back to Carter?" Joel asked curiously.

Jas turned around again. "He didn't want me hanging around anymore," she said. "He liked to keep a low profile wherever he went, and I was much too noticeable. After telling me for months that I can't survive without him, he suddenly says I can take care of myself just fine. And I did." She spread her wings out, then let them drop back down. "So now you know why I avoid having anything to do with gods. If they decide to judge and sentence you, there's nothing you can do about it, and they can really make a mess of your life. Not that Finder hasn't been a decent guy," she added hastily.

"But you're still afraid to face Tymora," Joel said.

"Wouldn't you be?" Jas asked with an exasperated tone.

"Well, the fact that you're trying to get rid of the dark stalker in you shows that you aren't flying away from your problems," Joel said. "At least, that's what it looks like to me."

Jas tilted her head thoughtfully.

"What's the worst that could happen?" Joel asked. "After all, Iyachtu Xvim put a dark stalker in you and made you look like an owl."

"Tymora could make me look like something else," Jas said darkly.

"Something worse than an overgrown pixie? That would be bad," Joel joked.

Jas glared at the bard. "She might say it serves me right and turn me down."

"She might. If she does, we'll leave. I don't think she will, though," Joel said. "She's been a good friend to Finder."

"So you think I should go to Brightwater to see Tymora?"

"Jas, it doesn't matter what I think. It's your decision."

"Fine," Jas said shortly. "Then I'll go."

"Good," Joel answered.

Behind the Scenes

The little figures babbled with excitement as the dark servant entered the tent carrying a wooden box inscribed with ancient text.

A tall figure stepped forward and loomed over the servant. "Open the box," the figure ordered in a deep voice.

The servant flipped up the lid of the box. Within, embedded in white velvet, was a small crystal sphere of the deepest blue.

"Take up the sphere," the figure commanded, "and hold it between the rose and the coin."

The servant drew out the sphere with a trembling hand and held it over the center of the altar of stone. On one side of the sphere, suspended magically in midair, was a white rose, still sparkling with crystals of ice from the Desertsmouth Mountains of Toril. On the other side, also held in the air by magic, was an old platinum coin stamped with the profile of an elven woman on one side and the sigil of the ancient and long since ruined kingdom of Myth Drannor on the other. The servant released the blue crystal sphere, and it hovered between the rose and the coin.

"Now it is time to begin the spell," the looming figure said, pulling the servant away from the altar. And time, the figure thought privately, to drink of Tymora's power.

Offstage

Somewhere in the Prime Material Plane on the world known as Toril in Realmspace, the renowned mage Volothamp Geddarm, known simply as Volo to his friends, was sweating profusely. It was alarming how quickly the friendly game of table dice with the barbarian mercenary leader had turned ugly. Not that Volo was losing. If he were losing, he could extricate himself with a smile and an excuse. No. Volo was winning, winning against an ogre-sized man with a hairy back and a deer-skinning knife that could serve a halfling as a short sword.

On his first roll of doubles, Volo allowed himself a chuckle. When his next roll also turned up doubles, the mage merely smiled. By his fifth consecutive roll of doubles, Volo felt the first trickle of sweat dripping down the side of his face. His opponent's scowl had grown so deep that his heavy brow shadowed half his nose and turned his eyes into deep black pits. On Volo's sixth roll of doubles, the barbarian pulled out a whetstone and tugged at the clasps of his knife sheath. On Volo's seventh roll, snake eyes, the barbarian pulled out his knife and began running it across the stone.

Volo was sweating so hard he felt as if he was steaming away and wished that he could. It would be a clever escape, to turn to vapor and drift away, too insubstantial to pursue. The barbarian reached for the dice cup. He, too, looked hot, but not from terror. He rolled a five. Enraged, he flung the ale in his mug to the floor and slammed the dice into the emptied ale mug, obviously convinced Volo was using an enchanted dice cup.

"Perhaps we should leave this for—" Volo began.

"Roll," the barbarian growled. He tested his sharpened

knife blade by whittling off a layer of the maple dicing
table.

Volo rolled . . . double sixes. There were tears in his
eyes.

The barbarian cursed Volo and Volo's gods as he
snatched up the dice and rattled them around in the ale
mug. He slammed the mug down and lifted it. A one and a
three. Making an ugly declaration about the ancestry of
Volo's father, the barbarian pushed the mug back toward
Volo.

"I don't understand how—" Volo squeaked.

"Roll, damn your bones!" shouted the barbarian. Volo
could swear he saw a fire glowing in the pits of his opponent's eyes.

Volo slid the dice into the mug, gripping the handle as
if it might escape. He hesitated for a moment, then flung
the mug full force at his opponent as he dodged sideways.

The barbarian raised a hand to fend off the missile and
threw the deer knife across the table. The knife buried itself several inches into the door, but Volo had made his
exit through the second-story window.

The barbarian stood up and retrieved his knife. That's
when he spotted the dice on the floor beside the ale mug.
Double sixes.

With a roar, the barbarian ran from the room, determined to chase down and destroy the fiend before it
wreaked worse havoc.

Limping on a twisted ankle and shivering in the warm
Elturel night, Volo whimpered a chiding prayer to the
goddess Tymora. "Lady, what were you thinking, to waste
so much good luck on me?"

Act Two
Scene 2

Once Joel, Jas, and Emilo had bathed and changed into clean clothes, they joined Finder out in the garden for a light supper. Over the meal, Emilo asked to journey with them to meet Tymora, and Finder acquiesced. When they finished off the wine, they made a chain with their hands, and Finder teleported to Brightwater with them.

They arrived in the middle of a broad avenue and were nearly run over by a pair of horses, each ridden by a young woman in a nightgown. Finder pulled the adventurers off to the side in the nick of time. One of the horses, startled by the sudden appearance of the adventurers, fell a length behind the other.

Joel gave a low whistle of relief. He looked around in astonishment as he followed Finder up the street.

All about them, the town of Brightwater glittered in the setting sun. Joel couldn't remember having seen so much gilt in a city before. Great mansions sported golden domes like the Gilded Hall. Each of the stores and taverns featured some architectural aspect to attract the eye— gaudy statues, magnificent fountains and archways, charming stained-glass windows, structures with un- usual, even impossible shapes. Even the meanest of shacks displayed some touch of trim that gleamed with the look of a precious metal or stone.

His eyes wide with wonder, Emilo whispered, "Even the streets are paved with gold!"

Finder chuckled. "It's only an illusion. Gold streets wouldn't last long. Gold is too soft a metal. Here we are. The Hall of Chance." The god stepped through a marble archway and seemed to disappear. Hastily the others followed.

They found themselves in a vast room opulently decorated with red carpeting and crystal chandeliers. Crowds of people stood or sat about tables of polished obsidian playing every game of chance known to the Realms, including some games Joel had never seen before. Their ears were assaulted with the din of the gamblers' voices. Some were calling out wagers; others announced the outcomes of freshly rolled dice; still others called for extra cards to be dealt. Within a minute, though, the din had subsided to a hushed murmur as the gamblers turned their attention from their games and focused on Finder and his party.

As Finder moved forward, people stepped aside until there was a clear path between him and a table at the back of the room. Seated at the table, on a high stool, was a slender woman with short, dark hair. She wore a short, gold-trimmed tunic of white satin, a brown leather vest, and high leather boots, which hugged a pair of shapely legs. A slender silver coronet encircled her head and glittered in the light. The woman turned about on the stool as Finder approached.

Joel would have known her for the goddess of good fortune were she dressed as a scullery maid. The songs of her grace and charm were not exaggerated. The bard could understand immediately why Finder put so much faith in her. Joel himself was instantly smitten, and he halted in his tracks a little afraid of how eager he felt to approach her. Jas remained beside Joel as Finder continued forward. Undaunted, Emilo followed close on the heels of Joel's god.

Three paces before the goddess, Finder stopped. He made a very low and formal bow, then stepped up to accept the hand that Tymora held out to him. He brushed his lips against her fingertips.

"Finder, you reckless fool," the goddess greeted him. She ran her hand over the god's beard and tugged playfully at it. "What mischief have you been up to? I have heard the most alarming and unbelievable stories," she teased.

"Since you know me, lady, you no doubt believe them," Finder replied.

"Oh, yes," Tymora agreed.

Emilo laughed.

Tymora leaned to one side to get a better look at Emilo. "And who is this gentleman?" she asked.

"My lady, allow me to present Emilo Haversack of Tengrapes," Finder said.

Emilo imitated Finder's bow. "Pleased to meet you, lady," he said when he'd risen.

"And how did you come to be in the entourage of this godling rogue, Mr. Haversack?" Tymora asked the kender.

"Well, first I stepped through a magical vortex to the city of Sigil. That's where I met Jas and Joel. Joel offered to bring me to Finder so he could help me to go home, but when Joel and Jas said they were coming here, I asked to come with them so I could see you, too," Emilo replied. "I'd never met a goddess before—that I know of, anyway. But having met you, I realize it would be hard not to know, since you just seem to shine. . . . "

Tymora laughed softly and the babbling kender's voice trailed off.

"Does Mr. Haversack refer to Joel the Rebel Bard?" Tymora asked Finder. "Your very young and very talented protégé?"

Finder motioned for Joel to step forward. The bard joined his god and bowed before the goddess. "I am Finder's very charmed protégé, lady," Joel said.

Tymora laughed with delight. "Finder has told me so much about you," she said, "though he failed to mention how very handsome you are."

Joel felt his cheeks warm as they flushed with color.

"And the last member of my entourage I believe you know," Finder said, motioning toward Jas.

Jas remained frozen in place. Joel could sense the anxiety and anger in her.

"Yes," Tymora said softly, sliding off her stool. She strode forward and stopped just before the winged woman.

Uncertainty gripped Joel. Although he'd told Jas that making this visit was her decision, he'd given her every

reason in its favor without really knowing how Tymora
felt about Jas.

Then Lady Luck kissed Jas on the forehead and said,
"Welcome to Brightwater, Jasmine. You have grown since
last we met."

Joel breathed a silent sigh of relief.

Jas bowed her head and muttered a reply that Joel
couldn't hear. Tymora took the winged woman's arm.
"Let's go out into the garden, shall we? Finder, you can
follow behind with these gentlemen," the goddess said,
nodding at Joel at Emilo. "Winnie, will you bring us re-
freshments?" she requested of a halfling priestess seated
at a nearby table.

"My pleasure," the priestess replied. She laid down her
hand of cards—four queens and a goddess—and hurried
off.

Tymora led Jas from the Hall of Chance. Finder followed in Lady Luck's wake, and Joel and Emilo brought
up the rear.

The garden was a hodgepodge of plantings, as if someone had just thrown seeds anywhere and left them to
thrive or not on their own. In the deepening twilight,
Joel could discern no real paths. Tymora just picked her
way through some of the shorter growth. Tymora
stopped beside a wooden bench beneath a birch tree. The
tree's white bark seemed to glow in the light of the rising
moon, and the stars twinkled through the slender
branches. Fireflies sparked all around them. The goddess sat down on the bench, with Jas at her side. Finder
settled on the ground at Tymora's feet, and Joel and
Emilo did likewise.

"Your parents were great favorites of mine," the goddess told Jas. "So passionate, so daring. It really irritated
me to learn that their daughter was traveling with a
weasel like Chaos Carter."

"Well, the wings got rid of him fast enough," Jas noted.
Her tone was completely neutral. Joel couldn't even
fathom a guess at what she was feeling.

"But you still ran from your grief," Tymora noted.
"Saerloon wasn't far enough from Waterdeep, so you had
to leave Realmspace and travel to other spheres."

"I tried going home a couple times," Jas said. "Things just kept coming up."

"And when you finally returned to Realmspace, your crew was murdered and you were abducted by a mad priestess of Bane," Tymora added, "who delivered you to the priests of Iyachtu Xvim for sacrifice. You escaped, but then you were recaptured and transformed into a dark stalker."

"I guess Finder's told you everything," Jas said, giving the god a sharp look.

"No," Finder said. "I kept your confidences, as you asked."

"My ability to sense things is even more powerful than Finder's. I am aware of what occurs around the worshipers of my allies as well as my own worshipers," Tymora explained. "Lathander is one of my allies," she explained.

"You know all this from Holly?" Jas realized aloud.

And from me, Joel realized silently. Since Finder was also an ally of Tymora's, the goddess would sense things that happened to Finder's worshipers.

"I know you're here to rid yourself of the dark stalker. But since Holly wasn't with you when the priests of Xvim captured you, I don't know how they came to transform you," Tymora said.

Jas stared into the darkness for several moments without replying. Then she sighed and began. "The priests of Iyachtu Xvim gave me a choice—die or agree to be transformed into a dark stalker. I let them transform me. Then they sent me to Sigil to hunt down Walinda, Joel, and Holly. The priests told me once I killed someone, the transformation would be complete and I would be able to sense the power of my prey. But I didn't want to kill anyone. Except Walinda."

"So you attacked Walinda, and Holly got in the way, and you thought you'd killed her. Is that the first time you sensed the dark stalker in you?" Tymora asked.

Jas closed her eyes, trying to remember back. "I think so, yes."

"Even though you hadn't killed anyone yet?" Tymora asked.

"If Holly's friend Bors hadn't healed her, Holly would have died," Jas insisted.

"When the priests of Iyachtu Xvim transformed you, how did they do it?"

"They used a spell," Jas said.

"A mage spell or a priest spell?" Tymora asked.

"A mage spell. They had this crazy wizard with them. He kept tearing off his clothes and throwing fireballs at monsters that only he could see. He talked to himself and to people who weren't there. Just being near him was scary. They told me not to resist when he cast his spell. If I didn't transform, then they'd kill me." Jas shrugged. "Maybe I resisted a little, and that's why I could partially control the transformation by keeping calm."

Tymora exchanged a glance with Finder.

"I managed to transform Jasmine back to her true form," Finder explained, "but she can still sense the dark stalker within her."

"I see," Tymora said. Her brow furrowed with concern.

"But I suspect that since you're a far greater power than Iyachtu Xvim, you should have no trouble removing the curse from her soul," Finder said to Tymora.

The goddess raised an eyebrow. "Indeed," she replied.

At that moment, the halfling priestess, Winnie, appeared, followed by two human servants carrying trays of food and drink.

"Winnie, your timing is excellent, as always," Tymora said. "Jasmine, drink some of the wine; it will make the ordeal to come easier to bear." The goddess stood up. "Winnie, Finder, I need to have a word with both of you," she said. She led the halfling and the god some distance away from the bench beneath the birch tree.

The human servants set the trays of wine and food on the bench beside Jas, then left without a word.

Jas looked at the wine as if it might be poisoned. Joel laughed. He stood up and filled three goblets. He sampled the drink and sighed. "Only the finest, as my grandfather used to say." He handed goblet to Jas. "To your happiness, lady," he said.

Jas took a swallow from the goblet as if it were filled with water. A moment later she gasped and her eyes grew round. "It *is* good," she whispered.

"Told you so," Joel said. He turned around with a goblet for Emilo, but the kender wasn't there. "Where did Emilo go?"

Jas looked about her, but not with much effort. "Don't know," she said. She took another deep swallow from her goblet, then held it out to Joel. "More, please," she requested.

Joel looked at the winged woman with surprise. He'd never seen her drink anything stronger than ale, and then she always nursed her drink carefully. It was possible that the quality of the wine was behind her current lack of self-restraint, but the bard suspected it had more to do with her anxiety. He filled her goblet halfway. Jas took another long swallow.

"I could learn to like this stuff," the woman said. She smiled up at Joel. Her eyes already appeared unfocused.

An uneasy suspicion seized the bard. He knelt down before Jas and put his hand around her goblet. "Jas, do you remember what you said about how Tymora reacted when you said you wanted to be able to fly. She gave you a sad little smile as if you were a kid who asked for cake for dinner? If it was a test, you failed, but she gave you what you asked for anyway."

"Yes . . . so?" Jas replied, tugging her goblet away from Joel's hand and sloshing some of it on herself in the process. It looked like blood dripping down her leather vest.

"I was thinking of those drunken revelers last night—the ones we hid from on the road to the Gilded Hall. They were fighting over the wine, remember? Finder called them the bacchae. They travel in mobs, with no purpose but to drink. I'm wondering if they all had a dark stalker."

"What are you talking about?" Jas asked, clearly confused by Joel's line of thought.

"Metaphorically speaking. They might all have something inside them that they can't get rid of. Maybe that's what made them more susceptible to the wine."

Jas stared at the bard for several moments, seemingly without comprehension. Understanding, when it came, caused her to start. She set the goblet back down on the

tray. Her body shook. At first Joel thought it was from
rage, until he saw the tears in her eyes.

Joel set his goblet down as well. He took Jas's hands in
his own. "It's going to be all right. Tymora will get rid of
the dark stalker."

"It doesn't matter," Jas sobbed. Her tears fell from her
cheeks and mixed in rivulets with the wine on her vest.
"Arandes is dead. All the others are dead. I shouldn't even
be alive. I should have died with my crew."

"No," Joel insisted. "They wouldn't want you to feel that
way. Your being alive means they'll be remembered." Joel
hesitated for a moment. Reminding Jas of Walinda might
only encourage her to renew her futile quest for vengeance, but it was a risk the bard felt he had to take. He
phrased his words carefully. "Your being alive is a symbol
of Walinda's failure to resurrect Bane. Fighting off the
dark stalker as long as you have is a symbol of the failure
of Iyachtu Xvim's priest to spread their darkness."

Jas looked up at Joel and laughed in spite of herself
through her tears. "You bards are such smooth talkers.
Everything's a symbol to you."

Joel shrugged. "After all those years of training at the
bard college, I can't help myself anymore."

"Can't help what?" Emilo asked, suddenly popping out
from behind a weigela bush.

"The propensity to put reality into poetical context,"
Joel said. He released Jas's hands and stood up. "Where
have you been?"

"I went to investigate something that caught my eye,"
Emilo replied. He looked at Jas with surprise. "You've
been crying," he noted. He pulled out an enormous baby
blue handkerchief from one of the many pockets in his
vest. "Here, you can dry your eyes with this. It's clean. Unless you'd rather keep crying. That would be all right, too."

"No, I'm finished now," Jas said, taking the proffered
cloth. She dabbed at her eyes, then wiped off her leather
vest.

Emilo snagged a slice of melon from the tray of food on
the bench and slurped at it noisily.

Tymora, Finder, and the priestess Winnie returned
from their private conference.

Jas stood as they approached. "Will you help me now, please?" she asked the goddess. She held chin up and met Tymora's gaze, but there was only earnestness, not pride, in her tone.

"Of course I'll help you," Tymora answered. She smiled warmly and placed both her hands on the winged woman's shoulders.

Joel stepped away from the pair to stand at Finder's side. Emilo took a position beside Winnie. He flashed the halfling priestess a cheery smile. Winnie eyed the kender with a look of indifference, but a tiny smile played across her lips when the kender looked away from her.

Tymora whispered a few words Joel couldn't hear. Suddenly blue light glowed about her hands; then the blue light began to turn white, like a poker in a fire. The light soaked into Jas's body. The winged woman began to glow, and her skin took on a translucent look, as if a gauze curtain were blocking the sun. A tiny sliver of black appeared in the light. It began to rise like a mist, expelled by Tymora's power flooding through Jas.

Something overhead rumbled in the sky. Joel looked up with surprise. A dark cloud had blocked the light from a patch of stars overhead. Then the ground shook beneath their feet. A moment later the ground moved like a wave of water. The bench beneath the birch tree toppled over, and the birch was uprooted from the ground by the violence of the tremors.

Joel was knocked from his feet. He tried to rise, but the heaving of the ground convinced him to remain down. When he looked up, the goddess was pushing the winged woman away from her. Tymora's head snapped up and her body arched back with a jerk. Sparks danced about her. She began breathing very quickly.

Finder cried out, "Tymora!" at the same time as Winnie shrieked, "My lady!" Finder leapt forward and wrapped his arms around the goddess's body. A bolt of lightning shot upward from Lady Luck straight into the darkness overhead. The goddess collapsed in Finder's arms, as limp as a doll.

The ground stilled, and the darkness overhead disappeared, leaving the stars twinkling above as if nothing had happened.

Jas lay on the ground, stunned. Winnie looked at her in alarm. "You *do* have something inside you, don't you?" the halfling priestess whispered.

"No," Tymora whispered. It seemed to Joel that in the silence that followed the upheaval, the goddess's soft voice could be heard throughout her realm. Finder lowered her gently to the ground, cradling her shoulders and head against his chest.

"Winnie, listen," Tymora said. "It was not Jasmine. Something caused me to lose control of my power. I sensed . . . I sensed . . . " The goddess's voice faded.

"Tymora," Finder whispered urgently. "What did you sense? Or was it a person?"

Tymora's eyes flew open wide. "Beshaba!" she growled. Then her eyes closed again and she collapsed against Finder.

The ground gave one last tiny rumble, as if Tymora's realm was shuddering from the name the goddess had just uttered.

"Who's Beshaba?" Emilo asked curiously.

"Her sister," Finder replied.

"Her enemy," Winnie answered.

Behind the Scenes

"I am having a problem harnessing Tymora's power," the looming figure growled. "She is too generous with it. It leaks away whenever her followers call upon her. Worse, when she casts a spell, my power conduits cannot contain the energy bursts, and they overload and spew the power back out. It has attracted the attention of her allies."

"So what is to be done?" the summoner asked with concern.

"She is greatly weakened. If we can capture her and bring her here, her allies will not be able to investigate the power drain and trace it back to us. Should she regain consciousness and cast another spell, we will not have to rely on the energy conduits—the fusion chamber can absorb the power. Then it will not be wasted. More importantly, if she is within the circle of darkness, she will not sense her followers calling upon her, and her power will not leak away when she shares it with them. Can your forces capture her?"

"I will make it so," the summoner said.

"Good," the looming figure replied. Then, the figure thought, no more of her power will be squandered on her foolish followers. It will all be mine.

Act Two
Scene 3

In the earthquake-ravaged garden, Finder had cast all the spells he could think of to help revive Tymora, but the goddess remained in a swoon. Joel had never seen Finder so pale and grave, not even when the god had returned to mortality to enter Sigil and his own life was threatened.

Joel realized his god was not just reacting in fear of anything that could so injure a power as great as Tymora. When Joel had first met Finder, Finder had assumed the identity of an old priest named Jedidiah and told Joel about Finder's life and transformation into a god. Jedidiah had told Joel how much Finder owed to Tymora, how grateful the god was to the goddess for her help. He'd also spoken of Tymora's grace and charm with so much passion that Joel had wondered if Jedidiah were speaking of his own feelings or those of Finder. Later, when Finder revealed that Jedidiah was only a ruse, Joel realized that his god had revealed his heart. Finder was smitten with Lady Luck.

Now Finder found himself powerless to help the patroness he cared for. As a mortal Finder had always been a man of action. As a god, he would feel no less frustrated by his helplessness.

Tymora's priestess, Winnie, faced a critical dilemma. As Finder had pointed out to her, any spells she cast on her mistress would ultimately draw from her mistress's power, so it was perhaps best for her to take a different role in the crisis. At the god's advice, the halfling priestess had hurried off to arrange security for the area and to request the aid of Tymora's oldest ally, the goddess Selune.

Finder, Joel, Jas, and Emilo had formed a circle about

Tymora, anticipating an attack, perhaps from Beshaba, perhaps from some unknown enemy.

"How is it," Emilo asked, "that Tymora and her sister are enemies?"

"Joel," Finder said, "tell Emilo the story of Tyche."

"Tyche?" Joel asked, his mind fixated on danger, not old tales.

"Yes, Tyche. They still teach her tale at that fancy barding college in Berdusk, don't they?" the god snapped at his priest.

"Yes," Joel said, realizing that his god was far more worried than he let on. The bard paused for a moment, trying to remember the traditional beginning to the tale of Tyche.

"Feel free to improvise," Finder said with a more even humor.

"Right. A long time ago," Joel began, "even before the fall of Myth Drannor, there was a great war between the gods of Toril over who would be their leader. It was known as the Dawn Cataclysm because it was started by Lathander when he decided that he should be that leader. Lathander is the god of beginnings," Joel added for Emilo's benefit. "Births, spring, and dawn are all his purview. Also called the Morninglord, he's a god of good. At the time of the Dawn Cataclysm, Lathander was favored with the love of Tyche, the goddess of all luck, good and bad, but Tyche wanted no part in the conflict Lathander had begun. She kissed Lathander with misfortune and left him to his war.

"Tyche wandered about the Realms for some time. As she rested on a snow-capped mountain surveying the land all about her, a rosebud burst through the snow at her feet. The bud showed no sign of damage from the harsh setting in which it had grown. It was just on the verge of opening its petals and promised to be perfect in every way. Because of the circumstances of the rose's appearance, Tyche took it to be an overture of peace from Lathander.

"The goddess of luck reached down to pluck the rose, but the stem wouldn't break. Tyche yanked harder, only to be rewarded by thorns in her fingers. She cursed the young blossom with bad luck, and the stem snapped right

off. Annoyed that the gift had proved so difficult, Tyche
decided to keep Lathander waiting a while longer. She
continued wandering about the Realms, with the rose fastened in her hair above her ear.

"The rose, however, was not an offering from Lathander but a trap set by Moander the Darkbringer, god of
decay. The rose blossomed, and its pollen drifted into her
ear, where it began to rot her from the inside out. Thus
the Darkbringer hoped to gain for himself Tyche's power
over luck.

"When Tyche returned to her home in the outer planes,
Selune, goddess of the moon, was there waiting to speak
with her. Selune was instantly aware of the corruption
eating away at her friend. Without a moment's hesita-
tion—"

"—she lashed out," said another voice, "with a bolt of
purifying light that split Tyche down the center of her rotting core. All that was good and kind in Tyche coalesced
into a single form and stepped out from Tyche's rotting
corpse. That was Tymora. I brought her forth from the
tragedy of Tyche's corruption, and she possessed power
over good fortune." The speaker appeared to be an elderly
matron with long, black hair streaked with silver. There
was something extraordinarily regal about her. Joel was
filled with a sense of awe. Although he realized her elderly appearance was probably a godly illusion, the bard
was certain he was in the presence of someone far older
than either Finder or Tymora, and far more powerful.
With Winnie trailing along behind her, the speaker approached Finder.

"Lady Selune," Finder greeted her. His demeanor was
grave as he bowed low. His mortal companions did likewise.

"Finder," Selune said, recognizing the god with a cur-
sory nod. She knelt beside Tymora's unconscious form and
set her hand over Lady Luck's heart. A white light far
brighter than that which Tymora had summoned flowed
from the older goddess's hand and covered Tymora's body.
The light appeared to seep into the unconscious goddess.
Finder gasped.

"Did you see that?" Selune asked Finder.

"I think so," the younger god said.

"Let's try it again, shall we?" Selune asked. Once again the white light flowed from her hand over Tymora, then disappeared.

"Something's drawing it off," Finder whispered.

"What are you talking about?" Jas demanded. "The energy's going into her."

"No," Selune said. "It appears that way to your mortal eyes because you do not sense all that we do. Something is drawing off the power surrounding Tymora in such a way that it only appears to be sinking into her form. But that's only part of the problem. Close your eyes, Finder, and concentrate on Tymora. What do you sense?"

Finder closed his eyes. In less than two heartbeats, they flew open again. "She's leaking like a sieve," he said in a shocked voice.

Selune nodded. "Something has pierced the very source of her power. She can no longer control its release. Every time she uses her power, her control weakens so that more spills out of her. When she was casting her blessing on Jasmine, the power burst out. Whatever or whoever is siphoning her energy away was unprepared to absorb the surge. Some of the power went into the land, so the land quaked."

"So it wouldn't have happened if she hadn't tried to cure me," Jas said.

Selune leaned back on her heels and looked up at Jas. "The guilt is not your own, Jasmine. Do not rush to claim it," the older goddess said curtly. "Only another god would have the power to cause such damage. Had Tymora not attempted to cure you, we might not have discovered the drain until it was far too late."

Jas's body stiffened, and the feathers on her wings quivered until Selune looked back down at Tymora. The winged woman tilted her head in puzzlement. "You look like someone I knew a long time ago," she said softly.

"No," Selune replied without looking up at Jas again. "Someone you knew a long time ago looked like me." She stroked Tymora's forehead and said, "We must find a way to stop this drain and restore Tymora's ability to control her power."

"Tymora believed Beshaba was behind this," Winnie said.

"Please, who is Beshaba?" Emilo asked, stepping up beside the elderly goddess.

Selune turned toward the kender, and a look of surprise crossed her face. Perhaps she was surprised the kender had addressed her so directly, but Joel was left with the unmistakable impression that the goddess had not sensed the kender before.

"Beshaba, like Tymora," the goddess explained, "arose from the corrupted form of Tyche. Once Tymora came forth, all that was tainted by Moander coalesced and stepped out as the goddess of ill fortune, Beshaba. Beshaba was lovely to behold, but her heart was malicious and spiteful. She is called Tymora's sister only because they shared the same origin. Beshaba and Tymora hated one another instantly and tried to destroy each other. Fortunately other powerful gods were present at the time and helped separate the battling sisters. Beshaba fled to live on the dark planes, which were more suited to her spirit."

"We must discover out how Beshaba is draining my lady and stop her somehow," Winnie said.

Selune nodded. "Before we begin to investigate Beshaba, we need to take certain precautions. We can slow the drain from spells that Tymora grants to her priests. Winnie, as circumspectly as possible, you will have to spread word to Tymora's churches that Finder and I will grant their spells for now. The drain from adventurers who call on Lady Luck will be more difficult to control. It is already causing problems in Faerûn, the sort of problems that could soon spread throughout the Realms. Tymora has always been generous. Even in her unconscious state, she's still sending good fortune to those she favors. Too much luck is disrupting their lives as assuredly as bad luck would."

"Can we stop that?" Finder asked.

"We must find a way," Selune said. "Or the consequences will be horrible."

"How can too much good luck be a bad thing?" Emilo asked.

"In more ways than you can imagine, but mostly it's a

case of flood or famine," Selune replied. "Think a minute. When the good luck is all gone, what will be left?"

"Nothing but bad luck," Jas said, beginning to sense what the regal goddess was driving at.

"Perhaps another power could conceal from Tymora's senses any adventurers who call on her," Finder suggested. "That should help to control her releases of power."

Selune nodded. "Lathander might be able to do that. I will speak with him. Wait here." The goddess vanished.

Joel went to Finder's side. "Will you be going to investigate Beshaba?" he asked softly.

Winnie flashed a look of utter disbelief at Joel. "He really is one of the clueless, isn't he?" the halfling priestess asked Finder.

"What's that supposed to mean?" Jas snapped, glaring at Winnie.

"Easy, Jasmine," Finder warned. "No," he said to Joel, "I will do everything I can for Tymora, but I don't dare approach Beshaba's realm. She would detect another power in an instant. For another god to enter her realm without invitation would be tantamount to a declaration of war. And Beshaba is Tymora's equal in power. In a fight with her, I wouldn't stand a chance."

"But Selune is more powerful than Beshaba, isn't she?" Joel asked.

"Selune will do what she can to avoid a war with another power," Finder replied. "It's a messy business."

"We'll have to send in a discreet party on a reconnaissance mission," Winnie explained. "They'll have to take care not to set off any magical alarms that Beshaba may have cast upon her realm. If they cannot stop whatever it is that is draining my lady's power, if they find there is nothing to be done short of warring with Beshaba, then Selune may act."

"I can go on your behalf," Joel said to Finder.

Finder smiled sadly at his priest. "I know you would do anything for me, but you don't realize the dangers you would be facing. Beshaba's realm is in the Abyss, a place of infinite evil, cruelty, and bloody war. Moreover, the nature of the realm will weaken your ability to cast your priestly spells."

"If Beshaba has set up magical alarms, it will be to warn her of the arrival of the minions of Tymora or Selune, mighty warriors and powerful mages. What could be more harmless than the priest of a god she has no reason to fear?" Joel insisted. "I can at least spy out the territory."

"He has a point," Winnie said.

Finder shot Winnie a withering glare.

Joel set a hand on his god's arm and said, "When you were forced to trade the Hand of Bane in return for your power, you let me make the decision. You trusted me to make the right one for all involved. I know your heart, Finder. Let me help."

"I'll go with Joel," Jas said. "I'll keep him out of trouble."

Finder looked at Jas with surprise. It was unlike the winged woman to volunteer for anything dangerous. "Why?" Finder asked.

Jas threw up her hands. "You heard Selune. If we don't stop this, the Realms will run out of good luck. Everyone will be at Beshaba's mercy. I've been away for ten years, but Toril is still my home." She shrugged. "Besides, Tymora tried to help me."

"Is this the same Abyss where the Queen of Darkness reigns?" Emilo asked.

"Who?" Joel asked.

Finder sighed. "On Emilo's world," the god explained, "all the Lower Planes are referred to as the Abyss. The Queen of Darkness inhabits a realm in a lower plane we refer to as Baator. When we speak of the Abyss, we mean a completely different plane."

"Then I'll go with them," Emilo said. "I've never been to *that* Abyss. I should take a look around."

"Perhaps you haven't been paying careful attention, Mr. Haversack," Winnie said sternly. "The Abyss is an evil, horrible place. No one goes there to 'take a look around.' Take my word for it."

"Have you been there?" Emilo asked.

"Once, which was one time too many," Winnie retorted.

"So you couldn't resist either," Emilo noted.

"Resist?" Winnie squeaked. "It had nothing to do with—"

Finder put up his hand to silence the priestess. "Forget it, Winnie. A kender's curiosity can't be quenched with tales of horror. They're completely fearless. I think Mr. Haversack will make an excellent addition to the party. Joel and Jas could use someone older and wiser."

Winnie sighed. "Very well."

"The sooner we go, the better," Joel suggested.

"Wait here while I fetch some things you'll need," Winnie said. Once again she left them alone in the garden.

Finder pulled out half of the finder's stone. He sang a single note, and a blue light burst about his hand, then seeped into the stone. He handed the stone to Joel. "Take this," he said. "I've imbued it with enough power so it can serve you as a power key for a few days, at least."

"A what?" Joel asked.

"A power key," Finder repeated. "As I said before, in Beshaba's realm, your ability to cast priest spells will be greatly weakened. A power key will lessen that effect. It will also keep your spells from being twisted by the nature of the realm."

"Can I still use the finder's stone to find Beshaba?" Joel asked.

Finder shook his head. "It can only locate people you know. I wouldn't recommend using it that way even if you could. Beshaba would be certain to detect it, and you don't want to attract her notice. Still, the stone has other powers I have never fully understood. Sometimes it functions as if it has a mind of its own, sending out a light to guide the lost. That may work for you. At the very least, it can serve you as a magical torch."

Selune reappeared before the party. "Lathander will do what he can to obscure Tymora's sensing ability in the Realms. Lathander suspects that Tymora's power has been overmanifesting itself all day."

"We've arranged a party to investigate Beshaba's realm," Joel said.

The goddess gave Joel a look of motherly reproach and said, "I may have been in another plane, but I had no trouble sensing the plans you were making here. There can be no doubt you are a priest of Finder. You're as reckless a fool as he."

Joel lowered his eyes, unable to face the goddess's disapproval.

Finder stepped between the goddess and his priest. "They stand as good a chance as any other adventurers. It would be no more difficult for Beshaba to destroy the strongest proxy in your court, my lady, than to destroy a lowly follower of mine. With any luck, Beshaba may take no note of their arrival."

"We may not be able to count on luck," Selune said darkly. She looked again at Joel and warned, "Do not lose the power key. It could be used against Finder as long as it holds some of his power. I hope you will guard it better than Finder did the last time he filled it with power."

"Yes, ma'am," Joel said nervously. Less than a month ago Finder had stored more than half his power in the stone, then had it stolen by the evil priestess Walinda, who had given it to her master, a crazed banelich. Joel and Finder had been forced to do the banelich's bidding until they'd managed to wrest it away from the evil undead creature.

"It would be impossible to guard it worse than I did," the god pointed out with a smile.

Selune gave a derisive snort.

Winnie returned, carrying a sheathed sword. Two human servants behind her carried backpacks of gear. The halfling stood before Jas.

"It is the custom of my lady to loan this sword to those who perform a mission for her," she explained to the winged woman. "It's a fine weapon, and it will bring you luck."

Jas looked at the others uncertainly.

"If you're intending to help Tymora, save the Realms, and keep Joel out of trouble," Selune said, "you'd better accept the sword."

Jas took the weapon from Winnie. She slid its sheath onto her weapons belt, then drew it out to examine it. She tested its balance and smiled.

"When you're ready to return, you can use the sword to wish your party back here," Winnie said. "Wish aloud, and wish carefully, so no one is left behind. A wish will attract the attention of everyone from Beshaba to the tanar'ri lords, so you don't want to remain in the Abyss after you've made one. Just use the wish to get home, nothing else," the priestess warned. "In the backpacks, you will find food and water, a tarp for shelter, a magical lantern, rope, some healing potions, and a few magical scrolls that you may find useful. There is also some gold; creatures in the Abyss are not above accepting bribes."

"Beshaba's realm is the thirteenth layer of the Abyss," Selune explained. "Long ago the layer was flooded to prevent the baatezu from ever invading it again. Umberlee, the evil goddess of the sea, makes her realm in those waters. Towering over the waters is the Blood Tor, a massive rocky peak that some sages say rivals Mt. Olympus in size. Beshaba and her court live in a cavern complex within the mountain, somewhere near the pinnacle. I will make you a gateway in the mountainside. You will have to discover your own route into Beshaba's caverns. Many other evil things live on and within the Blood Tor. Take care to avoid as many of them as you can."

Joel nodded.

"Finder and I will be able to detect what is going on throughout Beshaba's realm the moment you arrive, but the longer you stay, the more we can learn. You do not need to get close to Beshaba for us to sense her, but you may be safer near the heart of her realm," the goddess explained. "The fiends in the Abyss avoid tangling with the powers. If creatures there think you are one of Beshaba's minions, they will avoid you. You do not need to take risks. For now, we only need you to be our eyes, not our armies. Do you understand?"

Joel nodded in agreement.

Selune motioned with her hand, and a magical portal formed beside the root ball of the fallen birch tree. A barren wind-blasted slope appeared on the opposite side of the portal, and an unpleasant odor issued forth, which Joel recognized as the stench of blood.

Joel felt a twinge of fear, but his determination did not waiver. Finder was relying on him to help Lady Luck, and so were the luckless Realms, although no one there probably yet realized their peril.

Finder embraced his priest. "Be careful. I don't want

you as a petitioner yet," the god said.

"I will," Joel promised. He picked up one of the back-packs provided by Winnie. Jas picked up the other one. Together they stepped into the Abyss.

"Hey, wait for me," Emilo called out and leapt after them.

Offstage

Somewhere in the Prime Material Plane on the world known as Toril in Realmspace, Mirt the Moneylender settled his prodigious girth on a heavy ironwood chair and said, "You are the last person I ever expected to see in my office."

Joshuan Havabuck—"Fast Joshy," as he was known on the street—squirmed in his chair, his furry halfling feet dangling a good foot off the floor. "Would that you were not seeing me, guv'nor," the halfling said, "but I appreciate your willingness to aid my situation."

Mirt folded his hands over his belly and smiled. His aid always came at a hefty, if deferred, cost. "It's hard to believe that you, of all people, are short of ready money," Mirt stated. "You've lectured me many a time about keeping your eggs in numerous baskets."

"Diversification," Havabuck said with a sage bob of his head.

"Numbers running, smuggling, pornographic Talis cards, stolen goods . . . " Mirt enumerated Havabuck's baskets, ticking them off on his sausage-sized fingers.

"All solid enterprises," the halfling boasted, "though subject to normal irregularities and marketing fluxes."

"So why are you here?" Mirt asked.

The halfling sighed, a sigh that ended in a shuddering sob. A moment later Havabuck pulled himself together and explained. "It's my core business, guv'nor. The ready money for all the others comes from a lottery I run in Dock Ward. A bet on the total daily tonnage that comes into Waterdeep, as reported by the dockmaster."

"An honest man," said Mirt solemnly.

The halfling nodded. "Incorruptible, and best of all, a

man with a trustworthy demeanor. The lottery costs a
gold lion a ticket, and it pays out a thousand gold lions.
Normal take is ten thousand lions, so I get a tidy profit,
which I can use to cover losses of other, less dependable
operations."

"Unless more than ten people pick the winning number," said Mirt.

The halfling suppressed another shudder and nodded.

"So I take it more than ten people won?" Mirt queried

The halfling nodded again.

"Fifteen people?"

The halfling pressed his lips together and did not re-
spond.

"Twenty?"

Havabuck shook his head.

Mirt's eyes widened in surprise. "Thirty people all
picked the same number?" he asked in a breathless
whisper.

"All of them," the halfling declared in a piteous whine.
"All ten thousand miserable souls picked the same bleeding number. And it was the right number. They're all expecting payment tonight."

A silence pervaded the room as Mirt marveled at the
anguished halfling before him. A lesser being might have
taken the ten-thousand-gold-lion take and fled the city.
Yet Havabuck was prepared to take on the obligation of
paying out the ten million gold lions, not to mention the
interest payments on the loan. Mirt suspected the halfling
was prepared to pay any price to retain the honor of being
a major crime lord of Waterdeep.

With such round figures, Mirt did not require his abacus to calculate the interest. He slid the wooden frame
aside and drew up the papers.

"You have enough armed guards to cart away the prin-
cipal?" Mirt asked as the halfling signed the papers.

Havabuck nodded. He was nothing if not efficient.

It only took four hours to clear the one hundred thousand bags of gold from Mirt's treasury, since Havabuck
had not thought it necessary to count the coin in each
sack. Mirt's reputation was unimpeachable

Much later that evening, as Mirt sat calculating which

gems, magical artifacts, and art pieces he would be selling to partially replenish his stock of coin, a masked figure appeared before him. Mirt was not startled. The mask was one of the helms worn by the members of the council who ruled the city. The council members kept their identities secret.

"I was wondering if you would be dropping by," Mirt said, motioning for the anonymous figure to have a seat. "You've heard about Havabuck. What do you think? Godly influence? Did Havabuck enrage Mask, Master of All Thieves, or simply annoy Beshaba? Or perhaps this is a mad plot of Cyric, Prince of Lies."

"Havabuck isn't the only victim," the figure said.

Mirt's eyes widened in surprise.

"The Cassalanters have made two similar loans, one to Widow Silvermane for a similar lottery that she runs in the North Ward, the other to the Field of Triumph Race Track in Sea Ward. Over four hundred people placed bets averaging fifty gold lions on a horse named Song of the Wind before the track could post new odds. The horse ran as if Kesef the Chaos Hound was chasing him. Won three lengths ahead of the favorite. Then there's the good luck of a venture capital company called The Rock, which funded an adventuring group that took out two beholders and raided their lair. That's another million to be divided between the company's one hundred and sixty shareholders."

"So do you have a theory?"

"Don't need a theory. There's something wrong with Tymora," the figure said. "Her priests are keeping it hushed up, but they've made a private off-the-record admission to Lord Piergeiron. Lord Piergeiron sent me with a question for you."

"Yes?"

"Could we be in the same trouble as Amn?"

"Amn?" Mirt asked.

"Yes. Remember a few years back when Amn invaded Maztica and brought back all that gold? A bushel of corn cost fifty gold there after the war. You said it was because there was more money circulating through their kingdom than actual goods that the money is supposed to represent."

Mirt nodded slowly. "It's a theory espoused by some sages."

"Could Waterdeep be in the same danger?" the masked figure asked.

Mirt slid a few beads across his abacus. His fingers were quick and sure. "I don't think so," he said finally, but his tone was not certain.

"Suppose similar things happened again tomorrow?" the masked figure asked. "Suppose that much money came in all week?"

Mirt gave a low whistle. He slid all the beads on the abacus to one side with a violent sweep of his hand. "Then," he said, "we'd be in a lot of trouble."

Act Two
Scene 4

Joel, Jas, and Emilo stepped through Selune's gate
onto a wind-blasted mountainside. The party's first prior-
ity became shelter. The wind blew stinging particles of
dirt into their face and made walking difficult. They
huddled on the leeward side of a large boulder and surveyed their surroundings.

The Blood Tor was no simple conical peak, but a complex series of steep boulder-strewn faces, sloping, but-
tresslike ridges, and cliff-walled ravines. The adventurers
couldn't even see the pinnacle from their current position
because their view was blocked by steep faces above them.
Downwind, the slope grew progressively steeper, until it
was almost a cliff wall. Upwind, the slope was steep but
manageable. If they walked into the wind, they would
come to another face that rose to a ridge. The ridge climbed
until it ran into another mountain face at a considerably
higher altitude some distance away. There was no evidence of any caves.

Joel pulled out the finder's stone and tried imagining a
cave opening in the side of the mountain. Whether the
stone was reacting to his mental image or just trying to
keep him from heading into danger, Joel had no way of
knowing, but it issued a weak beam of light in the direction of the higher mountain face off in the distance.

"We're going to have to walk into the wind," Joel said.

"What?" Jas shouted.

Joel repeated his words, shouting to be heard over the
roar of the wind.

Jas nodded. Her wings, Joel noted, had altered once
more. Now they were bat-shaped, but their color was

bright scarlet with golden flecks. Ignoring the transformation, as she always did, Jas opened one of the backpacks Winnie had supplied for them and rummaged around until she found several kerchiefs made of some lightweight fabric. They wrapped the kerchiefs around their faces, shouldered their backpacks, and stepped out into the furious wind.

There was no trail that Joel could perceive, and the slope was treacherous. Rocks gave way beneath their feet and slid and rattled down the mountainside. Far, far below, the waves of a blood-red sea pounded at the mountainside and shot upward in frothy spumes. Overhead, the sky was completely overcast. Black clouds flickered with sheet lightning. It was unclear what illuminated Beshaba's realm, but it was bright enough on the mountainside for their shadows to pool at their feet. Nothing grew on the wind-blasted slope but the red and black lichen that covered the gray rocks all around. They traveled in silence, unable to make themselves heard over the wind.

Time was hard to judge, but it had to be at least an hour before they made it to a notch in the ridge. The climb had exhausted them, and the roar of the wind left them dazed. They passed through the notch. On the other side of the ridge, the slope was less steep, dropping gradually into a great sheltered bowl where a few stunted trees grew. A ledge just wide enough to serve as a trail traveled along the ridge on the sheltered side. There, out of the wind, it seemed almost quiet, and they rested and made a general inventory of the equipment Winnie had packed in the backpacks.

Jas pulled out a padded flask of water and took a few sips. As she handed the flask to Emilo, something large and dark leapt through the notch in the ridge. The creature, a great black stag with red eyes, bounded surefootedly down the slope. Its rack might have gored an elephant with ease. The beast so startled Emilo that he dropped the water flask. The flask rolled down the hill, spilling its precious contents.

"Rotten luck," Emilo muttered, prepared to lunge after it, but Joel held him back by grabbing the kender's vest.

"Careful," the bard said. "It would be worse luck if you went rolling after it and fell down a cliff."

"Sorry," the kender said. "I never drop things like that."

"The black stag is *her* symbol," Joel said, purposefully avoiding using Beshaba's name. Without Selune and Finder to shield them, using the goddess's name could attract unwanted attention.

Joel lowered Emilo down the slope with a rope attached to his belt so he could fetch the flask, then hauled him back up. The flask was more than half empty, but at least they had it back. If they were desperate enough, Joel could create water to fill it. The party traveled along the ledge on the sheltered side of the ridge. As the ridge climbed higher, the adventurers grew tired quickly and were forced to rest often.

"I feel old all of a sudden," Emilo noted with some surprise.

"The higher you go, the less air there is," Jas explained.

"Of course, here in the Abyss, it could just be there's less air as you approach dangerous powers," Joel suggested.

The ridge and the ledge ended abruptly at a deep gorge and continued on the opposite side. A towering stream of water poured down a cliffside nearly half a mile away. It was the longest waterfall Joel had ever seen, and he could hear the roar of the water in the distance. It was the color of the water, however, that made the sight so eerie. It was blood-red.

The water, Joel thought, must be why the mountain is called the Blood Tor. It looks like blood pouring from a wounded land. He wondered briefly why the water was red, then decided he didn't want to know.

The water surged down the gorge below them toward the sea, where the goddess Umberlee made her realm. There was a rope bridge over the gorge, but it wasn't sheltered by the ridge. Consequently the bridge had been battered by the wind with such violence that it was a knotted tangle of ropes and reeds that appeared completely uncrossable.

"You want to try unravelling the bridge, or should I just fly us across?" Jas asked Joel.

Joel watched the bridge flap about as the wind came ripping up the gully. "Do you think you can fly in that wind?" he asked.

Jas shrugged. "I trust my wings more than I trust that contraption."

"I knew a caravan guard who used to say all the luck in the world won't make up for willful stupidity. I'm thinking we should test the reverse of that rule. Perhaps some willful reasoning will make up for all the bad luck in this realm. We're not going to leave anything to chance."

Since Emilo was the smallest, and together Joel and Jas could bear his weight easily, they rigged up a harness for the kender to use while he tried to unravel the bridge. They attached the harness to two lines of rope. Joel held one line and Jas took the other. Should the bridge collapse, Joel would keep the kender from falling into the gorge and Jas would risk flying upward to keep him from slamming into the sides of the ravine.

Emilo started down the rope bridge, untangling it as he went with his dexterous hands. The moment the kender had gotten all of the reed walkway to lie flat, he dashed across the rest of the bridge like a startled rabbit. The whistling wind made communication impossible, so they weren't sure what had alarmed Emilo. The kender turned, and to demonstrate the bridge's unreliability, he gave a sharp tug on one of the old worn ropes.

The ropes snapped in the center of the bridge, and the bridge flopped sideways. Emilo removed both lines from his harness and attached them around a boulder. Joel held both lines on the opposite bank. With a lead rope attached to the lines, Jas flew across with the first knapsack. The winds buffeted her, but the lead rope held and kept her from losing control of her direction. She checked the lines Emilo had affixed before flying back for the second backpack.

Before Jas carried him across, Joel hammered a piton into the rocky ridge, slipped one line through the piton, and joined the lines into one. Jas had more trouble with the bard's weight. She lost altitude rapidly shortly after taking off. Joel's stomach lurched. Then the wind forced the winged woman back upward. When they reached the other side, she ducked behind the ridge and collapsed onto the ledge.

Joel untied the knot joining the two lines Emilo had affixed about the boulder. He tugged the rope through the piton. Somehow he'd forgotten to check the ends of the line before he began pulling. A knot near the end of the line caught in the piton. He tried yanking at the piton to no avail. Then he cut the rope and let it fall back into the gorge, where it hung forlornly from the piton until a gust of wind caught it and sent it flapping about until it was tangled with the useless rope bridge.

When they reached the mountain slope where the ridge ended, the finder's stone's light pointed to the right of the ridge, which meant walking once again into the wind. Wearily they started out again.

They'd only been traveling a short while on the new face when there was a tremor in the ground and a great thunderous rumble all around them. Small rocks tumbled down the slopes, pelting the adventurers until they took shelter downslope of a great boulder. All the while, Joel prayed that the boulder wouldn't suddenly start rolling. The tremor subsided. Then suddenly the wind died and they were encased in a thick gray fog.

"Are earthquakes followed by fog regular occurrences in the Abyss?" Jas asked Joel. "Or do you think it had something to do with you-know-who and her sister?"

Joel shrugged. It was possible that Tymora had released another burst of power, and Beshaba, unable to absorb it quickly, had to disperse it into her realm. It made sense, but it was mere speculation.

Fearful of the terrain's uncertainties, the adventurers decided to make camp right where they were. The ground sloped at least thirty degrees where they halted, but Joel doubted they'd find a gentler incline if they continued. They fixed a rope between two boulders and stretched a tarp overhead. Huddled in their makeshift tent, they feasted on the contents of Winnie's backpacks.

There were packages of fresh berries that had been magically enchanted. Just a few berries left them feeling reasonably nourished. To dispel the chill brought on by

the fog-laden air, Joel heated one of the metal flasks with
a spell to boil the water within.

With his back against the boulder, Joel kept watch
while Jas and Emilo slept. By the light of the finder's
stone, the bard perused the magical scrolls Winnie had
placed in the backpacks. Some time later Emilo woke and
took over the watch. From one of Winnie's packs, Joel
pulled out a magically glowing lantern and gave it to
Emilo. Then the bard rolled the finder's stone into a spare
tunic and used the tunic for a pillow.

The kender stared into the fog, imagining all sorts of
creatures in the swirling mists. He began whistling softly
to keep awake and to fight off the cheerlessness of this
place. Whenever he fell prey to bad dreams, this was the
sort of place in which the dreams were set. He whistled a
second tune, and just as he began whistling a third
melody he spotted a flame burning somewhere off in the
mists downhill from their camp.

It's a campfire, Emilo thought, and not too far off. He
wondered whether something evil had settled nearby. He
knew he should wake the others, but he suspected Joel
would be overly cautious and insist they avoid going anywhere near the light. His curiosity roused, Emilo couldn't
stand that thought. The flame seemed to draw the kender
like a moth. He had to see it up close.

Leaving the magically glowing lantern behind, Emilo
slipped out from under the tarp and padded silently
downhill toward the flame. As he got closer, he slowed his
steps and proceeded more cautiously. The kender ducked
behind a boulder no more than twenty feet from the fire
and peered around the edge. The flame flickered a foot off
the ground with nothing to fuel it, as if it were an illusion
or some other sort of magical fire.

Emilo could see no one around the fire. The kender
wondered if whoever had created the fire was invisible.
He watched carefully for shadows across the flame or an
outline in the fog and listened for the noise of breathing,
but there was no sign of anyone.

Unable to contain his curiosity, Emilo stepped out from
behind the boulder and walked right up to the fire. He put
a hand out. Heat emanated from the flame.

Welcome, Emilo Haversack, a voice whispered inside his head.

Emilo whirled around in surprise, but there was no one behind him.

Turn and look at me, the voice in his head ordered.

Emilo spun around and looked back at the flame. "Are you talking to me, fire?" he asked with amazement.

I am forming thoughts inside your head, the voice explained. *The fire is only a manifestation of my being that I created to draw you away from your companions so I could speak with you in private.*

"Who are you?" Emilo asked.

Can you not guess? the voice asked. *You find yourself in a perilous adventure fraught with gods. Does it surprise you that one of your own gods takes an interest in your safety?*

Emilo's jaw dropped. He shook himself. "You're a god, too?" the kender whispered. "Which one are—wait, I know. Are you Sirrion? The Flowing Flame?"

The fire flared high over the halfling's head. Emilo thought he saw a red rose blossoming in the tongues of flame.

I cannot manifest in this dark place for long, kender. You must listen carefully and do as I say.

"Yes, sir," Emilo said with a nod.

You must take the finder's stone from the bard-priest and dispose of it where it will never be found.

"Why?" the kender asked with astonishment.

The stone is cursed. It will lead your friends to their doom, but your companions will not believe you if you try to warn them. They will use the stone anyway, unless you take it from them. Toss it down the mountain so it will never be found. You will find a safer entrance to Beshaba's realm down this hill. When the fog clears, look for the bats returning to the cave.

"But Finder made the stone into a power key. Without it, Joel can't cast spells in the Abyss," Emilo objected.

Joel will need no more spells. Have faith. The path I have prepared for you is clear. Take the finder's stone and throw it away. It is the only way to save your friends.

The fire flared higher, then suddenly vanished. Emilo

was left alone in the fog.

The kender turned in the direction of the tarp. Through the fog, he could spy the lantern he'd left in the entrance. He made his way back to the camp and slipped beneath the tarp. Ever so carefully he slid his hand into the rolled-up shirt beneath Joel's head until fingers felt the finder's stone. Slowly he eased it out from beneath the bard's head. Joel stirred slightly as his head sank deeper into the rolled-up shirt, but he did not awaken.

Emilo slipped out of the tent again with an uncomfortable feeling that something wasn't quite right. Once outside, he held up the yellow crystal and examined it. The stone was a thing of beauty. Cut and polished to perfection, it reflected back dozens of Emilos.

It's a shame that it's cursed, Emilo thought. He pulled back his arm to pitch the stone downhill, but he couldn't bring himself to release it. Even though he'd taken it for a good reason, it was still Joel's property. It didn't feel right to cast it away.

Surely, the kender thought, it will be enough to hide it from Joel so he can't use it. Once we find Sirrion's entrance to Beshaba's realm, we'll be safe. Then I can give it back to Joel.

The kender tucked the stone into his knapsack, feeling a little less uneasy about the compromise he'd made.

Offstage

Somewhere in the Prime Material Plane on the world known as Toril in Realmspace, Amberlee Wyvernspur watched from an upper window as her two younger brothers joined the flock of cousins in the courtyard. They were up to some mischief, led, no doubt, by Aunt Julia's twin sons, Tavan and Toran Sudacar. Uncle Giogi's son, Cory, and Amberlee's brothers, Lumen and Ferrin, followed them like moths to the flame.

As the oldest and most mature at nine years old, Amberlee generally made an effort to ignore her cousins' antics, but today the youngest cousins, Uncle Giogi's daughter, Olivia, and Aunt Julia's daughter, Heather, and even Amberlee's littlest brother, Pars, were part of the flock. Tavan and Toran were not responsible enough to keep the little ones safe. All the adults but Uncle Steele and their great-grandaunt, Aunt Dorath, had gone to a wedding at one of the nearby farms. Amberlee realized it would be up to her to find out what the older children were up to and discourage them from including Heather, Olivia, and Pars.

As the Wyvernspur and Sudacar brood disappeared into the stables, Amberlee raced down the stairs of the castle out into the courtyard and hurried after her younger kinfolk. Just outside the stable, Cory sat upon his own pony. Olivia, Heather, and Pars were waiting in Olivia's pony cart. Inside the stable, Tavan, Toran, Ferrin, and Lumen were saddling up their own ponies. After hitching up the coaches for the adults to attend the wedding, all the stablehands had taken the rest of the day off.

"And just where do all of you think you're going?" Amberlee asked Cory. He had the most sense of all the boys, and she could usually get him to come clean.

"Don't tell her, Cory," his sister Olivia whispered. "She'll only go running to Aunt Dorath."

"No, she won't," Cory said, giving Amberlee his most charming smile. "She'll come with us. I've already saddled her pony."

"That's very presumptuous of you, Cory Wyvernspur," Amberlee retorted with a sniff.

"We all have to go," Cory said.

"Go where?" Amberlee demanded.

"To the family crypt to meet the guardian."

Amberlee gasped. The guardian was the spirit of a fierce wyvern who guarded the family's underground burial chamber. The girl's alarm was replaced a moment later by reason. "You can't do that," she said. "The crypt is locked."

From the back of the cart, Heather held up a silver key on a chain.

"Where did you get that?" Amberlee whispered anxiously.

"I took it from Uncle Steele's sock drawer when he was sleeping," Heather said with a giggle.

Uncle Steele referred to his nieces and nephew as a pestilence of brats and barred them from his quarters completely. Whenever he had too much to drink, however, he showed a partiality to Heather, whom he mistook for his little sister Julia, although Julia was now a matron. At such times Heather was able to coax coins and candy from her uncle and was allowed to rummage through his old toys, which he still hoarded in chests beneath his bed.

"When Uncle Steele finds out, you're going to be in a lot of trouble," Amberlee said.

"We'll return it before he notices," Cory said.

"Only if you're very lucky," Amberlee replied.

"That's the beauty of it," Cory said. "We *are* very lucky. I heard Mother Lleddew tell Father last night that Tymora's power is leaking. Anyone who calls upon her gets scads of luck. This morning we each tossed a toy in the well as an offering to Lady Luck. We should have more good fortune than we need."

"That's how I managed to get into Uncle Steele's room

without Aunt Dorath noticing and without Uncle Steele waking up," Heather explained.

"Cory, the crypt opens onto the catacombs, and the catacombs are filled with evil monsters," Amberlee said. "You can't go down there, especially not with the little children."

"We are not little children," Olivia snapped.

"I want to go," Pars shouted and began blubbering like the four-year-old that he was.

"We aren't going into the catacombs," Cory insisted, "just the crypt. We have to talk to the guardian and find out who's her favorite of the cousins so we know which one can use the wyvern's spur."

A horrible suspicion seized Amberlee. "Cory Wyvernspur, you didn't steal the wyvern's spur from your father, did you?"

With an unashamed grin, Cory held up the mummified piece of wyvern's foot that enabled the guardian's favorites to turn into a wyvern at will. "I took it out of his pocket."

"You can't do this," Amberlee insisted, stomping her foot on the ground. "It's too dangerous."

"We'll be too lucky to get hurt," Tavan said as he led his pony from the stable. Toran, Lumen, and Ferrin followed with Amberlee's and their own ponies in tow.

"Lumen and Ferrin and Pars, as your older sister, I forbid you to go," Amberlee said imperiously.

Lumen and Ferrin laughed and mounted their ponies.

"I want to go," Pars screeched.

"I'm going to tell Aunt Dorath," Amberlee declared.

Tavan grabbed Amberlee's arm. Although a year younger, Tavan was taller and far stronger than Amberlee. "You don't want to do that, Lady Amber," Tavan said with menace.

"And why not, Tavan Sudacar?" Amberlee asked.

"Because while you're telling Aunt Dorath, we'll go off without you. Aunt Dorath won't be able to catch us, and she'll spend the whole day fretting. Probably die of worry. And then we'll all be in the crypt for her funeral. And it will be your fault."

"Tavan, that wasn't very nice," Cory reprimanded.

"But probably true," Tavan's twin, Toran, said darkly.

"Aunt Dorath will send Uncle Steele after you."

"He's probably drunk half a flask of brandy by this time of the day. He'll be sleeping till supper," Tavan said.

"Please, Amberlee," Cory asked again. "We could use your help and advice."

Amberlee glared at her charming cousin, knowing full well his flattery could lead her to her doom. She looked back at Redstone Castle uncertainly. Tavan was right about Uncle Steele. Aunt Dorath was probably snoozing over her knitting as well. There was no one she could rely on. It was up to her. "All right, I'll go," Amberlee announced, "but only to keep you all out of trouble."

Act Two
Scene 5

Joel awoke with a start, feeling alarmed. He'd been having a nightmare. He lay very still, trying to piece together the dream. He'd been traveling with a group of children riding ponies, and they'd ridden into a graveyard. The children dismounted and took him into a large family tomb. It was dark and chill in the tomb, and Joel wanted to leave, but he was afraid to say so because then he would be left behind and the children would be alone. Ordinarily crypts held no fear for Joel. He could, after all, turn the undead and lay them to rest, but in this dream, he sensed he couldn't do that.

More disturbing than the feeling of dread was the sense that he knew the children in the dream. While traveling to Finder's temple in the Lost Vale, Joel had passed through Immersea in Cormyr and been welcomed into the home of Giogi Wyvernspur, a descendant of Finder's brother, Gerrin. Two of the children in the dream had been Giogi's son and daughter.

Joel wondered if the dream had any meaning. Perhaps he'd dreamed of children in crypts because he and Jas and Emilo were like children to the gods venturing in this deadly realm. He may only have dreamed of Giogi Wyvernspur's children because they'd been the last human children he'd seen in the Realms. On the other hand, there was the troubling possibility that he had dreamed of them because Tymora's troubles had directly affected them in some way.

"There, see," Emilo called out excitedly.

"Yes. I see them," Jas replied.

The bard rolled over. Emilo and Jas stood outside the

tarp. Joel yawned and crawled out to see what they were
looking at. They were camped on a little hillock at the foot
of a cliff. A talus field, left over from yesterday's earthquake, surrounded the hill. A mild breeze had dispersed
most of the fog. The sky far overhead was once again full
of black clouds and sheet lightning.

Joel rubbed his eyes and yawned. "What's up?" he
asked.

"See the bats fluttering around down there?" Emilo
whispered excitedly, pointing downhill. "It must mean
there's a cave nearby. It could be the entrance to Beshaba's realm. We should go look."

Joel and Jas agreed it would be worth checking out
after breakfast. Jas returned to the tarp and began rum-
maging through Winnie's knapsack for breakfast. They
split a loaf of bread and downed some more magical
berries.

They washed breakfast down with water, leaving the
second water flask half empty. Realizing he'd probably
have to magically create more water soon, Joel began
singing a soft prayer to Finder to grant him the spells he
would need. He felt curiously empty as he did so. It was
then he realized that perhaps he should be holding his
power key while he prayed.

When he couldn't find the stone in his rolled-up shirt,
Joel searched beneath the tarp. Then he began unpacking
the backpacks. His searching grew more frantic. He began
searching up and down the slope, fearing the stone had
rolled downhill in the mist.

Jas joined the search, going through the backpacks
again, more carefully this time. She felt in every fold of
the tarp and crawled around among the boulders that
held the tarp line, in case the stone had become lodged beneath one of them.

Emilo pretended he was joining in the search, but he
felt too foolish.

"Why don't we check out the cave?" he asked.

Joel glared at the kender and continued to stalk about
the campsite.

"You don't really need the stone now, do you?" Emilo
asked.

Joel whirled about, barely concealing his panic and anger. The kender's earnest expression softened him somewhat. He proceeded to explain patiently. "Emilo, the power key is a link to Finder's heart. I can't just leave it lying around on a mountainside in the Abyss. You heard Selune. It could be used against Finder. And it wouldn't be the first time, either. I would have failed him after all the trust he's placed in me."

"I don't think anything like that will happen," Emilo said calmly.

"How would you know?" Joel snapped angrily.

It was Jas who suddenly gained insight into Emilo's strange statement. "Emilo, do you know where the stone is?" the winged woman asked.

Emilo looked down at the ground, then at the humans, then back down at the ground. Slowly he pulled the stone from his knapsack.

A tiny sob escaped Joel's lips and he sighed with relief. He snatched the stone from the kender's hands.

"I'm sorry," the kender said. "I tried to explain to Sirrion how important it was to you, but he said it was cursed. I was only trying to protect you." The kender's voice cracked with emotion. "I'm really sorry," he added.

Joel slid the finder's stone into his shirt and pressed the cool crystal into the flesh over his heart. He began breathing more deeply, and his pulse slowed to normal.

"Who the heck is Sirrion?" Jas asked.

"He's a god on Krynn. Lord of the Flowing Flame. He said I should take the finder's stone because it was cursed. He's a god, so I thought he must be right."

"He said the stone was cursed? When?" Jas asked. "When did Sirrion say this?"

"Before you woke up," Emilo explained. "He appeared as a flame not far from here and told me about the cave. He said you wouldn't need the finder's stone, and I should take it so it didn't lead us to our doom."

"Why would a god from another world . . . " Jas started to ask. "You don't think it was *her*, do you?" she asked, referring obliquely to Beshaba. "An illusion she sent?"

Joel shook his head. "If she's noticed us, she could, and probably would, crush us like fruit flies. Maybe it's some other evil creature causing mischief."

"No," Emilo insisted. "It felt like a god. It was Sirrion.
I'm sure. The flame was very beautiful, and it felt . . . "
The kender struggled to find the words to describe his awe
and excitement upon speaking with the flame. "It felt god-
like," he concluded.

"So what sort of god is this Sirrion?" Jas asked.

"He controls fire so that it's useful and beautiful, not
destructive," Emilo explained. "He said he came to be sure
I was safe."

Joel looked up at the sky in disbelief.

"Why don't you pray for your spells," Jas said, "while
Emilo and I pack up the gear?"

Joel knelt beside the boulder and sang a prayer to his
god. With the finder's stone once again in his possession,
the prayer left him feeling strong and certain that his
spells would be granted.

"Are we going to look for the cave where the bats
went?" Emilo asked anxiously. "Sirrion said it was the
way into Beshaba's realm."

Joel and Jas exchanged glances, not certain they
trusted Emilo's vision.

"We may as well see what's there," Jas said.

Joel nodded. If there wasn't a cave, or it didn't lead to
Beshaba's realm, at least then Emilo would realize he'd
been duped.

There was indeed a cave. The opening was at the base
of the hillock where they had camped. Overhanging rock
had sheltered the cave entrance so it hadn't been blocked
by the avalanche. The entrance was wide but very low. Jas
and Joel had to duck to enter. They could hear water dripping, and deeper within the cave a shallow pool glittered,
reflecting back the light from the cave entrance.

Jas touched Joel's arm and pointed. A human figure sat
half hidden in the shadows of the cave, staring into the
pool of water. Suddenly the shadowy figure rose, shape-
changed into the form of a human man wearing armor
and wielding a sword, and dived into the water, disappearing completely from sight.

"It's times like this when I really miss Holly," Jas whispered. "With her paladin ability to detect evil, she could

warn us whether or not we should get any closer to that creature, whatever it is."

"In a place like this where everything is evil, Holly would have a ringing headache by now," Joel countered.

Seemingly unconcerned with the possible dangers, Emilo walked into the cave and approached the pool of water.

"Emilo," Jas called out in a warning tone.

"I can see him," the kender said excitedly. "This pool must be a portal to another place. He's in another room, fighting another man." The kender gave a little gasp. "No, wait. He's fighting himself."

Joel and Jas moved deeper into the cave. The limestone ceiling and walls glistened with water, and tiny crystals glittered all along the floor, crunching under their boots. Jas and Joel found they could stand up, though Joel's head brushed the cave roof in spots. Farther back in the shadows, they could see about twenty small, furry bats hanging from the ceiling.

Joel and Jas joined Emilo beside the pool of water. On the opposite side of the water's surface were two identical men, dressed in identical armor, fighting with identical swords. The adventurers couldn't hear the combat, but they could see that one man was gaining the upper hand in the duel. The room surrounding the men was a gaudily decorated bedroom. Joel would have guessed it was a visitor's room in a festhall, but where in all the worlds the room was, he had no way of knowing.

The bard knew what it was he was seeing, however. "A fetch," he whispered.

"A what?" Jas asked.

"It's an evil creature that dwells in the Abyss," the bard explained. "There's a creepy Turmish song about fetch that explains why Turmish law prohibits large mirrors. Fetch attack through portals that lead to mirrors in the Prime Material Plane, taking on the forms of their intended victims. Their attacks drain the life energy from their victims. Then the victim is dragged back to the Abyss, where he becomes another fetch. There's one thing that bothers me, though. Fetch are supposed to be invisible to all but their victims."

"Perhaps we can see him because we're on his home plane," Jas suggested.

"That could be," Joel agreed. He pulled out the finder's stone to illuminate the rest of the cave. The cavern didn't appear to extend back into the mountainside more than ten yards. Joel saw no evidence of passages that went any deeper. Sirrion's "passage" was a dead end.

The bard glanced back into pool. On the opposite side of the portal, four more armed men came running through a door into the room where the two fetch fought. Although they couldn't see the fetch, the armed men surrounded the fetch's victim, presumably their companion, with a circle of swords.

Joel whirled around. "We've got to get out of here before the fetch flees back through the portal," the bard insisted.

Joel's warning came in time for Jas and Emilo to retreat to the entrance, but the fetch reared out of the watery portal and splashed to the shore between Joel and his avenue of escape.

Upon spying the bard, the monster smiled coldly. Suddenly Joel found he was looking at himself. The fetch had assumed the bard's form and raised a sword identical to the one Finder had given to Joel. He retreated back several steps and drew his own weapon. It was unnerving enough knowing the fetch would be draining his life energy if it struck him; having to attack his twin made it worse. On top of all that, fetch were said to be excellent fighters.

The fetch had received some injuries from his last opponent. He was bleeding from a slash on his leg and a superficial stab in his gut. It wasn't enough of a handicap as far as Joel was concerned. The bard took a completely defensive stance, blocking the first strike with his sword and retreating from the second. He was now cornered in the back of the cave.

It was Jas who dealt the first blow to the creature, a deep cut to the shoulder. She followed it up quickly with a slice to the creature's ribs. The fetch whirled and hissed. This time it didn't bother to shapeshift again, but targeted the winged woman still wearing Joel's form. Its first blow glanced off Jas's shoulder guard, but the second drew blood, slicing through her leather wrist guard and penetrating the flesh beneath.

Jas reeled backward. The wound wasn't too serious, but it opened the mystical pathway by which the fetch could drain her life energy.

Joel charged at the creature and stabbed his sword deep into its back. Emilo hit the creature's leg with his sword.

The fetch turned again on Joel, but Jas blocked the creature's blade with her own. The fetch struck Jas across her ribs, slicing through her leather tunic, shirt, and skin. Jas's sword cut halfway through the fetch's neck.

The fetch fell to the ground, and Jas collapsed beside it.

"Make sure it's dead," the winged woman gasped to Emilo. "Make damn sure."

The kender stabbed at the fetch's throat with his sword, but it did not stir. The monster was dead.

Joel shuddered at the sight. The creature remained in the bard's form, though its skin was as pale as a corpse. That's how I'll look when I'm dead, the bard thought. He knelt beside Jas and hummed a prayer to heal her wounds. The skin at her wrist and ribs knit easily, but she remained leaning against Joel.

"Gods, I feel weak," the winged woman murmured.

"I can't restore your life energy," Joel said. "It may take years before you recover what's been drained from you. You didn't have to make yourself its only target."

"Better me than you," Jas said. "If it hit you, you wouldn't be able to cast the spells we might need."

Emilo, who had been looking about the cave, said, "I don't understand. This is a dead end. Why would Sirrion send us to a dead end?"

Joel sighed. "Perhaps he wanted us to kill the fetch. I think we'd better keep moving," he added.

Outside the cave, the finder's stone sent out a weak beam of light pointed back up the slope. "This way," Joel said with a nod of his head.

"But Sirrion said the finder's stone would lead us into danger," Emilo objected.

"Emilo, you can't still believe it was Sirrion you spoke with," Jas growled. "Someone impersonated Sirrion to lead us into a trap."

Emilo shook his head. "I just can't believe it. I was so sure," he murmured. Uncharacteristically, he remained silent for some time after that, lost in private musing.

The three heroes resumed the long trek upward. Farther up the slope, they spied the first sign of a true path, which had been cleared of all loose stones. The path weaved its way back and forth up the mountainside.

It was while they were taking their second rest that Emilo spotted three winged creatures circling overhead. They looked like giant vultures, but they had human arms and hands in which they carried spears. The three adventurers huddled behind a large boulder beside the trail and waited until the creatures flew off.

Unfortunately the light from the finder's stone indicated that they needed to proceed in the same direction as the vulture creatures. They proceeded along the trail more cautiously, with one eye to the sky at all times.

Jas seemed to linger behind, watching for the creatures. Joel was struck with an uneasy suspicion.

"You aren't planning on making yourself a target again just to keep me and Emilo safe, are you?" he murmured to the winged woman. "Because if you are, forget it."

"Why?" Jas asked. "Think about it, Joel. As long as I have the dark stalker in me, I may as well take risks. Dying is the only way I'm going to cheat Iyachtu Xvim. On the other hand, you're young. You have a lot to live for."

"Jas you're only six years older than I am. This fatalism is ridiculous," Joel declared.

"Is it? I killed that fetch. If the priests of Iyachtu Xvim were telling the truth, I've already sealed my fate. The only reason I don't look like a dark stalker is that Finder transformed me with magic."

"Do you feel like a dark stalker?" Joel asked. "Do you sense the power of your prey like they told you you would?"

"It's hard to say," Jas admitted. "With so much of my life energy drained, I can't be sure what I'm feeling."

Emilo, who was farther up trail, turned and ran back to the two humans. "The path leads to another cave," he said excitedly. "A really big one—big enough to hold a dragon, or even a couple of dragons."

From overhead, there came a horrible screech. One of the vulture creatures was diving straight toward them.

Joel grabbed Jas's hand and shouted, "Run for it!"

The three pelted down the trail.

The cave loomed up ahead. Its entrance was quite large, and Joel realized there was nothing to prevent the vulture creatures from following them inside. Darkness would be their only cover.

As they dashed into the opening, Jas yanked her hand away from Joel and turned to face the creature should it decide to enter.

Up ahead, in the darkness of the cave, Joel spotted two glowing red spots moving toward him. The bard grabbed Jas about the waist and dragged her off to the side of the entrance to hide in the shadows.

The vulture creature landed at the cave entrance and stood silhouetted in the light. The giant bird was a full two feet taller than Joel. A few moments later the vulture was flanked by two more of its kind.

The glowing red spots inside the cave grew larger. The vulture creatures, apparently having spotted what Joel assumed were the eyes of some far larger monster, backed away from the cave entrance. The glowing spots flashed past Joel, and he saw in the cave entrance a hideously misshapen spider at least ten feet long. From its spinneret, the spider shot a strand of webbing at the vultures.

There was a horrible shrieking sound outside the cave, but Joel turned his attention to the kender tugging on his vest.

"There's a way through the cave," Emilo whispered. "Hurry."

Joel and Jas followed the kender deeper into the cave. Great webs filled the passage, but Emilo had discovered a sinkhole four feet wide and nearly as deep that was free of webbing. Emilo scurried through the sinkhole as the humans, dragging their packs behind them, crawled on their hands and knees to avoid the webbing overhead. Joel speculated that the hole had been caused by the earth tremors they'd experienced the day before. Had it been formed less recently than that, the great spider surely would have detected it and filled it with webbing.

When they emerged from the sinkhole on the opposite side of the webbing, Joel pulled out the finder's stone once again. The stone shone down the passageway. The light seemed brighter underground, as if the stone sensed it was safer from detection in this dark place. The passageway twisted and turned and finally led them to a steep staircase that led upward.

Jas counted two hundred steps before they reached the first landing. The next flight of steps was set ninety degrees to the first flight. It was another two hundred steps to the second landing.

"Are we there yet?" Jas half joked, half whined.

"Beshaba's supposed to have her court somewhere near the pinnacle," Joel reminded Jas. "It could be a thousand, two thousand steps, maybe more."

Jas groaned and rummaged about in a backpack for the water bottle.

"Hello," Emilo murmured. He'd been tapping on the stones of the wall. "I think I've found something."

Joel turned to see what the kender had discovered. Emilo was pushing at a stone on the wall of the landing. A hidden doorway, some five feet high and two feet wide, popped open a crack.

"Shall we have a look?" the kender asked.

"It would be a nice break from all the stairs," Jas said, taking a gulp of water.

Joel stared uncertainly at the door. "We're more likely to discover what we need to know at the top of the stairs," he said.

"But perhaps we can learn something useful here," Emilo argued. "Maybe Beshaba keeps her secrets down here instead of up there," the kender suggested.

"Just a quick look," Joel agreed with a sigh.

They slipped through the door. The finder's stone light stubbornly shone back toward the stairs.

From his pack, the kender pulled out a torch and tinderbox. By the light of the torch, they proceeded down the narrow corridor.

The corridor opened into a larger hallway. To his left, Joel could hear the murmur of low, indistinct voices.

The bard led his companions in the direction of the

voices. The hallway emptied into a great room with rows of benches facing an altar covered with a red cloth and a rack of horns—an underground temple to Beshaba. The benches were packed with people praying, some silently and others mumbling their prayers with considerable fervor. Occasionally a worshiper approached one of the braziers that surrounded the altar and set fire to an offering.

A pretty young woman dressed in black from head to toe came up from behind them. "Beshaba provides," she whispered. "Bad things always happen. Only offerings and prayer to Lady Doom can save us."

"Mmmm," Joel responded noncommittally.

"Our goals are meaningless. Lady Doom can undermine them with but a thought," the woman insisted.

"Oh, yeah?" Jas replied with irritation. She didn't doubt Beshaba's power, but the other woman's fear of the goddess annoyed her.

The woman clutched Jas's arm. "Appease her so her wrath turns elsewhere—" the woman's eye's lit up—"perhaps even on your enemies," she concluded. Then she turned away from them to approach the altar.

"I feel a sudden urge to climb another few thousand stairs," Jas muttered to Joel.

"Me, too," Emilo agreed.

"Let's go," Joel said.

They hurried down the hallway, scurried down the narrow corridor, squeezed back through the secret door, and pushed it closed behind them. The finder's stone shone upward.

In unison, the adventurers sighed, then resumed their ascent. Every two hundred steps there was a landing, a secret door, which they ignored, and another flight of steps that turned ninety degrees.

On step 1313, Joel slipped on the stairs, slid down twenty steps, and twisted his ankle. He had already used his healing spell on the wounds Jas suffered at the hand of the fetch. In order to continue the climb, the bard was forced to cast a healing spell from one of Winnie's scrolls. They rested at the next landing, ate some more food, and finished off the water.

"We don't really have to go any farther," Joel said. "We could just sit here while Finder and Selune sense what's going on above."

"I don't want to just sit here in the dark while Finder and Selune are the only ones who get to see what's going on," Jas argued. "What do you think, Emilo?"

"It would be a shame to come all this way and not see what's at the top," the kender said.

"Two to one. You're outvoted, Joel," Jas announced.

"So much for trying to break away from my image as a reckless fool," the bard muttered.

After Joel cast a spell to fill their empty water flasks, the adventurers continued on their way.

The landing at step 2600 appeared to be a dead end, but Emilo had no trouble detecting the stone to push to open the landing's secret door.

They blinked in the sudden light that assaulted their eyes. In actuality, it wasn't particularly bright, but it was far brighter than they were used to. The light, coming from lanterns hanging from the ceiling, revealed a vast chamber or gathering hall. The floor was littered with human bodies, some moaning, some lying deathly still. A portion of the chamber's ceiling appeared to have collapsed recently. Some of the bodies lay beneath boulders and piles of rubble.

Other people stood around talking, apparently oblivious to the suffering and pain around them. One group of people squatted in a corner rolling dice and cursing loudly. Joel weaved a path through the fallen bodies. Jas and Emilo followed. They passed a group of men playing a bizarre game with a basket. As each man reached into the basket, the others chanted, "Beshaba, take him," over and over again. Each man drew out a snake, usually something harmless like a garter snake, but one man reached in, gave a hideous screech, and fell back, clutching his hand. A few moments later the man's body was wracked with a violent seizure. Joel forced himself to avert his eyes.

"Here's another player," a large bully of a man said, blocking Joel's path. "Have you done enough to appease the Maid of Misfortune, chum?" the man asked the bard.

Jas stepped forward with her sword drawn, pointing the weapon at the man's throat. "Leave him alone," she growled.

The man paled and stepped back. "Sorry, ma'am. Didn't realize he was with you."

Jas took a position beside Joel, and when people saw her determined expression and her weapon, they backed away from the adventurers.

"Someone you know?" Joel asked.

"Never seen him before in my life," Jas whispered.

They crossed the room and followed the light from the finder's stone through a doorway that led to another corridor. Farther down the corridor, their progress was halted by a gaping chasm in the floor. It was at least fifteen feet to the other side. Emilo dropped a pebble into the pit, and it took nearly four seconds before it *clink*ed on something below. Jas flew the two men and their gear across the chasm. After her exertions, the winged woman required several minutes rest before she could continue.

They proceeded far more cautiously along the corridor.

Somewhere up ahead, a soft red glow issued from a doorway. The three adventurers crept forward and peered into the room that lay beyond. The damage in this room was even worse than the last. Most of the ceiling had collapsed, as well as some of the floor. Moans arose from a pit approximately in the room's center. The red light shone out of a pool of water on one side of the room.

The people in this room were at least paying some attention to the fallen and injured. Two women in the mauve robes of Beshaban priestesses were tending to the injured, most of whom were other priestesses. Two beautiful winged women stood as armed guards beside another entrance across the room. Joel guessed they were alu-fiends, the half-human offspring of succubi. Now he realized why the men in the last hall had backed away from Jas. Her wings were the same size, shape. and color as the alu-fiends.

"Any sign of Beshaba?" Jas whispered.

Joel shook his head. "Something's not right here," he whispered.

"That's right. And you're it," a soft female voice said

from behind them.

The adventurers spun around. In the hallway behind them stood another alu-fiend. She was lovely to behold, with long, black hair that glittered like silk in the light of the finder's stone and a small, lithe frame. Her beauty was matched only by her deadliness. She held a sword point to Joel's throat.

From the shadows behind the alu-fiend appeared a tall figure in a dark cloak. The figure held the edge of a curved sword to the alu-fiend's throat and ordered, "Lower your weapon, fiend, and don't make a sound, or we will have to kill you and all your friends."

The alu-fiend stiffened angrily, then complied sullenly.

Joel peered intently at his rescuer and the curved blade. There was something familiar about her and her sword. "Holly?" the bard whispered in disbelief.

The tall figure lowered her hood, revealing the face of the paladin Holly Harrowslough. Beneath the black cloak, she was dressed in full battle armor.

"Holly!" Jas growled softly. "What are you doing here?"

"Lathander sent me," the paladin said softly. "What are *you* doing here?"

"Finder sent us," Joel said as he took the alu-fiend's sword from her hand. "I wish Lathander had mentioned to Selune that you'd be here," he added. "We could have teamed up sooner."

"What does Selune have to do with this?" Holly asked.

"She's helping Tymora," Joel said.

"What's wrong with Tymora?" Holly asked with confusion.

"Someone is draining her power. We think it's the mistress of this realm. Isn't that why Lathander sent you? To discover how she's doing it?"

"Beshaba has nothing to do with Tymora's troubles," the alu-fiend spat.

"I told you not to make a sound," Holly growled, pressing her sword blade against the flesh of the alu-fiend's neck.

"Hold on," Joel said, pushing Holly's hand back. He smiled sweetly at the alu-fiend. "What do you know about this?"

"It is Xvim. He sent a squad of hydroloths to attack my lady's court," the alu-fiend declared. "When my lady used her power to defend us, she lost control, and the mountain quaked. Xvim must have known such a thing would happen, or he would not have risked his forces."

"How do you know the hydroloths came from Xvim?" Jas asked.

"Because my mistress cursed his name before she teleported away," the alu-fiend said haughtily.

"Hydroloth? Aren't they the froglike things that Xvim sent to Sigil to bring back Jas?" Emilo asked Joel.

Holly started, as if she hadn't noticed the kender before. Emilo smiled up at the paladin and bowed. "Emilo Haversack. Pleased to meet you at last, Holly," he said. "I've heard a good deal about you."

"Why did your mistress teleport away?" Joel demanded of the alu-fiend.

The alu-fiend *tch*ed as if Joel were a simpleton. "To save her realm and her people from destruction," she said.

"Where did she go?" Holly asked.

"She did not say, but I would guess she has gone to Gehenna, to confront that mewling godling Xvim and make him pay for his treachery," the alu-fiend said.

"When?" Jas asked.

"During the quake," the alu-fiend said.

"That was yesterday," Joel said. "Why isn't she back?"

"Do you think something happened to her in Gehenna?" Jas asked Joel.

"I think," the bard said, "that we're going to have to go to Gehenna to find out."

Offstage

Somewhere in the Prime Material Plane, on the world known as Toril, in Realmspace, Daramos Lauthyr, High Lord Priest of Tymora, surveyed the wreckage of a once-secret shrine to Beshaba. Hidden in an underground chamber beneath a stable beside a respectable inn, the shrine had been a mere hundred yards from the shining spires of the Lady's House, also known as the temple of Tymora and Arabel's most resplendent cathedral. Beshaba's worshipers must have laughed at their proximity as they hid here in Lady Luck's shadow.

Now it was Lauthyr's turn to laugh. He toed one of the holy symbols of Beshaba, a crudely painted red plaque with black antlers, and allowed a tight smile to creep across his thin lips. As he looked around at the devastation, the smile grew into a full-fledged grin.

A week of heavy summer storms following hard after a season of steady spring rains had created a sinkhole over thirty feet across and twenty feet deep just beneath the stables. The secret shrine's earthen roof, insufficiently supported by wooden beams, had collapsed, as had the stable above, revealing the vipers' nest below. The worshipers had been crushed and smothered by dirt, slate rock, and lumber.

The town guard, aided by Lauthyr's priests, were now sorting through the tangle of rubble and timbers to pull free the corpses of Beshaba's unfortunate followers. Apparently the collapse had occurred during a service to the Maid of Misfortune, for there were many human corpses. A dozen had been discovered in the top layer of the ruins, along with a those of half a dozen horses that had been quartered in the stable above. So far the rescuer had found only one survivor—a stallion. Lauthyr had ordered that it be dug out, lifted from the sinkhole, and healed. It was unlikely that he would accord similar kindness to any of Beshaba's worshipers, should any of them be found alive. Lauthyr was not the sort to show mercy to an enemy.

Any other priest might have credited Chauntea for the bountiful rain that had revealed the temple, but Lauthyr attributed the destructive rain in full to Tymora, since it had revealed the shrine of her hate-filled sister. It was a clear sign, in Lauthyr's mind, that Tymora had chosen Arabel as her own, which meant Daramos Lauthyr, High Lord Priest of the Lady's House, was the chosen prophet of Tymora's church.

Lauthyr looked up beyond the pit's walls to the new spires of the Lady's House, with their finely wrought golden domes perched atop turrets of white marble veined with sea-green jade. It had cost as much as the price of the marble to haul the stone from Impiltur, but Lauthyr considered the money well spent. The new construction, made possible by the donations of Tymora's followers, announced the wonders of Tymora and demonstrated that Tymora's church in Arabel was the most faithful in the world.

Lauthyr decided he would have to convince Myrmeen Lhal, the local lord, to cede this land to Tymora's church. Once the sinkhole had been filled in, it would serve well as the site for a church school, or perhaps a rectory—a place where Lauthyr himself could reflect upon the marvels his rule had created.

The High Lord Priest was shaken out of his daydreaming by the sound of someone clearing his throat. Lauthyr stifled the frown that came naturally to his face whenever he was interrupted. Lord Priest Doust Sulwood stood before him.

"We've uncovered thirty-seven bodies so far," Sulwood reported. "There's likely to be four or five times that number by the time we're through."

"An impressive display of Tymora's vengeance," Lauthyr replied, sagely concealing any pleasure he felt. Doust Sulwood was an annoyingly kind person, not the sort to revel in a foe's misfortune. "This should make a wonderful sermon for this evening's service and for many evenings to come."

"Are you planning to speak from the pulpit about the Marliir noble we found?" Sulwood asked with a hint of sarcasm in his tone.

"What?" Lauthyr growled.

"Among the bodies is one of the Marliir nobles. A lesser cousin," Sulwood explained.

Lauthyr frowned for a moment. House Marliir was much favored in Arabel. The noble family wouldn't appreciate a priest implicating any member of their family in a scandal. With a more impassive expression, the High Lord Priest replied, "Such a pity that poor Marliir noble was in the stables when Tymora chose to weaken the supports of the temple below."

Sulwood snorted contemptuously. Lauthyr's political machinations never ceased to annoy him.

From the ground level above them, a woman called out urgently to the High Lord Priest. Lauthyr and Sulwood looked up. A young priestess stood on the edge of the sinkhole, waving down at Lauthyr.

"What is it, my child?" Lauthyr asked calmly.

The priestess knelt down before Lauthyr, a ridiculous formality in Sulwood's opinion, especially in light of the fact she was twenty feet above the Lord High Priest. As far as Sulwood was concerned, a bow of the head showed respect enough for a mortal being who was, after all, only a servant to the goddess he worshiped.

"Forgive me, High Lord, but there is an emergency back at the Lady's House."

Daramos Lauthyr looked back up at the resplendent spires of Tymora's temple with alarm. "What's wrong?" he asked less calmly.

"Apparently the collapse of Beshaba's shrine changed the channel of one of the city's springs. The water is now pouring into the Lady's House."

The High Lord Priest sighed with relief. "No doubt Lady Luck wished us to have a more convenient source of water," he informed the priestess.

"But, High Lord," the priestess called down, "it's

flooded out the scriptorium and the library. All our tomes and scrolls have been ruined."

Lauthyr paled. He had no insight into Lady Luck's motives for destroying the accumulated learning of her favored temple.

Sulwood gave Lauthyr a solicitous pat on the back. "Don't worry, High Lord," he said. "I'm sure you'll find some good explanation before tonight's sermon."

It has been said that being turned into a drider is the worst punishment that can be exacted on one of Menzoberranzan's drow. Untrue. The high priestesses have perfected the art of uttering unintelligible shrieking sounds that burn the ears and send disrupting shivers through the spine, much like the famed "quivering palm" of some clerical warriors. They call it opera.

—Drizzt Do'Urden

Intermezzo

Walinda of Beshaba eyed the creeping lava with excitement. Less than a mile down the slope from the molten magma stood a fortress built of lumber. When the lava reached the building, it would burst into flame. If the lava pushed out a mere streamlet, the fortress would incinerate itself long before the wall of lava covered its current position, but should the lava come all at once, a wall of molten rock, the fortress would be torn from its foundations first and carried along with the lava as it burned.

Having already watched two other fortresses fall to the lava, Walinda knew that either sight would be impressive. The only thing to mar the priestess's amusement was the knowledge that the fortresses were empty. Watching inhabitants scramble about to save themselves, or their possessions, or perhaps even to attempt to save their fortress by digging a channel to divert the flow of the lava—that would have been much more entertaining. As it was, the priestess was able to appreciate the display of raw force, whether or not it made someone's life a misery.

She wore a magical ring that protected her completely from the heat of Gehenna, yet she walked carefully along the crust of cooling rock. Nothing could protect her from the tons of liquid rock that would bury her should she make a misstep through the crust and tumble into the flow of lava.

Walinda hugged herself with a feeling of satisfaction. She felt whole again. She needed a power to serve, a power greater than herself. Once she had seen Beshaba, she knew that she had made the right decision. She would serve Beshaba as she would have served Bane, had he not betrayed her.

Turning from all the more organized faiths had not come easily to the priestess. All her life self-discipline had been her greatest strength. When Cyric had seized Bane's power, Walinda had utterly rejected her superiors' demands that she join Cyric's church with them. Cyric was a mad and capricious god whom she could not possibly understand. She had remained faithful to Bane. She might even had resurrected The Dark One had he not betrayed her merely because she was a woman. That was when she had come to realize contracts and laws were meaningless to the gods. So when she went to seek out a new power to serve, Walinda did not confine her exploration to those religions that paid lip service to order.

However, she continued to reject Cyric. She had escaped the Banedeath—the campaign of destruction of the last of Bane's faithful in Zhentil Keep—but many of her friends had not. And she couldn't forget that Cyric had destroyed Zhentil Keep with his self-serving bungling. A decade ago, Cyric had been a mere mortal. She could never truly respect him or his clergy.

Some might have seen Bane's son, Iyachtu Xvim, as a logical choice. One of Walinda's favorite paramours held a position of power in Iyachtu's church. But Bane was now her enemy and while Iyachtu had no love for his father, Walinda suspected the lesser god would prove just as deceitful and dishonorable. She had already been belittled and betrayed once by the priests of his church. She would not join them.

She had considered offering her services to Shar, Mistress of the Night, but Shar's church was veiled in too much secrecy. Walinda didn't want to waste time negotiating the twisted power structure. She belonged in the top

echelon of any hierarchy. She flirted briefly with the
church of Loviatar, but the priests of the Maiden of Pain
were too willing to accept suffering; indeed, it was one of
the requirements of their faith. In Walinda's opinion, suffering was for peasants.

In the end, she had chosen Beshaba. It was not a matter of settling for the least offensive of the evil gods.
Walinda truly felt Beshaba suited all her needs, and she
would suit Beshaba's. True, the Maiden of Misfortune was
mad and capricious, but it was a madness born of spite,
the sort of madness Walinda understood. The church's hierarchy was dominated by women, which would make her
climb in rank more challenging, but also more certain.
There would be no invisible wall blocking her progress to
the seats of power.

Her quest to resurrect Bane had broadened her outlook
considerably. Having traveled in the Outlands and Sigil
and the Astral Plane, the priestess realized she needn't
return to the Realms to some backwater underground
temple in order to pledge her fealty to Beshaba. The Sensates of Sigil had made it possible for her to travel directly
to Beshaba's realm, the Blood Tor.

The priestesses of the Blood Tor hadn't exactly welcomed the former priestess of Bane with open arms, but
they had accepted her as a novitiate. It was also thanks to
the Sensates that she had gained an audience with Beshaba. By betraying the information she possessed about
the Sensates, Walinda had gained the goddess's direct attention. Interested to learn of the mortals who'd had the
temerity to spy on her, Beshaba had Walinda summoned
to her court to describe the Sensates' activities in detail.
Walinda had arrived at a fateful hour.

She relived those moments over and over in her head.
Beshaba, in all her glory, reclining on a divan, had just
asked Walinda to describe the genasi scryer when hydroloths teleported into the goddess's court. Beshaba rose
to destroy the evil amphibians with a simple spell. That
was when the quakes began. The earth trembled, then
heaved. Beshaba created a barrier to protect her court,
but at that moment the cavern began caving in. The goddess could do nothing as her realm collapsed about her

followers, crushing them to death.

As Walinda dealt a death blow with her goad to a hydroloth who was attempting to attack Beshaba, the goddess channeled her power into the resurrection of a favored priestess. The solid rock of the mountain grew more frenzied, shaking like a cart on a rough cobblestone road. The dead priestess revived, but like the realm around her, she went into a seizure. For some reason, Beshaba had lost control of her power.

Walinda had quickly concluded that since the hydroloths were not generally suicidal creatures, it could only be assumed that they were aware in advance that Beshaba would be so weakened. Although without control of her powers, Beshaba still had the strength of a goddess, and she seized one of the hydroloths and squeezed it by the throat with her bare hands and demanded to know who had sent it to her realm. The creature must have answered telepathically, for in the next instant the goddess cursed Iyachtu Xvim with words both foul and ancient.

Then, having hurled the hydroloth to the floor like a rag doll, Beshaba grabbed the nearest living priestess, who not coincidentally proved to be Walinda, and teleported away to Gehenna. There, on the fiery slopes of Chamada, the goddess of ill luck had given Walinda a ring to protect her from the fires and lava all about them. Then she had imbued Walinda with some of her power, making Walinda the goddess's newest proxy.

It was a gift that Walinda had never experienced before. It gave her a window into Beshaba's bitter heart. Suddenly Walinda understood Beshaba completely, and agreed with her completely. Her will had been subsumed by the goddess's desires. The gift had left Walinda with a feeling of complete ruthlessness. She would now do anything for Beshaba, even die for her.

Beshaba did not ask for her death, however—only her faithful patience. The goddess had perched her newly anointed priestess down on a portion of the mount that afforded her a view of the Bastion of Hate, the realm of the god Iyachtu Xvim. The goddess instructed Walinda to wait on the slope until Beshaba called to her. Then the goddess had flown off to the Bastion of Hate.

That had been hours ago, possibly as long as a day. It was impossible to tell in the dawnless land of Gehenna. Yet Walinda was not the least bit tired or bored. Waiting for Beshaba was the most important thing in the world to her now. And while she waited, she had the amusement of watching the lava flows destroy the abandoned fortresses.

Offstage

Somewhere else in the Prime Material Plane known as Realmspace, Polly Thax unfastened the top four buttons on her blouse and put her hand on the doorknob of the palace's exhibition hall.

"Maiden of Misfortune, pass me by, kiss my enemies," Polly murmured as she turned the doorknob. The door was not locked; it opened noiselessly. Polly slipped into the exhibition hall and closed the door behind her.

The room was well lit from hundreds of magical lanterns suspended from the ceiling. Polly did not spy anyone else in the room. Wielding her feather duster over a row of nude statues, Polly made her way toward the center of the room.

"What do you think you're doing here?" a stern male voice demanded.

Polly started and whirled around. The Hulorn himself, the hereditary mayor of Selgaunt, stood there. Polly's eyes widened.

Once upon a time the Hulorn's blue eyes and curly black hair and boyish charm had attracted more than his share of women. But that was twenty years ago. Now he was a plump middle-aged man of average height. He was still a man of power, however.

"Well?" the Hulorn prompted.

"I'm dusting, sir," Polly replied in a quivering voice. "I'm sorry if I disturbed you, sir. I'll come back later."

The Hulorn put his arm out, resting his hand on a glass cabinet containing several ivory carvings of sea mammals, effectively blocking Polly's exit. "No one is to be in this hall without the presence of a guard," he said. "I suppose they forgot to tell you," he suggested with a grin that made clear he supposed no such thing.

"I don't know, sir," Polly replied. "I forget things sometimes."

The Hulorn licked his lips and gave Polly a thorough examination with his eyes. Then he tilted his head to one side and said, "I don't suppose you'd like to see the Eyes of the Sea Queen."

Polly's eyes widened with wonder. "Oh, yes, sir," she replied. "I would love to see them." The look the Hulorn had given her did not distress her in the least. In fact, she'd been counting on it.

The Hulorn led her to a glass case in the center of the room. There, on a white velvet pillow, shining softly like full moons, were two pearls the size of oranges. They were the largest ever discovered in the Realms.

"They're beautiful," Polly gasped.

"Nearly as lovely as your eyes," the Hulorn said, taking a step closer. "Though I suppose men say that sort of thing to you all the time."

Polly smiled, and her eyes met the Hulorn's gaze without a trace of modesty. "Those that have the courage," she replied.

"Would you like to hold them?" he asked.

"May I?" Polly asked.

The Hulorn whispered a brief incantation, and the glass case popped open with a *whoosh*. The Hulorn reached in and withdrew both pearls. He held them out. Polly tucked her feather duster under one arm and took a pearl in each hand. She held the smooth-surfaced gems to her cheeks and smiled with ecstasy. The feather duster under her arm clattered to the floor.

"Oh!" Polly exclaimed.

"Allow me," the Hulorn said. He knelt down, but instead of scooping up the feather duster, he slid his hands beneath her skirt and rested them on her calves.

While the Hulorn was thus occupied, Polly dropped the pearls down her blouse and drew out a leather blackjack from the pocket of her apron. With a quick, practiced motion Polly slammed the blackjack into the back of the Hulorn's head. He went out like a light, sprawling at Polly's feet.

With two pairs of long silk stockings pulled from another pocket, Polly bound and gagged the Hulorn. Then she took his keys from his pocket and retrieved her feather duster. Once she'd slipped from the exhibition hall, she locked the door behind her with the stolen key. After rebuttoning her blouse, she moved quite unhurriedly down the servant's staircase and hung her feather duster in the appropriate cabinet. Taking up a broom, she swept her way through the kitchen, brushing the dirt out the kitchen door. She left the broom by the door and made her way unhurriedly along the garden path, pulling weeds from the onion beds. No one seeing her would suspect she was anything but a parlor maid, kitchen maid, or gardener.

At the garden gate, she retrieved a sack containing a guard's leather jerkin and a helm, and slid the pearls into a hidden pocket in the leather jerkin. Then she slipped off her apron and skirt and donned the leather jerkin and helm. She hung the skirt on a line behind the laundry. At the castle gate, one of the guards gave her a saucy wink and she winked back.

She was strolling through the busy city streets when a horn sounded in the castle yard. Polly turned and looked as surprised as the other pedestrians as troops of guards charged down the street, stopping any woman dressed as a servant. For a while she leaned against a wall and watched the interrogations. As the guards moved down the street, she followed them, blending in with the guards, helping to search some poor, luckless women who looked like her in the most superficial of ways. Then she slipped down a side street and made her way to the dock, where her buyer awaited with payment—the papers that transferred ownership of a Selgaunt carrack and its load of rare cargo to her name.

As she slipped out of Selgaunt's harbor aboard her new ship, she breathed a sigh of pleasure. She was rid of this city of snobs forever.

"We're being flagged by one of Selgaunt's navy vessels, ma'am," the captain of the ship reported. "They're demanding to board us."

"Ignore them," Polly said.

"We may not be able to outrun them."

"I have every confidence in you, Captain," Polly said.

The captain left the ship owner to shout orders to the crew. Polly stood at the rail and once again called on her goddess. This time her request was more of a shout than a whisper. "Maid of Misfortune, pass by me; kiss my enemies."

Polly had no doubt Beshaba would come to her aid. She had made all the right offerings. She imagined a snapped rudder or perhaps a fallen mast, but Beshaba manifested her favor in a far more powerful way.

The ship rose and fell as a great swell passed beneath it. The swell grew as it approached the land. It caught the Selgaunt navy vessel chasing Polly's ship and carried it along on its crest. By the time it reached the city harbor, the swell had become a wall of water.

The water crashed down on Selgaunt, smashing the dockside buildings and depositing the navy vessel, plus several others, in the city streets. The Selgaunt docks were carried back out to sea.

Polly smiled wickedly.

"That's that," she said.

Then she heard a roar behind her. A second tidal wave, even more monstrous than the first, caught her ship on its gigantic crest and swept it inland at a breathtaking pace. Once more Polly called on Beshaba to take her enemies, but there were no enemies left. The water slammed into the Sembian peninsula two miles south of Selgaunt and heaved Polly's vessel inland a hundred feet, dashing it against a cliff. The ship splintered like a child's toy, and its crew and owner were scattered across the beach below. Their corpses were found mingled with the vessel's rare cargo; the farmer who buried them was richly rewarded.

Attending the opera would be interesting in Menzoberran-
zan. During the overture, the audience could place bets on
whether more drow will die onstage or off.

                                              —Liriel Baenre

Act Three
Scene 1

"How will we get to Gehenna?" Emilo asked, clearly
eager to add another Lower Plane to his list of places he'd
visited.

"We go back to Brightwater and have Selune open a
gate for us," Joel said.

"Or I could take you back to Morning Glory with me,
and Lord Lathander could open a gate for us," Holly said.
"There's a portal at the top of this mountain that leads to
his realm. There's a staircase at the end of this hall that
leads straight up to it."

"That figures," Jas said. "We come in by a portal near
the bottom of the mountain and have to climb for miles.
Holly comes in at the top of the mountain and merely has
to walk down a few steps."

"We can bring you back with us to Brightwater," Joel
said to Holly. "I need to talk to Finder about what we've
discovered."

Holly seemed to think a moment, then said, "Then we'll
go your way."

The alu-fiend prisoner declared, "You will never make
it out of here alive."

"I don't recall anyone asking your opinion," Jas said.

"Then perhaps you *should* ask," a woman's voice said.

Out of the shadows behind them stepped five more alu-
fiends. Eight more appeared in the doorway through

which they'd been spying.

Jas and Holly whirled back to back with their swords drawn. Joel slapped himself in the forehead. "How could I forget? Alu-fiends communicate telepathically. All this time our prisoner has been screaming for help."

Their former alu-fiend captive smiled at Joel and said, "Perhaps we will let *you* live a little while longer."

Holly grabbed the alu-fiend around the neck and, using her as a shield, advanced on the line of fiends blocking their exit.

Joel put his hand on Jas's arm. "The wish," he reminded her.

Jas nodded. She held out the sword Winnie had given her and announced, "I wish Holly, Joel, Emilo, and I were back in Tymora's garden in Brightwater."

The alu-fiends and the dark halls of the Blood Tor faded around them, to be replaced by flowers and sunshine. Holly found herself without an alu-fiend for a shield and her sword pointed at Finder's nose. Joel's god sat on a wooden bench beside the uprooted birch tree. Finder's eyebrow rose in amusement.

"Finder!" the paladin gasped.

"Welcome to Brightwater, Holly Harrowslough," Finder greeted her, "but I don't really need a shave," he joked, carefully pushing the paladin's curved blade away from his face.

Holly lowered her weapon, bowed her head, and said, "Excuse me, Lord Finder."

"One day in Morning Glory and suddenly I'm 'Lord' Finder. Just call me Finder, Holly," the god said.

The paladin looked up at Joel's god. "Not all gods are as informal as you," she pointed out.

"Not all gods are as reckless as I am," Finder replied, reminding the paladin of how she had chided him on her god's behalf the last time they had met.

"*None* of the gods are as reckless as you," Selune reprimanded. "Stop taunting the girl for having good manners, Finder. We have more important things to discuss."

Holly whirled to address the speaker, but when she beheld Selune, she fell speechless.

"Yes," the goddess said, as if in answer to Holly's

unspoken question. "I am Selune. Sit down, paladin. We need to decide what is to be done next."

Selune sat on the bench beside Finder and Holly. Joel and Jas sat on the ground at the gods' feet. Emilo paced behind them.

"Beshaba wasn't at the Blood Tor," the kender reported excitedly. "The winged lady said she went to—"

"Gehenna. Yes, we know," Finder said. "Just as Selune said we would be, she and I were aware of everything occurring in the Blood Tor as soon as Joel arrived. Including what was going on in Beshaba's court."

"That's a really neat trick," Emilo said. "You never need to get a letter to know what's going on in your friends' lives, do you? But it must make it hard for them to surprise you. For birthdays and such."

"I am constantly surprised by what's in their hearts," Finder said, smiling at Joel.

"We don't know if the alu-fiend was telling the truth about the attack," Jas said.

"She was," Finder replied. "We sensed the attack on Beshaba."

"Where's Tymora?" Jas asked, having suddenly noticed that the goddess was not in the garden.

"Her minions have taken her someplace to keep her safe. It is probably best that you do not know where for now," Selune explained.

Jas looked down at the ground. "It's because I have the dark stalker in me, isn't it?" she asked.

"No," Finder said, lifting Jas's chin in the cup of his hand so that she was forced to meet his eyes. "It's because if you choose to travel to Gehenna, Iyachtu's minions might be able to read it inside your mind."

"So you're sure the hydroloths that attacked Beshaba were sent by Iyachtu Xvim?" Joel asked.

"That isn't something we could really tell," Finder explained. "Though Beshaba did curse his name before she fled her realm."

"If Xvim is behind this, then why did Tymora sense Beshaba instead of Xvim?" Joel asked. "And if Xvim is draining both of them, why did Tymora fall unconscious while Beshaba was able to teleport away?"

"As to the first question, we do not know," Selune answered. "As to the second . . . either Xvim started draining Tymora's power first or else Beshaba had more power in reserve. Tymora is extremely free with her gifts. She has endowed a number of items with her power and shared them with adventurers. She also gives out power keys to her priests who travel the planes. She has even lent her power to her ally gods and their priests. Beshaba, on the other hand, tends to hoard her power. She grants her priests their spells and spends a small portion of her power getting even with mortals who neglect her when they make large offerings to Tymora. It appears that Beshaba is indeed losing control of her power. In addition to the earthquake in her own realm, she is causing a good deal of destruction granting boons to some of her worshipers on your world."

"But if we do another reconnaissance into Gehenna, you and Finder can sense what Xvim is up to, right?" Emilo asked.

Selune shot a disapproving glance at the eager kender. "Know this," she said. "When you arrived on the Blood Tor, Beshaba surely sensed your presence. You were simply not sufficiently interesting for her to take particular notice. She was intent on a story being told to her concerning the Sensates of Sigil. Eventually, she presumed, one of the many evil creatures who live on the surface of the mountain would dine on your flesh. If Beshaba had sensed you approaching an entrance to her underground fortress, she would have dispatched someone to destroy you. But she was forced to flee her realm to keep it from collapsing around her followers and petitioners. Had she been present, you would never have made it to her lower temple, let alone her court. We have no reason to expect you will be that lucky in Gehenna. Xvim trusts no one."

"But won't he be preoccupied with Beshaba?" Joel asked.

"If she is not already drained and unconscious," Finder said. "Furthermore, there is the question of Sirrion's involvement."

"Sirrion?" Holly asked with a start.

"Sirrion is a god of neutrality who dwells in Limbo,"

Finder explained to the paladin. "A power meant to balance good and evil in the world of Krynn, where Emilo is from. The manifestation he sent to speak with Emilo said it was interested in protecting Emilo. If that is true, why? Is he the reason Emilo appeared in Sigil? The powers of the Realms have had few dealings with the powers of Krynn thus far. Sirrion may have reason to involve himself in this affair, but if Iyachtu is using a god from an alien pantheon for some scheme against Tymora and Beshaba, he is violating the compact the powers of the Outer Planes have agreed upon. Beshaba may not have left Gehenna yet because Sirrion challenged her there. She is more powerful than Iyachtu Xvim, but Sirrion is her equal in power."

"All this is speculation," Joel said. "If we go to Gehenna, you'll have more information."

"The Blood Tor wasn't the worst the Abyss had to offer, and Gehenna is worse than the Abyss," Finder warned. "The Bastion of Hate, Xvim's realm, is perched on Chamada, the second mount of Gehenna. The land itself is violent. It gushes, bleeds, and seeps molten rock from every crack and pore. There is no flat place on the outer slope to rest, and the inner canyons are home to the shapeshifting barghests, the deadly gas phiuhl, the razor-winged slasrath, and the yugoloths, the most evil creatures known to the Outer Planes. Iyachtu hires yugoloths as mercenaries."

Joel listened carefully and nodded. "I presume, like the Abyss, the nature of Gehenna will weaken my ability to cast priestly spells."

"He learns fast," a voice said from behind them. It was Tymora's priestess, Winnie, with two human servants carrying a large rolled carpet.

Finder nodded in response to Joel's comment. "I will have to pour more power into the finder's stone," he explained, holding out his hand to take the stone from his priest. Once again he siphoned blue energy into the crystal. He handed the stone back to Joel. "Even now, with the stone as powerful as I dare make it, you will be able to cast only the simplest of your priestly spells."

At Winnie's signal, the human servants set the carpet

down on the ground and unrolled it. The carpet was woven into a geometric pattern of red and gold.

"This flying carpet will keep your feet off the burning ground," the priestess of Tymora explained. "These rings," she added as she handed each of the four adventurers a silver ring, "are to help protect you from fire, should you get careless and fall off the flying carpet. The carpet's command word is "Airheart." Once it's off the ground, you need to tell it aloud which way to go, how fast, and how high."

"I would suggest you let Mr. Haversack take command of the carpet," Finder said. "He's less likely to be attacked and will have the best control."

"Why is he less likely to be attacked?" Holly asked.

"I've observed that when Mr. Haversack isn't speaking, he tends to go unnoticed," Finder said. "Perhaps he can tell you why."

Holly looked at the kender.

Emilo shrugged. "We can't all stand out in a crowd," he said.

Odd words, Joel thought, coming from someone dressed in blue pants and shirt, a red vest, and an orange cloak. Remembering Finder's observation that Emilo had come to them under highly mysterious circumstances, the bard exchanged a glance with his god. Finder shook his head slightly, warning Joel not to question the kender further. The god still wasn't prepared to interfere with whoever or whatever had sent Emilo their way.

Joel changed the subject before Holly could pursue the subject of Emilo's background. "There was one other thing. I had a dream about Giogi Wyvernspur's children and their cousins," he told Finder. "I think they may be in trouble."

Selune *tch*ed. "If it weren't for Tymora's luck," the goddess murmured, "that whole family would have died out years ago, even with my blessing. Present company included," she added, with a nod toward Finder. "I will look into it. Finder is busy helping Tymora's church."

Winnie loaded fresh water flasks and food into the backpacks, then began pulling out certain scrolls and replacing them with others. "Some of these spells will be useless in Gehenna," the halfling priestess explained, "while others that would not work in the Abyss will be effective in Gehenna."

Finder handed each adventurer a tiny harp carved from wood, "If you snap the harp in half and say 'Fermata,' you'll be returned instantly to my realm. With the harps, all of you do not have to return together, but if one of you is seriously injured or captured, you can escape."

"We have not exaggerated the dangers. None of you has to make this journey," Selune said. "There is no shame in remaining behind."

Jas looked at Holly and asked, "Are you sure Lathander would wish you to take this risk?"

"I was told to find Beshaba," Holly replied. "Just as Finder can sense Joel, Lord Lathander can sense all I do. If he wished me to abandon my quest, he would send a messenger to tell me so. He has not. I will go to Gehenna, whatever the risk."

"Jasmine, you are in the most danger from being in Xvim's realm. He considers you a runaway slave," Selune pointed out.

"Nothing's changed," Jas said. "Realmspace is still in danger of losing Tymora's luck and Tymora and Beshaba losing control of their power."

"We're all of one mind," Joel said.

"Very well," Selune said. "I can create a portal to the second mount of Gehenna, but it has been some time since any of my followers ventured into Gehenna, so I'm not sure where Iyachtu Xvim's realm is. The portal could be some distance away from the Bastion of Hate. It doesn't matter. Once you have entered Gehenna, I'll be able to sense what is happening in Xvim's realm. Finder will contact you with further instructions after I have assessed the situation."

"You'll want to ride the carpet through the portal," Winnie explained. "Don't fly too high above the sides of the mountain or you could become lost. The mountain is surrounded by a dark, cold void that only the most holy lights or evil eyes can penetrate."

"There's one other thing that might help you," Finder said. "As Selune mentioned, when you arrived at the

Blood Tor, Beshaba was listening to a report about the activities of the Sensates of Sigil. The report was given by
Beshaba's newest priestess . . . someone you already
know."

"Oh, no," Holly whispered. "Not Walinda?"

Finder nodded.

Jas cursed softly under her breath.

"When Beshaba teleported away, she took Walinda
with her," Finder explained. "Since you know Walinda,
you could use the finder's stone to track her and, presumably, to discover the whereabouts of her new mistress."

Jas's eyes narrowed. Walinda had tortured and murdered her spacejamming crew. Jas had sworn vengeance
on the priestess, but Walinda had been under the protection of a banelich. Now she was under the protection of a
goddess. It didn't matter. Jas would look for some way to
get at the evil priestess.

"Let's go," the winged woman said in a gruff voice.

The adventurers seated themselves on the magic carpet, their backpacks beside them. Selune motioned with
her hand and another portal opened up.

The stench of sulfur and a smell like burnt human hair
wafted from the planar opening. Inside the portal, it was
very dark. Then suddenly a fountain of burning rock
sprayed upward, lighting a barren slope. The Abyss
seemed almost cheery compared to Gehenna.

"Airheart," Emilo announced as if the command word
had been trying to burst from his lips all this while. The
flying carpet rose several feet off the ground. "Forward,"
the kender ordered.

"Slowly," Joel prompted.

"Slowly," Emilo added with a sigh.

The flying carpet passed from Brightwater through the
portal into the darkness of Gehenna.

Joel turned for one last look through the portal at Tymora's garden. The light from the opening shone like a
star, then winked out suddenly as the portal closed.

"Back away from the slope five feet," Emilo ordered the
carpet, "and remain in place."

The carpet hovered, not actually above the ground, but
beside a steep mountain slope glowing with hot magma. It

felt as if they were standing beside an open oven. No doubt it would have felt worse were they not wearing the rings Winnie had given them to protect them from fire.

As always in a new plane, Jas's wings had taken on a new form, the most unusual Joel had seen so far. Her wings had joined into a triangular sheet of black flesh, with the apex of the triangle hovering over her head while the other two corners fell downward in loose folds like a bridal train. When Jas stiffened the single wing, it fanned out to either side some ten feet. The flesh glittered with an oozy secretion. Jas let the wing droop about her ankles, then looked at it with disgust and sighed.

Joel pulled out the finder's stone and thought of Walinda. He had no trouble recalling her admittedly attractive features. Joel suspected she was far older than he, but some magic kept her looking young. She had long, silky black hair and dark eyes. Blood-red tattoos decorated her high cheekbones. She wasn't particularly tall, but very slender and very graceful. It was the way Walinda made Joel feel, however, that came more readily to mind.

The evil priestess had made no secret of her attraction to Joel. More than once she'd offered him a place at her side. But there were things that Joel found repulsive and frightening about Walinda beyond her worship of a cruel and evil god. Walinda took sick delight in humiliating and physically harming people, even as she was attempting to seduce them. When Joel had insulted her by calling her a slave, the priestess had been perversely excited by his attitude.

The finder's stone sent out a beam of light that arched upward and around the slope. Walinda was on another face of Mount Chamada, somewhere much higher up.

"That's all the direction we need," Holly said to Joel. "You'd better put it away for now. We don't want the light to attract any unwanted attention."

Joel slid the crystal into the top of his boot as Emilo gave orders to steer the flying carpet in the general direction indicated by the finder's stone. The sky overhead was completely black, without a sign of sun, moon or stars. Noxious vapors and steam rose from the mountain, but

the mists disappeared into the darkness; there were no
clouds to be seen. Conversely, the mountainside below
glowed with streams, pools, and fountains of lava, creating just enough illumination for them to travel without
running into the ground or getting lost in the void.

They flew for some time in silence, staring ahead into
the darkness or down at the glowering mountain, keeping
watch for any of the evil creatures who dwelt in this plane.
Joel glanced at his companions. Emilo wore an expression
of wonder, but Holly and Jas both looked grim. Joel wondered if both women were thinking of Walinda and her
treachery. When they'd last met, the evil priestess had abducted Holly and threatened to kill her if Joel didn't turn
the Hand of Bane over to her. Joel had been prepared to
pay the ransom for the paladin, but Jas had appeared
suddenly and rescued Holly. Ultimately Walinda had refused to resurrect Bane, but not for any noble reason. At
Joel's desperate urging, the priestess had chosen instead
to be the woman who denied Bane power, proving herself
stronger than the dead god.

After a while Joel began to feel weary. With no way to
measure the passage of time, the bard wasn't sure if he
was tired from lack of sleep, heat exhaustion, the noxious
vapors, or just boredom, but when he noticed Emilo's head
jerk up suddenly, he knew they had to sleep.

Uncomfortable with the notion of sleeping in the air, he
said to the others, "Look for somewhere safe and solid to
land. We need a rest."

Emilo spotted a canyon and maneuvered the flying carpet between the rocky slopes on either side. Joel pulled
out the finder's stone and searched for a patch of ground
that might be cool. Spying a touch of green on one slope,
he directed Emilo to head for it.

As the flying carpet closed in on the slope, Holly furrowed her brow. The green was an odd triangular shape,
and it seemed to reflect the light from the finder's stone.
Something snaked about the apex of the triangle and
raised itself in the direction of the adventurers.

"Eyestalks! That green thing is alive!" Holly gasped.

"Pull up! Fly backward!" Jas ordered.

The green thing suddenly rose from the ground to its

full height, revealing itself to be a giant slimy worm with razorlike fins along its back, large triangular wings attached along the length of its body, and a deadly-looking barbed tail. It soared forward, then arched back in their direction. The creature's wings spanned nearly fifteen feet. A gaping maw full of needle-sharp teeth opened on the lower part of the creature's head.

Jas assessed the creature as it fluttered toward them. It was swift and maneuverable. "We can't fight this thing in the air," she said to Joel. "You'll have to land. I'll distract it while you find a defensible position." She took off from the carpet, carrying only her sword. As she soared toward the creature, Joel noticed that Jas's wings and the creature's were very similar.

Emilo maneuvered the carpet straight down and commanded it to hover a foot from the ground. Joel poked experimentally at the rock with his sword to be sure it wasn't merely a thin crust over a magma flow.

In the sky above, Jas flew straight toward the creature. Both began to rise upward to try to gain the advantage. Seeing she would lose the struggle for superior altitude, Jas leveled off. She'd hoped to soar untouched beneath the beast, but it dropped suddenly, trying to force her to the ground.

Jas jabbed her sword upward as the creature glided over her body, tearing at its belly. At the same time, the creature jabbed at her with its tail. Both Jas and the creature screeched in pain. But while the creature continued to soar in the direction of the hovering carpet, Jas dived to the ground.

Holly leapt off the carpet and whirled around with her sword drawn. The sword glowed with a brilliant gold radiance that seemed to frighten the creature. It veered to its right in an attempt to avoid the paladin's blade, but before Holly could slice downward on the beast, the leading edge of its wing caught her in the chest. Holly gasped and fell backward. The creature soared on.

When Holly pulled herself to her feet, Joel noted that the paladin's breastplate had a gaping hole in it. The creature's wing had sliced right through the metal armor. He remembered Finder had warned them of a razor-winged slasrath. That must be what they battled now.

Joel ordered Emilo, "Go find Jas!"

The kender took off down the canyon in the direction they'd last seen Jas, carefully weaving his way through the pools of lava that dotted the canyon floor.

Joel rummaged hastily through one of the backpacks. He had spilled most of the contents over the flying carpet before he found the scroll he wanted. By the time he'd unrolled the vellum, the slasrath was closing in on him and Holly. This time the paladin took a stance beside Joel, nearer to the bottom of the narrow canyon where the razor-winged beast couldn't spread its wings without slicing at the rocky slope on either side.

That's when they discovered that the slasrath, like their carpet, could hover overhead. Its wings rippled above them as it stabbed down at Holly with its tail. The deadly stinger at the end of the creature's tail struck her in the chest but failed to pierce the paladin's damaged breastplate.

By the light of the finder's stone, Joel chanted the incantation inscribed on the scroll as Holly fought to hold off the slasrath. When the bard finished, he motioned toward the slasrath's eyestalks, both focused on the paladin.

A light as bright as day burst about the slasrath's head. The beast howled in terror and soared upward. It hovered high above them, shaking its head, trying to throw off the light spell that now blinded it. It flew about in a spiral until it hit the mountainside. Then it lay still against the slope.

Emilo came pelting back up to Joel as fast as his short legs could carry him.

"You've got to come quick," the kender said breathlessly. "I think Jas has been poisoned."

They hopped on the carpet and Emilo ordered it to fly low along the floor of the canyon.

Jas lay on the ground on her stomach with her wings spread around her, effectively camouflaging her from view. Her left calf had swollen to the size of a melon, and her breathing was strained and shallow.

Joel dug frantically through the scrolls until he discovered one to neutralize poison. He set his hand on Jas's injured leg and chanted from the scroll. Blue light flowed from his hand and seeped into the winged woman. The swelling subsided slightly and Jas moaned. After a few minutes her breathing grew steadier and less labored. Emilo pulled out a water flask and helped Jas take a few sips.

Holly looked back down the canyon while Joel and Emilo aided the winged woman. "I'm going to finish taking care of that creature," the paladin said. "I'll be back in a few minutes."

Before Joel could stop her, Holly began trekking back to where they'd last fought the slasrath. Joel called after her, but the paladin had already disappeared behind an outcropping of rock.

"Should I follow her?" Emilo asked.

Intent on casting a spell to heal Jas's injuries, Joel nodded without really thinking.

When the magical energy finished seeping into her, Jas sighed and sat up. "I'm getting too old for this," the winged woman grumbled.

Holly and Emilo returned a few minutes later. Holly sat down and proceeded to clean the slasrath's ichor from her blade.

"I wish you wouldn't run off like that," Joel snapped.

"You blinded the thing. It would be cruel not to put it out of its misery quickly," the paladin countered. "Now we can camp here without worrying about it coming back."

Joel sighed. There was no sense arguing with Holly. The paladin was always certain she was doing the right thing.

The canyon floor was covered with black flinty ash and broken hexagonal columns of stone that had sheared away from the mountainside above. The ground was warm but solid. It was also sterile. Nothing grew anywhere, not even lichen on the rocks.

The adventurers set up camp on the carpet so they could flee quickly if attacked. They shared a meal from Winnie's supplies. Holly insisted that she wasn't very tired and took the first watch along with Emilo.

Joel slept fitfully in the Gehennan heat. He dreamt of the Realms being beset with nothing but bad luck—

earthquakes, floods, and fires. Others died all around him, crushed, drowned, and burned, yet he remained unharmed. He realized he must be in a dream. Since he knew he was dreaming, he tried to qualm his fears of the disasters he witnessed. If Selune's suspicions were correct, it was not only Tymora's luck that was being drained, but Beshaba's as well. Eventually the bad luck would end, too. Yet that thought would not quell Joel's dream fears, and the bard thought he understood why.

When Beshaba and Tymora were salvaged from the poisoned Tyche, perhaps they didn't really each possess a different kind of luck. Perhaps their very nature shaped the luck they had. Even were it within her power, the selfish and vengeful Beshaba would never grant anyone good luck, just as the kind and generous Tymora would never curse someone with misfortune. Now another power, was stealing both Beshaba's and Tymora's luck. If an evil, selfish god had dominion over good luck, "good" luck would cease to exist.

Just when the bard thought his dreams couldn't get any worse, he dreamt again of the children.

Offstage

Somewhere else in the Prime Material Plane on the world known as Toril in Realmspace, Amber Wyvernspur watched with annoyance as her cousin Cory jumped across the marble tiles of the floor of the family mausoleum. Either Cory was especially lucky from being favored by Tymora or his father had been fool enough to demonstrate the secret pattern to him. A rectangular section of the floor dropped a foot lower than the surrounding floor and slid away, revealing a staircase leading downward.

"We have to hurry," Cory said. "The door doesn't stay open for long."

Tavan and Toran took up the torches they had just lit and took the lead. Cory, Lumen, and Ferrin hurried after them.

"Are there any spiders?" Heather asked uncertainly.

"Giant ones, as big as cats, with furry bodies," Olivia said gleefully. "We'll catch one and make it a pet."

"All right," Heather agreed. She didn't like spiders, but she loved cats.

The two younger girls headed down the stairs, leaving Amber with Pars.

"Pars, you don't have to come if you don't want to," the eldest Wyvernspur child said to her youngest brother.

"I'm not a baby," Pars shouted, and he started down the stairs, backward, so he could negotiate the steep steps without falling.

Amber sighed and followed behind him. The mausoleum had been chill, but on the stairs, warm air rose up from below. The warmth failed to dispel the gooseflesh on Amber's neck and arms.

At the bottom of the stairs the way was blocked with a heavy leaden door, on which was painted the image of a red wyvern. Heather pulled out Uncle Steele's key and turned it in the lock.

"What does that say?" Olivia asked, pointing to words engraved in the stone over the door.

Amber took Tavan's torch and held it up high. " 'None but Wyvernspurs shall pass this door and live,' " she read aloud.

"Neat!" Tavan said as he and his brother pushed open the door.

From the stairs above came a shout, a hoarse, growling war cry.

"What's that?" Ferrin whispered.

Amber looked back up the stairs with alarm. Something outside the mausoleum, something that must have been lurking in the graveyard, had followed them through the secret door. She squinted into the darkness and caught sight of glowing red eyes and the flash of a steel sword. A moment later she was able to make out the outline of a tall, hairy creature with a face like a pig's.

"It's an orc!" Amber shouted, throwing the torch she held at the creature. "Run!" she screamed.

The cousins raced through the door. Amber stopped only long enough to pick up Pars before dashing after the others. There was no time to close the door behind them.

The crypt beyond the door was a vast tunneled chamber with straight walls and a curved ceiling. The children's footfalls and screams echoed along the passage as they ran through the crypt. In the wall at the far end of the room was an arched opening that led to another stairway leading down.

"Wait!" Amber shouted as she passed beneath the arch. "Don't go down into the catacombs! It's dangerous down there!"

The others halted on the stairs and glared back at their eldest cousin.

"It's dangerous up here, too," Tavan whispered angrily. "Or hadn't you noticed, Lady Amber?"

"The orc can't get past the guardian," Amber said.

Tavan and Toran climbed back up to the landing beside

the arched entrance and looked back into the crypt. By the light of the torch Amber had thrown, the children could make out at least five orcs hovering at the doorway at the opposite end of the crypt.

The orcs were grunting and growling at one another as if they were arguing about something. Finally two of the orcs entered the crypt and began moving slowly across the length of the stone chamber as silently as cats. They were dressed in shabby, torn clothing, but they were both armed with swords.

"They're going to get us," Toran hissed.

"No. Look," Amber said, pointing toward the crypt's ceiling.

The shadow of a great wyvern, even more silent than the orcs, floated along the ceiling and hovered over the trespassers. Suddenly a great shadowy tail plunged downward twice—a quick stab into the back of each orc.

The orcs howled and fell forward stiffly, without any effort to break their fall. A shadowy wyvern's neck and head snaked down over its kill, lifted one of the orcs in its huge maw, and bit it in half with a sickening, crunching sound.

Pars began to cry. Amber covered his eyes, whispering, "Don't look, honey."

The orcs who had remained standing in the doorway screamed and shouted in their own language, but they made no effort to rescue their companions. Unfortunately they didn't leave, either, but stood eyeing the children at the other end of the room with hatred, waving their swords threateningly.

From the stairs where he stood transfixed with the other children, Cory murmured, "Uh-oh."

"I think we have another problem," Olivia said.

Amber looked down the stairs. Climbing up toward them were several black-scaled creatures with white horns and tails like rats. Amber recognized them as kobolds, monsters at least as vicious as orcs. They were no taller than Pars, but they held loaded crossbows, aimed directly at the children.

"I guess this is the proverbial rock and a hard place that Uncle Giogi's always talking about," Lumen muttered.

Inspired by the thought of his father, Cory declared, "Enough is enough!" He drew himself up to his full height and shouted down at the kobolds, "We carry the goddess Tymora's blessing. If you know what's good for you, you'll flee now."

The kobolds tittered and guffawed. The one in the lead drew himself up to his full height and, in a broken version of the common tongue, replied, "*We* carry blessings of Beshaba. We ask her kiss you with misfortune, you die."

Act Three
Scene 2

Joel awoke drenched in sweat and anxious. He'd dreamt the Wyvernspur children were trapped in a cave by foul monsters. They had called upon Tymora, but Tymora's luck was gone from the Realms, leaving them helpless. The bard shook his head. Selune had said she would check on the children, but perhaps his warning had come too late. Of course, it was possible that the dream had nothing to do with reality, but Joel doubted it. He rolled over, praying that Selune was able to do something for Finder's mortal family.

Soon after falling back asleep, the dreams returned. Joel dreamt of the earthquake in Tymora's garden. In his dream, however, the birch tree fell on top of him instead of away from him. He tried to push the trunk off his body, but it was soggy and rotten. A section broke off, leaving his hands covered with slime.

After several more attempts, Joel managed to wriggle out from beneath the tree.

"Joel," the tree called.

Joel whirled about. Buried within the rotting tree trunk was Finder. The tree fell away from the god. Then Finder began to age until he was an ancient, toothless old man. Joel gasped.

"Find Beshaba," Finder said. "Take her to the Spire."

"Is she here in Gehenna?" Joel asked. "And why the Spire? How do we get there?"

Finder didn't answer Joel's question. The god's flesh fell from his skeleton. Then the skeleton's mouth clacked, "Barghests use fear."

The ground began to shake once more, until gradually

Joel realized it wasn't the ground shaking. Emilo was shaking him awake, calling his name.

"I'm awake," Joel said, some unknown fear making his heart pound and bringing him to instant alertness. "What's wrong?" he demanded of the kender.

"It's Holly," Emilo explained. "She started muttering to herself. Then she cried out, 'Danger! Run!' and ran off." Emilo pointed deeper into the canyon.

Joel shivered despite the hot air. "There's something wrong here." His breathing grew very fast. "There's something terrible. Something dangerous all around us," he declared. With a rising sense of panic, he rose quickly to his feet, only to be seized with sudden, overwhelming fear. He started to run down the canyon and disappeared in the darkness.

Emilo shook his head with confusion. The bard had left in such a hurry that he'd left the finder's stone lying on the carpet. The kender was just about to wake Jas when it occurred to him that the winged woman might be better off left sleeping. Instead, he scooped all the party's gear into the center of the flying carpet. Then, with the finder's stone clutched in his hands, he ordered the carpet to fly after the terrified bard and paladin.

Joel ran pell-mell down the canyon, heedless of whether Emilo and Jas were following or were left behind and equally heedless of what lay ahead. He tripped over something metallic and sprawled across the rocky ground.

Joel rose to his hands and knees and looked around. A plume of molten lava shot into the sky on the slope overhead, and by its light, Joel was able to see what had impeded his flight. Holly lay on the ground nearby, unconscious but breathing.

A moment later something pounced heavily on Joel's back and sent him sprawling again. When he looked up, he was face-to-snout with a growling wild dog with glowing red eyes and horrible breath.

"N-N-Nice doggie," the bard whispered cautiously. He debated in his mind whether he should back away slowly or flee outright. His courage returned to him, however, and he held his ground, unwilling to abandon Holly to this beast.

Before his eyes, the dog transformed into a giant humanoid with a flat face, broad nose, pointed ears, and sharp teeth and fangs. It resembled some sort of overgrown goblin, except its skin had a strange purplish color. It raised a huge fist covered in a spiked gauntlet.

Joel could feel his heart racing, and a surge of energy rushed through his body. He ducked, but not fast enough. The gauntlet struck him in the side of the head with the force of a heavy club. Aware that his life depended on it, Joel spent several moments fighting against the darkness trying to claim him. In the end, he lost.

When he regained consciousness, the bard found himself lying on his stomach, his feet and his knees bound together and his hands tied behind his back. Holly lay beside him, similarly trussed with what appeared to be torn strips of blue fabric. The paladin was awake now, glaring at their captor.

About twenty feet away, seated beside a bubbling pool of lava, was the giant goblin who'd hit him. It was tearing strips of cloth from Joel's cloak and dangling them over the lava. When a strip caught fire, the barghest would shake it until it was about to burn his fingers, then drop it in the lava pool, where the cloth made a brilliant flash before finally incinerating completely.

"What's happening?" the bard whispered.

"We've been captured," Holly whispered back.

"I can see that," Joel muttered. "By what? I seem to have misplaced my Volo's guide to Gehenna."

"It's a barghest," Holly explained. "Remember? Finder mentioned them when he was telling us about Gehenna. They can shapeshift into wild dogs."

Joel recalled the last words Finder spoke in his dream. "Barghests use fear," he quoted.

"Yes," Holly said. "They can cast several different spells, including those to effect the emotions of their prey. This one must have cast magic to make us fear our own campsite. I was so afraid that I abandoned you and Jas and Emilo and fled right into a snare. Then something bashed me on the head."

"Me, too," Joel acknowledged. Even with Finder's warning, he hadn't managed to see through the barghest's trick. "Except I tripped on you before getting smashed in the head. What else do you know about barghests?" he asked the paladin, hoping to learn something that might help free them.

"They leave their young in the Realms to forage for themselves. The young tend to live with goblins. The immature barghests eat people, preferably heroes. That's how they grow in strength. There was one terrorizing travelers around Daggerdale a year or so ago. I was with the party that hunted it down. According to Elminster, when they gain enough power, barghests return to Gehenna, but sometimes they return sooner, before they're ready, if they're fireballed in their canine form. I think that's what happened to this one. It's not as tall as most of them and its skin isn't quite all blue. That's how you tell when a barghest is mature."

A great wolflike dog appeared out of the darkness and immediately transformed into another barghest. The second barghest sat down beside the first. This creature, like the first, was about seven feet tall with purplish skin. "Lucky us," the bard murmured. "There's two of them, but they're not fully grown."

The barghests made growling sounds at each other, speaking in a language Joel did not know.

Holly smiled suddenly. "Emilo took off on the carpet with Jas. They weren't captured."

Joel gave a sigh of relief. He'd been feeling guilty about abandoning the pair, but they were probably safer than he. "You can understand the barghests?" he asked the paladin.

Holly nodded. "A little," she said. "They're arguing about who gets which one of us."

"This might be a good time to break the harps Finder gave us and go back to Fermata," Joel said.

"Probably," Holly agreed. "Can you reach your harp?"

Joel wriggled in his bindings. "Um . . . no."

"Me either," Holly said.

Suddenly, from the outer ridge of the canyon, someone shouted, "Hey, dog-breath!"

"It's Emilo!" Joel whispered excitedly. He craned his neck, trying to get a glimpse of the kender, hoping to warn him away.

Emilo stood alone on the ridge, the finder's stone shining at his feet. He held his thumbs up to his temples and wriggled his fingers at the barghests. "Why don't you go back to your doggie shapes? Then you could round up some sheep."

The barghests rose to their feet. One moved farther down the canyon, while the other began to move toward Emilo.

"Isn't mutton your favorite meat?" the kender shouted. "But tough to catch, I bet. Those sheep are smart. Why, their brains must be two, three times larger than the ones in your thick skulls."

The barghest moving toward Emilo growled.

"I sure hope he knows what he's doing," Holly muttered. "That second one is sneaking off to come up behind him."

"Don't forget, Jas is out there somewhere, too," the bard said. He rolled over, sat up, and began wriggling toward the pool of lava.

"Joel, be careful," Holly whispered. "What are you doing?"

"Most monsters agree that there's no meat sweeter than kender," Emilo said chattily. "Unfortunately kender are just about the cleverest game around, so there's no chance you two will ever be able to judge for yourselves. Unless you find a dead one lying around somewhere. Not above eating carrion, are you?"

The barghest howled and began scrambling up the slope toward Emilo.

Joel sat with his back to the pool of lava and wriggled his hands and fingers until the knot in the bindings covered his left wrist. Then he leaned backward carefully. If he lost his balance, he'd be parboiled, ring of fire protection or no. Very slowly, he began lowering his wrists toward the molten rock a quarter of an inch at a time.

The heat was almost more than he could stand, but the bard did not withdraw. He continued to lower his hands until he heard a sizzling sound. Not until a searing pain shot up his arms did Joel jerk forward away from the lava pool. He began tugging on his bindings, struggling wildly.

The pain was excruciating.

Suddenly he felt the bindings snap, and Joel jerked his hands forward. His left wrist was free, but flaming fabric still encased his right wrist. The bard grabbed the remains of his cloak, which the barghest had left by the pool, and used it to smother the fire. Whimpering from the pain, Joel used his teeth to tear the last bit of the blackened fabric from his burnt flesh.

"You know, there's a nice dead slasrath around here somewhere," Emilo was saying to the barghest as it clawed its way up the steep slope. "It looks like a giant winged worm. A real gully dwarf treat, worms, and easy to catch, too. You might like it for breakfast."

With an enraged bellow, the barghest clamored up the last few feet of slope and lunged at the kender.

Emilo glided backward, riding on the magic carpet, until he disappeared from view. The barghest teetered on the edge of the ridge, growling and snarling. At that moment, Jas soared out of the darkness, coming up behind the barghest with one of Winnie's backpacks swaying beneath her. The pack hit the creature in the head with a *thunk*. The barghest stumbled, then tumbled down the other side of the ridge.

For several long seconds, they could hear the monster's anguished cries. Then the screams ceased abruptly.

Emilo brought the flying carpet swooping down near Joel and Holly.

"Hurry!" the paladin cried. "The other one could return any moment."

There was a shimmer in the air beside the pool of lava as a magical doorway opened onto the barghests' campsite. The second barghest stepped out from the shining portal. Joel tossed his tattered cloak in the barghest's face and raced toward the carpet.

From the sky plummeted another backpack, which struck the barghest square in the head. Rocks spilled out of the pack as the creature fell to its knees, howling and clutching its head.

Joel hurled himself onto the carpet, pulling Holly behind him. The paladin was armored in heavy plate mail, but the bard managed to drag her over the edge and onto the carpet. Joel could feel his injured wrists and hands throbbing. Holly rolled into the middle of the carpet, and Joel shouted, "Go! Go!"

Quickly Emilo ordered the carpet to rise twenty feet.

"Backward, quickly!" Holly shouted as the barghest took a leap into the air and levitated upward toward them.

The barghest clawed at the carpet, managed to grab at the fringe, and found itself being pulled along by the retreating carpet. Jas swooped out of the darkness, flying alongside the creature. She hacked at the monster's hand with her sword, and the barghest instinctively released his hold on the carpet.

The barghest hung motionless in the air, growling at them.

"It can levitate, but it can't fly," Holly said. "Better move away before it tries something else."

A howl echoed in the canyon as the first barghest also stepped from a magical door beside the pool of lava.

"I wasn't planning on hanging around, I assure you," Emilo retorted. He slowed the carpet just enough for Jas to settle down beside them, then continued the ascent up the mountain.

Once Jas had cut Holly free, the paladin laid her hands gently on Joel's burned wrist and used her gift of healing to soothe the pain. The scars were terrible to look at, but at least the bard hadn't lost the mobility of his wrists.

"Your ring of fire protection didn't do much good," Jas noted.

"The rings can only protect you from so much heat," Holly said. "Joel nearly dipped his wrists in molten lava. If it weren't for that ring, he wouldn't have any hands left."

"The important thing is we're all right," Joel said. He looked at Jas and Emilo. "Thanks to you two."

Jas shook her head. "Thank Emilo. He's the one who had the foresight to fly off before I could wake up and get scared, too."

"Finder tried to warn me," Joel said. "I wasn't paying enough attention."

"Finder warned you? How?" Holly asked.

"In a vision, when I was sleeping. He said the barghests use fear. And before that, he said we had to find Beshaba and take her to the Spire."

"Oh, great," Jas muttered. "First Holly has visions. Now Joel's getting them. How do you know it wasn't just a dream?" the winged woman demanded.

"He knew about the barghests," Joel pointed out.

Unable to argue with that fact, Jas threw up her hands. "Fine. We go find Beshaba, even if it takes us a century to find her in this hellhole. Then we take her to the Spire, presumably not against her will, since that's a little hard to do with goddesses."

"What's the Spire?" Emilo asked curiously.

"The Spire is the mount in the center of the Outlands," Holly explained. It lies just beneath the ring that holds the city of Sigil."

"Why do you think we're supposed to take her to the Spire?" the kender asked.

Joel shrugged. "It wasn't really clear in my dream. I asked, but Finder didn't have time to answer before Holly ran off and you woke me up."

"The Spire is a neutral ground for the gods to parley," Holly explained. "Rumor has it that even the most powerful of the gods are unable to cast magic there."

"Why do *we* have to take Beshaba there?" Jas wondered.

"Perhaps Selune has sensed that Iyachtu's magic has finally made Beshaba unconscious, like Tymora," Joel speculated. "Finder wouldn't have asked us to do something he knew would be impossible," the bard reasoned.

"Is this Finder, the god of reckless fools, we're talking about here?" Jas asked sarcastically.

"So we have to keep searching for Walinda," Holly said with a grim look.

Joel nodded. He took up the finder's stone from the jumble of gear on the carpet and thought once again of the evil priestess.

Once again the light arced upward, but now its beam curved back down to earth closer to their location.

"Not more than a few miles," Emilo judged. "Your friend Walinda isn't far off now."

"She's not our friend," Jas snapped.

"Sorry," Emilo replied, chastened.

"We're lucky, though," Holly said. "While Chamada isn't infinite like most Outer Planes, scholars believe that it's still hundreds of miles high. We could have been traveling and searching for Walinda for days if Selune's portal hadn't transported us to where it did."

"Oddly enough, I don't feel lucky," Jas murmured.

Feeling more alert since he'd had some sleep, Joel was prepared to take over flying the carpet so Holly and Emilo could get some rest. Emilo had no trouble whatsoever falling asleep on the flying carpet, but Holly couldn't seem to get comfortable. She lay awake, staring up into the darkness, until she reminded Joel of an owl. "I'm so hot, she sighed.

As the carpet soared ever higher up the mountain slope, Joel started singing a silly lullaby about goblins who put ice on the toes of sleeping girls in the middle of winter.

"Are you crazy?" Jas asked. "Do you want everyone to hear us coming?"

"Why not?" Joel retorted. "I'm tired of creeping around like a mouse. A little whistling in the graveyard might do us good."

"Actually, that may not be a bad idea," the paladin said. "They say a lot of creatures in Gehenna bluff their way to power. You just have to bluff better than they do."

"Bluffing," Jas gasped in mock shock. "Isn't that like lying? Are paladins allowed to do that?"

"Really, Jas, your notions of paladins are so old-fashioned," Holly said. "We're honest, not stupid. If some evil creature is prepared to believe I'm more powerful than he is, why should I disabuse him of the notion?"

"Especially when you're traveling in the company of the awesomely powerful, favored priest of the god of reckless fools," Joel said.

"Exactly," Holly agreed.

Jas snorted with amusement. "I'm tempted to say, 'You'll learn better when you're older,' but with that attitude, you aren't likely to get much older."

Joel began singing "The Circle Song," a folk song about

a boy who grows to be a man who woos and wins his true
love, then has lots of children who all grow up to woo and
win their true loves. He sang just loudly enough to entertain Holly, but quietly enough so as not to disturb Emilo.
When he began the lullaby again, Holly finally drifted off
to sleep.

Jas took over flying the carpet while Joel prayed for
new spells. When the bard was finished praying, he read
through the new scrolls Winnie had packed for them.
Since they'd lost a backpack during Jas's attack on the
barghest, Joel repacked their equipment, leaving out
some of the equipment they would be less likely to use,
such as blankets and tarps. He wrapped all the scrolls in a
scarf, which he fastened to his belt. The healing potions he
slipped into a vest pocket.

They began to fly over more violent sections of the
slope. Steam and rock and ash, even molten lava, spewed
up from secondary cones on the mountain slope. They had
to stay especially vigilant to avoid these hazards. While
dodging one eruption, the carpet jerked upward suddenly,
and Holly sat bolt upright. At first Joel thought she'd been
wakened by the jolt, but then he saw she was drenched in
sweat and shaking uncontrollably.

"Another vision?" he asked her softly.

The paladin nodded, but she didn't look happy. She
stared out over the violent land beneath them without
speaking.

"What's wrong, Holly?" the bard whispered anxiously.
"What did Lathander say? Is Tymora worse? Is it about
Beshaba? What?"

"No," the paladin said shaking her head. Tears ran
down her cheeks. "Lord Lathander said that in order to
bring Beshaba to him, I'm supposed to offer my aid to that
. . . that woman," she spat.

"You mean Walinda?" Joel asked.

Holly nodded wordlessly.

"Oh." Joel put an arm around Holly's shoulders and
held her gently.

"I don't understand," the paladin sobbed. "I've always
served Lathander well. Why do I have to work with that
awful woman? She makes me sick. She's horrid. I should

have let Jas kill her when she had the chance. She betrayed her people. She betrayed us. She betrayed the Sensates."

Joel sighed. "Well, fortunately, she also betrayed Bane."

Holly sniffed. "Do you think she might betray Beshaba?"

Joel shrugged. "When she was a priestess of Bane, she pursued power with a vengeance. That was her religion. If she's still in that frame of mind, she could just be using Beshaba. It's food for thought anyway," he said.

As if the mention of food had disturbed his sleep, Emilo rolled over, yawned, and asked, "What's for breakfast?"

Everything in the pack was warm—the water, the bread, the fruit—which would have been fine were the adventurers not already sweltering. Joel tried to conjure an image in his mind of a crisp, cool apple plucked from a tree on a frosty fall morning, but the apples in the pack were closer to becoming apple sauce. Even the magical berries had become the consistency of jam, though they still left one feeling nourished.

Joel held out the finder's stone again and thought of Walinda. The beam of light shot into a canyon somewhere above them. Joel estimated they would reach it within the hour. He slid the stone back inside his shirt.

They were all nervous now except for Emilo, who hung his head over the carpet, wide-eyed at the sight of towering sprays of lava and boulders being tumbled about in rivers of magma.

When they reached the mouth of the canyon, they hovered for a few moments to decide the best way to proceed.

Holly reached out with her paladin sense to detect evil. Not surprisingly, she sensed many evil things in the canyon. Far ahead, shadows and light played across the floor of the canyon in a curiously orderly pattern. At first Joel thought it might be another lava flow, but Jas had another idea.

"It's an army," she said with certainty, "bivouacked in the canyon."

"How can you know that?" Joel asked.

"She's right," Emilo agreed. "That's just what they look like. They're drilling in formation."

Joel didn't dare use the finder's stone again to search for Walinda for fear of being spotted by whoever was in the canyon. If Beshaba was with Walinda, the goddess would surely have sensed them by now. If Walinda was alone, however, they were better off approaching with stealth.

They floated over the canyon at an altitude that prevented them from being noticed, but which also kept them from spying out anything of use. When they came to the opening of the canyon they dropped down slowly, keeping an eye out for any signs of detection.

There were no signs, yet detected they were. Without warning, the flying carpet heaved and began to lose altitude. Jas flew off faster than a bird disturbed by a cat. Holly screamed, and Joel felt something grab at his wrists.

The air about them shimmered as their invisible attackers appeared before them. The attackers were shorter than Jas and looked like some sort of hairy apes, with reddish brown fur and long, sharp claws. At first there were only two of them; then a third appeared on the side of the canyon and leaped across the ten-foot gap to the carpet with amazing ease. The magical carpet drifted downward, unable to bear the extra weight of the attackers.

Aside from being great leapers, the creatures were amazingly strong. One swept Joel up in a bear hug, making it impossible for him to move. Another held Holly's wrists together over her head as if she were a doll.

"They're bar-lgura," Holly warned Joel. "One of the lesser tanar'ri." The creature holding the paladin gave her a vicious shake. Holly quieted instantly.

The tanar'ri, Joel recalled, were creatures from the Abyss who fought the endless Blood War with the baatezu from Baator. They sometimes fought outside of their home planes, which could explain what they were doing here.

The bar-lgura seemed not to notice or challenge Emilo. The kender, very much awake now, sat very still in the center of the carpet, not making a sound.

Joel recalled all the times Emilo had seemed to surprise people with his presence, even the goddess Selune. Finder was right—there was something very strange about the kender. The bard looked away from Emilo to avoid attracting attention to him. Perhaps whatever it was that shielded him from notice could be used to their advantage.

A voice in Joel's head threatened, *You will be killed if you do not hold still.* The words caused an awful pain behind Joel's eyes. The bar-lgura was communicating with him telepathically. He wondered if it could read his thoughts.

Joel remained motionless, trying not to think of Emilo. The carpet hit the slope, and the bar-lgura jumped off with their prisoners in hand. The third creature grabbed the carpet to keep it from escaping, forcing Emilo to hop off beside Joel. The creature who had grabbed the carpet rolled it up, with their gear inside, and tucked it under his arm as if it were no heavier than a magical scroll.

The three bar-lgura herded Joel and Holly roughly down the slope to the floor of the canyon where they were quickly surrounded by another twenty of the creatures.

This, the bard decided, was a good time for a bluff.

"We are here to see your leader!" Joel announced. "We have important news for her."

The bar-lgura looked at one another, puzzled, as if expecting that one of them would be able to come up with a reply that challenged the bard's assertion. When none did, Joel heard a voice in his head again.

What news? the voice demanded.

"That is for her ears alone," Joel snapped, glaring frostily at the bar-lgura, who maintained his none-too-gentle grip on his wrists.

The bar-lgura holding the carpet nodded to another of its kind. The other went running off down the canyon.

Holly looked at Joel in surprise. The bard shrugged. Assuming the tanar'ri leader was female wasn't such a gamble. If Beshaba were here, she would most certainly be the leader. If Walinda were here, she would find a way to become the leader. The bard knew she was an imperious woman, given to ordering people around. If Walinda weren't the leader, Joel figured it didn't really matter what he said.

The bar-lgura began marching Holly and Joel down the

canyon. Emilo trotted along beside them, taking care not to be tread upon by one of the hulking tanar'ri. Holly looked at Emilo with a puzzled expression, then looked at Joel. The bard shook his head to warn her, and the paladin looked away.

There was little light in the canyon, and most of what there was emanated from the hot lava that streamed down the small gullies in the side of the mountain and collected into bubbling pools on the canyon floor. Like the canyon where they'd last rested, the ground was covered with a black flinty ash. Broken, hexagonal-shaped columns that had sheered off the side of the mount above stood like rocky sentries. There were no trees or shrubs or plants of any kind anywhere. Only fiends from the lower planes could live and thrive in such a place.

The bar-lgura had marched them nearly half a mile through an encampment of hundreds of tanar'ri when Joel noted that the populace of the camp had begun to change, as had the atmosphere. The bar-lgura they had already passed had seemed content just to sit around, hardly giving the adventurers a glance. Now their guards led them through gangs of gaunt, filthy creatures who resembled minotaurs. Their behavior was aggressive and openly hostile. They fought with each other in vicious hand-to-hand combat, and several followed behind the guards, snarling at the adventurers.

"What are they?" Joel whispered, nodding to the minotaur-like creatures.

"Bulezau," Holly whispered back. "Tanar'ri pit bulls."

She was rewarded with a slap on her head for speaking.

As they continued on, they began passing tanar'ri troops, both bar-lgura and bulezau, drilling in attack formations. The bulezau who had been following gradually dropped behind. Joel could only assume their captors were approaching the army's headquarters. Soon afterward they came upon a large pavilion, lit all around the perimeter by torches. It was the only shelter in the canyon. Undoubtedly it had been erected for privacy, since it could hardly shelter anyone from the heat and stench of the plane. To one side of the tent stood a flag emblazoned with Beshaba's symbol—black stag horns on a field of red.

The bar-lgura pushed them toward the entrance of the pavilion and formed a semicircle around the prisoners, who were curious to see what would happen next.

A delicate hand moved the tent flap aside, and a small, graceful woman with long, silken black hair stepped out of the pavilion. A cold smile played across her lips.

"So, Poppin, we meet again," the priestess Walinda greeted the bard. Her eyes remained fixed on Joel like a viper's on its prey.

Joel bowed low before the priestess. Upon rising, he met her cold smile with a warmer one of his own. He realized he was mimicking the way Finder greeted women. "I have been searching for you," the bard explained. "You're looking well."

Indeed Walinda looked as lovely as ever, but there was something different about her, and Joel had to stare for a moment to realize what it was. She was wearing the same black plate armor she'd worn as a priestess of Bane. The ruby she'd worn on her forehead was gone, and over the blood-red tattoos on her cheek she had added Beshaba's stag-horn symbol. There was something else different, something even more remarkable. A dark aura surrounded Walinda, a pulsing, fluctuating dark shadow that silhouetted her slender figure. It made her appear more powerful, more forbidding, more seductive.

The bar-lgura holding the flying carpet dropped it at Walinda's feet.

Walinda acknowledged Holly's presence with no more than a glance. Like the bar-lgura, she did not seem to notice Emilo. She did, however, note Jas's absence. "So where is the pigeon girl?" she asked.

"Jas? Why do you ask?" Joel retorted evenly.

"The bar-lgura saw her fly off when you were captured," Walinda said.

"Oh, I imagine she's around somewhere," Joel replied, "inspecting the army you've got here. What does a priestess of Beshaba need with an army?" he asked.

"That needn't concern you," Walinda replied. "The bar-lgura said you had news for me."

Joel was momentarily taken aback. It was unlike

Walinda not to brag of the might of her forces, whatever they might be. For some reason, she held this proclivity in check now. "The news is for Lady Beshaba's ears," the bard answered.

"I am Beshaba's proxy," Walinda said. "You may relay your news to me."

Joel glanced at the bar-lgura. Taking the hint, the priestess dismissed the guards with a wave of her hand. Joel sensed in the apelike tanar'ri a certain reluctance to depart. They stepped back several paces, but they did not leave entirely, nor did they turn their backs on their prisoners.

When the tanar'ri were out of earshot, the bard explained in a quiet but urgent voice, "We know of the problem Lady Beshaba is having controlling her power. Lady Tymora is plagued with the same problem. Lord Finder is anxious to discover the cause and do away with it. He bade me to ask Lady Beshaba to meet him at the base of the Spire so they might discuss the situation and determine the solution."

"Beshaba already knows the cause of her misery. It is Iyachtu Xvim," Walinda declared.

"And yet the problem continues," Joel noted, "despite her knowledge."

Walinda squinted her eyes in anger.

"Lady Beshaba is a prisoner within the Bastion of Hate, isn't she?" Holly asked.

Walinda glared at the paladin.

"Walinda, Lord Lathander has sent me to render you whatever aid you need to free Lady Beshaba," Holly explained. Her voice was tight in an effort to control her anger that she was forced to deal with this woman.

The priestess's eyes widened. Then she burst out laughing. Just as suddenly she stopped, as if she were plunging a dagger into her prey, twisting it, then withdrawing it.

"You?" Walinda exclaimed. "A paladin of light, here in Gehenna to aid Beshaba?"

"Lord Lathander is an ally of Tymora," Joel interrupted. "Since Lady Beshaba and Lady Tymora share the same problem, why should an alliance seem unusual?"

Joel asked. "Furthermore, our own world is threatened by the goddesses' troubles. Who better to save the luck of the Realms than a paladin?"

Walinda tilted her head thoughtfully. Then she shrugged and said, "Beshaba has been so weakened that she is now unconscious. I need to reach her to restore her strength. She is indeed a prisoner inside Iyachtu Xvim's realm, which is guarded by Xvim's yugoloth mercenaries. Fortunately Xvim himself is not present. He hasn't been since Beshaba arrived. I await but one more ally and we will attack the Bastion of Hate. You may join the attack if you so choose."

"Against yugoloths?" Holly exclaimed. "Your troops will be slaughtered!"

"They are tanar'ri," Walinda said dismissively. "They live only to die in the Blood War. What difference does it make if they die instead to help Beshaba? At any rate, the bulezau are anxious to engage the enemy. They care little who that enemy is. Their lord loaned me their services so they would not grow bored waiting for their next encounter with the baatezu."

"And the bar-lgura?" Holly challenged.

"The bar-lgura are less eager," Walinda admitted. "The other tanar'ri consider them little more than animals. A balor lord has sold them to me to punish them for failing to obey orders during a recent battle. I promised I would free any survivors."

An easy promise to make if they all die, Joel thought.

"How far off is the Bastion of Hate?" Holly asked.

Walinda pointed to the outer canyon. "If you climb up on that ridge and look down to your left, you will see Iyachtu's fortress. Xvim has set a powerful enchantment about the Bastion of Hate so that no one can gate or teleport into the fortress."

"I want to see it," Holly said.

"Very well," Walinda said.

"We can take the carpet," Joel said.

Walinda unrolled the carpet a few feet with a nudge of her boot. "Nice workmanship," she commented. "It will serve as payment of your commission in Beshaba's army. You can walk up there. You'll forgive me if I cannot join you. As I explained before, I am awaiting the arrival of an ally." She turned to the bar-lgura. "Escort them to the ridge. They are to go no farther."

Holly and Joel trudged behind an honor guard of six bar-lgura. As they scrambled up the ridge, Joel noticed Emilo was missing. Joel wished fervently that he knew what the kender was up to.

From the top of the ridge, they could see a great lava flow below, wider than any river. Chunks of unmelted rock were carried along in the fiery flow, like ice in a thawing stream. Across the river of magma, perched on a ledge cut out of the mountain, was Iyachtu Xvim's fortress, the Bastion of Hate.

On one side, the fortress was shielded by a cliff wall, on the other, by a crescent-shaped wall fortified with six towers.

"If Iyachtu Xvim isn't in there, where is he?" Joel wondered aloud.

Holly's brow furrowed with puzzlement. "Visiting a friend?" she volunteered facetiously.

Joel snorted in amusement. The god of hatred and tyranny was said to have no allies at all. "How do you think they're planning on getting across that lava?" the bard asked.

"All the tanar'ri, even the least, can teleport," Holly said.

"But according to Walinda, Xvim has enchanted his realm so no one can teleport into the fortress. They'll have to climb over those walls," Joel said.

"Not necessarily," Holly countered. "They need only distract the yugoloth so Walinda can sneak in and reach Beshaba without being killed or captured."

"How is Walinda going to restore Beshaba's strength?"

"You saw that dark aura around her," Holly said. "Beshaba has imbued her with power."

"Like Finder pouring his energy into the finder's stone," Joel said, feeling the warmth of the crystal against his chest.

"Sort of," Holly replied. "But by putting some of her power into Walinda, Beshaba has made Walinda a part of her. When Walinda said she was the goddess's proxy, she meant it in a very special way. Beshaba's desires are now her own. She has no choice any longer but to serve Beshaba as Beshaba would wish her to." Holly spun around suddenly and looked back down into the canyon. Joel turned as well.

Directly in front of the tent stood three new arrivals. Flanked by two seven-foot-tall toadlike creatures was a very tall six-armed creature that appeared to be half-snake, half-woman. Walinda seemed to be greeting the snake-woman. Holly must have sensed them with her ability to detect evil.

"Are those toad things hydroloths?" the bard asked, remembering Emilo's description of the creatures in Sigil that had been sent to fetch Jas.

Holly shook her head from side to side. "Hydroloths are much taller. Those things are hezrou, one of the true tanar'ri species. They have human arms. The snake-woman is—"

"A marilith . . . yes, I know," Joel said. "The strategists and tacticians of the Blood War."

Holly looked at the bard with surprise. "How is it you didn't know about barghests, bar-lgura, or bulezau, but you know what a marilith is?" the paladin asked.

"For the same reason he knew all about alu-fiends and probably knows all about succubi, yochlol, and lamia," Jas said from just behind them.

The winged woman hovered just beyond the ridge, out of reach of the bar-lgura guards, who growled at her and tilted their heads in puzzlement. No doubt they were confused by the appearance of a human woman with slasrath wings and were trying to determine if she was a denizen of the plane or not.

"Relax," Jas said to the tanar'ri. "I'm a friend of theirs." She fluttered to the ridge and landed beside the bard and the paladin. "So how is Walinda?" she asked Joel. "On her deathbed, I hope."

"She's Beshaba's proxy," Holly explained.

"Yes, I heard you talking," Jas replied. "I've been hovering overhead since you came up here. Forgive me for flying off, but if I see Walinda again, I'm likely to lose my self-control and wring her scrawny little neck until her forked tongue pops out of her vicious mouth."

"She knows you're here," Joel pointed out.

"Good. I hope she loses sleep over it," Jas retorted.

"Jas, you mustn't try to attack her now," Holly warned. "She isn't the priestess of a dead god anymore. She can cast priest spells again, ones that could kill you in an instant. With Beshaba's power inside her, she's far stronger than ever before."

"Not that I ever succeeded in killing her when she was a mere mortal, unable to cast any magic at all," Jas said bitterly.

With no comforting reply to offer her friend, Holly changed the subject. "What did you mean about Joel knowing about mariliths for the same reason he knew about alu-fiends and succubi?" she asked.

"Well, I'm assuming there are all sorts of books describing monsters and fiends in the library of that fancy barding college Joel attended as a boy," Jas said. She draped a friendly arm around the bard's shoulder. "Am I right, matey?" she asked Joel.

"Yes, of course," Holly said. "We had such a tome at the church where I learned to read and write," the paladin said. "But why don't you remember all the creatures?" she asked the bard.

Joel could feel a blush rising to his face. "It's not important," he insisted.

"Assuming boys haven't changed that much since I was a girl," Jas said, "I'll bet that book in your church and the book in the barding college both open naturally to certain pages, usually pages with pictures of fiends and monsters who mimic the looks of very attractive women."

"It's important to arm oneself with knowledge of an enemy to which one might be particularly susceptible," Joel pointed out self-defensively.

Holly laughed.

"Too bad Walinda wasn't in that book," Jas said, giving the bard's shoulders a sisterly squeeze.

Joel had to nod in agreement. If he'd known when he'd first met Walinda what he knew now, he'd have never made any sort of alliance with her. Yet here he was, forced to do so again.

Holly looked back down at the Bastion of Hate. "This isn't good," the paladin said grimly.

"It's Iyachtu Xvim's realm," Jas retorted. "It's not supposed to be good."

"Not that," Holly said. "This whole situation. It's going to be a bloodbath."

"Of a bunch of evil, lawless creatures," Jas pointed out.

"It's still not right," Holly said, shaking her head, "whatever kind of creatures they are."

"You're too softhearted," Jas declared.

"So only the just deserve justice? Only the good deserve goodness? Is that what you think?" Holly asked sadly.

"That's right," Jas replied. There wasn't a shred of doubt in her tone, but her voice cracked, and Joel knew she was thinking of Walinda's torture and murder of her friends.

"Holly, there's nothing we can do about it," Joel said. "Walinda is going to use those creatures, and they're letting themselves be used."

"So what now?" Jas asked.

"I presume the marilith is advising Walinda on how best to attack. When they've come to a decision, we attack."

"We should be there to hear their plans. Maybe we can influence them," Holly said, taking a step in the direction of the canyon floor.

"Not me," Jas said. "I'm not going to be involved in any plan of Walinda's. If she knows what's good for her, she won't trust me in any event. I'll make my own plans for this fight. When you're ready to begin, you let me know. Send out a ray of light from the finder's stone in my direction and I'll join you. Just make sure you're not with Walinda when you summon me."

The winged woman took off from the ridge and disappeared into the darkness.

Holly began sliding back down into the canyon. Joel followed behind more slowly, distracted by a new worry. Holly hadn't been looking at Jas before she'd flown off, so the paladin hadn't noticed what Joel had seen. Jas's eyes had glowed like an owl's—the way they did when the dark stalker was taking control of her. The bard said nothing to the paladin, because he wasn't certain he hadn't imagined it; it might have been a trick of the malignant red light that pervaded the atmosphere.

Even if I'm right, he thought, there isn't a thing I can do about it.

Act Three
Scene 3

When Holly and Joel went to look at the Bastion of Hate, Emilo remained behind to keep an eye on Walinda. No one in the party had bothered to explain to the kender why they all seemed to dislike the priestess so, but upon listening to her, the kender had a pretty good idea. Walinda was not nice at all. Furthermore, Emilo hadn't cared for the way she had appropriated their flying carpet.

Walinda stepped into the pavilion and ordered one of the bar-lgura to bring her the carpet. Emilo followed the hulking tanar'ri inside. When the tanar'ri left, the kender settled himself in a dark corner and watched.

He had no fear of being detected. The gift he'd been given, by a mysterious old man at the end of the magical vortex by which he had arrived in this world, seemed to be holding up well. As long as Emilo kept quiet, wasn't introduced by a companion, and didn't attack anyone, he went completely unnoticed. The hardest part was keeping quiet. The gift had served him well in Sigil until he'd run into Jas.

The mysterious old man had warned him that anyone from Krynn would be able to notice him. Jas had surprised him. Emilo had never seen any winged women on his home world of Krynn, but Jas had indeed noticed him, even though she claimed she came from Joel's world. It was possible she was confused about that. Whatever the case, her knowledge of his presence had turned out all right.

Finder was another exception, which Emilo had to think about for a while. In the end, he decided that since

Finder was aware of everything that happened around
Joel, and since Emilo had talked to Joel, that explained
things. When Emilo had left Joel's side to eavesdrop on
Finder and Tymora and Winnie, neither the gods nor the
halfling had seemed to take notice of him. Selune had
been the ultimate test. When Emilo had surprised the
elder goddess with his presence, then he was certain the
gift was still working. The way Holly had started when he
had finally greeted her in the Abyss had been one more
confirmation.

Since the bar-lgura had captured Joel and Holly but ignored the kender, Joel and Holly seemed to have figured
out Emilo's secret. They had been careful to keep their
eyes away from Emilo and had not introduced him to
Walinda. So now Emilo was free to spy on the priestess.

The old man had not explained why he'd granted Emilo
such an unusual gift, but the kender assumed it was so he
could spy on people. In Walinda's case, the thought didn't
give the kender much pleasure. The priestess gave him
the shivers. Still, someone had to keep an eye on her.

Walinda unrolled the flying carpet, settled herself in
the center, and ran her hand over the heavy wool with a
look of pleasure. Then, assuming she was alone in the
pavilion, she began poking through the party's gear.

First she dumped out the contents of Holly's backpack.
With a disdainful look, she pawed through the paladin's
brightly colored clothing. A glittering glass sculpture
caught her eye, and she picked it up.

The priestess let out a cry and tossed the sculpture
aside as if it had burned her. It landed right at Emilo's
feet. As the priestess sucked on her fingers, Emilo scooped
up the piece of glass and examined it. It was a piece of red
glass, shaped like the sun, with a beaming smile on its
face. It was every bit as lovely as Jas's star-filled paperweight and Joel's finder's stone. Emilo slipped it into a
pocket of his vest, certain that Holly would not want it left
behind.

Walinda stuffed Holly's things back into her pack. Next
she looked through Joel's pack and the one Winnie had
given them, but she found nothing of particular interest.
Joel had kept the finder's stone and the scrolls with him,

Emilo remembered. Since the potions were missing, Emilo figured Joel must have taken them as well. The gold had been in the other backpack, the one Jas had filled with rocks to attack the barghest. Jas had scooped the gold into her own pack—the same pack she'd flown off with when the bar-lgura attacked.

Walinda was just stuffing the last of the party's gear back into Winnie's pack when the awaited ally arrived. Walinda left the pavilion to greet her. The priestess escorted a snake-woman with six arms into the pavilion. The snake-woman never spoke aloud, but Walinda kept saying "yes" and "no" as if she were answering questions. After a while the kender realized that the snake-woman must be speaking directly to Walinda's mind.

"This," Walinda said spreading out a map on the table, "is our objective." She pointed to a spot on the map. "These are our forces." The priestess stepped back while the snake-woman examined the map in silence. Emilo could see Walinda nod occasionally, so he knew she and the snake-woman were still having a telepathic conversation. He was mildly annoyed. What good was it to be able to spy on someone this close up and not hear half the conversation?

From outside the tent, Emilo heard what sounded like a brawl. Walinda and the snake-woman were so intent on studying the map that they failed to take note of it. Curious, Emilo slipped outside the pavilion to investigate the noise.

About fifty yards from the pavilion, a crowd of the minotaur-like bulezau stood in a tight circle, shouting and cheering. Emilo had to squeeze between the legs of one of the smelly creatures to see what they were watching.

The bulezau stood around a great circular pit some fifty feet across and twenty feet deep. Torches flared and sputtered near the top of the pit wall. At the bottom of the pit, three hydroloths fought against three bulezau. They fought without weapons, using their claws and teeth. The froglike hydroloths also spat yellow poison, and the bulezau smashed into their opponents with their horns and slashed at them with their spiky tails. When one hydroloth managed to bring down a bulezau, another leapt

into the pit to take its fellow's place. Between the poison,
the blood, and the ichor, the stench from the pit was un-
bearable. When one of the hydroloths lost an arm, Emilo
turned to squeeze his way through of the crowd. After a
few deep breaths of air, the kender was able to continue.

Spotting Joel and Holly making their way back toward
the pavilion, Emilo ran to intercept them.

Joel felt a tug at his sleeve. Out of the blue, there was
Emilo. The kender motioned for him to follow. Joel took
Holly's arm and led her toward the crowd of bulezau
around the pit.

As their bar-lgura escort approached the crowd, the
giant bulezau parted for the smaller apelike creatures
and their human charges. Joel was the first to see into the
pit, and he tried to keep Holly back, but the paladin would
not be deterred.

At the bottom of the pit, a dozen or so bulezau and two
giant frog creatures lay dead or too injured to move. One
giant frog, over ten feet tall, and a single bulezau still
fought. The gore caused an awful stench.

Holly's eyes narrowed to angry slits.

"Are those frog creatures hydroloths?" Joel asked.

"Yes," the paladin answered coldly.

"Entertaining, isn't it?" Walinda asked from behind
them. "Prisoners should always be made useful."

Joel spun about. The priestess and the marilith stood
beside one another. The marilith was an exceedingly
comely female, with bright blue eyes and shining blonde
hair that streamed down to her waist in a mass of curls. A
flimsy veil covered her upper torso. About her hips she
wore several scabbards. She rose from the coils of her
green tail, hovering at least a foot above Joel.

"This is Stentka Taran," Walinda introduced the
tanar'ri.

The bard bowed courteously. Since the marilith said
nothing, neither did he.

"We have just finished mapping out our plan of attack,"
Walinda said.

"I hope it didn't rely on the twelve dead warriors in the
pit," Holly growled. "Your foolish entertainment is a
shameful waste of lives."

"But it was an effective demonstration for the others," Walinda replied. "Magic has been dispelled in the pit, so the hydroloths were partially handicapped. They were quite effective nonetheless. Now the bulezau are aware of the physical strength of the opponents they will face."

"What difference will that make?" Holly argued. "You won't be fighting your battle in a pit."

"But we can, in a manner of speaking," Walinda said. She pointed to an iron pole, some six feet high, which was firmly planted in the center of the pit. Tied to the top of pole was an iron latticework sphere about as large as a man's head. A dark blue light seemed to glow within the sphere. "In the war between the tanar'ri and the baatezu, the sphere you see is called a magic killer. It negates all magic within thirty feet of it. If you were paying closer attention to the combat, you might have noticed that the hydroloths attempted to reach the sphere to destroy it, while the bulezau tried to prevent them from doing so."

As Walinda spoke, the remaining hydroloth slashed completely through the head of the bulezau it was fighting. Another bulezau leapt into the pit, but not before the hydroloth whipped its tongue across the pit and scooped into its mouth the magic killer with the iron pole still attached.

Walinda frowned. The hydroloth bit down on the magic killer. There was a flash of blue-white light, and a blast of energy tore through the pit. Bits and pieces of the hydroloth and the bulezau showered the audience at the rim of the pit.

"So much for your magic killer," Holly said.

"Oh, rest assured, paladin," the priestess replied. "We have more." She looked suddenly at the marilith and nodded. "Stentka Taran wishes to know if you will submit to a test," Walinda said.

Holly's eyes narrowed suspiciously. "What sort of test?" she asked.

"Merely a test of your skill in combat," Walinda said.

"I didn't come here to entertain you as a gladiator," the paladin replied.

"Stentka needs to assess your skill to decide where you will best fit in our assault plans." Walinda gave Holly a chill smile. "Unless you wish to rescind your offer to aid in our attack," she said.

Joel could see the paladin was struggling to control her anger at the implication she might go back on her word. Her nostrils flared and her shoulders shook. The marilith watched the paladin, too, and Joel had the sudden impression that Walinda's insult had been a test as well.

Holly took a deep breath. The true extent of her abilities was more knowledge than anyone in her right mind would wish to share with the evil priestess. In the end, however, the paladin's desire to obey Lathander superseded her heartfelt desire to deny Walinda her request. "Whom shall I fight?" Holly asked.

"Stentka will test you herself," Walinda explained. "You will use edgeless weapons."

The marilith slithered toward the paladin. From one of the many scabbards she wore about her hips, the tanar'ri drew out a long sword. Holding it by the unsharpened blade, she offered the hilt to the paladin.

Holly took the sword. The marilith drew out a second sword.

The bulezau and the bar-lgura drew back a respectful distance from the combatants. Walinda stepped back to stand beside Joel as Holly and the marilith began circling each other warily.

The marilith began with a broad, sweeping stroke, which Holly parried easily. The tanar'ri's second strike was quicker and closer to the paladin's heart, but Holly knocked it aside. Although the combat was only a test, the bulezau and Walinda were mesmerized by the dance of weapons. The bulezau cheered and shouted encouragement each time steel struck steel.

Once more Emilo tugged on the bard's sleeve. Joel stepped back away from Walinda. Without taking his eyes from the combatants, he squatted on his heels so the kender could whisper in his ear.

"I was trying to show you one of the hydroloths in the pit," Emilo whispered. "He's the one who came to Sigil to take Jas away."

"How can you tell? He looked just like the other two," the bard insisted, without bothering to look back down into the stinking pit.

"Before the bulezau cut him to pieces, his markings were very distinctive," Emilo said softly. "I know that's him."

"Well, he won't be bothering Jas anymore," Joel noted.

"Suppose he was here looking for Jas. Suppose the others were, too. Suppose," Emilo hissed urgently, "there are more of them out there looking for her."

Joel looked up into the dark sky. Unsurprisingly, he could see no sign of the winged woman. "Keep an eye on Holly," he whispered. Then he stood back up and pushed his way through the crowd of tanar'ri watching the combat. Walinda was too engrossed in the combat to notice the bard's departure. Only the bar-lgura honor guard followed him. He slipped behind a boulder. Facing the rock and using his body as a shield from any curious eyes, he pulled out the finder's stone and thought of Jas.

The beacon of light shot out toward the outer edge of the canyon. Joel waited several anxious moments before Jas came shooting out of the darkness and landed beside him. Her eyes were glowing like an owl's, and there was a tuft of feathers sticking out behind her ears and over her eyebrows.

"What's going on?" the winged woman asked, jerking her head toward the crowd of tanar'ri.

"Holly's fighting a marilith," Joel said. He grabbed Jas's arm before she could race to the paladin's aid. "It's Holly's choice. It's some sort of test. I brought you here in case—" Joel hesitated, not wanting to suggest Jas couldn't look out for herself.

"In case what?" Jas asked.

"Emilo spotted the hydroloth who was sent to bring you back to Xvim. The hydroloth's dead now, but there could be others around. I want you to stay in camp until the attack. You won't have to see or speak to Walinda. You can stay right here. If Xvim's minions know you're here, it won't be safe for you to be alone out there."

"Joel, what difference does it make?" Jas growled. "Look at me. The dark stalker is taking over again. I don't know if it's because I'm close to Xvim's realm or because I can't stop thinking about Walinda, but it doesn't matter.

It's going to get me in the end."

Joel put his hands on Jas's shoulders. "It does matter," he insisted. "Gods, if Holly can bring herself to ally with Walinda and a marilith to bring about a greater good, you can at least try. You can fight this thing."

"I'm tired of fighting it," Jas said with a sigh. "Since the fetch weakened me, it's harder to resist. I'm turning into a creature of darkness. You shouldn't trust me anymore."

"I won't accept that," the bard said. "You have to fight this. Too much depends on us, on you. If Xvim has found a way to steal Tymora's luck and Beshaba's misfortune, think what he can do with it. Think what Realmspace will be like when his priests have all the luck and his enemies are beset with misfortune."

"I can't stop that either," Jas snarled. "I can't stop anything. I'm useless."

"No, you aren't," Joel argued. He wracked his brains for something he could say that would convince Jas to at least make the attempt to hang on to her humanity. Finder would know what to say, the bard thought. Finder would give her a reason even if he had to make it up. Then an idea struck him. "We need *you* to make our plan work. There's no one else who can get us into the Bastion of Hate."

"What are you talking about?" Jas demanded.

"If they think you're a dark stalker, they'll let you into the bastion. I need Walinda to get us some more information from the hydroloth that was after you in Sigil."

"I thought you said he was dead," Jas argued.

"That shouldn't be a problem for Walinda," Joel said. "Will you wait here? Please?" the bard pleaded.

Jas shrugged, and her wings stiffened. Joel was afraid she was going to launch into flight. Then she nodded.

Joel turned around. The bar-lgura Walinda had assigned to escort him were standing behind him, watching curiously. Joel wondered just how much they understood, and how much they would report back to Walinda. The bard pointed to two of the apelike creatures and ordered, "Make sure no one bothers her." Then he headed back toward Walinda. The bar-lgura he'd appointed as Jas's guardians remained behind.

Joel felt a secret twinge of amusement that he'd actually ordered a tanar'ri to do his bidding. He wondered what Finder would say about that. He'd probably tell his priest not to let it go to his head.

With the help of his remaining bar-lgura escort, the bard squeezed his way through the bulezau and returned to Walinda's side. Emilo stood beside the priestess, hopping from foot to foot, silently cheering for Holly.

Holly was still battling the marilith, but even Joel could see she wasn't doing well. She was slowed by having to constantly watch her footing as the marilith tried to coil her snake tail about her feet. The marilith used only one weapon, but she switched it from hand to hand to hand, keeping the paladin off-balance. Holly did manage to strike one solid blow to the tanar'ri female's tail, and she successfully warded off all the thrusts aimed at her, but in the heat and the stench of the plane, she soon tired.

The marilith ended the combat suddenly by sheathing her weapon. She must have spoken to Holly with telepathy, for the paladin replied, "Yes, I did," as she handed back the unsharpened blade the marilith had given her for the test.

The marilith bowed to the paladin and slithered off to Walinda's pavilion. The bulezau and bar-lgura cleared a wide path for her and the two toadlike hezrou warriors who followed in her wake.

Holly returned to Joel's side.

"What did she say to you?" the bard asked.

"She said I fought well for someone so young, and that I must have had an excellent teacher," the paladin replied, wiping the sweat from her brow with a handkerchief.

"Your father trained you, didn't he?" the bard asked.

Holly nodded. Her father, Joel recalled, had been a warrior from Zhakara who had settled in Daggerdale, far from his native land, after having fallen in love with Holly's mother. He'd died only a year ago, murdered by orc raiders along with his wife and in-laws. Holly still used the curved blade he'd brought with him from Zhakara.

"I must confer with Stentka," Walinda said.

"Just a minute. I have some conferring I need to do myself," the bard said. "I think Jas and I could manage to get

into the fortress before your attack and perhaps sabotage
a few of their defenses."

"Oh?" Walinda prompted the bard, obviously interested.

"It depends on whether or not you can speak with the
dead," Joel explained.

"What dead?" Walinda asked.

Joel strode back to the edge of the pit. "Which one?" he
whispered to the kender.

"The one on the right, with his right arm missing," the
kender whispered back.

Joel turned back to face Walinda and motioned for her
to join him. "That hydroloth," he said, pointing into the
pit. "The one on the right, with the missing right arm.
How did he come to be a prisoner?"

"As I mentioned before, Xvim will not allow anything to
fly, teleport, or magically gate directly into his realm," the
priestess explained. "His agents must teleport outside the
walls of the Bastion of Hate and announce themselves at
the gate to gain entry. The hydroloths teleport to the lava
flows, where they delight in swimming before returning to
their hired lord. The bulezau fished all three of these creatures out of the lava several hours before you arrived."

"The hydroloth I mentioned was stalking Jas in Sigil to
bring her to Iyachtu Xvim. He was helped by a priest of
Xvim who we defeated in combat. If I can find out more
about his mission, I might get away with impersonating a
mercenary hired by the priest and the hydroloth to bring
Jas back," Joel explained.

Walinda nodded thoughtfully. She pointed out the hydroloth in question to the nearest bar-lgura. "Fetch that
corpse from the pit," she ordered. "You . . . bring me a
torch," she ordered a second bar-lgura.

Within a few minutes, a team of bar-lgura had hauled
the dead hydroloth from the pit and laid it at Walinda's
feet. The bar-lgura who'd been sent for a torch returned
with a piece of tar-drenched fabric wrapped about a pike.
Great clouds of smoke came from the torch, but it burned
brightly enough to cast shadows in the dark canyon.

"What question shall I start with?" the priestess asked.

"Ask him what the purpose of his mission in Sigil four

nights ago was," Joel suggested.

Walinda nodded. From a small pouch hanging from her armor, she drew out a stick of incense and lit it from the torch flame. She knelt beside the head of the stinking froglike corpse. Holding the incense in her left hand, she held it under the hydroloth's nose. With the fingers of her right hand, she stroked the emblem of Beshaba tattooed into her cheeks. Then she began chanting dark words that had no meaning to the bard, for which fact Joel was most grateful.

Walinda shoved the burning incense into the hydroloth's mouth. Smoke billowed from the corpse's mouth and nose.

"I command thee to answer my questions," the priestess cried out. Her voice echoed throughout the canyon. Then, in a whisper, she asked, "What was the purpose of your mission in Sigil four nights ago?"

There was no sound from the hydroloth, but Walinda seemed to be listening intently. Her eyes were closed and she nodded twice.

That's when the bard realized that the hydroloth, like the tanar'ri, was communicating by telepathy. Joel would have to rely on Walinda to give him an accurate report.

Walinda looked up from the hydroloth. "He was to oversee the capture of Jasmine by Hatemaster Perr and some hired thugs. Then he was to return with Jasmine and Hatemaster Perr to the Bastion of Hate."

Joel nodded. Besides assuring Joel that Emilo had correctly identified the hydroloth, the answer revealed the name of the priest who had deliberately killed himself struggling in the razorvine.

"What identity did he use in Sigil?" Joel asked.

Walinda asked the question, listened, then told Joel, "He shapeshifted to a tall human form, but used no name. The hirelings and the priest called him Boss."

"Ask him to whom he was to deliver Jasmine."

Walinda repeated the question Joel had asked, then listened.

"Tyrannar Neri," she replied.

Tyrannar, Joel knew, was the highest rank of clerics in the church of Iyachtu Xvim.

"Does the tyrannar know he's failed in his mission?" Joel asked.

Walinda shook her head. "He has no way of knowing that for sure," the priestess told Joel. "He will be forced to answer that he does not know. I will rephrase your question. . . . Have you or has anyone you know informed the tyrannar that your mission has failed?" she asked the corpse, then waited for the answer. "The answer is no," she told Joel.

"I want to try something more complicated," Joel said. "What does he think would happen to someone else who brought Jasmine to the tyrannar to collect a bounty and also brought him news of the death of the hydroloth and Hatemaster Perr?"

Walinda put the question to the dead hydroloth, then waited. Joel could see her smile slightly. Smoke ceased streaming from the corpse's mouth and nose. The spell had ended. Walinda could ask no more questions.

The priestess stood up. "The hydroloth said that if the tyrannar is sufficiently impressed by the bounty seeker, he will accept Jas as an offering to Xvim so that the bounty seeker can join Iyachtu Xvim's faithful. He will not pay a bounty for his lord's own property. If he isn't impressed by the bounty seeker, he'll simply have him enslaved."

"Is there a big difference?" Joel asked.

"Probably not much," Walinda replied. "So will you impersonate a bounty seeker? Do you think you can impress a tyrannar?" she asked.

"I impress everyone," Joel replied matter-of-factly, winking at Holly and Emilo.

"You have always impressed me," Walinda said, running one of her sharpened fingernails none too gently down the side of the bard's throat.

"Must be my bad luck," Joel retorted as he drew away from the evil priestess's touch.

Walinda gave the bard a predatory smile.

"So, if I go to the bastion now, how long can you postpone your attack?" the bard asked.

"No more than half a day," Walinda replied. "The bulezau grow agitated if they are not killing something, and I am loath to keep Beshaba waiting. No one knows when Iyachtu Xvim might return."

"I can't say for certain what we can accomplish," the bard said, "but if possible, we will attempt to learn the strength of the guard around Beshaba and weaken it. If we discover a way to destroy any cache of weapons, we will do that as well. After you begin your attack, we'll try to open the gate. If I find Beshaba, I'll try to use the finder's stone to summon you. If you or Stentka Taran have any other suggestions, I'll take them under advisement."

Walinda said, "I will speak with her."

"Fine. I'm going to speak with my associates. I'll join you shortly," the bard replied.

Walinda nodded and walked off to her pavilion. Joel led Holly and Emilo to where Jas was waiting. The winged woman crouched behind the boulder.

Holly gasped at the winged woman's appearance. "Jas! Are you all right?" she asked

Jas shrugged. Joel knew she'd never tell Holly how hopeless she felt. As far as Jas was concerned, Holly was still an innocent to be protected. "It's just that we're so close to Xvim's realm," she told the paladin. "When we leave, I'll get better. So what's the plan for getting into Xvim's fortress?" she asked Joel.

Hastily Joel explained his plan to his three companions. His original plan called for Emilo to stay with Holly, but Holly insisted the kender would be more useful, possibly even safer, with Joel and Jas. The paladin had also noted the kender's gift for remaining unnoticed. If it worked in the Bastion of Hate as well as it worked in Walinda's camp of tanar'ri, it would make Emilo the perfect saboteur.

Jas, who hadn't realized there was something unusual about the kender, was suddenly more curious. "I've never had any problem seeing you," she said.

"I think it's because you're different from everyone else," the kender replied.

Jas accepted that explanation without asking which difference Emilo meant.

"How'd you get this gift?" Jas wanted to know.

"I got it in the magical vortex that brought me to Sigil," the kender said. "I don't know why exactly. The last century of my life has been pretty confusing. I suppose it's a destiny thing."

Holly was more concerned about Joel's plan than the origin of the kender's gift. She asked the bard, "How are you going to disguise yourself?"

"I have a scroll," Joel explained. "I thought I'd disguise myself as a tiefling. That should strengthen my story that I'm a native of Sigil, and not some clueless prime."

"Are you going to make yourself shorter?" Emilo asked with surprise.

"Tieflings aren't just another kind of halfling or kender," Holly explained. "Tiefling are what Planers and Cagers call a person who has an ancestor from the Lower Planes. Not all tieflings are short."

Joel pulled out the appropriate scroll from the bundle he'd attached to his belt. As he read the scroll, he added a description to the spell words that served to reshape his form. He made himself a little taller, covered his skin with black scales, and grew long fangs. When he'd finished casting the spell, Holly drew back from him in shock.

"You look awful," the paladin said.

"Yeah, you really do," Jas agreed. "Perfect, actually. No one would ever suspect you're really a nice young man who's gotten in over his head in the affairs of the gods."

"You should put your hair up like mine," Emilo suggested. "It will make you look even taller."

Joel bound his hair into a topknot.

"It makes you look fierce," Holly said, "It looks like the horse-tail crests on the helmets of the Tuigan warriors.

Jas and Holly agreed it made him look quite fiendish.

"Now what?" the winged woman asked.

"I'm going to go get our backpack and take my leave of Walinda. I'll be back soon," Joel said.

Joel found Walinda in the pavilion with the marilith, poring over a map.

"Your tiefling features are most becoming, Poppin," the priestess commended him.

Without replying, Joel bent over and retrieved his backpack and Winnie's. Then he turned to face Walinda.

"I will do everything in my power to help free your goddess, but I don't want you using Holly as if she were some tanar'ri meant to die in the Blood War," he warned the priestess. "Don't put her in a dangerous position."

"We agree completely," Walinda assured him. "Someday, when she is much more powerful, I hope to sacrifice Holly Harrowslough. Stentka Taran, on the other hand, is already plotting ways to corrupt her. So you can rest assured we will keep her safe . . . for now."

The bard glared at the priestess. "Any other suggestions about the sabotage?" he asked coolly.

"As I mentioned before," Walinda said, "Iyachtu Xvim's realm is guarded by mercenary yugoloths. They are exceedingly greedy creatures. Stentka knows of a case in which a great deal of chaos was sown by leaving unclaimed money lying about." The priestess handed the bard a small sack.

Joel looked inside it. It was filled with small but rare gems. "Illusions?" he asked, slipping the sack into his shirt beside the finder's stone.

"You learn quickly, Poppin," the priestess said, stroking the bard's scaly cheek with a look of fascination.

"I'll be leaving now," Joel said, stepping backward.

"Give my regards to the pigeon girl," Walinda said.

"I don't think so," Joel said. "Good luck with your attack," he wished the priestess and the marilith.

"Misfortune take our enemies," Walinda responded.

Joel turned and hurried back to his companions. He embraced Holly. "Be careful," he warned the paladin. Remembering the incident with the barghests, he reminded her, "Make sure you keep the little harp Finder gave each of us handy."

"You make sure you do, too," Holly replied. Leaving the paladin behind in the camp of tanar'ri, Jas, Joel, and Emilo made their way up the canyon's slope. Just before they reached the crest, they turned and waved good-bye one last time.

Holly waved back.

The bar-lgura who'd accompanied them up the slope suddenly disappeared. They'd become invisible, no doubt planning on following the bard and the winged woman as long as they could.

The three adventurers made their way up to a high
point on the ridge to skirt around the lava flow between
the canyon ridge and the Bastion of Hate. It was the first
time they'd traveled by foot in Gehenna, and it was far
more difficult than Joel had imagined. It took them nearly
an hour to get down to the ledge where Xvim's fortress
was located.

They regrouped behind a boulder that shielded them
from view. Joel handed Emilo the fake gems and explained Walinda's suggestion to leave them lying about
where they might cause discord among the yugoloths.
After a moment's thought, he also gave the kender the
finder's stone. If the tyrannar had him searched, the high
priest might demand the stone to give to Iyachtu Xvim. In
addition, the kender could use it to find Joel and Jas
should they become separated. Jas gave the kender the
lucky sword Winnie had given her. Since Joel was suppos-
edly bringing her in as a prisoner, she had to be disarmed.
With a short length of rope from Winnie's backpack, Joel
bound Jas's hands in front of her so she looked like prisoner. Then he tied a lead rope to the bindings.

Before the three adventurers could continue, Emilo
said, "I don't get it. If Iyachtu Xvim is like the other gods,
he can sense what's going on with nearby followers, right?
Then he must sense us. He must sense Walinda. You don't
suppose this is all a trap, do you?"

"I've thought about that," Joel admitted. "I have another theory. If Xvim is stealing Tymora's luck and Beshaba's misfortune, he has more than enough power to
seize some other realm, perhaps in some less unpleasant
place. He could have already abandoned his fortress here
and is only leaving it operating as a distraction for us."

"I don't know which would be worse," Jas muttered.

They marched in near silence to the gate of Iyachtu
Xvim's fortress. The Bastion of Hate towered over them.
Its walls were encased in plates of iron as thick as Joel's
thumb. The air shimmered with heat around the iron
plates, and the rivets joining the plates together glowed
like coal. Horn-shaped iron spikes decorated the para-
pets. The closed gate was an iron grid, bristling with

spikes meant to keep visitors away.

Joel could see no signs of life. He shouted out, "Hello the gate!"

A voice from the wall called down, "Who goes there?"

"My name is Marin the Red," Joel shouted. "I've come to collect the bounty on Jasmine the Dark Stalker—that is, if Tyrannar Neri still wants her. Otherwise I have another buyer."

They waited several minutes, but there was no reply. Joel glanced over at Jas. Black feathers had regrown about her neck. The dark stalker's presence was growing more and more prominent. It helped their story, but it was unsettling nonetheless.

Joel moved close to Jas and whispered, "We can still flee."

Jas shook her head sharply, but Joel could see she was trembling. As long as she could keep it under control for a few more hours, the bard thought, everything would be fine.

From somewhere overhead came the squeak of wheels, and the portcullis gate raised up just enough for them to enter the fortress. For show, he tugged on the rope that bound Jas until she drew up beside him. Emilo slipped in alongside Joel.

They stood in a dark gatehouse, illuminated by a single smoky torch. A second spiked portcullis blocked their way. The portcullis behind them slammed back down to the ground. They were trapped inside the Bastion of Hate.

Jas whirled about and hissed. Joel breathed in sharply, trying to hide his shock and fear.

Feathers now completely covered Jas's face and hands. Her hands had transformed into talons. She yanked the lead rope from Joel's hands and flew at the closed gate with the frenzy of a wild bird. An inhuman screech came from her throat. It sounded to Joel like the cry of a snared hawk.

From two side doors streamed twelve yugoloth guards armed with pikes. The guards were several inches taller than Joel and resembled horned crickets, their chitinous armor the color of dirty ivory. Without Holly to explain, the bard had no idea what breed of yugoloths they were.

The guards separated Joel from his "bounty" and surrounded Jas. The inner portcullis opened. A human priest
of Iyachtu Xvim stood on the other side. He was a small
man, with a shaved head and an iron ring in his pierced
lip. He looked younger than Joel.

"I am Hatemaster Morr. If you will follow me, Marin
the Red, I will arrange for you to meet with Tyrannar
Neri."

Joel looked back at Jas. Her owl-like eyes were devoid
of expression, but Joel sensed that Jas felt betrayed. The
winged woman screeched once more as the yugoloths led
her away through a side door. She spoke no words; the
sounds she made were those of an enraged animal. A
sinking feeling took hold of Joel. Perhaps he'd been wrong
to bring Jas here. Perhaps here, in the Bastion of Hate,
the dark stalker had finally destroyed her humanity.

Act Three
Scene 4

In the empty stone chamber in the gate wall where Hatemaster Morr had instructed him to wait, Joel paced restlessly from wall to wall. The bard couldn't get out of his head Jas's screeches as she was dragged away. His only comfort was knowing that Emilo had followed Jas. The kender would find a way to calm her down.

Ordinarily the bard would have used the time to sing or compose something on his birdpipes. He was certain he was being observed, however, and a practiced musician was not the image he wanted to project. He tried to guess what sort of thing a tiefling bounty hunter would do while he waited. He thought of practicing drills with his sword, but that might give away just how meager his skill with a weapon was. So he paced . . . and worried.

After what seemed an eternity, Hatemaster Morr returned. "Follow me," he ordered.

Joel shouldered both Winnie's backpack and his own and fell into step beside the priest of Xvim. The hatemaster escorted the bard past several yugoloth guards, beyond the bastion's inner wall, into the courtyard of Xvim's fortress.

The courtyard was illuminated with lines of torches. To the right, a rectangular temple of black marble squatted atop a low hill. A great staircase, littered with human bones and skulls, climbed up to the temple.

Yugoloths surrounded the temple, rank upon rank of the giant horned crickets. Drilling these cricket yugoloths in marching in formation were several shorter yugoloths who resembled red lobsters with chicken feet. Joel did not spot any of the yellow froglike hydroloths.

Across the courtyard from the temple stood a great
tower, which rose several stories taller than the fortress
walls. It was guarded by more hordes of the cricket creatures.

At first Joel presumed the torches were lit for the benefit of Xvim's human followers until he spied some of the
small lobsterlike yugoloths carrying torches. Then Joel realized that at least some of the yugoloths were not gifted,
as were the tanar'ri in Walinda's camp, with the ability to
see in the dark.

Hatemaster Morr led Joel through the courtyard toward the temple. Joel followed the priest up the staircase and into the great marble building. There were no
yugoloths within the temple. A few human priests scurried from rooms on one side of the hall to rooms on the
other.

Joel and the hatemaster walked the length of the great
hall; at the other end, they passed into an audience chamber. There were no yugoloths in here either, only humans.
Some twenty of these, armored in plate mail and armed
with morningstars, served as guards. Over their armor
they wore green stoles embroidered with Xvim's symbol,
green eyes set in the palm of a black hand. From the relative plainness of their stoles, Joel guessed they were low-
ranking priests. Six other priests in robes of gray silk
trimmed with green, serving as scribes and advisers, attended the tyrannar. Only two of the priests were women;
both were serving as guards.

The tyrannar was seated in a chair upholstered with
human flesh. He was an ancient spider of a man, covered
with liver spots, wearing robes made from an elaborate
black and green brocade. From the tattoos on his cheeks,
Joel could tell that he had once been a priest of Bane, the
father of Iyachtu Xvim.

"So," the tyrannar croaked, "you've brought me the elusive Jasmine the Dark Stalker."

"Yeah," Joel said, being deliberately brief in an attempt
to imitate the toughs he'd encountered in Sigil.

"Tell me how you knew we were searching for her," said
the tyrannar.

"A priest called Perr hired me and my mates to bring

her down," Joel replied with a fairly passable Sigilian accent.

"And what happened to Hatemaster Perr?" the tyrannar demanded.

"Got himself caught up in a razorvine. Sliced himself up on it deliberately before the Hardheads could use their magic to get him to turn stag on us and the Boss," Joel replied.

"What happened to the Boss?" the tyrannar asked.

"When the Hardheads come beating down the door, he turned hisself into a big frog and attacked 'em," Joel explained. "But the Hardheads took him down. That's when I pinched the bird girl and give 'em the laugh. I remembered the Boss saying she was supposed to be delivered here to you, so I brought her myself. No need to thank me. Jink will do nicely."

The tyrannar glared long and hard at Joel, but the bard never lowered his eyes.

At last the tyrannar spoke again. "You should know, Marin the Red, that we do not pay for our own property. Which is not to say we will not offer you a reward."

"What sort of reward?" Joel asked, allowing a suspicious tone to creep into his voice.

"If you join the church of Iyachtu Xvim, I am prepared to offer you a position of honor, which, should you prove yourself, will be followed by a position of power."

"I'm not much of a joiner," Joel replied. "I don't like most other people."

The tyrannar chuckled. "As Iyachtu Xvim is the god of hatred and tyranny, that is considered a requirement of the faith."

"Yeah?" Joel asked, his tone hinting that he might be prepared to nibble on the tyrannar's offer.

"We need a new captain of the guard for Lord Xvim's throne room," the tyrannar explained.

"What happened to the old captain?" Joel asked suspiciously.

"He met with an unfortunate accident, along with several of his immediate underlings. Only one of his deputies survived, and none of the remaining guards are really leadership material. So, you see, we need to recruit someone to fill the position. It is important that the position not be left empty for any considerable period of time. Aside from the security concerns, it would be a serious breach of tradition."

"What about all these yugoloths you've got around here?" the bard demanded.

"The job requires certain skill beyond the yugoloths' capabilities. Traditionally it is held by a human, and we are loath to break with tradition," the tyrannar explained.

"Don't trust the big bugs, do you?" Joel asked with a vulgar wink. "So what's the garnish on this job?"

"Garnish? Oh, you mean pay. We're willing to pay a hundred gold pieces a week."

Joel bit down on his lip. The offer was quite generous, which, considering its source, had to make him even more suspicious. It didn't seem reasonable that they were prepared to recruit a complete unknown to serve as a guard in Xvim's throne room, so there had to be a catch. If he were to turn down the offer, however, he had a sneaking suspicion he'd become a slave or a sacrifice. He wasn't exactly in a position to bargain, but he didn't want to appear as if he knew that. "Make it three hundred," the bard offered, "and you have yourself a deal."

"As I said, we can only offer such a position of honor to a follower of our Lord Xvim," the tyrannar replied.

"Well, then, sign me up," Joel replied, wondering if he would be compelled to join if he refused.

"You must make an offering to Xvim," the tyrannar explained.

"Well, you can have the bird girl, then. I offer her to Xvim," Joel said blithely. He couldn't help but recall that Walinda had done the exact same thing to Jas not long ago.

"Welcome to the ranks of the Xvimlar," the tyrannar said. "Kneel before me, Marin the Red."

Joel set the backpacks aside and knelt before the ancient priest. He wondered if Finder was finding this performance amusing. Possibly not. The situation was too serious.

Tyrannar Neri laid his hand, twisted and emaciated with age, on Joel's head. "Know that you are part of the

New Darkness that will spread throughout the multiverse. By your faith will Lord Xvim rule as the greatest tyrant in history, and his hatred will fill the void."

Joel felt a sudden revulsion seize him. His stomach heaved, but fortunately it was empty. The tyrannar's touch seemed to sting like a wasp. Under the pretense of prostrating himself lower, the bard slipped out from under the tyrannar's hand.

"Rise, Xvimlar Marin," Hatemaster Morr pronounced.

Joel stood up. The tyrannar's eyes glittered with hatred and the corners of his lips curled upward with some unknown amusement. He obviously thought he'd fooled Joel somehow.

As he grabbed up his backpacks, Joel wondered just how much the old man knew.

The tyrannar waved his hand, and Hatemaster Morr said, "Follow me, Xvimlar Marin."

Joel turned from the tyrannar and followed the hatemaster from the audience chamber. He felt a horrible chill come over his whole body. He touched his hand to his chest to feel the warmth of the finder's stone, then remembered he'd given it to Emilo.

Although Joel was sure Finder would know his offer to Xvim was only a lie, the bard had a strong sense that evil had embraced him. In this place of hatred, he worried that his spoken words might have been more powerful than what was in his heart.

Hatemaster Morr led Joel out of the temple. As they stood atop the great staircase, the hatemaster pointed imperially across the courtyard.

"Within that tower," the priest of Xvim said, "is the throne room of Lord Xvim. That is your new post. Lord Xvim is not present at the moment, but he requires that there be a captain of the guard or his deputy on duty at all times. The yugoloths are not permitted in the temple or the tower."

"Where do the yugoloths live?" Joel asked curiously.

Hatemaster Morr pointed to the cliff that formed the bastion's rear wall. "The mount is honeycombed with caverns. As the yugoloths are not threatened by fire, the eruptions that occasionally occur within are no more than inconveniences for the creatures."

"So the deputy and the rest of the guards are in the tower?" Joel asked.

"Yes," the hatemaster said, signalling to one of the lobsterlike yugoloths.

The short red yugoloth tramped up the stairs with an honor guard of six of the giant cricket yugoloths.

"This is the new captain of the guard of Lord Xvim's throne room," the hatemaster informed the yugoloth. "Escort him to his post." He motioned for Joel to follow the yugoloths.

The bard followed his honor guard down the stairs of the temple and across the courtyard. As he passed by the units of giant marching yugoloths, he began to understand Holly's fears. Walinda's army was going to be slaughtered by the yugoloths; the priestess would reach her goddess only by walking on the tanar'ri's corpses.

Then Joel thought of Jas, and the problems of the tanar'ri and the yugoloths no longer concerned him. He worried instead about Jas, who deserved it. If Emilo didn't find him soon, Joel determined, he'd have to slip out of the throne room somehow and go looking for his friends.

The door to the tower was barred on the outside with the thighbone of some gargantuan beast. What, Joel wondered, were they keeping inside? Then it occurred to him: Beshaba was locked within. According to Walinda, however, the goddess was unconscious and thus didn't need to be locked up. Didn't the Xvimlar know that? Surely they didn't imagine that the doors would hold if Beshaba were conscious and desired to leave.

Perhaps, Joel thought, there's something else in the tower—something the tyrannar had assigned to guard the goddess, something even the yugoloth feared enough to want to lock it up.

The short yugoloth gave the order for the door to be opened. Two of the giant yugoloths lifted the bar, and a third pulled open the door. Darkness and a suffocating heat came from the doorway.

Suddenly one of the giant yugoloths gave Joel a shove that sent the bard sprawling through the door and across the floor of the tower. Then the yugoloths slammed the door shut, leaving the bard in total darkness. Joel could hear them set the bar in place.

Joel rose carefully to his feet.

"Finally," a voice whispered. The whisper echoed throughout the chamber, making it hard for Joel to judge the speaker's direction.

"Finally," the voice repeated, then added, "another sacrifice."

Act Three
Scene 5

Emilo hurried after the four yugoloths who were carrying off Jas. The creatures marched down twisting corridors through the fortress walls, then down a staircase that led into a swelteringly hot, humid dungeon. During the entire time, Jas never ceased screeching. The yugoloths entered a large room filled with vile implements of torture. As one lit the torches in the wall sconces, the others strapped the winged woman down on a huge table. Jas's screeching turned to a pitiable keening. The yugoloths pulled a sack over her head, and Jas grew instantly quiet. Her body became completely rigid. The yugoloths began searching her person, removing weapons and valuables and setting them on a tray.

One of the yugoloths spent a long time examining Jas's star-filled paperweight, until one of the others smacked him, grabbed the paperweight from his hands, and set it down on the tray. Alongside the paperweight, Jas's daggers, her ring of fire protection, and her water bottle, the yugoloths set the little wooden harp that could transport Jas back to the safety of Fermata. While the yugoloths were intent on dumping out the contents of Jas's backpack, the kender palmed the harp and the paperweight.

Winnie's gold spilled across the table, and a number of pieces rolled to the floor. That was Emilo's first experience with yugoloth greed. The creatures scurried frantically after the gold, each clawing at the others in order to gather up the most coins. Finally they returned to the tray. Although they only spoke to one another telepathically, it was obvious to Emilo from their gestures that they noticed the missing paperweight. They started to argue over its absence.

Another yugoloth, half as tall as the others, whose shape reminded Emilo of a crayfish, came into the room. The little yugoloth must have been a boss, because he got the big yugoloths to stop fighting and ordered them to leave the room. Then the little yugoloth looked over Jas's possessions for himself. He snatched up the ring of fire protection and scowled at the meager remains. After a more thorough search, he discovered a hidden pocket in Jas's backpack that held a small sack of gems and jewelry. He tied the sack to his weapons belt. For good measure, he took Jas's dagger. The silvered blade must be worth something, Emilo conjectured.

As the little yugoloth turned to go, Emilo gently slit the sack of gems and jewelry with his dagger, creating a hole in the bag from which a tiny gem spilled forth. In time, the hole would grow. Once the yugoloth left the room, Emilo hurried back to the table where Jas was bound and patted the winged woman's shoulder.

"They're gone, Jas. It's going to be all right now," the kender assured her in a soft voice. Very gently he pulled the hood from Jas's head. The winged woman turned her head and blinked in the light of the torch on the wall, but she didn't seem to see Emilo.

The kender unbuckled the leather straps that held Jas to the table.

Freed from her bonds, Jas suddenly sprang up and flew to the ceiling. She fluttered in a dark corner like a moth caught in a jar.

"Jas, come down," Emilo whispered. "What are you doing up there?"

Jas hissed at the kender.

Emilo sighed. Then an idea occurred to him. He pulled out Jas's star-filled paperweight and held it up to the light. "See what I have?" he asked softly. "Come down and look at the stars, Jas."

Jas's eyes followed the paperweight, entranced by the sparkles inside. Suddenly she swooped down and grabbed the ornament in her talons. As she crouched beside the kender and stared down at the flecks of glitter within the paperweight, her eyes ceased to glow. In another few moments, she took on human shape. Finally Jas collapsed to her knees, sobbing.

The kender stroked Jas's hair while she cried. She still said nothing, but the sobbing was definitely a human sound. After a few minutes, her crying grew less violent, and Emilo pulled out a purple handkerchief and pressed it into one of her talons. Jas looked up at the kender.

"You've got to go find Joel, Emilo," Jas said. "Leave me behind."

"I can't," Emilo replied. "Joel wouldn't want me to, and I don't want to. It's two to one. You're outvoted."

"Emilo, the dark stalker could take over again at any moment," Jas growled. "I could end up hunting you for Xvim's people. I could betray you and Joel. I don't deserve to live."

Emilo put his hands on Jas's cheeks and leaned his face very close to hers. "Jas, listen to me very carefully," he said. "There is no dark stalker in you. It's your heart playing tricks on your mind."

Jas drew away from the kender and glared at him angrily. "You don't know what you're talking about," she snapped.

"Maybe not," the kender said, "but Finder and Tymora seemed to think they did. When you and Joel were sampling the wine in Tymora's garden, I followed Finder and Tymora and Winnie to find out what they were talking about."

"So? What did they say?" Jas demanded.

"Finder said that the crazy Xvimlar wizard had cast an ordinary spell on you. The priests told you it would make you into a dark stalker, so you believed them. But all the spell really did was change your shape. When Finder changed you back to your true form, though, he couldn't make you believe you weren't a dark stalker. He told Tymora that your belief was too strong to overcome, but if Tymora cast a spell on you and made it look like it was very powerful, you would believe she had removed the dark stalker because she was so powerful."

"That's ridiculous," Jas hissed. "If the dark stalker wasn't inside me, I never would have changed back."

"Well, Finder had an explanation for that, too. He said the spell the Xvimlar cast on you unbalanced the magic in the wings that Tymora gave you. The magic in your wings is very powerful. So when the magic kind of leaked out into your whole body, your body changed to match your emotions. Kind of like the way your wings change when you go to a different place so that you always fit in. Anyway, there's really no such thing as a spell to make a person into a dark stalker."

"Bear was a dark stalker," Jas argued. "He hunted Finder all the way through Daggerdale."

"Finder was confused by that, too, but Tymora said Bear may have been driven mad by the wizard, and those who are driven mad can sometimes sense power intuitively."

"You're making all this up," Jas shouted. "There's no way I am wrong about the dark stalker. I can *feel* it inside me."

Emilo sighed. "That's because your heart is stronger than your reason. Winnie said it's quite common in cases like yours where you've not only suffered a recent tragedy, but you still haven't recovered from a childhood tragedy. Winnie said what you're feeling inside you isn't a dark stalker, Jas. It's your own guilt and bottled-up grief. You can't let go of them, so they've made a darkness on your soul, which you confused with the lie that the priests of Xvim told you. Winnie didn't think Tymora should go along with Finder's plan to try to fool you. She thought the only thing that could heal you was if you grieved for your parents and your friends and accepted the fact that it wasn't your fault that they died."

"How can I grieve when that murderess is walking around free?" Jas snarled angrily. "It's just like when my parents died. I couldn't do anything to avenge their deaths. My friends' deaths were even worse. Every time I tried to kill their murderer, I failed. I'm useless . . . worse than useless, in fact. I'm helping that bitch just so Tymora doesn't die."

A sudden realization came over the kender. "You mean it was Walinda who murdered your friends?" Emilo asked.

"Walinda tortured them to death," Jas keened. "She

made me watch." The winged woman began sobbing once more.

Emilo stroked her hair some more. After several minutes, Jas grew calm again.

"I thought the only way I was going to fight the dark stalker was to give up hating Walinda," Jas said. "I can't do that. And not just because we're so close to the Bastion of Hate."

"I can understand that," Emilo said. "You don't have to. You just have to accept that Walinda isn't dead yet."

"You tell me how to do that," Jas demanded angrily.

The kender squeezed Jas's shoulders and said fiercely, "Just focus on that word *yet.*"

Act Three
Scene 6

Joel turned about slowly, his eyes trying to adjust to the darkness. Fortunately the room wasn't truly pitch-black. Somewhere ahead was a smoldering brazier. There was a horrendous stench to the room, like an abattoir.

"Who's there?" the bard called out.

"Oooh, a curious one," the whispering voice replied. The echoes in the hall still made it seem to come from everywhere. There was a slight squeak to the whisper, as though it came from a woman or a child . . . or perhaps a halfling or kender.

"I'm Marin the Red," Joel announced, "the captain of the guard of Lord Xvim's throne room, and I demand to know who you are."

Raucous, high-pitched laughter rang through the hall. Leaving his backpacks on the floor, Joel drew his sword and moved forward cautiously.

"Watch out!" the high-pitched voice cried out.

The warning came too late as Joel tripped on something soft. He sprawled across the floor once more.

As he pulled himself to his aching knees, the bard's hands came in contact with what had tripped him—the legs of a human body. Joel ran his hands up the body. It was encased in plate mail. The bard felt around the body's throat. The flesh was cold. There was no pulse.

"That was the last captain of the guard," the voice announced matter-of-factly.

Hastily Joel muttered a spell to cast light upon his sword, but no light appeared. Without the finder's stone his power as a priest wasn't even great enough to cast a simple spell.

"Ouch," the voice said. "I'll bet that's embarrassing.
Can't even spit out a light spell. You must be a looong way
from your god."

Joel crawled back toward the door until he came upon
his backpacks. He rummaged around until he found a few
torches and tucked them under his belt. Then he crawled
toward the dimly glowing brazier. Nothing else blocked
his way. From the coals in the brazier, he lit one of the
torches. In the flickering light, he could see that the room
was littered with bodies, the corpses of priests of Xvim
and human guards. Joel estimated there were at least a
hundred.

"Quite a mess, eh?" the voice commented.

The voice no longer seemed to come from everywhere.
Joel got a fix on the speaker's direction. It was definitely
somewhere up ahead, in the darkness at the far end of the
chamber. Holding the torch in his left hand and his sword
in his right, the bard continued forward cautiously. The
throne room was a vast chamber. The floor was of marble,
and the walls were covered with tapestries depicting de-
tailed, vile scenes of murder. There were several braziers
scattered throughout the room, but all but the one near
the door were cold and dark. There were no other furnishings. At the far end of the room, a broad set of steps led up
to a raised dais. Joel continued to inch his way forward.

The voice laughed again and quipped, "Kid, if you're a
tiefling, I'm a faerie dragon."

Joel held the torch up higher and peered ahead. There,
atop the dais, slumped in a giant-sized throne, was a giant-
sized woman. Save for her size, which Joel estimated to
be over ten feet tall, the woman appeared to be a lovely
human maiden, slender and shapely. Her head lay
slumped upon one arm, and her long, white hair cascaded
to the floor. She wore a black velvet gown, which contrasted
sharply with her milky white skin. Brilliant gem-encrusted
gold jewelry glittered on her arms, about her throat, and in
her hair. The beauty of her features outshone the jewelry.
Joel could see a faint resemblance to Tymora. There could
be no doubt this was Lady Luck's "sister."

Joel climbed halfway up the steps and whispered, "Beshaba?"

"Oooo, aren't you well informed," the high-pitched voice commented with a hint of surprise in its tone.

Joel turned toward the sound and finally discovered the speaker. At the foot of the throne, beside Beshaba's legs, was a large gilded birdcage. Inside the cage was a winged male humanoid creature about a foot and a half high, with bright red skin and a long, scorpionlike tail. It had sharp teeth, an oversize nose, long, pointed ears, and two sharp-tipped, curved horns protruding from its brow, just above its eyes. Although it was completely naked, the creature showed not the least bit of shame as it stood casually leaning against the bars of its cage. Despite Jas's teasing that he only recognized female fiends, Joel knew this creature was an imp. Back home, they served as the familiars of evil wizards and priests. Joel also knew that the stings from their tails were deadly. He moved back a step, just to be sure the tail couldn't reach him through the bars.

"You wound me with your distrust," the imp said. "You have nothing to fear from me. I'm so bored and lonely that I'm grateful for your company. Allow me to introduce myself, Marin the Red. I am Ratagar Perivalious, former associate of the late Tyrannar Noxxe."

"Pleased to meet you, Ratagar," Joel said, letting a hint of sarcasm drip into his tone. He sat down on the step and set the torch down with its flaming end hanging over the edge of the dais. "What happened here?" he asked the imp.

"Ah, thereby hangs a tale," the imp replied. He pointed to Beshaba's unconscious form. "Her Highness showed up two nights ago in a foul mood. When she discovered Xvim wasn't here to meet her, she settled down to wait for him. While she waited, she took out her annoyance on Xvim's priests and followers. See that body just beside that brazier on the left? The one in the fancy green and black brocade?" The imp pointed in the direction of the body in question. "That's the late Tyrannar Noxxe. I tried to warn him not to get involved in these little spats between gods, but you know how young people are these days. You can't tell them anything."

"He didn't try to attack her, did he?" Joel asked in surprise.

"Nothing so courageous," Ratagar replied. "He tried to suggest she go home until Lord Xvim returned. Beshaba decided his beard was hideous—something else I've been trying to tell him for years. Anyway, Her Highness used a little magic to suggest Noxxe shave right there and then. Noxxe's hand slipped. Most unfortunate, wouldn't you say?"

"Definitely bad luck," Joel agreed.

"Most of the others met with similar fates. Those back there were the original guards." Ratagar pointed to a heap of about twenty bodies in a back corner. They had been burned and were still smoldering. "When Her Highness first appeared, they didn't realize how outmatched they were. They sent a lightning bolt in her direction, and the bolt ricocheted back on them. Then the ground started to shake. The floor and the ground beneath it collapsed. Poisonous gas rose up from the sinkhole. That's what killed most of the priests. The gas dissipated quickly when the next wave of priests came rushing in to check out the noise. Of course, they were more cautious, like Noxxe, but none of them groveled and sniveled sufficiently to please Her Highness."

"Except you?" Joel asked.

"Well, I *am* an imp, after all. It is part of my job. More importantly, I'm not one of the Dark One's followers, so she didn't waste her energy on me, except to imprison me into this cage so I couldn't run off. Shortly after that, she passed out. It was several hours before they sent anyone else in here. See that guy over there?" Ratagar pointed to a man lying at the base of the dais with the point of a sword sticking out of his back. "He thought he could attack Her Highness while she slept. He tripped on the stairs and fell on his sword."

"So even though she's unconscious, she's still leaking bad luck," Joel noted.

"A most accurate assessment. You're one clever fellow, even if you aren't a tiefling."

Joel ignored the comment. "What did you mean by calling me a sacrifice when I arrived?" he asked.

"Apparently," Ratagar said, "if there's no one around to soak up the bad luck, it leaks out of the building. So every

hour or so they toss someone in here to sponge it up, so to
speak. One guy choked on an apple. Another slipped on
some blood and cracked his head against the floor. He
moaned a long time before he finally expired. One of the
guards had the bright idea of sitting perfectly still. A
chunk of the ceiling fell on him. I take it Tyrannar Neri
the Nitwit has seized power out there."

"That's who sent me here," Joel said.

"He must be desperate to think sending you here would
work," Ratagar commented.

"Why?" Joel asked.

"Well, according to one of the captains of the guard
they sent in this morning, the one who choked on the
apple, Her Highness seems to be directing the bad luck
even in her unconscious state. He said the bad luck is
only affecting the followers of Xvim. It isn't influencing
the yugoloths. That's one reason there aren't any of them
in here. Not that they'd allow themselves to be used as
sponges anyway. They're mercenaries, not tremendously
devoted to Xvim. Anyway, the priests tossed a captive
barghest in here yesterday, but apparently barghests
aren't on Her Highness's cursed list either. Nothing happened to it, and the bad luck kept leaking out of the tower.
The next person they sent in here, a nasty little novitiate,
passed the time by torturing the barghest. The barghest
got free and tore the priestling to pieces. Then the barghest died."

"So that's why Neri insisted I join the Xvimlar before
he sent me in here," Joel realized.

"Yep. Dotardly old fool. Whatever made him think initi-
ating you would take?"

"Why do you say that?" Joel asked.

"For the same reason I know you're not a tiefling,"
Ratagar explained. "You've got the stink of goodness on
you. Not as bad a stench as a paladin, but I'm willing to
bet you're an honorable guy, a good friend, kind to animals, that sort of nonsense."

"I wouldn't be so sure about that," Joel said. "I'm afraid
I've done my share of evil." He was thinking of Jas's transformation and how his marvelous plan might actually
have been a betrayal.

"Ahhhh, the self-excoriating type. So rare these days. Too many people deny responsibility," the imp declaimed.

"So where's Xvim?" Joel asked.

"Ah! Now, that's the big question. No one knows. He told Noxxe he'd be incommunicado for a few days. Noxxe was supposed to hold down the fort, so to speak."

"Any other ways out of here besides the front door?" Joel asked.

"Of course. Let me out of this cage and I'll show you the way," Ratagar offered, waving his fingers in Joel's direction.

The bard felt an urge to free the fiend, but he realized immediately that the imp had used magic to make the suggestion seem more palatable. Joel shook his head. It was bad enough he was dealing with Walinda. Adding an imp to his list of associates didn't seem like a good idea. He also had to wonder why Beshaba had seen fit to cage the imp instead of killing him or letting him go. So far, Beshaba's bad luck hadn't touched the bard, but if the goddess perceived Joel freeing what she'd seen fit to imprison, he might be the target of her wrath. "I'll have to think about that for a while," Joel said. "I'll get back to you." He picked up his torch and started down the stairs.

"Hey! Where you going, pal?" Ratagar demanded. "Don't leave me here alone," he whined. "I'm afraid of the dark!"

"Don't worry," Joel said as he made his way toward the outer wall of the throne room. "This will all be over soon."

"What's *that* supposed to mean?" Ratagar said with rising panic.

Joel began pushing at the tapestries along the wall until he found one with no wall behind it. Behind the tapestry, he discovered a staircase leading upward. The steps were high and wide, made for the feet of a god with a form as large as the one Beshaba had assumed. Joel fetched his backpacks, then returned to the stairs and began climbing toward the top of Xvim's tower.

Act Three
Scene 7

Jas looked out over the Bastion of Hate from the roof of Xvim's tower. From here, she could see the dark outline of the canyon ridge where Walinda's bar-lgura kept watch in their invisible form. If she looked directly down, Jas could see the torches twinkling along the fortress wall and in the courtyard below. She and Emilo had witnessed the mezzoloths toss someone with a crest of red hair through the tower's front door and lock him inside. The finder's stone confirmed that Joel was somewhere beneath them, but its beam stubbornly pointed to a trapdoor entrance on the tower's roof, which was bolted securely from the other side.

The windows to the tower were blocked by invisible magical barriers, and there were at least twenty yugoloths guarding the front door, so the roof entry was the only way to reach Joel. Emilo was examining it now by the light of a torch, looking for some way to slip the bolt or break through the trapdoor.

After depositing Emilo on the roof of the tower, Jas had tried flying toward Walinda's camp, but the barrier that kept things from flying into the fortress also prevented her from flying away. As far as she could tell, the barrier was a dome that came to a peak over the tower, then fell straight down to the city walls. She returned to the tower roof, having ascertained there was no way out but the gate.

Now she leaned against the parapet and enjoyed the slight breeze. It was hot atop the tower, but not as hot as it was down below. She was feeling a lot calmer now. At first she'd been annoyed that Finder and Tymora had

allowed her to continue in her state of self-deception, but
she realized she wouldn't have believed them if they'd told
her the truth. She believed Emilo, though. She wasn't
sure why, but she was certain the kender was incapable of
deceiving her.

Her hands had returned to normal, but her face was
still covered with feathers and her eyes still glowed. She
suspected that in this unholy realm of the god of hate,
where she couldn't forget her hatred of Walinda, she could
never shed the dark stalker form entirely. The sense that
she was possessed by something evil had faded, however.
She had set aside her guilt that she had not yet destroyed
Walinda by focusing, as Emilo had suggested, on the word
yet. She would find a way to mete out justice to the evil
priestess. In the meantime, Jas was left with only her
grief, which was far more painful but much less frightening.

Frustrated by his failure to slip the bolt on the trapdoor, Emilo poured some lantern oil along the edge of the
door and set it alight. The door was made from stout
wood, though, and did not catch ablaze easily. The kender
succeeded only in charring the wood. Then Jas began
stabbing at it with her dagger, trying to create a hole large
enough for Emilo to get his slender arm through.

"How mad do you think Iyachtu Xvim would be if he
suddenly came home and discovered us vandalizing his
tower?" Emilo asked.

Jas snorted. "From what I've heard about him, you'd be
dead before you found out, which is probably preferable to
being left alive. The church of Xvim is known for its elaborate methods of torturing their sacrifices to death, which
they wouldn't do if it displeased their god."

"I wonder why they locked Joel in there," the kender
mused.

The tip of Jas's dagger chipped on an iron plate beneath the wood. "Damn!" she cursed, kicking the door
with irritation. She fingered the dagger blade to survey
the damage. "What I wouldn't give for a packet of smoke
powder," she said.

"What's that?" Emilo asked.

"Magic powder that causes explosions," Jas explained.

"The beauty of it is you don't have to be a wizard to use it."

"But wouldn't an explosion attract too much attention?" Emilo asked.

"Probably, but it would tear this door to shreds in moments," Jas replied.

Suddenly the door moved. Emilo, who'd been sitting on top of it, hopped off in alarm. Jas flew straight up into the darkness.

The door swung open, and a tall, black-scaled figure with a crest of red hair climbed out of the tower. He had his sword drawn and a grim look on his face.

Jas landed behind the figure with her sword at its back.

In Joel's voice, the figure cried out, "Hey, watch who you poke with that thing."

Sheepishly Jas lowered her weapon, remembering that Joel had disguised himself before they'd arrived. "About time you got up here," she chided the bard. "We've been trying to dig our way through this door for nearly an hour."

Joel collapsed on the rooftop, gasping for air. "You try climbing all those stairs in better time," he challenged Jas when he'd caught his breath once again. "That was worse than the staircase in the Blood Tor. The steps are huge. I had to abandon one of the backpacks after the first hundred steps." The bard tilted his head and peered at Jas. "So you're all right now?" he asked. "I thought—"

"That I'd lost my sanity?" Jas asked. She looked over at the kender and winked. "I gave a pretty good performance, didn't I?"

"You're telling me that was an act?" Joel demanded with disbelief. "What about the way you were transformed?"

"Well, that I can't help," Jas admitted.

"You really had me worried," Joel said.

"Sorry," Jas said.

There was an awkward silence as the bard stared at Jas, trying to discern if she was telling the truth about her earlier behavior.

"So what's down there?" Emilo asked as he peered down into the darkness of the tower.

Joel put the question of Jas's sanity aside for now. "I didn't stop to look into any of the rooms in the upper stories," he explained. "The first floor was interesting enough." The bard described what he'd seen in Xvim's throne room and related everything he'd learned from Ratagar Perivalious.

"Xvim didn't even come back to save his followers from Beshaba?" Emilo asked, wide-eyed with astonishment.

"It's not like he really cares about any of them," Jas pointed out.

Joel shook his head. "He may not care, but he must realize that without his followers, he has no power. And not coming to their defense is a tremendous display of weakness," Joel pointed out. "He didn't even return when Beshaba became unconscious. It's very strange. It's possible he can't return."

"So what now?" Jas asked.

"From what I can tell," Joel said, "all Xvim's priests and followers are cringing in the temple, trying to keep away from Beshaba's bad luck. I noticed one exception. There was a human at the gate. The priests don't dare leave the fortress's only access in the hands of yugoloth mercenaries. Xvim doesn't trust anyone or anything, but his priests preach that humans are the chosen people. My bet is there's a human priest at the gate. He could be fanatically loyal, or he could be dying to leave his post so he can cower in the temple with his fellow priests. I'm going to change my shape into another priest and check him out."

"What about Emilo and me?" Jas asked.

"Well, I thought the pair of you could just run around causing trouble . . . without getting caught, of course. One of the priests told me the yugoloths live in caverns in the cliff wall, but the lava from the mount makes it too dangerous there for humans. I saw several yugoloths coming and going from the bastion walls. Concentrate your sabotage there. Take advantage of any opportunities that present themselves. Scatter Walinda's false gemstones, steal or destroy any weapons or magic you can. When you're done, fly back up here and hide. I'll signal you with the finder's stone when I'm finished at the gate."

Joel used another scroll to change his shape back to

human form, creating the illusion of a shaved head and pierced lip and the robes of a hatemaster. In a superficial way, he now resembled Hatemaster Morr.

Joel took back the finder's stone from Emilo. He slid the stone into his shirt with a visible sense of relief. Then Jas flew the bard down to the bastion wall, as near to the gate as she dared to go. She landed in the shadows of the parapet. The eternal darkness of Gehenna, lit only by lava and torchlight, made sneaking around the fortress possible, especially since no one suspected the adventurers were roaming around unconstrained. The wall adjacent to the gate, though, was better lit.

As Joel made his way toward the gate, Jas returned for Emilo. Together she and the kender slipped into a window in the inner bastion wall that looked out over the courtyard. Then they began exploring.

Although the yugoloths lived in the caverns in the cliff, Jas and Emilo discovered several great mess halls on the ground floor of the structure built between the bastion walls. Most of the tables and benches were suited to the size of the giant cricket-shaped yugoloths, but there were smaller accommodations as well, either for humans or for the lobster-shaped yugoloths.

"This must be the mess hall," Emilo said.

"I thought Joel said the yugoloths live in the caverns in the cliff," Jas murmured. "Why would their mess halls be near the wall?"

"Maybe it's like oats and horses," Emilo suggested. "The food brings the yugoloths in from the cliff like oats bring horses to the stables. Then, after they've eaten, Xvim's men put them to work."

Jas nodded. It made sense. The yugoloths were mercenaries. They weren't going to assemble for work for the love of Xvim; they had to be bribed.

They discovered one mess hall where four human priests, acolytes by the look of their robes, were scooping some white gelatinous porridge into giant bowls and setting them out on the table. The priests finished serving and moved on to the next mess hall.

"This looks like a good place to start," Jas suggested.

An indescribable stench rose from the putrid white

globs in the bowls.

"That stuff would send any decent horse running back
to the pasture," Jas declared.

Emilo scampered down the benches alongside the yugoloths' mess tables as Jas kept watch from the doorway.
He sowed the tables with Walinda's phony gems at ran-
dom intervals. Occasionally he'd drop a gem into a bowl.
Some yugoloths would be rewarded at dinner, while
others would go wanting.

Somewhere nearby someone rang a gong four times.

"They're coming," Jas hissed, hurrying to one of the
narrow windows that looked out over the courtyard.
Emilo hopped down from a bench and hurried after her.
Jas squeezed through the window and perched on the
window's keystone while the kender watched from the
windowsill.

It was only a matter of minutes before discord erupted
as the large yugoloths and their shorter commanders set
to squabbling over the gemstones. Within another few
minutes, there was all-out warfare in the mess hall.

Jas scooped up the kender and moved on. They planted
the seeds of discontent in two more mess halls before they
ran out of gems. Then they sneaked in through a window
of the wall's upper level.

In a locked room, opened handily by Emilo, the pair
discovered an arsenal of missile weaponry: arrows, crossbows, and spears. The same room was lined with arrow
slits along the outer wall of the bastion.

Emilo poked an arrow out a window slit. There was no
invisible barrier to stop it, but when the kender tried to
draw the arrow back inside, the arrow stuck in midair.
"It's a one-way barrier," he noted. "We could push everything out the windows."

Jas shook her head. "The yugoloths stationed atop the
wall are likely to hear the clatter. We have to find someplace— Hello. What have we here?" The winged woman
held up a strange-looking device Emilo had never seen before. It looked like a short hollow wand with a wooden
handle.

"What is it?" Emilo asked.

"An arquebus. It's a weapon that uses smoke powder,"

Jas explained. With her sword, she began prying the lid off the small barrel next to which she'd found the arquebus. "Remember that stuff I mentioned before? The stuff that causes explosions?" Jas yanked the lid off the barrel to reveal a fine silver and black powder.

"Is that smoke powder?" Emilo asked, stepping closer and sniffing. "Ew. I once knew a gnome that smelled like that."

"Stay back with that torch," Jas ordered the kender. "Gods, if only Arandes was alive to see this," she murmured as she stirred her fingers gently through the powder that filled the barrel. "He was a gif," she explained to Emilo. "Gif measure their honor in part by how much smoke powder they possess."

"Is that a lot of smoke powder?" Emilo asked.

"Oh, yes," Jas replied, pressing the lid back onto the small barrel. "I wonder if there's any more around. . . ."

Act Three
Scene 8

Joel drew out a torch from his belt and lit it from another torch burning in a sconce on the parapet. If the giant yugoloths could see in the dark, they would spot him easily. He might as well appear as if he had every right to be on the wall. He strode with purpose along the road between the two walls in the direction of the gate.

Giant yugoloths milled about everywhere atop the walls. Some stared outward from the bastion, but most leaned along the inner wall, watching their fellows drilling in the courtyard below. Bored out of their minds, Joel expected. There were none of the smaller yugoloths atop the wall at the moment. No doubt they came up here only to make periodic inspections.

The bard halted when he stood over the gate. If the gatehouse was laid out as he expected, the controls for the gate would be in a room just above the gate—directly beneath his feet. There was a trapdoor near the outer wall that must lead down to the control room. Two yugoloths stood on it.

Joel looked out over the wall to the outside of the fortress with an expression of annoyance on his face. After a moment, he whirled around and addressed the nearest yugoloth. "Tyrannar Neri is expecting a visitor. She is late in arriving. Have you spotted anyone approaching the bastion?" he demanded imperiously.

The yugoloth shrugged and shook its head.

Joel tapped his foot impatiently and glared at the yugoloth as if it might be lying. After a moment, he said, "I need to speak with the gatekeeper immediately."

Joel felt a sharp pain in one side of his head, and the

yugoloth's telepathic words formed in his mind: *Not standard procedure*, the yugoloth informed him.

"I know it's not standard procedure," Joel snapped. "It's not standard procedure for the tyrannar to cower in the temple either, or for an angry goddess to take up residence in our lord's throne room, now, is it?"

Not our fault the gatekeeper let her in, the yugoloth insisted.

Joel rolled his eyes as if he were tired of the yugoloths excuses. "I know that," he said. "Unless you—"

An excuse not to pay us on time, the yugoloth argued.

"Since when does the tyrannar need an excuse?" Joel growled. "As I was saying, unless you want a repetition of the whole ugly affair with Beshaba, I suggest you let me speak with the gatekeeper."

Another power is coming? the yugoloth demanded. The creature chittered with its teeth in what Joel presumed was a nervous reaction.

"Beshaba has a sister, you know," Joel replied curtly.

Several of the yugoloths joined in a chorus of chittering. The yugoloth who was communicating with Joel motioned with its head, and the two standing on the trapdoor stepped aside. One of the yugoloths pulled on the ring that opened the door. A flicker of torchlight shone in the hole below. A ladder led downward. Joel could see no sign of the gatekeeper.

Joel handed his torch to the yugoloth spokesman and began climbing down the ladder. When he'd gone down four steps, he looked up at the yugoloth and ordered, "Close the door behind me. I'll knock when I'm ready to leave." Then the bard continued his descent.

With his hand clenched about the little wooden harp, Joel stepped down to the floor of the gate's control room. It was possible the gatekeeper would prove to be some creature he couldn't deceive. If such a creature, whatever it was, attacked him, he would be left with no choice but to flee to Fermata.

The air was suffocating in the room below. It took Joel's eyes a few minutes to adjust to the dim light of a single torch. A tiny window in the outer wall looked out over the gate, and another one on the opposite wall looked out over

the courtyard. An array of large gears, levers, and handles
occupied the other two walls.

There were signs that the gatekeeper actually lived in
the room. A cot stood against the outer window, and beneath that a chamber pot. On a small table beside the cot
rested a water bottle and a half-finished meat pie.

A figure stood beside the cot. Joel's eyes widened in
surprise. While his inductive reasoning had proved correct—the gatekeeper did indeed prove to be a human, and
a priest -the gatekeeper's identity came as a bit of a shock
to the bard. The gatekeeper wore the robes of a novice. He
was tall and handsome, with blue eyes and golden hair.

It was the same priest of Xvim Joel had battled four
nights ago in Sigil. The priest who had arranged for Jas's
abduction. The priest who had deliberately killed himself
by slicing his flesh to shreds on the razorvine. Upon his
death, the Xvimlar had returned here to his god's realm
as a petitioner.

Lucky I disguised my features, Joel thought. It was
lucky, too, that he had learned the priest's name from
Walinda's interrogation of the dead hydroloth. "I am Hatemaster Camfer, Hatemaster Perr," the bard greeted the
man.

The priest bowed. "Perr?" Was that my name?" he
asked.

Suddenly Joel remembered that petitioners recalled
nothing of their past lives. Finder had given his only two
petitioners their names again, but apparently the Xvimlar didn't bother with such niceties.

"Yes," Joel answered.

"I was powerful then," Perr noted, with a hint of anger
in his voice.

Joel was struck with an idea. An unsettled gatekeeper
was a poor gatekeeper. A true follower of Xvim would
never settle for such a lowly position. Even as a petitioner,
a follower of Xvim would be ambitious, would despise
others, especially those who kept him from the superior
position of power to which his faith entitled him.

"Yes," Joel replied. "Before you died, you were powerful.
If you had succeeded in your last mission, they would
have made you a ruinlord . . . possibly."

"Possibly? Why possibly?" Perr asked.

"Well, you know the political situa— Oh, excuse me. I'd forgotten. You don't remember, do you?" Joel asked.

"No," Perr replied with a chill tone.

"Suffice it to say you did not get along with Tyrannar Neri, but he might still have promoted you. After all, you were his man. Tyrannar Noxxe, on the other hand, never appreciated your devotion."

"But Tyrannar Noxxe is dead," Perr noted.

"But he wouldn't have died if Beshaba hadn't entered the fortress, which she might not have done if you had been successful in your last mission. But if you had been successful and lived, Noxxe might still be alive and you wouldn't be promoted. Hence, I qualified my statement with 'possibly.' "

"What was my last mission in life?" Perr asked.

"Well, your cover story was you were bringing back a runaway slave. Actually, you were involved in arranging an attack on Beshaba's fortress," Joel lied.

"Why?"

Joel shrugged. "I do not know. You would not tell me more before you left."

"I told you of my mission? Were we friends?" Perr asked.

"Hardly," Joel said with a sniff. "We are, after all, priests of Xvim. It would be more accurate to say we share most of the same enemies. Nonetheless, it irks me to see you reduced to this menial role. It's a waste of your talents."

"I am gatekeeper of the Bastion of Hate," Perr growled. "It is an honor accorded me for having died in service to Lord Xvim."

"Look around you. This is a slave's job. It's been pushed off on you because you're an expendable petitioner," Joel retorted. "Everyone of any power is in the temple trying to hide from Beshaba's spreading ill luck. Otherwise they'd put someone with more sense in here. Tell me, did you let Beshaba into the fortress because she enchanted you, or did you hope she might destroy Tyrannar Noxxe?"

"I did not *let* her in," Perr shouted angrily. "She tore both gates in half. Nearly a hundred yugoloths died trying to block her entry before they realized she was a goddess and fled before her mad eyes."

"Really?" Joel asked with astonishment. "Excuse me. I see that Tyrannar Neri has misinformed me concerning the goddess's arrival. He's convinced the surviving yugoloths that you let her in. No doubt Neri was eager to convince everyone that you were not worthy of this post, let alone one more challenging and suitable to one of your power."

"I had the gate repaired in less than two hours," Perr said proudly. "And it functions perfectly—better, in fact, than it did before."

"Well, that is hardly surprising," Joel said, "considering the talents you possessed in life. As I said before, your talents are wasted in this position."

"Are you prepared to offer me another position, Hatemaster Camfer?" Perr asked.

Joel smiled. "That all depends," he said. He turned to look out the window of the inner bastion wall, the one that overlooked the courtyard. The giant yugoloths were still performing marching drills down below.

"On what?" Perr asked.

Joel turned back to face the petitioner. "Tyrannar Neri has insulted you by placing you here," he insisted. "He may even have been behind the failure of your last mission. Just because the other tyrannars call him Neri the Nitwit doesn't mean that Neri isn't a cunning man. My offer depends on your hatred of this man whom you should call your enemy. Is your hate great enough to spur you to action? Are you prepared to seize the power that should rightfully be yours?"

Perr's lips were set in a sneer, and his blue eyes glittered in the torchlight like a fiend ready to do battle in the Blood War. Despite his hatred, Perr was no one's fool. "I presume you have a plan to do away with Tyrannar Neri that will put me at great risk," he stated bluntly.

Joel smiled coldly. "It will only put you at risk if it fails," he said. "Naturally the plan does not depend on you, though it will be easier if you help us. The risk you take will serve as proof you are worthy of the power with which you will be rewarded. Of course, you are free to turn down my offer should you prefer to serve out the rest of eternity as a slave."

"I am a petitioner. I will soon merge with Lord Xvim," Perr countered.

Merging with one's god was the ultimate goal for a petitioner, Finder had explained to Joel. When the petitioner's spirit was sufficiently like his god's, the two became as one. Of course, the spiritual growth necessary for a merger would be far different for petitioners of Xvim than the petitioners of any other god.

"Perhaps you have confused Lord Xvim with a god of obedient sheep," Joel retorted haughtily. "Slaves do not merge with the New Darkness. A petitioner must become as Lord Xvim himself is, consumed by hatred and a tyrant over all, before there can be a merger. We have never had to replace a gatekeeper because one merged with Lord Xvim."

Perr glared at Joel, but he did not deny the wisdom of the false hatemaster's words. "So what is your plan, and how will I be rewarded?" he asked.

"First," Joel said, "tell me, when someone calls at the gate, who decides to let him in?"

Perr shrugged. "I don't know exactly. I drop a note out that window," he said, pointing to the window looking out over the courtyard, "and a yugoloth carries it to the temple. I wait at the window until Hatemaster Morr arrives and signals me to open the gate. If he does not give me the signal to open the gate or does not come, I do not open the gate."

Which was why, Joel realized, Hatemaster Morr had been the one to greet "Marin the Red" at the gate. "And would you ever question Hatemaster Morr's signal?" Joel asked.

"Of course not," Perr insisted. "Tyrannar Neri ordered me to obey his commands."

"Suppose there were an army of tanar'ri sitting at the gate, commanded by a priestess of Beshaba?"

"Why would Hatemaster Morr signal me to open the gate to such an army?" Perr asked with surprise.

"Would that make a difference as to whether or not you would obey him?" Joel asked.

Perr looked confused. "Such at thing would be a betrayal of Lord Xvim," he said.

"Only if Lord Xvim gave a damn," Joel said. "Suppose Lord Xvim enticed Beshaba here as a test of his tyrannars—a test that I believe they have all failed. They cower in the temple waiting for Lord Xvim to return and save them all. Not one is filled with enough hatred to seize the opportunity offered them. Beshaba—the goddess herself, not merely one of her avatars—lies unconscious in Lord Xvim's throne room, no doubt from some magic set there by the lord himself. Yet not one of the tyrannar acts to destroy Lord Xvim's enemy."

"You can't kill a goddess," Perr insisted. Then, less certainly, he asked, "Can you?"

"A mortal, no. But another goddess could."

"What goddess?" Perr asked with obvious fascination.

"Tymora," Joel said. "She and her sister, Beshaba, have always hated one another. Of course, this works to the glory of Lord Xvim. He feeds on their hatred, for the hatred and tyranny of the gods can be far more powerful than that of mere mortals. I have lured Tymora here with the information that Xvim has abducted one of Tymora's favorites, the bird woman Jasmine, and plans to give her to Beshaba. Tymora is so enraged that she fully intends to destroy Beshaba. I think Lord Xvim would be most pleased if the death were to take place in his holy tower."

Perr's jaw dropped, and he remained speechless for several moments. Joel did not spoil the mood by breaking the silence. He waited patiently for Perr to react. Finally the petitioner said, "It is dangerous . . . but so brilliant." There was admiration in the look he gave Joel.

"I haven't much more time to waste," the bard said. "It doesn't really matter whether you open the gate or not, because Tymora can tear it in half as easily as Beshaba did. I am telling you this only to test your loyalties. Tymora will come disguised as a priestess of Beshaba, because she believes Beshaba is in league with Xvim and that we will admit a priestess to attend her mistress. If we fail to admit her, she will admit herself, and her army of tanar'ri will attack the yugoloths until she reaches Beshaba. The tyrannars know nothing of my plan."

"But Hatemaster Morr does?" Perr asked.

"Hatemaster Morr is dead," Joel replied, "though his body has not yet been discovered."

"Is that why you go shaven and pierced as Hatemaster Morr does—did? To imitate him?" Perr asked.

"It is satisfying to learn that death has not dulled your keen mind," Joel replied. "I have noticed that the yugoloths have nearly as much trouble distinguishing one human from another as we do telling the yugoloths apart. They recognize Hatemaster Morr's naked head and lip ring rather than his features."

"So you will give me the signal to open the gate. If I do, how will I be rewarded?" Perr asked, obviously excited. He was breathing more quickly now.

"That will depend on how Lord Xvim rewards me. Though I wear the robes of a hatemaster to imitate Hatemaster Morr, I am actually a ruinlord. I believe Lord Xvim will raise me to the rank of a tyrannar. I will then ask that you not only be restored to the rank and power of a hatemaster, but to the rank and power you should have attained had Tyrannar Neri not foiled your last mission. I will ask Lord Xvim to make you a ruinlord. Although you are a petitioner, he can grant you such power. That is, of course, assuming you have not yet by then merged with Lord Xvim. This scheme might be the chance you await. What greater tyranny can a mortal attain than to aid in the destruction of a god? What greater hatred can he show than betraying commanders who are actually his inferiors?"

Perr flicked his right hand backward at the wrist. "That is the signal Hatemaster Morr gives to open the gate," he said.

Joel imitated the signal. "Darkness falls," he intoned solemnly, imitating the greetings he had heard exchanged by other priests of Xvim.

"And darkness rises again," Perr responded.

Once Joel had crawled out of the gatekeeper's suffocating quarters, he began to shiver despite the warmth of the Gehennan air. He had the uncomfortable feeling he had been transformed into a priest of the god Cyric, Prince of Lies. He pressed his hand against the finder's stone inside

his shirt and was comforted by its warmth. Finder was
still with him.

The yugoloth he'd spoken to earlier was staring at him.
He stared back, debating whether or not to try to convince
these creatures not to defend the fortress when the
tanar'ri attack came. In the end, he decided not to try. It
would be far more complicated than it had been to convince Perr to open the gate. The yugoloths would take
their orders from a higher-ranking yugoloth, and Joel had
no way of knowing which one that would be. Without actually lying, he had already suggested to them that Tymora was coming. Considering what had happened to
their fellows when Beshaba had arrived, that deception
might keep them from attacking Walinda, providing this
yugoloth spread the rumor that Tymora was expected.

Joel knew better than to repeat the lie, though. It
would look manipulative. Either the yugoloths gossiped or
they didn't.

He strode off down the wall until he turned a corner.
There were more yugoloth guards up ahead. He noticed
another trapdoor at his feet. He opened it without a trace
of furtiveness. The ladder leading down into the darkness
below was scaled for a large yugoloth, but Joel managed to
make his way down it without breaking his neck.

Joel pulled out the finder's stone. By its light, he could
see that he was in a room with a window looking out over
the courtyard. The room was empty save for him, a table
and a chair, and a dead yugoloth, one of the short, lobsterlike ones. It lay on its back, its carapace sliced down the
center from its head to the bottom of its tail. Its entrails
had been pulled out and stomped on.

From somewhere in the walls, Joel caught the muffled
sounds of a battle with swords. He stood at the window
and thought of Jas. The finder's stone sent a beacon of
light up to another part of the wall. Joel hoped Jas was
paying attention, for he didn't dare use the beacon for
long. After only a few heartbeats, he slipped the magic
crystal back into his shirt and stepped to one side of the
window.

The bard counted to five hundred before returning to
the window to resignal the winged woman, but Jas

appeared in the window just as Joel was pulling out the finder's stone. She had Emilo with her.

"Sorry we took so long," Jas apologized. "We were just finishing up. Did you know that Walinda's troops are starting to mass outside the bastion?"

"She said she'd give me half a day," Joel replied.

"Well, apparently she got impatient," Jas retorted. She looked down at the dead yugoloth on the floor. "Your handiwork?" she asked.

Joel shook his head. "I take it it isn't yours either."

"No," Jas replied. "Looks like one of the bigger yugoloths got tired of taking orders from this guy."

"We started the fighting going on down the hall," Emilo said excitedly. "And Jas has set up fifteen barrels of smoke powder to explode."

"You did *what?*" Joel gasped. "Do you know how dangerous that stuff is? It's been outlawed in fifteen cities in the Heartlands."

"Trust me," Jas said. "I know what I'm doing. It may be enough to knock a hole in the outer wall, and maybe not. At any rate, it will make a great diversion. What did you find out about the gate?"

"I think I've got the gatekeeper convinced to open the gate on my signal. Unless he's got me completely fooled, or he changes his mind, or he figures out I'm not a ruinlord of Xvim."

Suddenly there was a tremendous boom, like a fireball cast by an ancient wizard, and the floor shook beneath them.

"Was that another quake from Beshaba?" Emilo asked.

Jas leaned out the window and peered out into the darkness. "Damn! I think my smoke powder went off a little early," she declared.

Joel looked out the window. A fire burned out of control on the wall across the courtyard from them.

"Does it look to you like the wall's collapsed a little?" Jas asked.

"It's too dark for me to tell," Joel replied. "This isn't good," he huffed. "Now the priests are going to be on the alert. I thought you said you knew what you were doing."

"Hey, as hot as it is in this place, anything could have

set it off," Jas retorted. "Maybe a yugoloth got careless with a torch, or a little fountain of lava sprouted up nearby. Walinda had to be near enough to hear it. Maybe she'll take it as a sign to begin her attack."

"I was hoping we might avoid a big battle," Joel said.

"What difference does it make?" Jas said. "So some yugoloths and some tanar'ri tear each other apart."

"Holly's out there," Joel reminded the winged woman. "You heard how upset she was about Walinda sacrificing her troops. She's likely to try to protect the bar-lgura."

Jas looked down at the floor, unable to argue with the bard's assessment.

"Maybe you better try summoning Walinda now with the finder's stone," Emilo suggested, "before the priests get themselves organized."

Joel nodded. "You're right," he agreed. "Jas, fly me down to the ground near the wall. I'll signal her through the gate. While I'm taking care of that, I want you to take Emilo back to the tower. Emilo, climb down the stairs to the throne room on the first floor and wait there without giving yourself away. Walinda's betrayed us more than once in the past. We need to keep you in reserve in case she proves ungrateful for all we've done for her. Stay away from the imp. Jas, I may not need you, but wait for my signal, just in case."

Once on the ground in the courtyard, Joel made his way along the wall toward the gate. The larger yugoloths were no longer drilling in formation but milling about in large, tight herds, while the shorter ones were trying to reorganize them. A group of novice priests emerged from a door in the wall and hurried toward him.

"Hatemaster, what's going on?" one of the novices asked.

"What's going on?" Joel imitated the man's panicked voice. "Tyrannar Neri is setting off fireworks to announce the start of his tea party," the bard replied sarcastically. "What do you think is going on, you ninny? We're under attack, of course. If you know what's good for you, you'll get back inside the wall."

"Wouldn't we be safer in the temple?" another novice asked.

It might be better, the bard realized, if he could keep the
novices separated from the temple so the higher-ranking
priests within received no information. He had to make
them think it was their idea, however.

"Fine. Go right ahead," Joel said. "The yugoloths are in
some sort of snit about not being paid, but if you want to
walk past them while they're in such a quarrelsome mood,
feel free," he added, waving his arm in the direction of the
courtyard.

The novices glanced nervously at the yugoloths milling
about in the courtyard, then turned and hurried back
through the door into the wall. Joel continued on toward
the gate.

When he came to the iron portcullis, he halted and
peered out into the darkness. Against the red glow of the
lava river, he saw the silhouettes of hundreds of bulezau.
There was no sign of the bar-lgura or Walinda. Joel pulled
out the finder's stone and concentrated on the priestess.
The beacon of light shot through the portcullises of the
inner and outer walls and struck a boulder not more than
a hundred yards away from the gate.

Come on, Walinda, the bard thought impatiently. I
can't signal for them to open the gate if they don't see you.
He slipped the finder's stone back into his shirt.

Joel didn't care whether the priestess made her appearance because of the signal from the finder's stone or
because she had read the bard's thoughts as long as her
appearance made an impressive spectacle. Suddenly the
air around the boulder shimmered and the priestess manifested herself. She was kneeling on the magic carpet,
which hovered five feet off the ground. As the carpet
glided forward, Holly stepped from the dark ranks of the
bulezau and walked along beside it. Then the marilith
slithered forward behind Holly.

The carpet halted directly before the gate. The ebon
aura of power that surrounded the evil priestess had
grown until it blocked out the light from the lava river behind her.

From the wall above, Joel heard the gatekeeper call
out, "Who goes there?"

Walinda, with her head held high and her back as

straight as an eastern princess's, called out, "I am
Walinda of Beshaba. I have come at the summons of Lady
Beshaba."

Joel stepped back away from the portcullis so that Petitioner Perr could see him from the window in the gate control room.

Perr looked down upon the bard disguised as Hatemaster Morr. Joel gave him the signal to open the gate.
Perr disappeared from the window.

All right, Perr, old buddy, Joel thought, this is it. Your
moment of destiny. Please don't make me look like a fool.

Both portcullises raised up all the way, as if Perr
wanted to be sure this woman he believed to be Beshaba's
sister didn't feel inclined to damage his newly repaired
gates.

"Enter and be welcome, Walinda of Beshaba," Joel
called out, "in the name of the New Darkness."

One of the larger yugoloths came running up to Joel
and halted at his side. An agonizing pain blazed across
the bard's head as the creature shouted telepathically,
*There are hundreds of invisible bar-lgura all around the
priestess!*

"I am aware of that," Joel lied, realizing that the yugoloths could see the invisible beings he had only suspected
were present. The magic carpet carried Walinda through
the gatehouse. Holly and the marilith entered beside her.
All three moved toward the bard.

The bar-lgura are entering the courtyard!

"It's all right," the bard said with a calm, reassuring
tone. "They are our allies."

The yugoloth grabbed at Joel's robe and shook him. *Allies do not enter with their weapons drawn!*

The marilith's tail whipped around the yugoloth, and
she yanked the struggling creature toward her. She lay all
six hands on the creature's body and hissed.

Joel's mind reeled with the yugoloth's telepathic
scream as the marilith's touch magically bruised and
burned the creature's body.

"Leave him be!" the bard shouted at the snake-woman.
The yugoloth vanished.

"What did you do to him?" Joel demanded.

He fled from my attack with his magic, the marilith answered telepathically.

Walinda leaned forward on the magic carpet. "Is that you, Poppin?" she asked with astonishment.

"Of course it's Joel," Holly snapped. "He's the only person here not radiating evil."

"I am impressed, priest of Finder," the priestess said. "I had no idea you would prove such a talented saboteur. You have ensured our victory."

"And you may have just thrown it away," Joel retorted sharply. "You still have to win your way to Beshaba. We might have reached her with stealth, but now that you've attacked one of the guards, we may not be able to avoid a fight."

Even as the bard spoke, the giant yugoloths in the courtyard surged toward the intruders.

"So there will be a fight," Walinda said. "That is what we have armies for."

The yugoloths stopped about a hundred feet away from the wall, and it soon became clear that they were blocked by invisible bar-lgura. The larger yugoloths apparently had no trouble seeing the shorter apelike tanar'ri, invisible or not, and engaged them in combat. As the bar-lgura began to fight back, they broke the spell of invisibility that surrounded them. Then Joel was able to see what had so alarmed the yugoloth who'd tried to warn him. Hordes of tanar'ri surrounded Walinda.

The marilith raised a horn to her lips and sounded a call to battle. Moments later the minotaurlike bulezau, in all their horrifying visibility, began streaming through the gates, flanking outward along the wall, territory which the bar-lgura had claimed for them. Several of the bulezau carried magic killers. As the iron latticework spheres passed near the invisible bar-lgura, they became visible again.

Joel looked toward the temple, but so far there was no sign that the priests of Xvim had chosen to leave their refuge to investigate either the explosion or the sounds of battle that they surely must have heard.

"Beshaba is on the first floor of that tower," Joel told the others. "If we hurry, we might still make it to the roof and down the stairs before it occurs to the yugoloths to block our access to your goddess."

Suddenly a shower of spears hailed down upon them from the bastion wall. Several struck the bulezau and the bar-lgura near the wall. One spear bounced off Holly's shoulder plate. Another struck Joel in the leg, just above his knee.

The bard cried out and fell forward.

"Get him on the carpet," Walinda ordered.

Invisible bar-lgura hands lifted the bard into the air and laid him on the magic carpet beside the evil priestess.

Joel ignored the fiery pain and called out to Holly to get on the carpet, too.

At that moment, a column of fire shot down from the sky and struck the paladin.

"Carpet, up fifty feet," Walinda commanded.

"No!" Joel shouted as the carpet began rising above the battle, leaving Holly on the ground. "Carpet, go down," he ordered.

"Silence him!" Walinda snapped.

Large, hairy arms belonging to an invisible bar-lgura grabbed the bard from behind and covered his mouth. As Joel struggled, the bar-lgura's invisibility dispelled, but the bard was unable to break from the apelike fiend's grasp.

"Carpet, go up another fifty feet," Walinda ordered. "Don't be foolish, Poppin," she said to Joel. "The paladin's holiness makes her a natural target. We cannot afford to keep her beside us."

Then Joel spotted Jas swooping down toward Holly, and he ceased his struggles. He turned to glare at the priestess as she directed the flying carpet up to the roof of the tower.

The marilith and her two hezrou lieutenants had used their power to teleport to the roof. By the time Joel and Walinda arrived, they already stood beside the parapet surrounding the roof. The toadlike hezrou were sniffing at the air as the snake-woman looked with a critical eye at the ground far below. Walinda settled the carpet just behind where the marilith stood. At a signal from the priestess, the bar-lgura released Joel. The apelike tanar'ri rolled off the carpet and began sniffing the air as well.

Walinda pulled the spear from Joel's leg, laid her hands on the bard's wound, and began a healing chant. Unlike the warmth of Holly's healing touch, Walinda's spell sent icy fire shooting through Joel's flesh. It stanched the blood and eased the pain, but it left the bard shivering and feeling numb with cold.

The priestess and the bard stood and joined the marilith at the parapet. Joel searched without success for any sign of Jas and Holly, although he did spot one of the giant frog hydroloths teleporting into the air and gliding down toward the bulezau who held the gate.

The marilith pointed toward several yugoloths who were massing at the front door of the tower nearly a hundred feet below. The yugoloths were pointing upward. They had spotted the carpet and were undoubtedly debating whether or not they should enter the tower from below to keep the adventurers from reaching the prisoner inside.

The marilith hissed and spat. A great, billowing yellowish green cloud appeared just beneath the top of the tower, blocking their view of the ground below. From the stench, Joel realized the vapor must be poisonous. The cloud slid down along the wall of the tower like a slithering creature. It sank to the ground, covering the hordes of yugoloths at the tower's front door.

Suddenly the bar-lgura standing beside them gave a horrible cry and fell to the ground. Four spears were buried in the creature's back.

Walinda, Joel, and the marilith spun about. One small lobsterlike yugoloth and six giant cricket companions stood on the roof between them and the trapdoor leading into the tower. More yugoloths of varying sizes quickly joined them.

The marilith drew out six ornate swords and engaged in battle with the front line of yugoloths, her tail lashing at those her arms couldn't reach. The hezrou, armed with spears, took up the fight on their mistress's flanks.

Jas landed on the roof, carrying Holly. The paladin's armor was scorched, and there was a coating of ash on her skin and hair. Despite the column of flame that had struck her, she was not only conscious but able to stand, much to Joel's relief.

"Are you all right?" the bard asked.

"Just fine," Holly growled through clenched teeth. She drew her sword and proceeded to engage the yugoloths in combat.

Then the bard remembered that Holly, too, had a ring of fire resistance.

Jas drew her weapon and took up a stance next to Holly.

The marilith struck at a yugoloth, and the giant cricket creature disappeared. At almost the same instant, Holly hit one of the giant cricket fiends, and it, too, vanished. Both had been illusions. The marilith and the hezrou struck two more yugoloths, but these yugoloths were real and did not disappear.

"They've mirror-imaged themselves," Walinda noted with annoyance. "They can continue to do so over and over again."

"And in the meantime, more can teleport up here," Joel pointed out. "But remember, you didn't mind a fight, as long as it was between your pawns and Xvim's pawns," he accused the priestess.

Walinda smiled coldly. "This is a minor problem, Poppin," she said. "Carpet, up twelve feet," she said.

Joel rolled from the carpet before the priestess was able to drag him away from his friends a second time.

Walinda hovered over the combat and called out," Yugoloths, hear me!" The priestess's voice was deep and booming. "I will offer one hundred gold pieces to each warrior who serves me for the next hour."

All the yugoloths looked up at the priestess. The yugoloths in the front line stepped away from Holly, Jas, and the marilith.

One of the shorter yugoloths stepped forward and looked up at Walinda. The creature must have addressed the priestess telepathically, for Walinda nodded and said, "Done."

With a gesture from the priestess, a brass chest appeared at the small yugoloth's feet. The yugoloth opened the chest. It was filled to the brim with gold coins.

"You will allow us to enter the tower, then you will guard the door behind us and keep any others from following us for one hour," Walinda said.

The yugoloth drew back from the trapdoor.

"Go," Walinda ordered Joel, Jas, and Holly.

The paladin and the winged woman hurried to the trapdoor and rushed down the stairs, but Joel sat down on the magic carpet. He was unwilling to leave it behind.

"The stairway is wide enough to fly down," he told the priestess.

"Is your leg still aching, Poppin?" the priestess asked in mock sympathy.

"Of course it's still aching. You're a lousy healer," Joel retorted.

Walinda smiled tightly and knelt down beside the bard. Then she gave orders for the carpet to rise a foot and glide forward.

Stentka Taran and the hezrou followed behind them. Joel pulled out the finder's stone to light the way as Walinda maneuvered the carpet expertly down the stairs.

As they soared down the vast staircase, the magic that gave Joel the form of a priest of Xvim faded, having reached the limit of the spell's power. Walinda made no comment when the bard changed appearance. She seemed to be lost in thought, occasionally glancing back at Stentka Taran.

The bard sat very still, trying to compose himself. He was still furious with Walinda for abandoning Holly, but he knew he couldn't allow that emotion to color his dealings with Beshaba. Finder had told him to bring the goddess to the spire, and Joel was determined not to disappoint his god.

The throne room was just as Joel had left it. Walinda landed the carpet on the dais beside Beshaba's unconscious figure. The priestess bowed her head before her goddess and held her hands before her. She appeared to be praying silently. Joel rose to his feet and backed away.

"Is that you Marin?" Ratagar called from his cage. "You've shed your scales, but I recognized the red hair. I knew you weren't a tiefling. I can't believe you came back. Are you nuts, kid?" he asked Joel.

The bard didn't reply. He was looking around anxiously for his friends.

He spied Holly standing at the base of the dais. The paladin was cradling her head in her hands. Either she was shocked by the death and destruction all around or overwhelmed by the tremendous sense of evil that pervaded the throne room. Probably both, Joel thought.

"You certainly have an eclectic group of friends, Marin the Red," the imp noted. "Paladins, mariliths, evil priestesses, pretty girls with wings . . ."

Jas landed just behind the bard.

"Where's Emilo?" Joel whispered.

"He's beside Holly," Jas said.

Then Joel spotted the kender, who was standing on the third step of the dais. Emilo reached out and stroked the paladin's hair in a comforting gesture. Even more odd than the kender's gift of being overlooked was the way Jas could always spot him. The bard shook his head, unable to understand it.

"You really have no idea of the evil you're perpetrating," Ratagar said to Joel.

Stentka Taran slithered up beside the paladin. Before Joel realized what was happening, the marilith wrapped two of her arms about Holly's waist, and with two more hands grabbed the paladin's wrists. With her third set of hands, the snake-woman manacled Holly's arms together. The marilith tossed the chain attached to the manacles to one of her hezrou lieutenants.

"No!" Joel shouted, leaping toward the stairs, but the marilith lunged forward and, with a single deft action, tossed him down the stairs. He landed on his uninjured leg, twisting his knee.

"Walinda!" Jas shrieked as she took to the air. "Stop that snake creature, you bitch!"

Walinda looked up from her prayer, slightly annoyed.

"I'm sorry, Poppin," she said, "but I was forced to pay the yugoloths on the roof with all the gold that was meant for Stentka Taran. She has agreed instead to take the paladin in payment."

"Ooooo! Betrayal," Ratagar squealed with glee. "What fun!"

Unable to stand, his knee burning with pain, Joel was forced to plead from the floor. "Walinda, think what you're doing." He struggled for some argument, no matter how useless, knowing only that he had to stall for time. Still unnoticed by all the evil beings, Emilo was even now picking the locks on the manacles that bound Holly's wrists.

"Lathander offered his paladin to help your goddess," Joel said fervently. "If you let this creature take Holly, you will be offending the Morninglord, and he is far more powerful than Beshaba."

"For all his goodness, Lathander has no interest in helping Beshaba," Walinda countered. "He only wants to know what she knows so that he might help Tymora. I care not whether he is offended."

Emilo finally finished picking the locks on the manacles. Holly jerked the restraints from her wrist and let them fall to the floor with a clatter. She leaped backward and drew her sword, leveling it at the belly of the hezrou.

"Hey," the imp cried out in surprise. "How'd she do that?"

Jas landed beside Holly, her sword also drawn. "You won't take her without bloodshed," the winged woman snarled at the marilith.

Stentka Taran looked toward Walinda.

The priestess sighed. "You will have to charge me interest on what I owe you," she said to the marilith. "We will settle accounts in a few days time."

The marilith nodded. She slithered away, back up the stairs. The hezrou hopped behind her.

Walinda glared at Holly. "You have cost me dearly," she said accusingly.

Holly laughed, completely astounded by the evil priestess's selfishness.

"That was an interesting trick. How did you do it?" she said, repeating the imp's question.

"Walinda, don't you think we should be getting on with reviving your goddess?" Joel asked, trying to keep the priestess from guessing at the presence of the unnoticed kender.

Walinda nodded. "Yes, of course," she agreed.

The priestess approached her goddess slowly and reverently. With an atypical tenderness, she reached out for one of the giant-sized hands, clasping it in both of her own. In a soft voice, she began to chant words Joel did not understand, but Walinda spoke them with joy in her face. She was smiling, and there were tears in her eyes.

Slowly the dark aura about Walinda faded away from her body as an even darker nimbus grew about Beshaba. Walinda began to look pale and haggard. She was giving more back to her goddess than the power her goddess had given her. Or perhaps her goddess was simply taking more.

"Nooo!" Ratagar shrieked. "You've got to stop her, Marin! This is a bad thing. Trust me."

Joel could not even stand up at the moment, let alone stop Walinda from restoring her goddess to power. Walinda's shiny black hair began to turn gray, then colorless. Lines etched themselves in her face, and her back grew stooped. Joel watched in horror as the goddess began to stir at the expense of her priestess's vitality.

Holly and Jas crept to the bard's side. Holly began a soft prayer to heal the bard's injured knee. Joel sighed with relief at the warm feeling that spread through him as Lathander's gift of healing passed through his paladin's hands. Jas and Holly helped the bard to stand.

Suddenly the goddess sat bolt upright, blinking in the light of the finder's stone. The whites of her eyes were shot with red, giving her a look of madness. The dark aura that surrounded her being seemed to spread throughout the whole room. The light from the finder's stone dimmed to the brightness of a single candle. Looking upon her, Joel felt an unknown fear grip at his heart.

Beshaba pulled her hand away from her priestess, and Walinda collapsed to her knees at her goddess's feet beside the imp's cage.

Seizing the moment, Ratagar lashed out with his tail, burying its tip in Walinda's back. "That's for the death of my Noxxe!" the imp screamed. "Your priestess for my priest, Beshaba!"

Walinda's body began to twitch with a violent seizure, poisoned by the imp's stinging tail. She looked up at her goddess, her mouth opening and closing, but no words came forth.

Beshaba slid her right hand through the bars of the cage, and with a single squeeze, crushed the life out of Ratagar Perivalious. She squeezed again until Ratagar was no more than a pulpy mass of red flesh and green ichor, then dropped his body on the floor of the cage.

The goddess turned her attention to Walinda. Without any trace of emotion, she watched as her priestess's body ceased twitching and lay still.

Holly ran toward the dais, clearly intent on trying to aid the very same woman who moments ago nearly made her slave to a fiend of the Abyss.

"Leave her be, paladin," Beshaba commanded. Her voice was soft and sweet, like a young girl's, but it echoed throughout the whole chamber. "She is among the honored dead now. I do not want her body defiled with Lathander's stench."

Holly pulled back, insulted and aghast, but she had the sense to choose her words carefully. "Is there nothing you can do for her, lady?" she asked the goddess.

"She has no need of aid. She had done her duty here. Her spirit is already returned to the Blood Tor, where it will serve as my petitioner."

Holly lowered her eyes to the ground so that her shock would not be so obvious. She was appalled that Beshaba did not value Walinda's life, but only the service the priestess rendered her goddess.

"So. The servants of Lathander, Finder, and my hateful sister Tymora have all come to my aid. How amusing," Beshaba said.

Joel bowed low, with a flourish of his hand, making sure his greeting was every bit as graceful as the one he'd first given Tymora. Beshaba was renowned for the jealousy she bore her sister. "Greetings, fair Beshaba," the bard said as he rose. "My lord, Finder, bids me to escort you to the spire, should you agree."

"The spire . . . aye," Beshaba replied. "There I might find sanctuary from this sickness. Then I can better plan how to avenge myself on the upstart Xvim."

"Forgive my impertinence, Lady Beshaba," Joel begged,

"but how is it you are so certain Iyachtu Xvim is behind your sickness?"

"I read Xvim's name in the minds of the hydroloths who attacked me in my realm. He sent the creatures to goad me into using my power, and then I discovered I could not control the power. This is his doing, I am sure. No doubt Lathander can discover exactly what Xvim is up to. Come, we will leave this place finally. Bring your flying carpet. You may need it."

Beshaba rose with a goddess's grace and flowed down the stairs of the dais like a ghost. She drifted over the bodies of the dead Xvimlar she'd slain days earlier.

Joel, Holly, Jas, and Emilo hurried up the dais, slipping past the corpses of Walinda and Ratagar, and sat down on the carpet.

"Airheart," Joel whispered, giving the carpet a pat. "Carpet, rise and go forward slowly."

The carpet glided along behind the Maid of Misfortune.

Beshaba stopped at the door to the tower. Joel halted the carpet beside her.

"Leave the bastion," Beshaba ordered, "and await me in the canyon where my proxy gathered her army. I will join you once I have taken care of some unfinished business."

Beshaba knocked softly three times on the door. The bar holding the door fell away, the door's hinges snapped, and the door collapsed outward. The ground began to tremble. Beshaba stepped out of the tower, and Joel ordered the carpet to follow on her heels. He was eager to be out in the open before the quake grew stronger.

Yugoloth corpses, felled by the marilith's deadly cloud, littered the stairs to the tower door. In the courtyard, yugoloths and tanar'ri continued to fight, even though the battle no longer served any purpose beyond the fiends' desire to shed blood.

Joel ordered the carpet to rise far above the combat and soar toward the only exit from the fortress. Joel slowed as they approached the gate. The gatehouse was choked with bar-lgura keeping the passage open for their fellow tanar'ri.

Fortunately the apelike creatures seemed to recognize the adventurers as allies. They did not attack, but neither did they clear the way for the carpet to exit through the gate.

Holly addressed the tanar'ri. She had to shout to be heard over the clashing and screaming of the battle. "The battle is over," the paladin announced. "Walinda is dead. Her goddess follows us. You have no reason to stay."

The bar-lgura looked at the paladin uncertainly. Holly raised her hands to her forehead, agonized by the barrage of telepathic queries the tanar'ri were sending.

"It is true," Holly insisted. "I do not lie. Tell your fellows to retreat while they still can."

The bar-lgura began backing out of the fortress. Joel ordered the carpet through the gatehouse.

Once free of the confines of the fortress, the bar-lgura began vanishing in beams of shimmering air, presumably teleporting back to their homes in the Abyss. Joel gave a last look up at the gatehouse, but he saw no sign of petitioner Perr. He wondered if the former priest of Xvim had any clue that he had been deceived. The bard ordered the carpet to rise twenty feet and sent it back toward the canyon as Beshaba had ordered.

Holly looked back at the fortress, shaking her head.

"What's wrong?" Emilo asked.

"The bar-lgura will flee," the paladin explained, "but they said the bulezau have gone into a battle frenzy and will never leave."

"Their loss," Jas said.

"Evil's gain," Holly argued. "No good is served by their deaths."

"Even dead, Walinda manages to ruin the lives of others," Jas commented. "And she never actually had to pay for any of it."

"She paid with her life," Holly said, aghast.

"That's not payment enough," Jas growled. "Now she's a petitioner, still serving an evil power."

"But that is all she will ever be now," Holly said, "until she merges with Beshaba. It is only as living beings that we can choose the course our spirits will take. Now Walinda can never be redeemed by the light. She will never know joy or love or mercy."

"Walinda could have lived a thousand years, and she

would never have changed," Jas declared. "She was evil incarnate."

They had just reached the ridge overlooking the Bastion of Hate when they heard another rumble.

"Beshaba's bad luck seeping out?" Holly asked.

"Pouring out is more like it," Joel replied. "She must be casting some very powerful magic."

Floating above the ground, the four carpet riders didn't feel the vibrations of the earthquake, but they still weren't safe from its violence. Geysers of ash and molten lava began to shoot up around them, and rocks from the slope above rained down on them. Joel ordered the carpet to back away from the mount a hundred feet.

Hovering near the darkness of the void, the adventurers could hardly even feel the heat, but they had an excellent view of the havoc wrought on the Gehennan mount.

The realm of Iyachtu Xvim trembled like jelly, yet neither the walls, nor the temple, nor the tower collapsed. Xvim had built them well. Finally Mount Chamada itself gave way. The great, wide ledge beneath the Bastion of Hate broke from the side of the mount and began to slide down the slope. It moved slowly at first, but soon picked up a terrifying speed, carrying with it Xvim's fortress.

The noise was deafening, a continuing roar that battered their ears and left an ache in their foreheads. Then the air grew foul with dust, ash, smoke, and foul vapors. The four adventurers lay on the carpet with their arms over their heads and their faces, choking and gasping.

Suddenly there was silence all about them, and bright light and clean, fresh air. They raised their heads and looked about. The carpet sat in a field of thistle and burdock. Overhead, the cloudless sky was bright blue, though there was no sun to be seen.

"I don't think we're in Gehenna anymore," Holly said after a long pause.

"But where are we?" Jas asked.

"Who cares?" the paladin said with a laugh. "Breathe that air. Isn't it wonderful?"

Indeed, the air was not only fresh, but it also seemed to make Joel's skin tingle. The feeling was a familiar one to the bard. "We're in the Outlands," he said.

"How'd we get here?" Jas asked.

"I brought you," a soft, girlish voice said from somewhere overhead.

The adventurers looked up.

Beshaba hovered above them, her feet grazing the thistle flowers. She was no longer a giant, but the size of a normal human woman. "Bringing you here has cost me more power than I thought it would. In payment, you will serve as my bodyguards on our journey to the spire."

Eager to keep the goddess on the path Finder had requested, Joel bowed his head and said, "We would be honored, Lady Beshaba."

Beshaba looked at Holly and Jas. "Does he speak for you as well?" she asked.

"Joel is our friend," Holly said. "We trust him to speak for us."

"Your friend? Well, that is a good thing," Beshaba said. "You will protect me the better for it. For if my person comes to any harm, I will hold your friend Joel responsible and he will forfeit his life."

*Opera? I loved the opera. So much jewelry, so much profit
. . . The music? I was too busy to listen.*
                                —His Royal Highness Pinch I

Intermezzo

"She really is a mean old witch, isn't she?" Annali Webspinner commented as she watched the goddess Beshaba
threaten the Rebel Bard's life after all he'd done for the
Maid of Misfortune.

"It's no wonder Walinda worshiped her, is it?" Bors
Sunseed retorted with a dry tone.

The bariaur made a face at the paladin. She had been
prepared to argue to the death her admission of Walinda
into the Sensates. That was before they'd learned Walinda
had betrayed a secret she had sworn to keep. Annali had
felt a trifle embarrassed, but she wasn't going to take crit-
icism lying down from the snotty paladin.

"I think perhaps this would be a good time for a break,"
Cuatha Da'nanin said. "Ayryn, you have exhausted yourself for us, and we thank you, but now you must rest."

The genasi scryer covered her crystal ball, and the vision of the goddess and Joel and his companions and the
thistle field in the Outlands faded from view.

The wizard Quellig took up the crystal ball and proceeded to summon a view of Joel's party. Quellig's sensations were not as incorporeal as Ayryn's, so the rest of the
Sensates in the room were not treated to Quellig's vision,
but the tiefling wizard held a recorder stone so that everything he saw could later be shared with the others should
any of it prove interesting.

The Sensates had scried upon the Rebel Bard nonstop
since he'd reached Arborea, and many of those hours had

been tedious. There was nothing quite so boring as watching a man sleep. Erin Montgomery had been adamant, however, that they record Joel's journey to Fermata to meet with Finder.

When it looked as if Joel's party would pay a visit to Tymora, Erin had insisted the watch continue. At Da'nanin's suggestion, she had agreed to halt once they'd witnessed Tymora exorcising the dark stalker from the winged woman, Jasmine.

For that event, Ayryn had been asked to scry once more, and the Sensates who'd shared the first viewing of the gods had been asked to return. All but Walinda, who could not be found, had come back for the experience. Since Joel, not Tymora, was the target of Ayryn's scrying, the genasi's vision had not been misdirected. The Sensates witnessed Joel's meeting with Lady Luck with mild interest. Many of them had actually visited Brightwater and had already seen the goddess from afar. Finder's charm had impressed more than a few of the ladies. Ultimately it was the goddess's seizure that had made it a night to remember.

After witnessing Tymora collapse, nothing in the multiverse—not even her lover, Da'nanin—could have convinced Factol Montgomery to cease watching over the young adventurers who had agreed to risk their lives to discover the cause of the goddess's weakness.

Montgomery had presented three arguments in defense of continuing to spy upon Joel and his party. First, Tymora's realm, Brightwater, being so close to the Gilded Hall of the Sensates, was a favorite spot for Sensates visiting the plane of Arborea. Tymora was a desirable neighbor. Her loss could change the area about the Gilded Hall in an unfavorable way. The Sensates needed to be informed should Lady Luck's power be about to fade. Secondly, if the Sensates could uncover useful information to pass on to Tymora's allies, it would gain them the favor of those powerful allies, so they needed to follow Joel to see what information he and his companions might need. Lastly, the Sensates could use their magical recording stones to chronicle the entire crisis from beginning to end, whatever the end might be. Such a saga could end up

making the Civic Festhall sensoriums a fortune when
peddled to the masses of Cagers eager for entertainment
of a heroic bent.

Privately, Cuatha Da'nanin knew that Erin's true reason for continuing was simple, insatiable curiosity. He
held his peace, though, bowed to his lover's reasoning, and
did not hold her to her promise to cease the scrying.

All the resources at the factol's disposal, and these
were considerable, were brought to bear on the mystery of
Tymora's weakness. Forty mages and seven priests were
kept on call at the Civic Festhall, and two other crystal
balls were located and purchased so that Joel's party
could be monitored. Sages were hired to determine how
the goddess was being drained. Any persons known to be
in Sigil with knowledge of the gods of Realmspace were
brought in and interviewed. Envoys were sent out to
Realmspace to gather information on the effects of the crisis on the people of the Realms. Once the connection to
Xvim was known, Xvim had been scried for—unsuccess-
fully. Thus spies had been dispatched to discover if the
church of Xvim had any insight into the whereabouts of
its god.

Ayryn had been brought back to scry for Walinda's entrance into the Bastion of Hate. Very few were interested
in the battle. The endless Blood War between the tanar'ri
and the baatezu, which often included the yugoloth mercenaries, had made such combats seem monotonous to the
experienced Sensates. All assembled, though, had been
more interested in watching the traitor Sensate Walinda
awaken her goddess. Witnessing Walinda's death had
proved even more satisfying to some.

Da'nanin looked unhappily about the sensorium, which
had become the center of the investigation. The air had
become stale with the odor of unwashed bodies. Dirty
dishes and empty cartons of food were strewn about the
floor. Since Ayryn was no longer broadcasting her sensations, several of the Sensates got up to leave, but just as
many remained. Some sat down beside Quellig and listened as he described the activities of the Rebel Bard. A
few curled up in a dark corner of the room to nap until
someone woke them to tell them the next important

development. Others hurried off to search for sources of information that might solve the mystery. The mystery had become a shared obsession.

The factol was standing off to one side of the sensorium, speaking in hushed whispers with Annali and Bors. The half-elf returned to Erin's side. A servant entered the room and handed a note to Annali.

Annali perused the missive and shared the information with the others. "One of my sources claims this god, Sirrion of the Flame, has his realm in the plane of Limbo. He is a power of complete neutrality."

"Well, if he's in Limbo, that could explain why Quellig failed in his attempt to scry for him," Da'nanin said. "It's nearly impossible to discern anything in the chaos of Limbo."

"The rest of the information concerns the kender," Annali reported. "My source insists they do not have the power to become invisible naturally. Emilo must have some sort of magic artifact, probably a ring."

"I have watched very closely. The only ring he has is the one that protects him from fire," Cuatha insisted.

"That is, assuming Emilo really is a kender," Bors said.

"Finder would know if he weren't, wouldn't he?" Annali asked somewhat uncertainly.

"Whatever he is, I'm prepared to wager that he is hiding something," Bors replied.

"Any explanation why the manifestation of Sirrion misguided the party by sending them into the fetch's lair?" Erin asked.

"No,"Annali admitted, "but Sirrion may have allied himself with Xvim in some effort to restore a balance between good and evil."

"We have no proof the flame manifestation was really Sirrion. The flame did not even actually claim to be Sirrion. It got the kender to guess, as if the flame could not lie," Bors pointed out.

"Or was afraid the kender would recognize an outright lie," Cuatha Da'nanin suggested.

Kenda Fretterstag, having just left the sensorium a few minutes ago, reentered the room, with a smug look on her face. The statuesque blonde sauntered toward the group

surrounding Montgomery. Bors had a strong suspicion he
would not like whatever news the sorceress brought.

Erin Montgomery was more welcoming. "Kenda, I
know that look. What have you brought for me?" the factol
asked excitedly.

"There is a dark region in Lathander's realm," Kenda
answered, "which defies all attempts to scry into it. Lathander goes in and out of it frequently."

"Perhaps that's where they are keeping Tymora," Bors
suggested.

"Yes," Kenda agreed, "but why? What is it they don't
want anyone to see?"

"That she is weakened?" Da'nanin suggested.

"Everyone already knows that. Her church in the
Realms has more or less admitted there is a problem,"
Kenda countered. "Yet Lathander shields her from all
eyes."

"What are you implying?" Bors asked suspiciously.

"Why, simply that Lathander has something to hide,"
Kenda insisted.

"Are you suggesting Lathander has something to do
with this?" Bors demanded angrily. "Holly Harrowslough
serves Lathander. He is a god of goodness and light."

"Yes, I know, Bors darling," Kenda replied. "I saw him
hanging about Chauntea when we scried upon her. As I
recall, she told him to get lost. That sort of suggestion always seems to annoy members of your sex. In my experience, men scorned in such a way either mope or try to get
even."

"Not surprising, considering the kind of men in your
experience," Bors retorted.

"Men are men," Kenda declared. "And Lathander is a
man whose lover just suggested he entertain himself with
Tymora or Beshaba."

"That is pure coincidence," Bors argued.

"Is it? What about the other creatures that have been
in and out of the dark region of Lathander's realm?"

"What sort of creatures?" Montgomery asked.

Kenda held her hands out in a dramatic gesture.
"Gnomes," she said.

"Gnomes?" Annali asked.

"What do gnomes have to do with this?" Da'nanin queried.

"What sort of gnomes?" Bors asked.

"Ah, paladin. You always ask the right question," Kenda complimented Bors. "Tinker gnomes, to be specific. The kind that originated on the world of Krynn. And all these tinker gnomes wore little red badges in the shape of a flame."

"As in Sirrion, the Flowing Flame?" Montgomery asked.

"Quite a coincidence, wouldn't you say?" Kenda commented.

"What were the gnomes doing?" Bors asked.

"Well, talking mostly, like all tinker gnomes, too fast and all at the same time. They carried eggs into the dark region."

"Eggs?" Annali asked with a laugh.

"Eggs," Kenda repeated.

"And then what happened?" Montgomery asked.

"Well, later, when they came out of the dark regions, they brought out something completely different."

"What?" Montgomery demanded.

"Omelets," Kenda replied soberly.

Offstage

In the Prime Material Plane on the world known as Toril in Realmspace, Amber Wyvernspur decided it was time to take charge of the situation. Handing Pars to Tavan, she slipped down the stairs until she stood between the other children and the kobolds. "We are very sorry to have trespassed," she said, curtsying to the kobold leader. "We'll be leaving now." Without turning around, she ordered her cousins, "Go back into the crypt."

"But the orcs—" Ferrin began.

"They can't enter the crypt," Amber snapped. "Now, go!"

Behind her, Amber could hear the others hustling back into the crypt. Amber started to back up the stairs, then bumped into Cory, who had remained behind.

"Halt or we fire," the kobold leader said. "You must pay for invading our kingdom."

"I have some silver coins," Amber said, pulling out the velvet purse Aunt Dorath had given her for her birthday. She tossed the purse down the stairs.

One of the other kobolds snatched it up and looked inside.

"Not enough," the kobold leader said. "Your people owe for torture of my mother."

"You must be mistaken," Amber replied. "No Wyvernspur would do such a thing."

"He means Uncle Steele," Cory whispered. "Father told me about it. It happened a long time ago."

Amber huffed with annoyance. First Uncle Steele went and lost his key to Heather, and now they had to pay for the bad behavior of his youth. She unfastened the locket about her neck. Her mother had given it to her, and she was very unhappy to have to part with it, but it was better than being dead. She held it out to the kobold. "This locket is real gold," she said.

"Not enough!" the kobold leader growled. "Must give us slave!"

"Now, see here," Cory retorted hotly, "we are not about to give you a slave."

"Give me the wyvern's spur," Amber ordered Cory.

"What?" Cory asked, aghast. "You can't be serious. We can't give the spur to a bunch of kobolds."

"Give it to me," Amber snarled.

Cory pulled out the spur from his shirt pocket. The family heirloom looked like an ugly chunk of moldy, dried meat. Amber snatched it from Cory's hand. Then she turned around and faced the kobold leader again.

"Don't want your magic," the kobold insisted. "Give slave or die."

"You will take the locket or you will regret it," Amber growled.

The kobold leader howled something in his own language. All the kobolds cried out something that included the name of Beshaba and fired their crossbows at Amber.

Cory screamed, expecting to see his cousin collapse dead at his feet. Instead he saw a blur in the air. Then there was a large emerald-green, serpentlike creature, with two legs and wings for arms, and it was standing where Amber had been standing a moment earlier. Amber, Cory realized suddenly, had used the family heirloom to transform into a wyvern—a small wyvern, admittedly, only ten feet long, but a wyvern nonetheless.

Cursed by Beshaba, every one of the kobolds' crossbow bolts struck Amber, but only two stuck in her scaly wyvern hide. The rest bounced away and clattered to the floor.

Amber hissed. The kobolds screamed and clambered back down the stairs. Amber turned around and nudged Cory with her scaly horned head. Cory raced up the stairs, with Amber trundling clumsily after him.

The other children, who had not witnessed Amber's transformation, cowered against the wall of the crypt when they saw the wyvern. The orcs at the other entrance to the crypt gave a shout and retreated up the stairs.

Amber changed back into her normal form and immediately sank to the floor, whimpering softly. The two crossbow bolts, which hadn't slowed her in the least when she
was a wyvern, were far more painful now that they were
buried in human flesh. One missile stuck from her thigh
and the other protruded from her shoulder. Blood seeped
out from under the bolts, but at least it didn't gush.

Pars ran to his sister and threw himself into her arms,
clinging to her dress.

Cory looked at his older cousin with a mixture of jealousy and respect. Only one Wyvernspur in each genera-
tion was capable of using the spur. Naturally he had
hoped it was he, but if it had to be someone else, he was
glad it was Amber. He liked Amber best of all his cousins.
He even liked her more than his own sister. He knelt beside Amber and pressed a clean handkerchief to the
wound in her shoulder. "You knew all along that you were
the one who could use the spur, didn't you?" he asked her.

Amber nodded. "Last summer I started having the
same dreams Uncle Giogi has. He brought me down here
to meet the guardian and showed me how to use the spur,
just in case anything ever happened to him."

"Why didn't you say anything?" Tavan asked.

"Would you have believed me if I had?" Amber asked.

"No," Tavan admitted.

"Amberlee," a sensuous, husky voice whispered
through the crypt. The wyvern shadow that had destroyed
the two orcs reappeared on the wall. The dark silhouette
swayed back and forth above the children's heads.

"Hello, guardian," Amber replied.

"You have gotten yourself cornered," the guardian
noted.

"But the kobolds and the orcs have fled," Cory said.

"The kobolds still lurk on the stairs to the catacombs,
and the orcs still wait on the stairs to the mausoleum," the
guardian replied. "I can hear them. The orcs know you
must come out eventually. The kobolds are praying to Beshaba to bring you ruin."

"We'll just have to wait here," Amber said.

"Wait!" Toran complained. "Wait for what?"

"When Uncle Giogi gets back and finds out we haven't come home for supper, he'll look for the wyvern's spur so he can turn into a wyvern to search for us. When he sees the spur is gone, he'll guess we took it and know where to look for us," Amber said. "Then he and Uncle Sam and Aunt Cat can fight off the orcs and free us."

"She's right," Cory agreed.

"I'm not sitting around here waiting all day," Tavan said. "We made a sacrifice to Tymora. If we attack the orcs, we'll be lucky and break through." He pulled out a dagger from his belt.

"No," Toran said. "We should attack the kobolds and try to find the exit from the catacombs into the woods."

"We'll flip for it," Tavan said. "I call heads."

Toran pulled out a coin and tossed it in the air, but he didn't manage to catch it. The coin hit the floor of the crypt and spun about on its side like a top. When it stopped spinning, it did not fall over. Instead, it remained balanced on edge, neither heads nor tails.

"Interesting," the guardian hissed. "I'd take that as a sign."

"We stay here," Amber growled to Tavan and Toran.

From the catacombs, the kobolds began shrieking loudly. The clamor upset the children.

Suddenly a terrible rumbling noise came from the catacombs, and the whole crypt began to shake. Pieces of stone from the arched ceiling of the crypt began to tumble to the floor.

"If we stay here, we'll be crushed!" Toran shouted.

Now not only Pars, but also Ferrin and Heather, began to cry and scream as well. Dust filled the air as more stone and dirt collapsed around them.

"Tymora," Cory called out, "we need your help!"

The other children took up the call, shouting out Lady Luck's name. Amber bent over her young brother to shield him from the falling stone. She whispered a prayer to Selune, since the goddess of the moon was the patron of shapeshifters.

The ground ceased moving as suddenly as it had started. In a few minutes, the dust cleared enough for them to survey the damage. The ceiling of the crypt had collapsed on either side of them, so that both the entrance to the catacombs and the exit to the mausoleum were both completely blocked off.

Amazingly, the ceiling over their heads remained intact. They were safe from the orcs and kobolds, but they were now sealed alive in the crypt of their ancestors.

Behind the Scenes

The looming figure hovered over the altar of stone and stroked the gold coin and the pink rose. Swollen with the power of two goddesses, they glowed with a light so bright it was painful for mortals to behold. The figure coveted that power, but it was not yet time to claim it. Soon, very soon, Beshaba and Tymora would be no more. Then their power would be his, and no one could stop him from claiming it.

Then he would claim the goddesses' worshipers as well. Beshaba's followers would turn to him readily, eager for the ruin he would bring to their enemies. Tymora's priests, of course, would balk, but they would be powerless without him. They would turn to Selune for protection, but they couldn't cower in Selune's temples forever. When they emerged, they would be captured and given a choice—join him or die. It mattered not to him which they chose.

It was the adventurers who followed Tymora that he coveted. Adventurers were a power to be reckoned with in the Realms, and many of them relied on Tymora's luck to survive the hardships of their professions. They wouldn't dare to risk his wrath. They would call on him for sustenance, and their strength would be his. And then, in time, the Realms would be his.

Opera is the one medium that provides a venue for the composer to express vastly differing emotions simultaneously through song. The many voices weave together to form a single tapestry of song that may reveal not only wrenching pain and darkest evil, but sublime joy, noblest sacrifice. Thus, music that is already beautiful and moving is further enhanced by chilling ironies and dramatic overtones. The enjoyment of opera is an acquired taste, but to my mind, those who put forth the effort to study it and appreciate it will be richly rewarded.

—Raistlin Majere

Act Four
Scene 1

Jas landed on a rocky butte and folded back her wings, which here in the Outlands were reddish brown at the base and speckled with white and black flecks at the tips. After all the awful shapes and colors her wings had taken, Jas rather liked them they way they looked now—like a hawk's. Even better, her eyes had returned to normal, and she was slowly molting her feathers. She felt human again.

She peered out across the prairies, but she could see nothing for miles and miles but the spire. The infinite peak rose in the distance, seemingly no closer today than it had been yesterday. Jas did not hurry back down to the party, but sat for a few minutes to enjoy the peaceful solitude.

Traveling across Gehenna on foot would be preferable to traveling anywhere with Beshaba. Despite having shrunk to the size of a human, the goddess was still a giant terror. Although she made perfectly clear that she could destroy the party in an instant, the goddess was so exhausted by the drain on her power she rode on the carpet. Since the carpet couldn't take the weight of five persons, Jas was forced to fly alongside it, for which she might have been grateful. She was plagued, however, with the sensation that she was once again watching her friends being tortured, only this time by Walinda's goddess.

Beshaba never stopped complaining or criticizing or scheming. The magic carpet moved too slow. The light of the Outlands was too bright. Holly's smile was annoying. Joel's good manners were a pretense. Jas reeked of Tymora's magic. They'd been forced to introduce Emilo, to keep Beshaba from tripping over him, and the goddess had been especially aggravated by the kender's presence. Halflings and kender were vermin. On occasion, she would launch into a tirade about how Xvim would rue the day he tangled with her. She would see that he choked on his own tongue.

Then there was the bad luck that dogged not only the adventurers but Beshaba herself. A freak wind blew the magic carpet into a tree. In the collision, a branch tore a great hole in the rug so that it would no longer fly. Emilo had been crushed at the loss of so spectacular an item of magic.

The party was forced to walk. They passed too close to a burr bush and ended up picking prickles out of their clothes for hours. Their boots began to fall apart, and before long, they all had blisters, even the goddess, who also broke a nail trying to adjust the straps on her sandals.

When they set up camp for the night, Holly cut her hand cleaning a bird she had caught for them to eat, Joel hurt his knee breaking a branch to feed the fire to cook the bird, and Emilo burned his hand building the fire. Beshaba, who, as Holly pointed out, didn't really need to eat as did the humans, insisted on tasting the bird and burned her tongue. The injury soured the goddess's mood even further.

After spending half an hour fruitlessly searching for a holy symbol that was missing from her backpack, Holly threw herself, frustrated and tearful, to the ground to sleep. She was up again in only a few minutes, having lain

on an anthill. She had to remove all her armor to get the
ants off her, and she was badly bitten. While Joel sorted
through their remaining magical scrolls, the wind
whipped the pages away in the dark. Then, while Jas was
on watch, the bard was beset with nightmares about children suffocating in a cave and cried out in his sleep, waking Holly and Emilo and alarming everyone.

Only Jas seemed immune to the problems besetting the
party. Reeking of Tymora's magic apparently had a posi-
tive side. Ordinarily this many tribulations would have
resulted in bickering, but no one was comfortable speaking in the goddess's presence except the goddess. The
angry silence of the others was infinitely more wearying
than any fight would have been, and Jas couldn't help but
think the others resented her lack of misfortune.

During the second day's travel, Beshaba grew more
suspicious and distrustful, not only of the surrounding
area, but of her escorts as well. She demanded that Jas fly
up ahead to scout, Emilo and Holly walk in front where
she could see them, and Joel stay right at her side. She
would become livid when she took her eyes off Emilo and
didn't see him when she looked again. From some of her
jewelry and a string, the goddess created a jangling collar
for the kender, so that she could hear him and he wouldn't
become "unnoticed" again. Emilo looked as mortified as a
cat with a bell around the neck.

After having desired Walinda's death since the day she
met her, Jas now regretted that the priestess wasn't here
to suffer under her goddess's spiteful eye. Of course,
Walinda was so perverse that she had thrived on the
abuse her previous master had heaped on her, so there
was no guarantee Beshaba would actually make Walinda
miserable even were she still alive.

Now that her friends' murderess was dead and the
dark stalker was just a phantom of her mind, Jas found
the fires that had driven her had grown cold. She didn't
want to go back on her promise to help Tymora, but the
thought of traveling day after day with Beshaba was in-
tolerable. And when they finally reached the spire, what
would happen next? The uncertainty, the inability to plan
her life beyond tomorrow was exhausting her.

Suddenly, off in the distance, Jas caught sight of a beam of light. The beam looked familiar, a line of yellow just like the light from the finder's stone Joel had used to summon her when they were in Gehenna. There were two finder's stones, Jas remembered, or rather two halves of one stone. Joel had one half, and the other . . .

"Finder," Jas whispered. "It's about time you showed up."

The thought that Finder would soon be there lifted Jas's spirits slightly. Finder would deal with Beshaba, god to goddess. Jas flew back to the group to give them the good news.

Beshaba didn't seem pleased. She didn't trust any of the gods, and apparently she suspected Finder of some treachery. She awaited his arrival holding a dagger next to Joel's ribs so she would have the upper hand over Joel's god.

Soon it appeared as if a sun had blossomed on the horizon and was moving toward them. With Beshaba's attention fixed on the sky, Emilo sat down beside Jas and pulled out a piece of red glass from one of his many vest pockets. He held the glass up to his eye so he could view the approaching light without squinting. "It looks like a chariot of fire," the kender said excitedly. "Want to see?" he asked Jas.

Jas took the glass and looked at the approaching light. "It looks more like a fiery carriage and four," she noted. "Leave it to Finder to travel in style."

Jas was about to hand the piece of glass back to Emilo when she noticed the depiction of the sun and the face carved on its surface. It looked like the holy symbol of Lathander.

"Emilo," the winged woman whispered, "where did you get this?"

"Walinda took it from Holly's backpack," the kender said. "I picked it up when she tossed it aside. Can you imagine doing that—as pretty as it is? I think it stung her."

"Holly was looking everywhere for that last night," Jas said. "She was in tears about losing it."

"Really?" Emilo asked with astonishment. "I must have

been sleeping. I'll give it back to her."

The kender rose and hurried over to Holly and tugged on her sleeve to get her attention.

Finder landed his fiery flying carriage pulled by four flaming stallions. The god pulled the carriage up beside Beshaba and reined in the horses.

"I've come to offer you a ride, Lady Beshaba," Finder said with a cocky wink. "I'll even let you drive if you promise not to murder my priest."

Beshaba glared at Finder. "I have been in the Outlands nearly a whole day. What took you so long to come for me?" she demanded.

"I've been busy. Assassins and saboteurs have begun to strike against Tymora's church, and Lady Selune and I have been hard pressed to keep her priests safe," Finder explained.

"Or perhaps you were busy preparing some scheme at the base of the spire to betray me?" the goddess accused him.

"My lady, you know the natives of the region of the spire, the rilmani, would never allow that," Finder replied. "They serve only the Balance and will preserve our truce. I suggested the spire as a neutral ground where you would feel safe for just that reason."

"Ha!" Beshaba laughed coldly, but she removed her dagger from Joel's ribs. "The rilmani are just as likely to let you destroy me, then destroy you, all in the name of their precious Balance."

"I may be a reckless fool," Finder replied, "but I have no desire to quarrel with the rilmani. Hence you are safe."

"Where is my hateful sister?" Beshaba demanded.

"Lathander has set up a dead magic zone in Elysium to protect her from the drain on her power. Since we did not think you would wish to travel to Elysium, you will have to make do with the dead magic zone near the spire."

As Finder and Beshaba bickered, Emilo slipped Holly the red glass. "Walinda took this from your pack, but I saved it," he said. "Sorry I forgot to give it back right away."

Holly's eyes lit with joy. "Oh, thank goodness!" she declared.

Then the paladin did something the kender hadn't expected. Indeed, if he'd known what she was going to do, he would have stopped her.

Holly gripped the glass firmly in her right hand, rocked back on her heels, and hurled the glass ornament at a rock, smashing it to pieces.

Finder's head snapped up and Beshaba whirled around. Both powers looked at the paladin, Finder with horror, Beshaba with fury.

"What was that?" Beshaba demanded.

"I broke a piece of glass," Holly said.

"What sort of glass, girl?" the goddess hissed as she moved toward the paladin with her dagger drawn.

"It was a holy symbol," Holly said. "To let Lord Lathander know I'd found you."

"Lathander senses all you do," Beshaba growled. "You broke it so he would know exactly where you were, didn't you?"

"I suppose so," Holly replied.

Something overhead gave an ear-piercing shriek.

Everyone looked up. Swooping toward them was a huge bird with the most brilliant plumage Jas had ever seen. Every color of the setting sun was reflected in its feathers. Its eyes were as red and shiny as rubies. It also flew faster than any bird Jas had ever seen.

"It's a phoenix! Some trick of Lathander's!" Beshaba gasped. "I warned you the bard's life would be forfeit," she growled to Holly. She turned about and lunged for Joel, grabbing him by his ponytail.

"No, Beshaba!" Finder cried out. "He had nothing to do with this. Leave my priest out of it." The phoenix's shadow covered them all.

Finder leapt forward to grab Beshaba, but he was too late. The goddess was snatched up in the talons of the phoenix and carried aloft, screeching like a banshee. Joel was carried off with her, dangling from her hand by his hair like a doll carried by a small child.

Finder jumped back into his carriage, snapped the reins, and gave chase. Within seconds, both the bird and the fiery carriage had become mere dots on the horizon.

Jas and Emilo looked at Holly.

"I had to do it," the paladin whispered, but there were tears pooling in her eyes.

A minute later Finder returned in the carriage. He didn't have Joel or Beshaba with him.

"What happened?" Jas asked.

"The phoenix went through a magic gate that closed before I could reach it," Finder said coldly. He stepped down from the carriage and strode up to Holly. Jas had never seen him look so angry before. His eyes blazed with light and his body shook.

"You," he said, thrusting a finger in Holly's face, "have some explaining to do."

Act Four
Scene 2

Once he'd recovered from the initial shock of being yanked into the air by his hair, Joel grabbed at Beshaba's wrist with both hands and hung on for dear life. The phoenix flew with such speed that the wind in his face made it hard to breathe. Far below, the plains of the Outlands became a blur. For a moment, Joel thought he saw Finder in his flaming carriage, but it might just have been a flash of light in the back of his eyes from the pain in his head.

The phoenix's talons were wrapped about Beshaba's waist and hips, so her arms were free. Although she was now the size of a human woman, she was still possessed of godly strength. With one arm, she raised Joel so that they faced each other eye to eye. The goddess gave the bard a cruel smile, one that reminded Joel of Walinda.

Joel was sure Beshaba was about to drop him to avenge herself on everyone she believed had betrayed her.

"Rat," the goddess murmured, and it appeared suddenly to Joel that the goddess and the phoenix overhead were growing larger.

A great blast of wind hit the phoenix sideways, very likely caused by Beshaba's bad luck. The phoenix lost altitude but recovered quickly.

The bard was beginning to feel relieved that Beshaba hadn't dropped him when he noticed with alarm that there was gray fur on his arms. He felt his nose, and was shocked to discover that it had become a snout. Beshaba had called him a rat, and a rat he had indeed become. Fearful that he might forget he was human, Joel writhed and called out to Finder, but all that came from his mouth

was a pathetic squeak. A moment later Beshaba grabbed
him about the belly with one hand and slipped him into a
pocket of her gown. It was dark inside the pocket, but Joel
fought back his sense of helplessness by reminding himself that at least he still remembered who and what he
was.

It was also hot and stuffy inside the pocket of Beshaba's gown, but infinitely preferable to being dropped
from such a height. In the relative safety of the warm
darkness surrounding him, Joel was left to wonder why
Beshaba didn't simply destroy the phoenix.

There was the possibility she no longer possessed
enough power to attack the great creature. Yet she had
wreaked havoc upon the Bastion of Hate, even after she
had lapsed into unconsciousness. She may have thought
to confront Xvim on an angry impulse, but if she had gone
with the understanding that her lack of control could be
used against Xvim, then she was very cunning indeed.
She could be faking her weakness so that she could confront Lathander and cause the same sort of destruction in
his realm.

This left Joel wondering just what kind of game Lathander was playing. He'd sent Holly to retrieve Beshaba,
that much was obvious. But why? Did he think, as Tymora had, that Beshaba was behind Tymora's loss of
power? Then why hadn't he told Finder what he was planning?

After a few minutes, Joel felt his stomach drop out from
under him, which he hoped meant the phoenix was landing and hadn't released Beshaba in midair. A moment
later all sense of motion ceased.

The bard heard a man's voice, loud but muffled by the
fabric of Beshaba's gown, order someone else, "Hurry, before she regains consciousness. Get her into the fusion
chamber."

Something growled. Joel felt Beshaba being jostled
about, then set down. There was the sound of wheels
rolling on a wooden floor, and then the rolling gradually
stopped.

The goddess stirred and moaned softly. Suddenly she
gasped and leapt to her feet. Joel could feel her pacing

about. He remained very still, unsure whether or not he wanted to draw attention to himself.

Beshaba screamed, "Show yourself, Lathander, you arrogant peacock! I know you're here."

There was no reply.

"I'll use my power to bring your puny realm collapsing about your head," Beshaba declared.

Still there was no reply.

"Rat," Beshaba muttered, and from the pocket of her gown, she drew Joel out by the scruff of his neck. "Thought I'd forgotten about you, didn't you? No such luck for you, bard."

Joel looked around. He and Beshaba were alone in a stone-walled room with a single high window, covered with bars. Joel could see no door. Either they'd been shoved into the room through a magical portal that had now closed or the door was well hidden.

Upon one wall was a wheel of torture, painted in brilliant colors. In a far corner, beneath a chain fastened to the wall, Joel saw an urn, a scepter, and a pile of what looked like human bones. Otherwise the room was bare.

Beshaba motioned with her fingers, and Joel felt his body stretch and contort until he had transformed back into a man.

"Thank you, my lady," he said, anxious to let the goddess know he was grateful she had not destroyed him when she had the chance.

Mercy was not on Beshaba's mind, however. With her godly strength, she slammed him against the wheel of torture and forced his arms and then his legs into manacles fastened to the wheel.

"Now we will discuss why I was brought here," the goddess said, stepping back from the wheel.

"I assure you, my lady, I have no idea," Joel insisted.

"The paladin was your companion. She signaled for the phoenix to come. Do you expect me to believe that you knew nothing of her plans?"

"It's true, my lady," the bard said. He chose his words carefully, aware that each one might be his last. "Lord Finder told me to escort you to the spire. Lord Lathander must have given Holly other instructions."

Beshaba pulled out her dagger and hurled it at Joel. It buried itself deep in the wood of the wheel, inches from the bard's face. "Do you know where we are?" she asked.

"I was in your pocket when we arrived, my lady. I did not see where the phoenix landed."

Beshaba stepped forward to retrieve her dagger.

"This room is like the dungeon in the Blood Tor, but there is no door," Beshaba said. "Why was I brought here?" she demanded, holding her dagger at Joel's throat.

Joel took a deep breath, trying to control himself. "I do not know, my lady."

Beshaba gave the wheel a nudge and it began to spin. Joel felt his stomach churn as he was turned upside down, then right side up once more.

"I am not very talented at throwing daggers," Beshaba said. "I hope you're feeling lucky, bard." She stepped back and tossed her dagger once more. It landed beside Joel's wrist, close enough to nick his flesh.

"What is Lathander's purpose?"

"Lady Beshaba, you accomplish nothing with this petty game," Joel retorted, barely managing to keep his tone civil as his stomach churned from the motion of the wheel.

"Petty game?" Beshaba growled. She stepped forward and grabbed at her dagger, stopping the wheel's spinning. "It is not I playing petty games, but Xvim and Lathander and Finder. My power leaks from my very being. It is being sucked away. Do you know what that feels like, bard? Perhaps when you come closer to kissing death you will understand. Now, tell me what you know."

"I don't know anything," Joel declared again. "Finder isn't involved. I don't know what Xvim's or Lathander's plans are."

Beshaba snapped her fingers, and a double-pronged goad and a barb-tipped scourge appeared in her hands. "For some reason, I feel less weak now, and when I use my powers, it does not leak into the earth. What has changed? Why has some of my strength been returned to me?"

"I don't know, my lady."

Beshaba lashed out with the barbed scourge, striking Joel about the shoulders and chest and tearing his shirt and tunic. Large welts appeared on his upper arms. Joel gasped with the pain.

"Lady Beshaba, I could lie and start making up things," the bard said, "but it wouldn't help you learn what your enemies have planned."

Beshaba blew on the goad, and it glowed as if it had been heated in coals. "I would be interested in the lies you tell, bard. For in every lie, they say, is a grain of truth."

"I don't know anything," Joel whispered, closing his eyes at the sight of the heated goad.

"Beshaba!" a woman's voice shouted. "Leave the mortal be."

Joel opened his eyes with surprise. Tymora stood in a doorway that had appeared out of nowhere. The bard allowed himself a silent sigh of relief. Lady Luck held a long sword, much like the one Winnie had given to Jas. The goddess of good luck stepped forward, gracefully blocking Beshaba from the bard.

"Is it not enough that your treachery has weakened me and all my faithful on Toril? Now you must torment a priest of a new godling. To what end, Beshaba?"

"*My* treachery?" Beshaba shrieked, jabbing her heated goad at Tymora's face. Lady Luck parried the attack with her sword, and streaks of lightninglike energy sparked off the surface of her blade.

"It is *your* allies who betrayed *me*," Beshaba snarled. "*They* brought me to this place. When I reached out and sensed it was your power draining me, I did not believe it. Like a fool, I thought you to be incapable of such treachery. But you and those peacocks, Lathander and Finder, have allied with Xvim."

Beshaba lashed out with her scourge at Tymora's legs, but Tymora leapt aside gracefully.

"That's preposterous," Tymora declared, slicing at the scourge with her sword. Beshaba twisted her body and blocked the blow with her goad. More bolts of energy flashed off the tip of Tymora's blade.

"When I reached out, I sensed it was your power draining me. "I have been your prisoner here for days."

"You lie!" Beshaba snarled. "I do not even know where 'here' is."

Joel decided it was time to speak up. "While I don't

really know for sure," the bard said, "if I had to hazard a
guess, I'd say we were somewhere in Elysium, since that's
where Lathander's realm is."

"Yes!" Beshaba declared, slashing and smashing furi-
ously at Tymora with both weapons. "Now this slave
speaks the truth."

With amazing reflexes, Tymora blocked each of Beshaba's attacks. "You have addled the mortal's brain with
your tortures," Lady Luck insisted. "He does not know
what he is saying."

"Speak more truth, slave," Beshaba shouted and threw
her goad like a spear over Tymora's head. The goad's
prongs struck Joel's right thigh, piercing and searing his
flesh at the same time. Joel struggled to fight back the
pain.

Tymora slammed her body into Beshaba's, knocking
her farther away from Joel. Lady Luck got her foot caught
in a strand of Beshaba's goad and tripped, but she fell into
Beshaba with her full weight. Both goddesses fell to the
floor in a tangle of thrashing arms and legs. Beshaba
squeezed at Tymora's throat with her free hand.

Joel recovered some of his senses and realized he must
convince both goddesses that they were both victims or
this struggle could go on endlessly.

"It's true, Lady Tymora," the bard cried out. "It was
Lord Lathander's paladin who summoned the phoenix
that abducted Lady Beshaba. It must have brought us
back to his realm."

Tymora jerked her head back and rolled away from Beshaba. "If it is true that Lathander abducted Beshaba,
then he did so to make her return my power," Lady Luck
declared.

"So how have you come to be in the same prison with
Lady Beshaba?" Joel asked. "Lady Selune and Lord
Finder wouldn't tell us where you were, but they wouldn't
have delivered you to Lady Beshaba. They would have en-
trusted you to Lord Lathander's care."

Tymora hesitated before she answered. "Perhaps I
must be near her to regain my power," she said, though
her voice was uncertain.

"But Lady Beshaba is as weakened as you are," Joel

pointed out. "When you fought, you were evenly matched. Neither of you could defeat the other. Someone has drained both of you."

Tymora and Beshaba both stood up, keeping a wary eye on one another.

"Beshaba must be faking her weakness to confuse you," Tymora said.

"Lady Beshaba's church and faithful are also weakened. Her bad luck has leaked out across the Realms just as yours has."

"It's a trick," Tymora said.

"Could such a trick fool Lady Selune?" Joel asked. "For it was she who told us this news."

Tymora said nothing for several moments.

"Why did you say that I had allied myself with Xvim?" she asked Beshaba.

"Because Lathander is your ally, and he appears to have allied with Xvim," Beshaba explained.

"That's impossible. What proof do you have that Xvim is involved in any of this?" Tymora demanded.

"Xvim sent creatures to attack me in my realm," Beshaba said. "He must have been trying to force me to use my power," Beshaba said. "I went to confront him in his realm, but he was nowhere to be found. I sent the Bastion of Hate tumbling down Mount Chamada, and still the little weasel did not appear."

"Is this true?" Tymora asked Joel.

"Lord Finder and Lady Selune sensed the attack, my lady," Joel confirmed. "And I witnessed the destruction of Xvim's fortress. Xvim seems to be missing or perhaps in hiding."

"You must be mistaken about Lathander," Tymora insisted.

"I know the stench of Lathander's paladins," Beshaba growled.

"It's possible that Holly was misled somehow," Joel said softly.

"Misled? How?" Beshaba asked.

"Perhaps someone like Xvim sent her a false vision, or he found a neutral minion to impersonate one of Lathander's servants," Joel suggested.

It was Beshaba's turn to appear thoughtful. Joel took advantage of the moment to ask Tymora, "Could you please let me down, my lady?"

Tymora stepped forward, but Beshaba moved to block her. "I still have no proof that you are not faking your loss of power. I cannot trust this slave, since he is priest of your lackey. The two of you together might overpower me."

"Lady Beshaba," Joel said. "You and Lady Tymora are trapped in this place together, put here by some common enemy. If you do not ally at least temporarily, you will no doubt fall to this enemy. Undoubtedly this enemy, whoever he is, is counting on you two to distrust each other while he finishes draining off your power."

"Perhaps," Beshaba said. "But that is still no reason to release *you*."

"I was hidden in your pocket when we arrived. I don't think whoever locked you in here realizes I'm here. I could be your secret weapon," Joel suggested.

Beshaba tilted her head and smiled. It was obvious Joel had chosen the just the right words. "Secret weapon." The Maid of Misfortune laughed. "Very well," she said, giving Tymora a nod.

Lady Luck released Joel from his bonds and removed the goad piercing his thigh. As quickly as possible, she healed the wounds Beshaba had inflicted on his body. Her touch not only removed his pain, but left him feeling mildly refreshed.

"Thank you," the bard whispered to Tymora.

"Well, what now?" Beshaba asked. "You say you have been here for days. How might we escape this place?"

Tymora shrugged. "I was unconscious all the while. I only awoke a short time ago. I was surrounded by chaos, matter without order, which, like that from the plane of Limbo, I could shape with my mind. When I heard your voices, I imagined a hallway and a door to reach you."

"When we first arrived here," Joel said, "I heard someone order someone else to put Lady Beshaba into the fusion chamber. What's a fusion chamber?"

Tymora and Beshaba looked at one another with a puzzled expression.

"I don't know," Tymora admitted.

"Nor I," Beshaba said. "I, too, was surrounded by chaos when I first awoke," Beshaba said, "but I, too, found I could arrange it about me. I expected to be in a prison. Perhaps that is why it looked like my dungeon in the Blood Tor, even down to the detail of the bones and scepter of the wizard Zorn."

The Maid of Misfortune closed her eyes for a moment. Instantly the room transformed into an underground temple dedicated to Beshaba, lit by two braziers. Joel felt a breeze from a slanted shaft near the ceiling.

Something white beside the stag's antlers on the altar caught Joel's eyes. He reached out and picked it up. "Lady Beshaba," he asked curiously, "why did you imagine an egg was here?"

"I did not imagine any such thing," Beshaba replied.

Joel examined the egg by the light of the brazier.

"What do you see?" Tymora asked.

"The shell is covered with fine lines, but it doesn't seem to be cracked," Joel said. He tapped and broke the egg on the side of the brazier and let its contents slide into the burning fire.

"How odd. There are two yolks," Tymora noted.

Act Four
Scene 3

Guilt-ridden that she had endangered Joel and faced with Finder's wrath, Holly lowered her head and sobbed like a child.

The paladin's tears did not soften the god's mood. "No tears," Finder snapped. "Like a desert will your eyes and heart be until my priest is returned."

Holly looked up fearfully. Finder's curse removed the tears from her cheeks and the corners of her eyes.

"Now tell me why you summoned the phoenix," Finder ordered.

"Dawnbringer Aurora told me I was to collect whatever materials Sirrion of the Flowing Flame needed for the spell he was casting with Lord Lathander," the paladin explained.

"Sirrion?" Jas asked. "Would this be Emilo's Sirrion, the one who nearly got us killed in the fetch's lair?"

"I don't know," Holly whispered.

"Who's Dawnbringer Aurora?" Emilo asked.

"Lathander's proxy," Finder said. "A very powerful priestess. Go on, paladin," he instructed Holly.

"Dawnbringer Aurora and Lord Sirrion said the spell would right an ancient wrong. Lord Sirrion sent me to fetch an odd assortment of things, symbols of bad luck and good, including chickens and an old coin from Myth Drannor and a rose from the Desertsmouth Mountains and a blue crystal ball that Dawnbringer Aurora kept in a locked box in the temple in Morning Glory. He set them on an altar. Then Lord Sirrion sent me to fetch Lady Beshaba. He didn't think I could do it, but Dawnbringer Aurora said Lord Lathander had every confidence in me. I didn't think I could do it either, so I asked Dawnbringer Aurora how. She gave me the holy symbol made of red glass and told me it would summon a phoenix, who would grab Lady Beshaba and bring her to Lord Sirrion. She told me not to be afraid for myself or the phoenix because Lady Beshaba would be very weak when I stepped through the gate to the Abyss."

"But when you stepped through the gate, Beshaba wasn't there," Finder said. "She'd already fled."

Holly nodded. "So I went with Joel and Jas and Emilo to find her in Gehenna, and Lord Lathander sent me a vision telling me to help Walinda so I could reach Beshaba. I didn't summon the phoenix right away because Walinda said nothing could get in or out of the Bastion of Hate except through the gate."

"But when you reached the Outlands, you couldn't find the summoning stone in your backpack because Emilo had it," Finder said. "But the moment he returned it, you used it, even though Beshaba had threatened Joel's life if you did not protect her."

There was such hard fury in Finder's tone that Jas felt she should say something in Holly's defense. "Surely Lathander won't let Joel come to any harm," she said.

"That is, assuming he is alive by the time the phoenix delivers Beshaba to Lord Sirrion," the god growled.

"But you can still sense him, right?" Jas asked. "With that god sense you have?"

Finder closed his eyes. "He is over Elysium, flying toward Morning Glory."

"All right," Jas said. "So he's not dead yet. We go to Elysium—"

"No!" Finder gasped. He opened his eyes. "He's gone! I can't sense him any longer!"

Fearing the absolute worst, Jas shoved Holly aside and placed herself between the god and the paladin.

"You have to be able to sense him," Jas insisted, putting her hands on Finder's arms. "Even if he's died and become a petitioner, you would sense him in Fermata."

"That witch has killed him," the god screamed at Holly, "and it's your fault!"

Dark clouds filled with lightning rolled toward them.

Jas stepped backward as Finder moved toward the paladin. The god tried to push Jas aside, but the winged woman clung to his sleeves. "Finder, you're still pretty new at this god thing. You could be wrong. Don't do something you'll regret," Jas begged.

"Lord Finder," a voice called out from behind the god. "Wait, please."

Finder whirled around. Two persons stood there. One was a statuesque blonde woman wearing a white gown of sheer fabric, and the other was a tall, pale warrior with cat eyes.

"Bors! Kenda!" Holly gasped.

Finder obviously recognized the warrior, for he addressed him. "If you've come for your treacherous friend, Sensate Bors," the god growled, "you had best abandon your mission now."

"Lord Finder," Kenda Fretterstag said hastily, making a slight curtsy, "Factol Montgomery bids us inform you there is a dark region in Lathander's realm that defies all attempts to scry into it. You cannot sense your priest because he was taken inside this region. But if he still lives, you will still be able to sense the area in Elysium surrounding the dark region."

It took only a moment for Finder to take in what the Sensate wizardess was saying, but it seemed to Jas like an eternity before the god relaxed the muscles in his neck and closed his eyes to follow Kenda's suggestion.

"Yes," Finder whispered. "It is like a dark spot on my inner eye." The god looked up at the Sensates. "What is the purpose of this darkness?"

"We do not know," Bors replied.

Kenda snorted derisively and said, "But some of us suspect Lathander has imprisoned both Tymora and Beshaba. We have scried tinker gnomes moving in and out of this dark region."

"Gnomes!" Emilo said excitedly. "What were they building?"

"We cannot see," Bors said.

Finder looked at Holly. "What is it, paladin?" he demanded.

"It is a great clockwork machine," Holly explained,

"which Lord Sirrion is building for Lord Lathander to help cast the spell that will right an ancient wrong. Lord Sirrion wouldn't tell me anything more, but I heard the gnomes call it a 'few chin chamber.' "

"A fusion chamber?" Emilo suggested.

"That could have been it," Holly agreed.

"Those are neat," the kender said. "I would love to see another one work."

"What does a fusion chamber do?" Finder asked.

"Well, when the gnomes make scrambled eggs for a large group of people," Emilo explained, "they beat up all the eggs with a little milk and salt and pepper, and then they cook the eggs. But there's always leftover egg mixture. They pour the leftover egg mixture in a fusion chamber, and the fusion chamber puts the eggs back into their shells so the gnomes can use them again later. I'm not sure what happens to the milk and salt and pepper. I'm not sure the gnomes know either."

"The gnomes were making omelets, not scrambled eggs," Kenda said.

Emilo shrugged. "I guess it doesn't make much difference."

"Somehow I don't suspect Lord Sirrion is in Elysium just to oversee tinker gnomes making omelets," Finder said irately.

"Well, it does explain why Sirrion wanted Holly to fetch some chickens," Emilo pointed out.

"But what were the other things for?" Jas asked. "The luck charms and the rose and the coin and the crystal sphere?"

"Spell keys?" Kenda suggested.

"What?" Finder asked in surprise.

"What are spell keys?" Emilo asked.

"They're special requirements necessary for a wizard to cast magic in different planes," Kenda explained. "Spell keys vary greatly from plane to plane and spell to spell. Sometimes the wizard must perform a certain action, such as free a bird or sacrifice a goat or spit in the wind or sing a song. Other times the wizard need only possess a certain item, like a dagger or cat or a feather or some sort of gemstone."

"Or something like the power key that Finder gave Joel?" Emilo asked.

"Well, similar to that, yes," Kenda replied. "But power keys are created by gods for their priests."

"That's it!" Finder said excitedly. "Lathander must know some of Tymora's major power keys. He may have guessed at some of Beshaba's."

"Is that important?" Jas asked.

"A power key allows a priest to siphon off some of his god's power," Finder explained. "That's why they're kept secret, or made to be temporary, or made so they can only be used by one person. If they aren't, they can be used by the wrong person to drain a god's powers."

Finder turned to Holly and asked sternly, "So what is this ancient wrong Lathander intends to right, paladin?"

"I—I don't know," Holly said, her voice trembling.

"But you suspect something," Finder said. "I can sense it. Tell me what it is," he growled.

"Dawnbringer Aurora said Lord Lathander would right an ancient wrong, but when Lord Sirrion said the same thing, I knew he was lying. I didn't know how that could be . . . unless . . ."

"Unless Lord Sirrion has lied to Lord Lathander, and Lord Lathander and his priestess were taken in by the lie," Finder suggested to the paladin.

"Yes," Holly whispered.

"So perhaps Sirrion only intends to drain away the two goddesses' powers," Bors suggested.

"But what's the ancient wrong that Lathander thinks he's righting?" Jas asked.

"Oh! I get it! He's going to put Tymora and Beshaba back together again!" Emilo cried out excitedly.

"What are you talking about?" Holly demanded.

"The kender has the dark of it," Kenda said. "Lathander wants to put Tyche back together as if she were a cracked egg."

Act Four
Scene 4

After discovering that their teleport, dimensional doorways, and magical portal spells all failed within the chamber, the bard and the two goddesses set about to explore their prison from top to bottom. The fusion chamber was filled with the chaotic matter that Tymora had said was very similar to that found in the plane of Limbo. Both goddesses could manipulate the matter into an organized form with a mere thought, and once they did so, the matter stayed fixed in place. With much concentration, Joel found that he, too, could manipulate the matter, but the moment he ceased concentrating on it, it reverted to a swirling chaos of earth, air, water, and fire that threatened to choke, drown, or burn him unless one of the goddesses re-formed it for him.

By forcing the chaotic matter to the side, forming vast spaces of air only, the prisoners puzzled out that the fusion chamber was actually a large pyramid nearly a hundred feet high, with a square base over a hundred feet on each side. The temple that Beshaba had created actually took up very little of the space within the fusion chamber. The boundaries of the chamber were silvery, shimmering magical walls of force. The prisoners could find no doors, so they began testing the nearest wall. They smashed at it with weaponry, magic missiles, lightning bolts, and fireballs. They rubbed at it with water and acid and lye created out of the chaos matter. They chanted ancient spells of disintegration at it and spells to dispel it. They cursed it and blessed it. Nothing they tried seemed to penetrate or even weaken the barrier.

Tymora and Beshaba began exploring every inch of the

walls in greater detail, looking for a flaw they could work
on. Because the bard was unable to travel safely through
the Limbo-like chaos outside the region the goddesses had
formed, they left him in Beshaba's temple. There Joel
practiced manipulating the chaotic matter with his mind,
feeling much like a child who'd been given a lump of clay
to play with while his parents went about their adult
business.

The bard found that fields of grass and groves of trees
were the easiest to create, while rooms took a great deal
more concentration. He challenged himself by creating
rooms he remembered well, like his grandmother's parlor,
the mess hall of the barding college he'd attended as a boy,
and the tavern where he first met Finder and spent a long
night discussing music and art.

His creations were nowhere near as organized or de-
tailed as the goddesses'; nonetheless, it was an amazingly
powerful sensation manipulating the chaos into order.
Concentrating proved to be taxing work, however, and
Joel was forced to retreat periodically to the temple so he
could rest without thinking.

As he played with the Limbo matter, Joel began to recognize a certain common denominator in each the envi-
ronments he created—the window. It appeared in each of
the interiors Joel created, although he was certain there
was no window in the real mess hall or the tavern. He
tried hard to envision the space without the window, but it
would not go away.

The temple Beshaba had created had a tunnel shaft,
and the dungeon that Beshaba's mind had formed without
even consciously thinking about it had a window. Joel concentrated on forming the hull of the spelljammer he'd ridden in, which definitely had no windows, but his creation
was marred by a ragged hole in the hull. Something, or
someone, was keeping the Limbo matter from completely
surrounding him.

Joel could think of only one reason for the opening:
Someone outside the fusion chamber wanted a window in
order to watch the prisoners.

Joel imagined some sacks of sand along the hull of the
imaginary spelljammer and climbed atop them so he

could peer through the hole. A dim, rosy light shone through.

In the dim light, on the other side of the spelljammer hull, Joel could make out what looked like a stone altar, adorned with glowing crystals and sparking balls of glass. Strewn about the table were varying tokens of luck both good and bad—a horseshoe, a luck stone, a four-leaf clover, a broken mirror, a new knife, and a black cat curled into a ball, sleeping. Suspended magically above the table were three items: an old coin and a pink rose, both of which glowed as bright as a lightning flash, and a blue crystal sphere.

The space beyond the stone altar looked like a grassy clearing beneath a bright red tent large enough to hold a wedding party.

The hole in the hull seemed to Joel like a magical portal out of the fusion chamber. Joel tried to put his hand through the hole, but found his way blocked by an invisible magical barrier. Unlike the shimmering walls of the fusion chamber, the barrier that blocked the portal was not completely impenetrable. Joel poked at it with his dagger, and in doing so discovered that nonliving objects could penetrate through the magical opening. Standing this close to the hole, he became aware of a faint clanking sound. Then he heard voices, muffled, he suspected, by the magical barrier.

In his excitement, Joel's concentration on the hull ceased, and he was surrounded again by chaos. Staving off panic, he swam back through the swirling matter until he reached Beshaba's temple. He coughed up the water and dirt he had inadvertently breathed in and smacked out the tiny patches of flame dancing in his clothing and hair.

Once he'd caught his breath, the bard concentrated on the tunnel near the ceiling. He reformed the chaos matter so the shaft was considerably larger, reaching down to the floor. In doing so, he uncovered another magical portal through which he could look out of the fusion chamber. Oddly enough, this portal opened to the exact same spot as the hole in the spelljammer hull—above the altar in the tent. Apparently only portals to the altar functioned. Just like the one in the spelljammer hull, this portal was

blocked by a magical barrier through which Joel could
push his dagger but not his hand.

Joel listened carefully for the voices again and was rewarded when he heard someone say, "My lord, I do not
recommend that you speak with them. It will only cause
them unnecessary anxiety, which is likely to affect your
ability to control the spell."

The voice was deep and familiar. Joel was pretty sure it
was the same voice that had ordered Beshaba to be placed
in the fusion chamber.

The second speaker's voice was also deep, but softer
than the first, making it hard for Joel to distinguish the
words.

" . . . would think . . . anxiety . . . happening to them
would be worse. . . . ease the transition . . . be cowardly
. . . Nothing will alter my will" were all the words Joel
caught.

Suddenly two tall male figures appeared in the doorway of the tent. One was particularly handsome, with the
body of a tall, slender, youthful athlete and fiery red-
orange hair. He was dressed in a tunic of opalescent reds
and golds. He could only be the god Lathander, Joel
thought. The other figure was even taller, with hair, eyebrows, and beard of living flames. His robe shimmered
with the colors of fire. Joel guessed this was the mysterious Sirrion of the Flowing Flame. Each god possessed an
aura so bright that Joel stood blinking like an owl in day-
light.

"What is he doing in the fusion chamber?" Lathander
demanded, pointing directly at the bard.

Immediately Joel dived behind the cover of the altar.

"In our haste to place Beshaba into the fusion chamber," Joel heard Sirrion reply, "I neglected to have your
servants search her. She must have smuggled him in as a
smaller creature. It will make no difference to our spell.
He is a mere mortal and cannot affect the outcome."

"But he will die in the chaos of the creation," Lathander
objected.

"I warned you, my lord, that some sacrifices would
have to be made," Sirrion said. A slight impatient whine
had crept into his voice.

"No," Lathander insisted, "not one such as this. He is the priest of another god. He must be taken out. I sense him hiding there behind that altar. Open the portal so the guardinals can fetch him."

"My lord," Sirrion objected, "it's too risky. Lady Beshaba and Lady Tymora are both conscious. They may sense the exit and seize the opportunity to escape."

"Then you must drain enough power from them so that they become unconscious again," Lathander ordered.

"That could delay the spell by nearly another day," Sirrion declared. "Selune's suspicions have already been aroused because you placed Tymora where she cannot sense her presence. If we don't hurry, Selune may enter this place unbidden and discover our plan. She isn't likely to agree with your decision. She may find a way to thwart us."

"And what exactly is this plan, Lord Lathander?" Tymora asked suddenly in an angry tone. "I was doubtful of Beshaba's claim that you were involved in this, but I see you have betrayed my trust." Lady Luck pointed to the gold coin suspended above the stone altar outside the fusion chamber. "You have drained my power from me by using the power key I gave to one of your priests as a favor to you."

Joel peered out from behind the altar. Tymora and Beshaba had just flown into the temple. They stood on either side of the tunnel window Joel had enlarged and glared out of the fusion chamber at their captors.

"Lady Tymora, Lady Beshaba, welcome to Elysium," Lathander said with a low bow. "Please forgive me for your abduction and imprisonment, but it is for a good cause, I assure you."

"I don't give a damn about your 'good cause,'" Beshaba retorted. "Free me this instant, you arrogant peacock."

Lathander gave Beshaba a coldly polite smile and said, "I did not expect you to care, Lady Beshaba. But I will explain our plan for Lady Tymora's sake. Please feel free to listen."

Lady Beshaba scowled at the Morninglord.

"Do go on, Lord Lathander," Tymora said with mock sarcasm.

"Some time ago," Lathander began, "Lord Sirrion peti-
tioned me to become a patron of an important cause. He
seemed to feel that there was an imbalance among the
gods of Faerûn that, if left unchecked, could lead to bloody
wars on Toril."

"Sirrion isn't worshiped on Faerûn," Beshaba said.
"Why should he care?"

"Lord Sirrion," Lathander explained, "has reason to believe that an imbalance of good on Faerûn would lead to
an exodus of evil. which would end up on Krynn, where he
does have worshipers. Krynn is already beset with much
evil, and Lord Sirrion is anxious to avoid the influx of any
more. From the first I found his arguments in favor of his
plan quite compelling, but I didn't agree to sponsor him
immediately. I am not as rash as many of the gods believe
me to be."

"Please get to the point, Lathander," Tymora snapped.
"My attention tends to wander when I'm a captive audience."

Joel peered around another corner of the altar so that
he could view Lathander and Sirrion. Sirrion had started
to manipulate the crystals and glass balls on the altar just
outside the fusion chamber.

"Lord Sirrion seemed to feel that your church, Lady Tymora, was about to face a grave conflict with that of Lady
Beshaba's, which would lead to horrendous wars. The only
way to prevent this catastrophe," Lathander said resigned-
ly, "was to bring the two of you, and hence your followers,
together. To accomplish this, you need to be united once
again in the form of Tyche, the goddess you once were."

Beshaba guffawed loudly. "Have you lost your wits?"
she asked Lathander.

"Lathander," Tymora said with horror, "Tyche is dead.
You can't mean you're going to try to resurrect her."

"No, Lady Tymora. Tyche is not dead. She lives in you
and your sister, and when the two of you are fused into
one with the aid of this machine and the power of our
magic, Tyche will be whole again. Toril will remain at
peace, and Krynn will not be disturbed by our troubles."

"But only at our expense," Tymora declared. "Lathander, I am happy as I am. I do not want to be united with

Beshaba. You have no right to force this upon us."

"Yes. For a long time, that is what kept me from supporting Sirrion's plan. But then I was left to dwell on a matter of equal importance." The Morninglord looked away from Tymora and stared off into space with a haunted look. "An ancient wrong will be righted by this plan," he said. "Tyche was a great goddess. She should never have been destroyed. To this day, I blame myself for that tragedy. Had I not started the Dawn Cataclysm, Moander might never have corrupted Tyche, and she would yet live."

"It's a little late to think of that now," Beshaba said accusingly. "You tried to claim power that was not yours. Only a fool would be surprised the other gods of Faerûn chose to war against you. By the time the Dawn Cataclysm ended, your allies had suffered more losses than the enemies you hoped to contain in your bid for leadership."

"You may come to regret this move as well," Tymora warned.

"I'm sorry you are unwilling, my lady," Lathander said, "but believe me, this is for the greater good. It will serve both Toril and Krynn as well as restore Tyche."

"Not to mention that it will help you assuage your guilt," Beshaba growled. "You're a complete fool, Lathander. It's no wonder the others wouldn't accept your leadership, nor that Tyche left you."

"Soon, Lady Beshaba," the Morninglord replied softly, "you will be free from the spite and malice that enslaves your heart. You will become happier and more beloved than you have ever been. Although I realize you would never agree, you, even more than Lady Tymora, should appreciate what I am about to do for you."

"Hear me, Lathander," Beshaba vowed. "If any part of me truly remains in Tyche, she will claw out your eyes the first chance she gets."

"Lathander, Selune will never let you get away with this," Tymora said fiercely. "You cannot hope to keep her from discovering this. She is your ally. She is aware of all that happens wherever you have followers, even here in your realm. Even if you've renounced your alliance, Finder's priest is here, and Finder is an ally of Selune's as well. Your scheme is already uncovered."

"Not really," Lathander said. "With Sirrion's aid, I have
created a dark zone about this machine that makes it impossible for anyone, even a god, to sense what goes on
within. Besides, Selune is far too busy searching for the
elusive Iyachtu Xvim and helping keep your church on its
feet in your absence."

"So you *are* in league with Xvim," Beshaba declared.

"Hardly," Lathander replied with a tone that suggested
he found the idea extremely distasteful.

"Then how did he know when to attack my realm?" Beshaba demanded.

"That was an unfortunate mistake on my part, Lady
Beshaba," Sirrion said. "The priests of Xvim had stolen
one of your power keys from your temple in Waterdeep.
The minion I sent to purchase it said far more than he
should have, and the priests of Xvim figured out the rest.
Thus, soon after rumors of Tymora's weakness began to
spread, Xvim, realizing you, too, must also be weakened,
took advantage of the knowledge to attack you. Unfortunately for him I had not yet drained as much power from
you as I had from Tymora. He fled from your wrath and is
hiding in Baator."

"And why is it necessary for you to drain away our
power?" Beshaba asked.

"First, so that we could capture you," Lathander explained. "Second, so that the fusion chamber could handle
the job of uniting the two of you. It's an ingenious device,
but hardly up to the task of containing and fusing that
much godly power. We returned some of your power so you
would regain consciousness and I could explain to you
what was about to happen. Now, however, we must drain
you again so that you will once more fall unconscious and
we can remove the bard from the fusion chamber. He
couldn't possibly survive the fusion process."

"What's going to happen to all the power you drain
from us?" Tymora asked bitterly.

"It's being transferred into the blue crystal sphere,"
Lathander said. "It was the last power key Tyche ever
made."

"Yes, I remember," Tymora snapped.

"When you and Beshaba are united, all the power will be restored to you," Lathander promised. "You will be more powerful than ever."

"Interesting," Beshaba said. Suddenly a great spear appeared in her hand. She drew it back and pointed it at Tymora, who was so engrossed with glaring at Lathander and Sirrion that she didn't seem to notice.

"Look out!" Joel cried out as Beshaba hurled the weapon. In the nick of time, he threw himself at Lady Luck, knocking her out of the spear's path.

"Beshaba, what are you doing?" Lathander shouted.

Tymora leapt to her feet and took cover with Joel behind a large shield she created from the chaos matter.

"If Tymora is dead, Lathander," Beshaba replied, "obviously you cannot shackle me to her side." She addressed Tymora. "You would do well to follow my lead, Sister. Soon we will be too weak to act on our own behalf. If you destroy me, so be it. I am willing to risk my life to spite this arrogant peacock. We are now at war," Beshaba declared. She pointed one hand at Tymora, and a bolt of lightning crashed down just to the left of Tymora.

Tymora responded by conjuring a magical dagger and hurling it at the Maid of Misfortune. As Beshaba ducked, Tymora grabbed Joel's hand and fled from the temple, flying into the chaos.

Act Four
Scene 5

Back in the wilderness of the Outlands, Finder nodded to Bors and Kenda. "Give Factol Montgomery my thanks for your timely information." Then he looked at Holly. "We have a report to make to Selune," he said, reaching out and grabbing the paladin's shoulder. He held his other hand out to Jas. The winged woman grabbed Emilo, then took up Finder's hand. The god whispered, "Argentil," and teleported the three adventurers away from the Outlands.

The next moment Jas found herself swimming beneath a bright full moon in a cold sea. She burst from the water, pulling the kender with her. Of Finder and Holly there was no sign. Cradling Emilo in her arms, she fluttered above the surface of the choppy water with huge white mothlike wings, shouting for the god and the paladin. The moonlight glittered along the waves, but Jas was too panic-stricken to appreciate the beauty all about her.

She couldn't understand why Finder had teleported to this place, but she knew that Holly, in her heavy plate armor, would never be able to make it to the water's surface. For a second, she wondered if Finder was still so angry with the paladin that he would allow her to drown, but she dismissed the idea with a shake of her head. She was sure Finder couldn't be so cruel.

After several fearful moments, Finder bobbed to the surface of the water, cradling Holly, coughing and spluttering, in his arms.

"What went wrong?" Jas asked.

"I tried to teleport to Argentil, Selune's hall, but someone has placed a barrier about the Isle of the Gates of the Moon. We slid into the sea when I hit the barrier."

"Lathander," Holly whispered. "He knows you know his plan. He's trying to keep Selune from discovering it."

"Can't Selune sense us out in the ocean?" Jas asked.

"Not if Lathander's taken the precaution to shield us magically from her senses. He's much more powerful than I," Finder said. "I can't beat him at this game."

"My presence will give away your every move," Holly said. She held up a small white flower and ripped it in half, whispering, "Morning Glory." The paladin vanished.

"What happened?" Emilo gasped. "Where did Holly go?"

"She returned to Lathander with a piece of magic, like the one I gave you to return to Fermata," Finder explained.

"So what now?" Jas asked. "Back to Fermata?"

"No," Finder said. He set one hand on Jas's head and the other on Emilo's and murmured the word, "Precipice."

Then next moment they stood at the top of a high cliff covered with heather and overlooking a river. The river poured into a lagoon before it plunged over an even higher cliff. Spray from the waterfall rose all the way to the top of the highest cliff, moistening the heather and making the air smell sweet. The sun shone brightly, creating rainbows in the mist.

As Jas set Emilo down beside her, the kender held his hands over his stomach. "I think I'm getting dizzy from all this popping in and out," he said. "Oooh. Jas, your wings look just like the phoenix's wings," the kender added.

Jas looked at the flame-colored feathers sprouting from her back and grimaced. "That's just ducky," she muttered. "Where are we, anyway?"

"Somewhere near Lathander's realm, or at least as near as I dare try to teleport," Finder replied. "If Lathander has a barrier around Selune's realm, he's sure to have one around his own."

"So what now?" Jas asked.

"We make our way toward his realm and hope we can sneak up on him," Finder said.

"How do you sneak up on a god?" Jas asked.

"Well, between maintaining the barrier around Selune's isle, shielding me from Selune's senses, keeping the dark region in his realm from prying eyes, and trying to put Tyche together again, he has a good deal on his mind," Finder said. "We'll have to seize any chance that comes our way and hope he's too distracted to notice."

"Distracted," a quavering voice said behind them. "I get distracted all the time."

The god and his companions whirled around. There stood an ancient old man in gray robes, his face and head covered with long, flowing, white hair.

"Sometimes the least little thing can distract me," the old man said. "I reach for the cheese cutter, and I remember I've left the barn door open. Of course, eventually all the cows come home to roost, but still, if you let them wander in strange corn, they start claiming alien spelljammers took them jumping over the moon. Then I sit down to dinner and realize I've forgotten to bring out not only the cheese cutter but the cheese as well."

"Oh, boy," Jas murmured, having met more than a few senile old men in her life.

In spite of the dire nature of his quest, Finder was so amused by the old man's ramblings that he chuckled in spite of himself. "Sir, I know just how you feel," Finder answered the old man. "Allow me to introduce myself. I'm Finder Wyvernspur, and these are my companions, Jasmine and Emilo Haversack."

"Haversack?" the old man asked. "Have we met somewhere?"

"Yes, sir," Emilo said. "A few days ago, in some other place. You made me unnoticeable except to people from Krynn so I could help you discover if someone was an impostor or not."

Jas and Finder exchanged surprised glances.

"See," the old man said, holding a finger up in front of Finder, "you don't have to remember everything. Sometimes you can get other people to do it for you."

"I'll find someone to remember that for me, sir," Finder replied.

"Ha!" the old man laughed. "You are a sharp one, aren't you?" Then he turned to Jas. He put a hand on the woman's cheek. "You've grown to be a lovely young lass," he said. "Why, I remember when you were just a wee tiny baby."

"Are you sure you don't have me confused with someone else?" Jas asked in a kindly tone.

"You are Rose and Michael's little girl, aren't you?" he asked.

Jas's jaw dropped. "Those were my parents' names," she said, surprised.

"You look just like your mother," the old man said. "Now, Finder, my boy—"

"Yes, sir?" Finder said.

"This is for you," the old man said, handing Finder an envelope.

Finder turned over the envelope. It was addressed simply to "Our Friend." The god opened the envelope and pulled out a plain white card edged in gold. "It's a wedding invitation," he noted.

"Yes. Someone I know threw it away. Very unlike him. I had to wonder if it was really him."

"But it isn't addressed to us," Finder said.

"It doesn't matter. That's the wonderful thing about weddings. Everyone is welcome. Turning away a guest would be very bad form," the old man said.

"But this invitation is for a wedding that took place last month," Finder pointed out.

"Oh, that doesn't matter," the old man said. "Better late than never to give best wishes to the happy couple. Anyway, it will get you where you want to go. It's a portal key. Just hold it up and say . . . and say . . . Oh, dear, I seem to have forgotten. Let me think for a moment. 'Don't leave me in the lurch?' 'Stop on a dime?' Hmmm . . . That's not it. How about, 'Plant a little birch, make a little rhyme?' No. Oh, now I remember. You say, 'Get me to the church on time,' and you'll be there."

Finder laughed at the irony of the words. "I really appreciate this, sir. Thank you," he said. "But it occurs to me you haven't told me your name."

"My name?" the old man repeated. "My name is Fuzzbat. . . . No, wait. Fezbutt," he said with less certainty. "Or maybe it's Fizz . . . Fizz . . . Fizz Something. I'm quite sure."

"Oh. I thought it might be something else," Finder said. "But I'm pleased to meet you, Mr. Fizz Something."

"What did you think my name was?" Fizz Something asked.

"Well, the way you've come to the rescue, completely out of the blue, I thought you might be Ao," Finder replied. "The Overpower of the Cosmos."

Fizz Something laughed hard for several moments until he started to cough and wheeze. When he had recovered, he looked up at Finder. "What an interesting guess," he said. Then he teleported away.

"What was that all about?" Jas asked, completely confused by the exchange between the god and the old man.

"That was Fizz Something," Finder said. "A god from your world, I believe," he said to Emilo.

"No," Emilo replied. "He's just a nice old wizard."

"Right," Finder said. "Just a nice old wizard."

"So the invitation is a portal key?" Jas asked. "It must have been someone pretty important for such a fancy invitation."

"It's for the marriage of Aurora Brightday to Allain Crimson, to be held in the realm of Morning Glory," Finder explained. "And it's high time we wished the happy couple joy." He reached out for Jas's hand. Jas, in turn, took Emilo's hand. Finder held up the wedding invitation and called out, "Get me to the church on time."

The heather-covered precipice over the river disappeared, replaced by an orchard of peach trees. The sun was just rising over a distant mountain ridge. Birds flitted about over their heads, twittering excitedly.

Suddenly a tall, dark girl in plate armor came running toward them.

"It's Holly!" Jas said.

Holly ran straight to Finder. "Hurry!" she begged. "Lady Beshaba is trying to kill Lady Tymora, and Lord Lathander won't do anything to interfere."

Act Four
Scene 6

Joel spat out the dirt in his mouth as Tymora formed a protective cocoon around them.

"My hero," the goddess called him as she helped pat out the fire that singed his hair and clothing.

The Limbo-like chaos they had just flown through left Joel dazed. The disorganized elements didn't seem to bother the goddess in the least.

"Thank you for saving my life," Lady Luck said. "You are lucky for me, Rebel Bard. But I think it's time you were going."

"Going where, my lady?" Joel asked.

"You cannot stay in the fusion chamber. You cannot negotiate the chaos matter, and I cannot protect you and defend myself from Beshaba at the same time. Beshaba will either kill you or use you against me, and I cannot allow that."

"The magical barrier surrounding this place holds living matter prisoner," Joel said. "There is no way for me to leave."

"I think I have a way around that," the goddess replied.

"Lady Tymora," Joel objected, "if I leave the fusion chamber, Lathander and Sirrion will begin to merge you with Beshaba immediately. The longer I stay here, the more time I buy for Finder to rescue you."

Tymora smiled and placed her palm on Joel's cheek. "You are so like Finder was when he was young, before he grew afraid of death. Such valor is commendable. Still, you must go."

"Finder will not be pleased if I do not render you every assistance I can," Joel insisted.

"Finder would be less pleased if you should die, though he does not know that," Tymora said. "He needs you. Take care of him, Rebel Bard. Be his luck, as you were mine." She kissed him on the cheek.

Joel opened his mouth to object more strenuously, but his face was suddenly too stiff to move. His limbs felt as stiff as stone. Then he realized that his limbs *were* stone. His whole body had become a statue. Then his mind went black.

* * * * *

Finder, Jas, Holly, and Emilo burst into the clearing beside the tent near the intersecting streams.

"They're in there!" Holly cried out, pointing to a shimmering portal hovering over a stone altar.

Just as the paladin spoke, a stone statue came sliding out of the portal. It was covered with dirt and dripping with water. Little patches of flame flickered over its surface. Nonetheless, they were able to recognize the statue.

"It's Joel!" Jas gasped. "He's been turned to stone."

Finder motioned with one hand, and the statue levitated to his side. Then he touched the stone, and Joel slumped into his god's arms, flesh and blood once more. The bard moaned softly. He felt as if he'd been sleeping on rocks for days.

As Joel's head cleared, he noticed Lathander, standing beneath the portal with his back turned toward them. The god spun around to face the intruders. He looked surprised to see Holly standing with Finder.

"Paladin, what is the meaning of this? Why have you brought Finder here?" the Morninglord asked Holly.

"Forgive me, Lord Lathander," Holly said, "but something isn't right here. Lord Finder should have an opportunity to speak on behalf of Lady Tymora."

"There is no time, paladin," Lathander said. "If we delay the fusion any longer, Beshaba may destroy Tymora or vice versa. Then Tyche can never be resurrected. Lord Sirrion, are you ready?"

"It will take only a few moments more to drain off enough power from both goddesses to make the fusion safe," Sirrion replied.

"You have your priest, Lord Finder," Lathander said. "I suggest you leave now, before I grow annoyed by your intrusion."

Finder set Joel down beside Jas. The bard leaned heavily on the winged woman, hardly able to move a muscle.

"You can grow peeved, piqued, and provoked, for all I care," Finder said. "I'm not leaving without Tymora."

"You cannot hope to defeat my plan," Lathander said. "I am far, far more powerful than you."

"I need only hold you off until Selune grows suspicious," Finder said.

Lathander glowered at the younger god. "You cannot stop me," he said.

"Did you think that if you succeeded, Selune would forgive you?" Finder asked. "That because she was friends with Tyche, she would be pleased that you sacrificed Tymora?"

"Once it is done, Selune will have no choice but to accept it," Lathander argued.

"If you thought your cause was truly just, you wouldn't be reluctant for the Moon Maiden to know what you intend," Finder retorted.

As the two gods argued, Emilo climbed up on the stone altar where Lord Sirrion's attention was fixed on the crystals and glass spheres, which glowed and sparked with increasing brilliance. To Jas's alarm, the kender began making all sorts of rude gestures and faces directly in front of the god of the Flowing Flame. He's really pushing his luck, Jas thought as she watched Emilo caper about.

Then Jas remembered with a start that Emilo said Fizz Something had made him unnoticeable except to people from Krynn. Sirrion was from Krynn, yet he obviously wasn't noticing the kender.

"It's time, Lord Lathander," Sirrion said, turning to face his fellow god.

"Keep Lord Finder occupied," Lathander ordered the Flowing Flame.

Sirrion stepped between Finder and the fusion chamber as Lathander went to the altar and took up the blue crystal sphere.

"Lathander, no!" Finder shouted. He made a rush for the altar, but Lord Sirrion grabbed him and held him fast.

Holly was right behind the god. "My lord," she whispered to Lathander, "must you do this? How can it be right if it must be done without the knowledge of your allies?"

"I require your silence now, paladin," Lathander said warningly.

"But—"

The Morninglord glared at Holly as if she were a creature from the Abyss. "I will not tolerate disobedience," he said with a chill in his voice that could freeze the sun. The paladin collapsed to the floor, sobbing, unable to face her god's wrath.

Lathander held up the blue crystal sphere and began chanting Tyche's name. Simultaneously shrieks of "No!" came from inside the fusion chamber as Beshaba and Tymora felt their souls begin to merge against their wills.

Emilo, who still stood on the altar, placed himself squarely in front of the Morninglord and said boldly, "Excuse me, Lord Lathander."

When the kender spoke, Lathander pulled back as if he'd seen a ghost.

"I realize you don't want to be interrupted," Emilo said, "but I really think you should know something." The kender pointed directly at Lord Sirrion, who was grappling with Finder. "That god is a fraud. He is not Sirrion of the Flowing Flame."

Lathander looked at the kender with fury, but he glanced back uncertainly at Sirrion.

"He's not even from Krynn," Emilo insisted. "There, I've done what I came to do," the kender said, hopping down from the altar and running to Jas's side.

"This is ridiculous," Lathander snapped. "If he's not Sirrion, who is he?"

"Now, there's an interesting question," Joel replied. "Can you think of another power who would want to impersonate Sirrion?"

"One with an interest in destroying two goddesses and harming Lord Lathander's reputation at the same time," Finder suggested.

"One who'd like to grab the power of those two goddesses for himself," Jas guessed.

Holly gasped with a horrible suspicion. "One who's been missing from his realm for days, not even returning when Beshaba destroyed it," she said as she looked up into Sirrion's glowing green eyes and realized why they were familiar. She had seen eyes just like them on a statue in a temple of evil. "My lord," the paladin shouted, "this impostor is none other than Iyachtu Xvim!"

Lathander whirled around to face the accused. The god who called himself Sirrion had released Finder, but as soon as he let go, Finder had grabbed onto him. The other god growled, a low, feral noise full of hatred. In a burst of godly power, he threw Finder from him.

"The farce is ended," the god said, transforming into the figure of a man with black scales and shaggy black hair, wearing nothing but a loincloth. It was indeed Iyachtu Xvim. "I will take what I am owed," he declared as he leapt across the tent to the altar, scattering the luck fetishes and startling the black cat who had sat so calmly through the whole proceedings. Xvim grabbed the pink rose and the old coin suspended magically over the altar.

"That power is not for you!" Lathander shouted, grabbing at Xvim's arm.

The god of hatred slammed Lathander in the face with the heel of his hand. Stunned, the Morninglord dropped the blue crystal sphere and fell backward. Xvim spun about to leave the tent, but he tripped over the black cat, which howled in outrage. Both power keys flew from the evil god's hands. Joel caught the rose and Jas caught the coin.

"Lucky catches?" Jas wondered aloud.

"And an unlucky trip," Joel said, pointing to the portal leading into the fusion chamber where Beshaba and Tymora stood side by side. The goddesses had cast their magic out of the fusion chamber, protecting their power keys even though they themselves could not escape.

Lathander leapt upon Xvim and held him down on the floor of the tent. Holly retrieved the blue crystal sphere.

"Put Tyche's power key back on the altar, Holly Harrowslough," Lathander ordered.

Holly stood up with the power key of the goddess her lord intended to resurrect and walked toward the altar.

"So, knowing this isn't really Sirrion doesn't change your mind?" Emilo asked Lathander with surprise. "Even though he's an evil god who lied to you?"

Lathander glared at the kender, but then his face grew thoughtful. His head snapped around just in time to see Holly toss Tyche's power key into the fusion chamber.

Lathander's eyes widened in surprise. In a shocked voice, he demanded of his paladin, "What have you done?"

"Now Tymora and Beshaba can use Tyche's power key to escape the fusion chamber," Holly explained.

"What compels you to disobey me?" Lathander asked in an amazed tone. "How dare you risk falling from my grace?"

Tears flowed freely from Holly's eyes. "It would be evil to join the goddesses against their will, my lord," she said.

In the fusion chamber, Tymora snatched up the blue sphere. The shimmering portal flashed with a bright light as the two goddesses flew out of the fusion chamber.

Like hawks swooping down upon their prey, Tymora and Beshaba landed before Lathander and Xvim, who still lay locked together. Tymora slammed Tyche's power key to the ground near Xvim's head. The crystal blue sphere splintered into a thousand pieces, spraying both Xvim and Lathander with the shards.

Offstage

In the Prime Material Plane on the world known as Toril in Realmspace, Amber Wyvernspur cried out with surprise and then delight at the sudden appearance of her great-granduncle, Drone Wyvernspur, who carried a lantern and a picnic basket. He arrived by dimensional doorway some time after the children's torches had burned out, but before panic had set in. Amber and the children had been in the dark long enough to sing fourteen rounds of a silly halfling song Cory had taught them.

"You found us!" Amber cried out in relief. "I knew you would."

"I didn't know I had lost you," the shaggy old wizard retorted. He looked around at the collapsed ceiling disapprovingly. "What a mess you children have made," he muttered. "You'll be cleaning this up until you're old enough to leave home. Of course, you could get out of the work if you want to leave home now," he added with a dark look at Tavan, Toran, and Cory. Uncle Drone had an uncanny understanding of who was responsible for any mishaps that occurred in the family.

"Are you going to take us home now, Uncle Drone?" Olivia asked.

"Do I look like a pack mule?" the old wizard retorted. "I brought you something to eat," he said, handing the basket to Cory.

As her younger kin began to devour the sandwiches and fruit in the basket, Amber sat patiently while Uncle Drone examined her wounds. He spread some healing salve on them and then made her down a potion that tasted like peppermint.

"Are our parents worried?" Tavan asked as he sipped a cup of tea.

"Not really," Drone said. "We've known something like this would happen for days now."

"What do you mean?" Toran asked, looking puzzled.

"Mother Lleddew came to check on you a few days ago," the old wizard explained. "Apparently she had a vision that you were trapped in a cave. Since you were all snug in your beds at the time, we guessed it was some sort of future vision brought on by Tymora's troubles. We've just been waiting for the shoe to drop, so to speak. Should have known you'd pick a day when we were all away, leaving your poor Aunt Dorath to fret about you."

"Aunt Dorath likes to fret," Heather said.

"Yes, well, your Uncle Steele likes to drink, but that doesn't mean we should indulge him. Speaking of Steele, let's have that key."

Heather pulled out the key to the crypt that she had taken from Uncle Steele's sock drawer.

Carrying Heather on his back and Olivia and Pars in his arms, the wizard left by another dimensional door, groaning all the way about how much weight they'd all put on. The other children had to wait until morning for the old wizard to replenish his spells. Amber often wondered if that wasn't just an excuse to make them stay the night to teach them a lesson. She didn't mind, however. She had a good time chatting with the guardian. The next day Uncle Drone, with Aunt Cat's help, managed to bring everyone out from the crypt.

Then the whole family began digging out the collapsed crypt and repairing the stonework. True to his threat, Drone saw that the children all helped to dig out the mess.

Years later the Wyvernspur cousins would always refer to any sort of hard labor, like digging, as the fruits of Tymora's luck, but it never kept any of them from calling on Lady Luck from time to time in the course of their adventures.

Act Four
Scene 7

In the realm of Morning Glory, the two goddesses faced their tormentors. Lathander released his hold on Xvim, though whether he meant to hand him over to Tyche's daughters, or was simply preparing to defend himself from attack Joel could not be certain.

Iyachtu Xvim cackled fiendishly in the face of the wrath of Beshaba and Tymora. "The paladin's foolish act has come too late to save you," he gloated. "You cannot stop the fusion once it has begun. See how the chaos matter comes to bind you!"

Xvim's words appeared to be true. A wisp of the chaos matter drifted out of the fusion chamber and wrapped itself around both goddesses. As the others watched, transfixed, more chaos matter swirled out into the tent and began to weave a cocoon around Beshaba and Tymora.

The goddesses' bodies grew translucent and fluid like melting wax. Their torsos joined, then merged, until there was only one torso between the two of them. They had become a misshapen creature with four arms and legs struggling against the bonds of the chaos matter and two heads screaming in rage and pain.

Tymora's head cried out, "Lathander, help me, please!"

"Lathander, do something!" Finder shouted. "Can't you see they're in agony?" he demanded.

"Xvim is right," Lathander said. "Once the spell has begun, there is no stopping it."

"There must be something you can do, my lord," Holly said with a tone of desperation.

"No," Lathander answered. "The fusion chamber will not stop until it has united something that had previously been separated," he insisted.

"What if we threw a whole bunch of broken eggs into it?" Emilo asked.

Lathander shook his head. "It must be something of power," the god explained.

"The finder's stone?" Joel asked Finder excitedly.

"It's worth a try," Finder agreed. He pulled his half of the stone from his boot, and Joel pulled his out from his shirt.

"Ready . . . set . . . go!" Finder shouted.

Together both halves of the finder's stone arced through the air and into the portal. The portal flashed with a brilliant light. Immediately the chaos matter around Tymora and Beshaba fell away and streamed back into the fusion chamber like a river running into the sea.

The partially merged Tymora and Beshaba squirmed and wriggled until they lost their balance and toppled onto the ground. The torso ripped in two, dripping chaos matter like ichor until Tymora and Beshaba emerged as two separate individuals.

Beshaba stood and shook herself like a dog. From Joel's hand, she grabbed the pink rose that held her power and disappeared.

Tymora sat up and shook her head sadly at Lathander. Jas knelt beside the goddess and handed her the ancient coin from Myth Drannor. Tymora slid the coin down her shirt and sighed.

"You know, I think there's something wrong with the fusion chamber," Emilo said. "I'm not sure, mind you, but I don't think it's supposed to look like that."

The others looked back at the portal to the fusion chamber. It had begun to glow with a brilliant white light.

"It's not properly calibrated to join the stone," Xvim screamed. "It's going to explode! Run!"

"Grab Emilo!" Finder ordered Jas as he scooped up Joel.

Tymora disappeared. Jas flew from the tent, with Finder close behind her.

Last of all, Lathander snatched up Holly and fled.

The blast from the fusion chamber expanded outward like a blossoming flower of solid light. The shock wave caught the fleeing Morninglord and his disobedient paladin and tossed them about like corks on a raging sea, propelling them across the god's realm. Then a blast of sound shook their bodies. As Joel looked back, Lathander and Holly appeared to Joel as two black specks. Then the specks were gone.

Slowly, but inexorably, the brilliant light faded. When the dust finally settled, a crater the size of a small town had appeared where there once had been a meadow.

I don't like opera at all. All that deception just rubs me the wrong way. It's too much like real life.

Vangerdahast

Curtain Call

The vision of Ayryn, the genasi scryer, was so lifelike that the Sensates had to shield their eyes from the explosion of the fusion chamber projected into the sensorium.

Kenda Fretterstag rose to leave. "I was really looking forward to experiencing the creation of a new power," she sighed.

"You did get to witness a paladin disobey her god," Bors pointed out.

"Why, yes, I did," Kenda noted. "Any chance you might risk your god's wrath?"

Bors frowned. While he had been proud of Holly's strength of character, the thought of what she had risked filled him with fear.

"Thought not," Kenda taunted as she grabbed her fur coat and made her way to the exit.

Ayryn continued to project the images of Lathander, Holly, Jasmine, Emilo, and Tymora. There was no sign of Joel or Finder. Though the others stood on the steps of Lathander's temple, it appeared to the Sensates as if the gods and adventurers were sitting among the Sensates in the sensorium.

Lathander and Holly Harrowslough stood off to one side, their image projected so that they appeared to stand beside Ayryn. They had been blasted from Lathander's realm and had only just returned. They were engaged in earnest discussion. Now the Morninglord cupped Holly's face in his hands and kissed her on the

forehead. Apparently the god of beginnings had decided
that his paladin's good sense and stout heart outweighed
her disobedience.

Quellig, the tiefling wizard, sat up and leaned forward
as Jasmine asked Emilo Haversack, "So, your friend Fiz
Whatever made you unnoticeable to all but people from
Krynn just so you could uncover Xvim's fraud? Why?
What's it to him?"

"Well, it's a little more complicated than that," the
kender said. "The way Fizban explained it, gods from one
world aren't supposed to let gods from another world
harm each other, whether they're good or evil. It's against
the rules. It could start a war between the gods from
Krynn and the gods from Toril. If it really was Sirrion
helping Lathander to drain the power from Tymora and
Beshaba, or some other god from Krynn impersonating
Sirrion, Fizban was going to have to step in and make him
stop. But since it wasn't a god from Krynn, Fizban didn't
have to get involved. He didn't want to get into an argument with Lathander if he could help it. That could
start—"

"All right, all right," Jas said. "I don't need to know any
more about the gods. What I want to know is, if you're unnoticeable to everyone except people from Krynn, why is it
that I can see you perfectly?" she asked. "I wasn't born on
Krynn."

"Actually, you were," Tymora said, laying a hand on the
winged woman's shoulder. "Your mother and father took a
spelljammer to Krynn, and you were born there before
they returned to Toril."

"So Jas has been spelljamming since she was a baby,"
Emilo said. "No wonder she likes the stars."

At that moment, Beshaba suddenly appeared in front
of Lathander. "I've teleported here to share my gift with
you, Lathander," she said, and she gave him a quick kiss
on the mouth. Then the Maid of Misfortune vanished
again.

The Morninglord looked mildly alarmed. "I don't suppose you'd care to balance out Beshaba's ill luck with a
kiss of your own?" he asked Lady Luck.

Tymora stepped back and pointed at Holly. "You were

blessed with far more than your share of luck the day this
girl entered your service," she informed him.

"Yes . . . I've come to realize that," Lathander said.

Finder and Joel appeared and approached the gods and
mortals assembled on the temple stairs. Finder casually
tossed the finder's stone in the air and caught it again.
The magic crystal was once again intact.

"No sign of Xvim," Joel reported. "We've searched
everywhere."

"I can't believe he let Beshaba destroy his bastion and
didn't raise a finger," Tymora said.

"He was playing for high stakes," Finder said. "He
couldn't bring himself to abandon the evil deception he'd
set up. If he had been successful, he would have possessed
all of your power, Tymora, and all of Beshaba's power as
well. He never intended to return it to Tyche."

Tymora put a hand on Jas's shoulder. "We have much
to talk about," she said. "Will you accompany me back to
Brightwater?"

"Yes," Jas agreed. "As long as you don't serve me any
more of that wine."

"I think you'll find that wine tastes quite different
now," the goddess replied. "Finder, Rebel Bard . . . until
we meet again," she added, saluting the god and his
priest.

Tymora teleported herself and Jas from Morning Glory,
and their projected image disappeared from the sensorium.

Finder bowed low to the Morninglord. "Well, Lord
Lathander, it's always interesting when we disagree," he
said.

"Good-bye, god of reckless fools," Lathander said. "Fare
thee well."

Finder chuckled. He bent over and kissed Lathander's
paladin. "Good-bye, Holly Harrowslough. May songs of
purity fill your heart, and may you always hear them
singing."

"Good-bye, Lord Finder," the paladin whispered. She
looked down at the ground, unable to meet Joel's eyes. She
couldn't forget that she had risked his life.

The bard stooped in front of her. "It's all right, Holly,"

he said, kissing her cheek. "I know how hard your decisions were. In the end, you made the right ones."

Holly threw her arms around the bard's neck and hugged him unashamedly.

Finder and Joel strolled away from the temple to have one last look at the crater made by the gnomes' fusion chamber.

"Hey," Emilo cried. "Wait for me."

"I'm sorry, Mr. Haversack," Finder said. "I thought you had gone with Jas. I'll be glad to take you home to Krynn if you'd like."

"Not yet," the kender said. "First I want to see this place you call the Realms. I'd like to meet some halflings."

"And I'll wager the halflings would like to meet you," Joel said.

In the sensorium on Sigil, Factol Erin Montgomery laughed. She had spied on the Rebel Bard long enough. She had seen all she desired. As far as she was concerned, this adventure was over. She rose to leave. Cuatha Da'nanin and Annali Webspinner followed her from the sensorium. Slowly the other Sensates began to depart as well.

"A kender in the Realms . . ." Bors said thoughtfully as he found himself left alone with Ayryn in the sensorium.

"It could be most interesting," Ayryn commented.

"Yes, most interesting indeed . . ." Bors agreed.

THE LOST GODS BOOKS

Finder's Bane
by Kate Novak and Jeff Grubb

Fistandantilus Reborn
by Douglas Niles

Tymora's Luck
by Kate Novak and Jeff Grubb